De'Ath in Venice

By Paul Humber

PART ONE

THE WORLD ACCORDING TO EMILY

ONE

Ever woken up handcuffed to a corpse? No, of course not; it's vanishingly rare.

I had woken early because my bladder was full.

I was lying on my front, and my right hand wouldn't move. I wasn't concerned at first; why would I be?

I tugged on my arm. I tugged again.

I raised my head to see why my hand was caught.

There was a naked man next to me. Yeah okay fine, that happens. Then I saw the handcuff.

My right wrist was handcuffed to the man's left wrist.

And they weren't the pink fluffy pretend handcuffs you sometimes see in lingerie stores. They were real metal handcuffs. Police style. Designed to immobilise a suspect. They were probably still intended for sex and sold by some dodgy store that specialised in such things, but they were more solid than you would expect; I wasn't going to be able to get out of them without a key. Oh joy.

And I needed a pee.

A lot.

My bladder was really full. Painfully full.

What is a rational person supposed to do in a situation like this? As a courtesy, I didn't initially attempt to wake him up; it would be reasonable to assume the key to open the cuffs would be within reach. But my scope for looking around me was pretty limited by my position, and my scope for retrieving an object from elsewhere in the room without waking him was pretty much zero.

I couldn't see a key.

I scanned my brain for what I could remember from during the night.

Nothing from after about eleven. Absolutely nothing. Nothing at all? It was both reassuring and alarming at the same time.

Okay, time to prod him.

'Hey!' I tried.

He didn't stir.

I leant up on my right elbow as best I could, and I pinched his nose. It's something I do with men who snore. Just pinch their nose and count to ten. The snoring will improve; roughly when you get to ten, and largely because you have just woken them up. Sometimes you have to close their mouth as well. It's also a sex move I sometimes do. Just sharing.

It didn't have any effect.

How about twenty seconds? It was the logical thing to do.

Twenty seconds later, and any reasonable person would conclude he might be dead. Under any circumstances this is a really horrible heart-stopping conclusion, the sort of conclusion that hits your whole metabolism; but it was worse in this instance because I had drunk far too much the night before and had a profound sense I had been poisoned.

I elbowed him in the ribs. I elbowed him some more. I shoved him.

His head lolled.

Was he cold? I felt his chest with my palm. He wasn't unduly cold, he wasn't fresh from the morgue cold, but it was quite warm in the room generally and presumably you can't drop below the temperature in the room, so it was hard to tell; and obviously I'm a total novice at this waking up chained to a corpse lark.

What else could I do? I felt under his nose. There was no sign of any breath.

I pinched his nose again with a view to counting to thirty, but now that it was clear he was dead, it was suddenly an immoral thing to do; disrespectful at least.

When I did reach the count of thirty however, it was beyond all doubt.

I was handcuffed to a naked dead man.

TWO

I had no clothes on, which is not unusual; I sometimes wear an old t shirt in bed, but nothing fancy. If I have a boyfriend round for a sleepover then I might make a bit of effort, but frankly I believe they should be pleased with who I am, not what I can squeeze into on a slim day; and besides there had been fewer slim days of late. I had put on an alarming amount of weight in the last year; I just didn't seem to fit anything anymore. I'd even had to reach into the back of the closet to fetch the dread dungarees of shame. In fact, my weight gain had been so rapid that I had even developed some stretchmarks over my arse and stomach. Stretchmarks for heaven's sake. I am not an excessively vain person, but stretchmarks? And the man I went to bed with last night, who I now realised was an idiot, had even pointed them out. 'I didn't know you'd had children,' he said. His exact words. 'I haven't,' I replied. He didn't look convinced. He just stared at them. They weren't even white; they were angry red streaks. He was young and had never seen the like. Okay, so they weren't that severe, but they were severe enough to be spotted and they played into a general sense I had been having of late that my body was getting much older.

But none of that was important now. What was important was to be very orderly about what you would do in a situation like this. There was no point in panicking; there was every point in doing things in a logical order. What would a rational person do next?

I wasn't in my own home which didn't help; I had been living in an Airbnb in Venice for a couple of months. I had been seconded onto the island to help process the mass of insurance claims that had been made after the recent flooding. If someone tells you they are going to pay you to live and work in Venice for six months, you say yes; so I volunteered. The trouble was, when you aren't on home territory it is much harder to deal with unexpected problems; you know hardly anyone local who could help, you might not even know the local number to ring for the police. At home if I woke up chained to a dead body; I might, for example, know where the nearest bolt cutters might be sourced, and I could ring my brother to come and help, and I have friends in the local police. But what could I do in Venice?

Think Emily, think.

I looked around again for a key. I padded my hand among the pillows. I peered around the sides of his body. I really couldn't remember anything from the night itself, but I could remember plenty about the evening up to about eleven.

There was no key. I could keep looking, but I knew there was no point. What else was I supposed to do in a situation like this?

Okay what about a phone? I don't tend to take my phone to bed with me. I am not a total phone addict; I usually leave my phone in the kitchen every night, on charge; usually but not always.

I could see his phone.

It was on a bedside table.

Perhaps I could ring for help.

But who? If I rang the police, then they would have to knock the door down to rescue me. Then I would be in trouble with the landlady, which wasn't the end of the world, but it would be one problem fewer if we didn't damage the historic door. I figured it would be better to ring the landlady first and she could let the police in. She only lived two floors above, so only had to pop downstairs. But how could I get her number?

I brought myself up on my knees and reached over for his phone. I clicked the side to bring it to life. It needed a PIN; of course, it did. I didn't know his PIN. I noticed also his battery was low. Typical of youngsters; they never seem to recharge their phones.

Should I just accept that the phone would probably let me make emergency calls, or try and activate the phone with a fingerprint? Oh dear. How macabre was this? I was going to get a dead man's fingers and try them out on the fingerprint recognition sensor. Sad to relate I have done this sort of thing before, when a boyfriend once passed out from drinking too much. One day I might have to sit down with myself and wonder what sort of life I'm leading that I get myself into scrapes like this.

Which finger was it? I was pretty sure it was nearly always the first finger that people used. Left hand or right hand? Either way, it made sense to try his free hand first; his right hand.

I tried it. Nothing. It was rejected.

I was pretty sure you only get five attempts at opening the phone this way, so I needed to choose my strategy carefully. I tried the same finger but a different angle.

Again it was rejected.

Perhaps when you die, the finger is less sweaty and it doesn't work for fingerprint recognition? Perhaps the skin loses tone and is a subtly different shape?

I decided to try the other hand – his left hand. This was more tricky. It was the hand that was handcuffed to my own hand; it made for more of a contortion.

I scrambled on top of his naked body. My living naked body was now astride his dead naked clammy body. It was really clammy. His clammy, slightly oily, cold flesh, was against my naked thighs; it doesn't get more gruesome than this. I dry heaved. The dry heave put pressure on my bladder. I really, really, needed to go to the bathroom and I was making no progress.

I tried his first finger of his left hand.

No dice.

I tried some different fingers. I was soon locked out of the phone.

I was stuffed.

What was I going to do?

I couldn't bear straddling him for a moment more, and got off.

Despite my lack of progress, my mind was wondering what I would do if I did ever get a phone to work. How would I get my landlady's number? It wouldn't be on the Airbnb website.

Perhaps I would ring my work and they could help. What time was it? 7.10am. Even if I did ring work, who would I call exactly? Perhaps my boss Marco; I needed someone with a bit of authority who wouldn't flap. But could I wait until nine o'clock when the office was open? My bladder was telling me no. Ringing the office would have to be my backstop option. What was I thinking? I didn't even have a phone that worked yet.

Who lived in the apartment above? Perhaps they could raise the alarm? Was it worth shouting?

'Help! Help!'

I paused to listen, to see if anyone was responding. I looked up at the ancient timbered ceiling. In the three months I had lived here, I had occasionally heard the scrape of a chair or a creak where someone was moving about on the floor above, but I had never come across anyone in the hallway.

I shouted louder. 'Help!'

Still nothing.

There was a chance the upstairs apartment was rented out on Airbnb just like mine, and wasn't always occupied. It was very common in Venice; in fact, it was a major bone of contention. On my first day at the office, a sundry colleague in a meeting had asked me what I was doing for accommodation and when I said 'Airbnb' he had virtually spat at me and refused to address me for the next two hours. At lunchtime I asked another colleague what the issue was.

'You have to understand,' he replied. 'That since Airbnb and similar websites came along, the landlords have been renting out their properties to tourists at twice the price they would rent out to locals. Locals have to bring up children and make ends meet, and now the rents have doubled. There is a lot of bitterness.' He shrugged and smiled; this was an issue you could see from everyone's point of view; the landlords, the holidaymakers, the locals trying to make ends meet.

'Yeah but he almost spat at me,' I said.

'It doesn't help that you have been sent here specifically to turn down insurance claims for the winter flooding,' he said. 'This is people's lives we are talking about and they thought they were insured.'

'Flooding was a foreseeable risk,' I replied. It was the company's official line. 'When people took out their policies, they knew that flooding was likely, and it clearly states that foreseeable risks are not insured.'

'But it's hidden in the small print,' he said. This time there was no shrug and smile; this wasn't something you could see from everyone's point of view. 'Flooding was a foreseeable risk, but flooding this severe was not. Those were record high tides.'

Is that where this all began? With that conversation about turning down the insurance claims? Whatever its significance, it was of little consequence now; now I needed to get in touch with the police. I decided to no longer worry about the damage to the front door. I had done my best to unlock the phone; I would simply have to use the emergency system instead.

I clicked the side of the phone to bring it to life.

Nothing.

Seriously? Had it been so hopelessly low on battery that it had run out of juice completely? Seriously? That was unbelievably bad luck; it was ridiculous. I pressed the button on the side of the phone for six seconds. Nothing. I tried ten seconds. Nothing. Coming to think of it, both the men I shared an office with - Angelo and Adam - were forever moaning about their battery charge. Neither of them ever thought of charging overnight; they would just wait until they were out of electricity and then act surprised. Every time; surprise. Angelo. Angelo. Angelo. He was dead. And Adam's dead too. What a tale.

But dwelling on the death of those two men wasn't going to get me any help. I must have used up the last of the charge trying to get it to recognise fingerprints; I needed to accept it and move on.

Okay. I was going to need to find my own phone, or wave from a window. Either way, that meant I was going to need to see if I could drag this body to another room.

THREE

Could I drag the body of a grown man across a floor? They are a bit of a dead weight; pardon the pun. It would at least help if I could get him flat on the floor and not hemmed in, or bunched up in any way.

I knelt beside his body on the bed and tried to pull him upright and forwards. It proved possible after a lot of heaving; but when he was finally upright, he slumped in slow motion to his left and we collapsed together onto the wooden floor; me on top. Another dry heave from me. By any measure, I was having a terrible day. It took a further minute to get him flat and in a position to pull him by his arms.

My next job was to ascertain where my phone would be. Usually in the kitchen, but not always; there would be no point dragging a body around from room to room, if I didn't even know where I was going.

I grabbed both of his wrists and I pulled. His body didn't move, so much as stretch.

I pulled again. His mouth made a puffing kind of retching noise. Maybe it was air being pulled out of his lungs. I felt sick.

In the absence of any other plan I decided to try his phone again. It might have found a little power by having a rest. It was a forlorn hope, but what else could I do?

I stretched back over the bed. And my own phone came into my line of vision. It was on a chair beyond. It was surprising I hadn't noticed it before; but as I said, I usually leave it on charge in the kitchen so it had been reasonable to assume it wouldn't be in the room.

It was going to be a stretch to reach it. I heaved at his body and propped it up as best I could against the side of the bed and then pulled his hand out hard.

I managed to drag the phone with my foot and made it spin towards me, albeit it fell off the chair and was now on the floor and under the bed. I then had to manoeuvre myself back over the dead body and down under the bed to get it.

Pitifully grateful to have a phone, I rang my landlady.

She didn't pick up.

I decided not to leave a message; a rambling message about waking up handcuffed to a naked man was - well I don't know what that was - but it felt wrong to leave a message like that.

I rang the police, which in Italy is 113. I got straight through. I should have done that all along.

'Hello police. I am stuck in my apartment with a dead body. I cannot get out. Please come and help me. I am literally chained to the dead body of a man.' I refrained from adding that I needed a pee because it would have sounded flippant. But I really, really needed to pee, so I added, 'Please hurry.'

The woman on the other end of the line did not sound at all fazed. I wondered what you would have to say to someone like that to alarm them; after all, over the years they must have heard it all. The woman took my details and asked a number of pre-set questions.

The next problem was that of my location. There is a huge issue in Venice over addresses. Venice is split into six areas called sestieri, and rather than have a street name and a number, each building has a sequential number in the area as a whole. Street names, where they do exist, are not in fact official addresses; sometimes they are little more than rambling descriptions. One example I came across was a street called 'River will have the bend and parsley' and that wasn't even in Italian as we know it, but an amalgamation of words and sentences derived partly from old Venetian dialect and, as far as I could tell, Portuguese. And as for the official system of numbering houses sequentially; there is an eatery I often frequent on the bank of a nearby canal and the street numbers go in a sequence like 2552, 2543A, 2543B, 2530. The missing numbers are somewhere else entirely. Basically, the system makes no sense.

As a result of all of this I explained my location to the police operator using local landmarks and directions by boat.

The operator cut me short. 'Don't worry Signora. We do have computers,' she said. 'We know exactly where you are.' So much for my theories about Venetian addresses being impossible.

She summarised what I had said to her and then said, 'Okay stay with the body.'

'I have no choice. I am chained to him.'

'Oh yes.' She allowed herself a laugh. I could hear tapping on a keyboard her end. She said, 'And you say the room backs onto a canal?'

'Yes, the bedroom window is perhaps three metres above the water level.'

'Well, that's lucky,' she said. Was this a reference to the recent floods? My apartment would not have been affected by being high up? Probably not; it was just that I'd spent too much time at work obsessing about the layouts of buildings in this town and which floors are liable to be flooded. 'Can you hang something out the window, so you can be seen from the canal?' she asked.

'Like what?'

'Like a sheet. If we need to enter your property from the river it is sometimes useful.'

'Sure,' I said. 'I could dangle a white sheet out the window.' It was at least something I could busy myself with for the next ten minutes. Anything to distract me from having to gaze at the dead body.

'Okay,' she concluded. 'Stay with the body, and we will be with you as soon as we can.'

I untucked the sheet at the head of the bed and then had to pull the body along the floor as best I could so that I could reach the foot of the bed to untuck the sheet at that end. The body wasn't stiff. It was the first time I had thought about it. Surely bodies go stiff when they are dead? But how quickly does that happen after death, and for how long? Or perhaps his muscles were indeed stiff, and I didn't know what I was looking for.

I now had the bedsheet in my left hand and was dragging the body towards the window. I was able to achieve the journey in short sharp bursts; I would rest, then psych myself up, then pull the body a few inches and then rest again, in a cycle. Eventually, I made it.

I went to unlock the window. The window catch was a wrought iron affair that was centuries old; it was the sort of ornate detail that attracted me to renting the apartment in the first place, but today I was angry with it because it didn't want to open.

As a result, I was standing in the window, stark naked, jiggling up and down, one arm chained to a dead man, trying to free it. A gondola went past slowly. The gondolier was young and attractive and neatly turned out; he wore a boater with a red ribbon. He caught my eye. He then double took and squinted at me; then he looked appalled, shocked. He paddled on, shaking his head. I felt like shouting after him, 'Have you never seen a naked woman before?' or 'Okay, so I've put on a few pounds but I am in pretty good shape for a woman in her thirties!' But he was soon out of view.

I had definitely opened the window for a while the night before; my memory loss allowed me that, so why was it so stuck now? I banged the window catch with my fist and it somehow freed up. In no time I was bundling the sheet out of the window and it was draped down the side of the house. I closed the window on it to wedge the top end.

Right. Was there any chance I could get a piece of clothing on before the police turned up? I needed to get to the chest of drawers, and that meant dragging the body again in fits and starts.

I found a t shirt and it was already in my hand before I realised that it isn't possible to put on a shirt if you have someone handcuffed to you; you can't get your cuffed arm through the sleeve. A cardigan then.

When I was packing to come to Venice, I had somehow assumed it would be warm here; after much dithering I decided to pack one cardigan 'Just in case.' It turned out it got quite cold during the winter, so I was glad I did pack it; much more so now, however. I put it over one arm and draped the other side around me. It would have to do. The minimum requirement was to not alarm any policeman with - oh I don't know - my newfound stretchmarks. Despite everything, the stretchmark situation kept popping back into my head; if my brain was to be believed it was almost as traumatic a discovery as waking up chained to a dead lover.

I had a thought. What about his clothes? I should have checked the pockets of his trousers to look for the key for the padlock. It's what a logical person would have done.

There was a loud knock on the main door. Too late to check his pockets, then. I should have put some knickers on. Why hadn't I thought to put some knickers on?

'Hang on!' I shouted. Then I added, 'I am afraid you will need to knock the door down.'

There was a knock again. It was louder. They hadn't heard me.

'I am just putting on some clothes!' I shouted. I suppose it was just about possible I could drag the body all the way down the corridor to the front door, but it would take a very long time.

'Signora! Go to the window!' shouted someone; I wasn't sure who or from where.

The cardigan would have to do. I managed to do up an extra button around my waist.

'Go to the window, Signora!'

'Okay!' I shouted back. 'Give me a minute.'

I looked down at the body. Sorry mate; another unedifying drag across the 18th century wooden floor for you.

My dragging technique was improving a little – it seemed to be all about momentum - so I got us both across the room to look out of the window in a slightly reduced time than before.

I looked out to the canal below.

There were two boats there already. A blue and white police boat and a red fire brigade boat. Beyond that I would see another boat motoring into view; a yellow and orange ambulance boat.

'Signora Fisher?' called a policeman. He was standing with his head about four feet below my window.

'Yes.'

'You said your door was locked,' he called.

'Yes,' I replied.

'We will come up from the river?' he asked. He was a capable looking man with thick dark hair. He looked just the sort of person I needed; someone solid and experienced.

The lowest windows of almost any building in Venice will have iron bars on the outside. He used these as a foothold to climb up to my window above. He was soon swinging his legs into my room.

He managed to land his first leg onto the dead body.

'Oh Lordy!' he said. What a quaint thing to say. 'But this is just awful.' He sounded mortified. Although, not as mortified as the corpse, obviously.

'Yes, I know,' I replied. 'But he's dead, like I said.' It sounded horribly flippant; I was feeling much more positive since the police had turned up.

And then I realised the policeman hadn't been referring to the fact that he had stood on the dead body, at all. The reason he was so shocked was to do with me.

'What the hell has happened?' he said. 'To you? What the hell has happened to you?'

'What do you mean?' I asked.

'Your face!' he said.

'My face?'

'It's covered in bruises. Your face is covered in bruises.'

FOUR

It turns out that with the basic distraction of being manacled to a corpse, I hadn't looked at myself. I certainly hadn't dragged the corpse off so that I could stand in front of a mirror and check my appearance for the day.

'And your body!' said the policeman.

I looked down at my body. I had nasty looking red and black bruises on my thighs.

'Are you okay?' asked the policeman. He was clearly very concerned.

'Yeah. I'm okay. I mean I'm handcuffed to a dead man. I feel ill and shocked. I feel poisoned and bruised. But I'm okay,' I said.

The policeman went off to open the front door to let his colleagues in. I took the chance to open my cardigan a little. I had bruising and swelling around my genitalia and some on my stomach; any sentient person would have noticed that before. It wasn't plausible that I hadn't noticed it just because I was hungover or poisoned; perhaps a more reasonable explanation was that I was in some kind of shock.

My next thought, bizarrely, was how much work I had waiting for me at the office; presumably I wouldn't be going in today. How did my brain think that that should be a top worry when I had so much else to process?

The policeman returned with two colleagues. He then leant out the window and shouted commands to the people in the boats below. I heard the sound of engines starting; presumably they were going to moor up and come round to the front of my apartment on foot, or perhaps just move on.

'I really need a pee,' I said in my creaky Italian.

He looked at me. He was uncertain.

'And we need to cut the handcuff off,' I said.

'Is there a key?' he asked.

'The key doesn't seem to be in the room,' I replied. 'Have a quick look by all means, but perhaps get some bolt cutters?'

'Did you lock these handcuffs?' he asked.

'I have no memory at all about large amounts of the night,' I said.

'Who is he?' he asked.

'I would rather not say.'

'What do you mean you would rather not say?'

'I will tell a detective,' I said.

'I don't understand.'

'When I can tell a detective in strictest confidence, I will say who this is.'

The policeman scrutinised the body with renewed interest. 'Is he famous?' he asked.

'Sort of,' I replied.

'Where do you work?' he asked. Why would he ask me that?

'Um. I am happy to answer lots of questions, obviously,' I said. 'But I really need to go to the bathroom as a priority and it would then be nice to have some clothes to wear.'

'Were you wearing this when the man died?' He pointed to my cardigan.

'No, I have just put this on.' He wasn't a detective, so I wasn't sure how much I had to answer his questions.

Two paramedics had entered the room; they were a man and a woman, and they were bent over the body. The woman took the temperature of the body using one of those sensors that you stick in the ear. She wrote down the reading and time on her rubber glove.

'Bolt cutters? I asked.

The policeman called to a colleague in the doorway. They said something fast in Italian that I didn't catch, and the man disappeared.

Then a man appeared who had the look of a detective. He talked to the policeman awhile and they stole glances at me as they progressed through their side of story. Events seemed to be going very fast; it had only been a few minutes and we already had a lot people present, in what was actually quite a small room.

Eventually the detective turned to me. 'My name is Detective Inspector Gilles Grimandi,' he said. 'I will be taking your statement.'

'Nice to meet you inspector. Actually, can I make a request?' I asked. 'What if I was drugged? Would it be possible for you to provide a way of analysing my urine?'

The detective appeared not to hear me.

One of the policemen returned with a fireman. He had some posh looking mechanical bolt cutters. They whirred into action, and in no time he cut through the link between the two cuffs.

'I am serious inspector,' I said. 'I think my urine should be analysed.'

He nodded and talked to the policeman.

'If you can wait. We will get the necessary support,' he said.

'I am bursting to go.'

'We will try and be quick.'

'Perhaps even a blood test?'

'A blood test?' he asked.

There was a good chance they were going to wonder if I had killed this man; perhaps through some sort of sex game gone wrong. I needed to be on my front foot from the outset, and make sure all possible evidence was gathered. After all, the deceased was a fit young man; why would he have died of natural causes?

I realised I was very thirsty. And hungry.

'I know this sounds vain, but can I pop in the bathroom and see what my face looks like in a mirror?'

The detective nodded but also signalled to the policeman to walk with me. The detective started looking at the dead body instead.

'You have moved this?'

'Yes,' I replied. 'I woke up in bed with him. He was dead when I woke up. I have no recollection of the night at all, so I want a blood test.' I pointed out where we were both lying when we woke. When I woke.

I took a pair of knickers out of the chest of drawers and walked the half dozen paces it takes to get to the bathroom. Before I could get in the room, the policeman had a thought and went in there first to have a quick look around. He then gave me a brief nod and I went in and locked the door. Why the suspicion?

I took a deep breath and faced myself in the bathroom mirror.

I realised now that the passing gondolier who was so alarmed, had been reacting to how my face looked. My left cheek was bruised and swollen, particularly below the eye and around the cheekbone. It was largely black. My forehead was probably the worst of it. It had a vertical gash that had clotted but had left blood all over my brow and there was general bruising each side of it. Shouldn't there have been blood on the sheets or on the pillow? I hadn't noticed anything, but perhaps there was. Okay, the evidence was all pointing to me being drugged or in shock, if I was repeatedly not noticing basics.

I looked at the toilet. It was so tempting to use it, but I definitely needed all the evidence I could gather in case the police blamed me for anything. That didn't stop the chronic ache in my bladder though; it was very painful.

I put on my knickers and went back to the police.

'The forensic team are coming soon. And a doctor has been alerted. Would you object to being photographed?' asked the detective.

'Not at all,' I said. 'I think you need to record everything you can. This is just, well, what can I say?'

'What can you remember about last night?' he asked.

'Right,' I replied. 'Can we sit in the kitchen or something?'

We moved to the kitchen area. There was a knock on the front door and a few moments later a policewoman appeared; she had a long plait of hair going down her back.

'You needed me?' she asked.

'Yes,' said the detective. 'This is Emily Fisher. She is an Englishwoman. She woke up this morning and the man next to her was dead. They were tied to each other with a handcuff. Signora Fisher has agreed it would be a good idea to have a urine sample. So you will need to supervise.' He looked at me. It was a look of concern. 'And chaperone,' he added. 'When the forensics come or the police doctor.'

The detective got an official pad of paper out of his bag along with a decent quality fountain pen; he took the top off and placed it on the table, then looked at it and straightened it to conform to some imaginary line. This was a meticulous man.

'Tell me what you remember about last night. Start at the beginning, but first I understand you did not want to tell the policeman the identity of the deceased man.'

'I felt that this was a potential embarrassment for him and his family. He comes from a notable local family and so I felt that discretion was important at least at first.'

'But you are going to tell me?' asked the detective.

'Yes. If you want to release his details, then that is of course your judgement. I just didn't want it to be my judgement. I am not a local. So, I don't want to do the wrong thing.'

The detective nodded that he understood. 'Could you write his name down for me? And his address if you know it?'

I wrote down his name and address.

The detective looked at it.

'This surname. It is the same family that is very important in Venice?'

'Exactly, yes.'

He considered this impassively.

'Thank you for your discretion Signora,' he said. A thank you on behalf of Venice, no less.

He passed the name of the dead man to the policewoman with the plait. She read it and gasped.

FIVE

'So start at the beginning,' said the detective. 'How long have you lived here?'

'A couple of months.'

'And how long have you known the deceased?'

'A couple of months.'

'Tell me how you met him,' he said. 'Tell me all that's happened to get to this point.'

And this is the story I told the inspector, all the while hoping the medical person would turn up so that I could have a pee.

At this juncture I would stress that I was at pains not to lie to the detective in any way at all. I am a reliable narrator. I did however leave out key elements that weren't going to help me personally. My experience in life is that there is rarely any mileage in lying, because some little detail will trip you up and you have to remember all the lies you've told forever more.

When I first came out to Venice, it was a few weeks after the worst of the floods. The regional office dealing with insurance was being overwhelmed with claims; we were the biggest insurer in the area by volume so an estimated 30% to 40% of all claims were coming our way. All the major insurance companies were finding ways to not pay out, not just us; they hadn't acted as a cartel, they had just come to the same conclusions individually and then held firm together. So when I was parachuted into the local office I found that everyone was stressed, but also wary of outsiders; an attitude that seemed to even permeate my own little department. The only true exception was my assistant Adam. On day one he beamed at me and put out his hand.

'I'm Adzio,' he said. 'But people call me Adam. Well apart from my mother. My second name is Amelio so people got the Ad from Adzio and Am from Amelio... wow I am boring you already.'

'No, I am interested,' I protested. 'It's just my first day and I have a lot to take in. I am feeling a bit dazed.'

Adam was one of those youngsters whose clothes were always ostentatiously trendy; a trait that is particularly prevalent, of course, amongst Italians in general. He was actively and energetically kind to me. But then I noticed he was also actively and energetically kind to everyone else, so it sort of counted for nothing. It was welcome nonetheless, because I was new and so far had no friends.

'I have bought you some pastries as a welcome,' said Adam. He'd spent a lot of money on fancy pastries for me; they came in a box with a bow. Then soon his face was in my face. 'How are you enjoying the pastries?' he asked. Then later, 'You haven't eaten your pastries.' I would have held it against him that he was so eager to please, but he was disarmingly good-looking. So good-looking it completely threw me. He was a bit like a young Leonardo DiCaprio in his Romeo and Juliet days, but with the frame of a Timothée Chalamet – handsome, but also boyish and slight. I wanted to jump his bones. I really wanted to jump his bones. But not too hard, obviously; because they might prove a bit fey and fragile, particularly given that I was a bit hefty of late.

I looked at him in his trendy Picasso sailor top and his tight blue chinos. On a whim I put my hand out to his neck and checked out the label in the collar. I almost fainted at which fashion house it was. How did he afford endless ludicrously-priced designer clothes on his underling's salary? And was it worth paying twenty times the going rate for the marginally better cut and the extra quality of fabric that the fashion house allowed? Evidently for Adam it was.

The third and final person in our office was Angelo. He had the desk in the corner. He was closer to me in age than Adam but still young; and unlike Adam, he was dour and careworn. He always seemed to wear grey; grey trousers, grey jacket, often a grey shirt, and mostly kept his thoughts to himself. He barely spoke to either of us; he just sat working. Although I'd occasionally catch him staring at me, which was just plain freaky.

'What's the deal with him?' I once asked Adam, after a particularly quiet day from Angelo.

'He married young to a woman named Gianna. She was a complete handful and he was totally traumatized by it,' he said. 'Italian women can be a force of nature,' he added.

Adam's explanation felt correct; Angelo had the air of someone who had long been battered into submission, his spirit first dulled, then broken. But beyond that though, he came across as someone profoundly dependable, and that counted for a lot. And what he did say tended to make perfect sense and was cheerful enough in content. Someone who'd married the wrong person; he would have been good-looking if the stuffing hadn't been knocked out of him quite so thoroughly.

'Or maybe he's just gloomy,' shrugged Adam.

As if to prove he was the polar opposite of gloomy, Adam would spend all day, every day, displaying his many enthusiasms. He was like a Jack-in-the-box; unexpectedly springing up to chat to other colleagues around the building. He was always telling us about some upcoming weekend party on Lake Como 'Where George Clooney has a house, you know', or a day spent snowboarding in the Dolomites, or a balmy week on the Adriatic sailing on some rich person's yacht. At 5 o'clock on the dot every day, he would jump up – often mid-sentence - fetch his jacket and scram to get on with the excitement of his evening. This left Angelo and I to smile weakly at each other and make a little small talk while packing up our stuff.

'There are some cocktail bars on the quayside,' said Angelo.

'Yes,' I replied.

'The area has been refurbished. They are putting in trees and fancy lampposts and a new bridge.'

'Yes,' I replied.

Angelo had spoken to me even less than usual that particular day, so much so that I had come to the conclusion I'd offended him.

'The quayside has a nice view over the water to Giudecca,' he persevered.

Then he just stared at me.

'Oh, you're asking me out?' I said at last. I just blurted it out. It was the wrong thing to say. I was correct – he was indeed asking me out - but by stating the fact so boldly, and in a tone that could be mistaken for incredulity, I had made him embarrassed. He reddened and looked ashamed. It turned out that reason he had been so quiet all day was that he had been plucking up the courage to ask me on a date, and even the thought of having to put his offer into words had made him more shy than ever.

'No, I was just...' he backtracked.

'No that's fine,' I said. 'A drink after work. Great. I didn't mean date. I mean it's a good idea. A drink.' But now I was the one a bit shocked. If we were stuck alone together, what the hell were we going to talk about?

Surprised by his unexpected success at getting me to agree to a drink, Angelo clammed up again. He looked thrown and out of ideas.

'I'll tell you what,' I said. 'Why don't you show me round the area a bit. We could loop round and then end up in a bar?'

Giving him a specific task perked him up. He nodded to himself. He could do this. Was I really so intimidating? Was he really so lacking in confidence? I was hardly out of his league; it was just that I was relatively full of life and colour, and he was so, well, on the face of it, dull.

Our offices were in an area called San Basilio; it is largely a residential area that was undergoing a bit of a refurb at the time. Five minutes' walk due north, however, there is Campo Santa Margherita which is a lively market square with shops and cafés; I had walked around the area in my lunch hours so I did know where everything was, but I linked my arm through Angelo's to be friendly, and encouraged him to show me places and tell me what he knew about the locality.

The detective interrupted me.

'You seem to be telling me about both Adam and Angelo. Are you implying that one was jealous of the other and it was part of the motive for what then happened?'

'Yes, possibly,' I replied. 'If you consider the situation, jealousy is a very likely motive for what occurred last night. Also though, I think part of the problem is I've been rambling when explaining things to you.'

'To clarify; you had relationships with both of them? Adam and Angelo?' asked the detective. Would he have asked a man a similar question so readily?

'I got to know them both well, in time,' I replied. 'I slept with them both, yes, but the relationships were out of sync with each other; they ran at their different paces.'

The detective wrote that down.

'Also,' I hurried to add. 'I know this all makes me look like the office floozy, but that is a total of two relationships over the whole winter. And it is now spring.'

Detective Grimandi scrutinised me. He looked puzzled.

'What's an office floozy?' he asked.

'Er.'

'How about we call the deceased X, what with everyone coming and going who might be listening, and perhaps just stick to talking about him for a while? Not the both of them,' he suggested. 'I can always ask more general questions as we go along.'

'No,' I said. 'Not X. A – let's call him A because that is his name. So, to recap, A was one of the first colleagues I got to know. And for my sins we ended up sleeping together. But he was also a work colleague so I decided we should stop. And then it started again, obviously; because you can see for yourself what happened last night.'

'How did he take it?' asked the inspector.

'Take what?'

'Being dumped. The first time.'

'I thought he took it well. He's local and I subsequently discovered he was well-connected; thus the secrecy today. So I didn't feel he would have trouble getting another woman. I didn't think much about it at the time.'

'How did he treat you around the office after you stopped the relationship?' asked the detective.

'Fine the first time,' I replied. 'They were both there to help, after all. They still helped me.'

A man came through the doorway wearing a plastic disposable gown with long sleeves.

'Someone wants a blood and urine sample?' he asked.

The detective pointed to me.

'You have no idea how pleased I am to see you,' I said. 'I am bursting. And would it be possible to have coffee soon? I could make it in a minute?'

'I'll make it,' said the detective. 'You two have a date in the bathroom.' He meant me and the woman police officer.

She accompanied me to the bathroom and watched me as I settled on the toilet. She actually watched me.

'Pee a bit first, then get some mid-stream pee into the plastic beaker,' she said.

I stared at her to see if she would look away as I peed. She didn't.

Back in the kitchen and much relieved – literally and figuratively – I settled down with the detective. He'd claimed he was going to make the coffee, but in my absence had delegated the task to a sundry female. Just when I thought he was a nice guy.

'So we had a month or two of working side by side, no trouble,' I said. 'Then there was the big event that happened to me that was in the news.' I stopped to see if I had to explain that further.

The female police officer piped up, 'Oh you're Emily Fisher. The Emily Fisher who has been in the news? Of course!'

'Nice to know I am famous amongst the Venice law enforcement,' I said.

'I was a good friend of the person who died,' she said. 'So, you're *the* Emily Fisher? And of course, you knew the other person who died that day. And there was another guy injured on the doorstep...'

'Death is following me around,' I said.

'But it must have been terrifying,' said the policewoman. 'Just terrifying.' She looked at me with alarm just considering it. 'Well, good for you anyway,' she concluded.

'So, there was the big event that you obviously know about,' I continued. 'And when that was all finally cleared up I still had to do my job of work, and after a week or so I felt a shadow over my desk and it was him: it was A. He obviously had something he wanted to say so I agreed to have a drink with him that evening. Oh, and we'd previously been to the same masked ball, a few days before that. It was the Venice carnival.'

I paused to drink my coffee.

'We went out to a charming little bar restaurant and he came over a little bit emotional. He said I had been too quick to dismiss what we had, and I was perhaps thinking too much about me being older. I only had so much time in Venice and I should enjoy myself and, well, the next thing I knew we were back at this apartment.'

'Was that yesterday?' asked the detective.

'No, maybe two weeks ago or a bit less,' I replied. 'Oh and we went to the opera.'

'So you renewed your sexual relationship with him about two weeks ago?' he asked.

'Yes.' I was actually getting myself a bit tangled up here, but it didn't matter too much. 'We dated,' I tried to clarify. 'Then I stopped it again. I think that was part of the problem and I should take some blame for this. I shouldn't have agreed to going out with him then stopped again then started again. So anyway, that was two weeks ago. I almost immediately thought it was a bad idea; we were colleagues.'

'Colleagues? You were his boss, or?'

'No I wasn't his boss. We were colleagues,' I said. 'So I stopped it again and then that is when things went wrong.'

'In what way did they go wrong?'

'He started getting emotional and abusive. He would wait until we were alone, and he would threaten me.'

'What kind of threats?' asked the detective.

'Nothing good ever comes of the way you behave. Sluts like you get their comeuppance in this part of the world. We have morals here in Italy.'

'That's not actually a threat,' said the detective.

'"You should be grateful I haven't fucking killed you." was one of his more kind remarks. "You think you are better than us, but you will end up floating dead in a canal," was another charming contribution. He always made sure no one could overhear him. I got the feeling he got a perverse enjoyment from hissing these things, but he was on the face of it smiling as he said them so that if a colleague saw us through a doorway he looked amicable. He was a nasty piece of knitting.'

The detective had been intermittently making notes.

'And you have proof for this?'

'No. As I said, he waited until no one could overhear us,' I said. Also it wasn't really what happened per se; I was smearing the dead man to a degree but not too much. I wanted to try and keep the narrative simple for the detective, but I didn't want to get too carried away saying how awful he'd been, when we all knew the punchline was that I then slept with him last night. It can go from him being suspect, to me being suspect for agreeing to being alone with him; such is the lot of women.

'And yet you ended up in bed with him?' he asked, as if to prove my point.

'I have no memory at all after a certain time last night,' I said. I was back to 100% truth which felt a lot better.

'So do you remember being assaulted?'

'No. Not in the slightest,' I replied.

'And you will be happy to put all this in writing in a statement?' he asked.

'Yes, of course,' I said. 'So after two weeks of this, I said to him that we should have a meet up and clear the air. I offered to have a drink with him. Like a peace offering.'

'And that was last night?' asked the detective.

'Yes. I had quite a few things to do over the weekend, so we agreed to meet last night. We had agreed to go to a bar at eight. But at about seven thirty, seven forty, there was a knock on my door and he was standing there holding two bottles of wine. He said, "I thought it would make more sense to stay in." He was holding a bottle of red wine and a bottle of white wine.'

Mentioning the wine reminded me that I had planned to alert the police to testing it.

'Those glasses,' I said, pointing across the kitchen to the seating area. 'Test the wine in those glasses.'

'Why?' asked the inspector.

'I drank white wine and he drank red wine. Seriously. Please test the wine left in those glasses.'

'Yes, but why?'

'Because I can't remember what happened after about eleven.' Was he being dim? 'I usually have a very good memory for events. These are the sort of events you would remember, yes? I was handcuffed to a man, it is clear I have been assaulted; it should all be very memorable. What does this all say to you?'

He nodded. 'We'll test the wine.'

The forensics man was in the bedroom with the dead body. The detective called to him and he came through to see us. The detective pointed to the wine glasses and asked that they be analysed.

'So you had a drink with him,' prompted the detective.

'Yes, and I tried to be pleasant and positive, but I wanted to bring things to a head with our relationship,' I said. 'We couldn't go on the way we were. But another thing you need to know...'

'Yes.'

'I was leading him on a bit.'

'How so?' asked the detective.

'I spent the evening trying to get him drunk. I had my phone on record and was trying to lull him into confessing a few of his misdemeanours. As well as what I was saying earlier, he was involved in the deaths that we mentioned before.'

'We don't know that,' said the inspector. He was far too quick to say it. I was suddenly aware he knew far more about the whole situation than I thought.

'Either way,' I said. 'I wanted to be able to prove to the world what he was like. That was how the evening began, anyway.'

'Hang on,' said the detective. 'So you are saying you have an audio recording of what happened last night?'

'Yes. I haven't listened to it, so I don't know if it came out clearly.'

'Well this is huge news. Let's get the phone,' he said.

My phone was fetched. I played with it a little. I checked the beginning of the recording, and there was some general chatter between me and him about making cocktails and it was clear enough. I ran forward to about halfway to check if it was still audible later in the evening; it was. We were discussing something about work.

'I'll go to the very end of the recording and see where it stops recording,' I suggested.

The detective nodded.

The audio was a bit more muddled now. It sounded like we were now in the bedroom and clothes were being removed. I scanned my memory for what embarrassments might lie in store for me. Oh what was I thinking? I had been caught by the police chained to a dead man with bruises on my genitalia. How much more embarrassing could it all possibly get?

The detective, the policewoman and I all craned over the phone.

We could hear some rustling and then a man's voice.

'If I really am the psychopath you claim,' he said. 'And you are the only person on my case, doesn't it make sense if I kill you now?'

Then it was my voice. 'No, you have to listen.' I was pleading.

'I am so angry with you,' he said.

Then there was a clear thumping noise. About four thumps.

I turned off the recording. We all exhaled. Thank heavens for modern technology.

'There is hours of it,' I said. 'So I suggest you listen to it yourselves and perhaps ask me about what you hear? But first I really would like to prioritise me being examined and photographed.'

'Well I want to hear the tape,' he said.

'Inspector,' I said. 'I have worked on a lot of insurance cases and I myself like as much evidence as possible that is gathered as early as possible. I have a lot of the night missing from my memory, so I would like to prioritise forensics rather than totally rely on my recall. The audio won't change if we listen to it later.'

The detective nodded. 'Would you feel comfortable having a male doctor examine you,' he asked. 'Or would you prefer a female doctor. It might take longer to get a female.'

'A male doctor would be fine. So long as he doesn't get handsy.' I have no idea why I attempted a joke. And given my Italian is not great, it was not clear - even to me – if I'd managed to make a joke at all.

I said to the detective, 'How about you photograph me now and take samples from me and under my fingernails and so forth? And then perhaps do it again with the doctor?'

'Why?' he asked. 'Why twice?'

'So I can get some proper clothes on.'

'Yes, some clothes,' he replied.

The odd thing was that although I had woken up chained to a dead body and had dragged it around, I now didn't want to see the body again; now I would find it distressing to even be in the same room as him. I asked the woman police officer to pick out some clothes for me from the bedroom and we then got on with some initial forensics. I egged them on to be as thorough as possible. I suggested areas they could swab and extra photos they could take.

We then figured that it would be best for me to wear loose fitting clothing in case we somehow disturbed any other evidence on my body, so I was soon sitting with the detective wearing a loose t shirt and some tracksuit bottoms.

I started to provide the detective with a few more details of the night before when the forensic man re-appeared.

'I've got a few issues,' said the forensics man. 'Firstly, I can't find the deceased's keys. Phone, yes. Wallet, yes. But no keys. That's odd. But there is more than that.' He beckoned to the detective to come and look at something in the bedroom together.

The detective was gone some time and then I heard him making a phone call, then another phone call. There was lots of discussion going on. I smiled at the policewoman with the plait, but we didn't make conversation. What was there to say?

When the detective returned, he stood in front of me.

'Emily Fisher I am arresting you on suspicion of murder.'

He started reading me my rights and the policewoman stood as if she was going to handcuff me. The way she moved so fluently, the way she showed no surprise, it was like she knew this was going to happen all along.

I went to stand, but found I couldn't. All the strength had gone from me.

'Perhaps I've been framed?' I asked.

No one was listening.

'When you think about what happened before,' I said. 'Perhaps I've been framed. Perhaps they wanted him out of the way and me discredited.' But I was talking to no one. Everyone was now bustling around; they all had their jobs to do. My head was swirling. They had not heard me, and I could no longer hear them.

For the second time that morning, I had handcuffs on my wrists.

SIX

I spent the day in a cell. I had no information to go on. No one to talk to. I was going out of my mind with worry. Why had they suddenly been so adamant that I should be arrested? Presumably they had seen something in the bedroom, or something on the dead body that made them come to the conclusion that I had done something, but what? I was the one covered in bruises, not the deceased; I had even provided audio of what had occurred. It was a complete and utter outrage that they had looked at the evidence in front of them and come to the conclusion that I was the criminal here, when clearly the overwhelming evidence was that I was the victim.

I was brought a meal on a plastic tray and some coffee. It was brought by hand by a woman who smiled at me. It struck me as trusting; I could easily have attacked her with the hot liquid. Then I went to drink the coffee; by accident or design it was lukewarm; perhaps she knew that. Perhaps it was even policy.

'Don't you even want to question me?' I asked. The guard shrugged as if she didn't understand what I was saying. Perhaps she didn't; Italian dialects vary considerably, and my Italian is perfunctory at best.

'Do I even get a phone call? One phone call?'

'No,' she replied. So she did understand me. 'It is not like in the movies,' she said.

At about four o'clock there was a clanking at my door and a warden appeared.

'You've got a visitor, come with me,' he said.

A visitor, not an interview.

I was led to an interview room where there was a tiny woman in black – black skirt, black blouse, black hair, black eyeliner, black expression. I think the effect she was going for was black. She had a file in front of her.

'Allegra de Vivo,' she said, not holding out her hand. 'I have been appointed as your lawyer.'

'By whom?' I asked. 'I haven't even made a phone call yet.'

She was a busy looking person with distraught-looking hair. She was tapping the interview table rhythmically and at high speed, as though I was somehow holding her up. She was the sort of person whose sole calorific intake each day was coffee; which, no doubt, was black. I used to worry about such people; I used to discretely push a pastry towards them in the hope they would eat it by accident. With my newfound weight gain my attitude had altered somewhat; it occurred to me that if I was a little more like her I might lose a few pounds.

'Well that's the way it is,' she replied. I'd already forgotten my question. 'If you would like other representation that is fine, but I assure you I will do my best to get you out of here if that is what you want.'

'That's exactly what I want.' I smiled at her warmly to see if she responded to that kind of thing. She didn't. She was the sort of person who was too busy having thoughts of her own to care about the thoughts of others.

'How did you get appointed?' I asked.

'Someone up high appointed me.' She shrugged at the recollection. 'You gave the police a urine sample.' She said this as a statement.

'I insisted on it. I think I had drugs in my system. Date rape drugs.'

'They will have had the preliminary results of that in three to four hours. If the results favoured their case, they would have made their move. Have you been interviewed after your arrest?'

'No. I've had a doctor look at me, and photos taken and stuff.'

'Perhaps the police are dithering. Perhaps they are gathering evidence. Perhaps they are just having a lengthy lunch break.' As she spoke, she was leafing through the file, scanning it at a rate of about five seconds per page. Is it even possible to read like that?

'In Italy we have one of the worst records for not allowing a suspect to have bail,' she continued. 'The European Court of Human Rights has issued numerous judgments that the courts and police keep suspects in prison too often, and for too long, prior to trial. They do not even consider the use of house arrest or an appropriate sum paid for bail. As a result, I have told the police that I have registered your case with the Observatory of Italian Prison Conditions. And I explained that it is up to them if they want to see their reputation further tarnished or if they want to see their reputation improved by their exemplary behaviour. It is possible that if I pursue this line you will be released on house arrest very soon. But maybe not. Either way, perhaps they will charge you later. Are you going to sign that or not?'

'Sign what?'

I had been so mesmerised by this fast-talking speed-reading caffeine junky of a woman that I hadn't noticed the piece of paper and pen she had placed in front of me; the document that officially allowed her to represent me.

'I suppose you're my only option,' I said.

The lawyer pierced me with her eyes, like I was being totally ungrateful.

'You sound great,' I tried. 'I'll sign. But you do think they will charge me?'

She didn't acknowledge what I said or my signature, she just placed the paper back in her file while simultaneously turning a page she was reading.

'I can't see any specific allegations against you. But it has to be murder or manslaughter. There is no warrant. When you are arrested in the act of committing a crime, or immediately after a crime, you have no right to be informed of the allegations until the prosecutor gets directly involved or a hearing for the validation of the arrest occurs. This is done by a judge and must be within four days of your arrest.' She said this like she was reciting something standard, and didn't have to listen to herself as she spoke; certainly she was reading something entirely different at the same time.

She suddenly looked at me. 'So your story is that this man slipped you a date rape drug and the next thing you knew you woke up covered in bruises and he was dead?'

'Just about,' I said. 'By chance I was able to provide audio from my phone that covered the whole evening.'

'What?' Asked the lawyer.

'I provided the police with audio of the whole evening.'

The lawyer started skimming through the file again. 'Not as far as I am aware,' she said.

'But I gave them my phone,' I protested.

'Not according to this. Did you back up the audio? Did you keep a copy?'

'No. There was no time. I thought I could trust the police,' I said.

The lawyer's pen tapped even faster. 'You thought you could trust the police?' she asked. She made it sound the most astonishing thing she had ever heard. 'Well what is on this audio?'

'Everything. It exonerates me.'

'Well the other evidence is here,' she said. 'Certainly the evidence is that he attacked you. I can see bruises. I am told there are other bruises?'

'Correct.'

'But there were no obvious bruises on the man.'

'I was flustered this morning, so I couldn't be sure. I didn't check his body thoroughly or anything; I was too flustered.'

'Well it is shocking that they have arrested a probable rape victim. Shocking that the audio you gave them has disappeared,' she said. 'I will try and get you out of here tonight, but don't raise your hopes. The dead man is from an important family. They may want to hush up anything that smeared his reputation. They may charge you with murder so...' In one motion she had gathered up her papers and was standing.

That was it? The meeting was over? I blinked and she was now by the door.

'Do everything the police tell you,' she said.

'I will.'

She knocked on the door to be let out.

'Do I not even get one phone call under Italian law?' I asked. 'To alert my friends or family.'

'No,' she said.

'Seriously?'

'It's not the movies.'

'When the other woman said that, I thought it was a joke.'

'I can contact your relatives for you,' she said. 'Or the police can do it. Your brother is called Peter, yes? Peter De'Ath? A Belgian name, I presume.'

'Yes.'

'Consider it done.' The door was now opening. 'Oh and you might want to spend your time thinking about the explanation that apparently the dead man died from a puncture.'

'A puncture?'

'Yes. They found a puncture wound on the skin of his chest, directly above his heart. It was a bruise with a puncture wound. The puncture wound was tiny but it was there. It was the evidence they used to arrest you.'

And with that she was gone. The whole encounter took at most four minutes.

Back in the cell and I was going out of my mind even more than before. I had handed over my phone with the audio on it and now it had disappeared. A puncture wound over his heart? These same two thoughts kept swirling in my head; but swirling them endlessly doesn't make them any clearer; it doesn't then create any extra information. Why does the brain do this to us? But then what else *was* I going to think about?

Hours later, or maybe less, there was a noise at my door. Food perhaps? I was starving. It was the lady warden, and she took me to an office where a policeman sat and smiled at me.

'You have a very efficient lawyer,' he said.

'Sounds good to me.' It was the first good bit of news that day.

'She is very forceful,' he said. 'If you insist on being released then there are a lot of conditions.'

'Which are?' I asked.

'You cannot leave the island. You cannot go to your home. You have to surrender your passport.'

'Which is at home,' I said. Where was I supposed to go if I couldn't go home?

'Your apartment is a crime scene,' he said. 'So we can accompany you to your home to pick up your passport and your toiletries and some clothes, and then you must nominate a hotel to stay in. You must not leave that hotel. We can phone you any time to check you are there. Do you understand and agree?'

'The alternative is staying in the cell?'

'Yes.'

In Britain if you agree to police bail it can mean you have to do the police's bidding for months or even years thereafter; it can be better for the suspect to simply stay in the police custody and wait out the 24 hours or 48 hours or whatever and then when released, you are released for good with no strings attached. I might happen to know. Because I might have been in trouble before. I had no idea if the same logic applied in Italy, however; my instinct was to get the hell out of the police station as soon as I could and on any terms.

'If I stay in the hotel does this affect me being allowed my freedom in four days?' I asked.

'No, it doesn't affect your rights.' It was one of those answers that was both precise and vague at the same time. But it would have to do. I wondered how much a hotel would cost me, but I signed the forms anyway.

SEVEN

The next day at ten o'clock I had an appointment with the detective, Gilles Grimandi. I still hadn't been charged with anything, but my heart fell when I saw him because he looked in a very sombre mood; nervous, even. What was he nervous about? Getting rid of my phone evidence? On the plus side, we weren't in an interview room; we were in the main police offices. I decided to take that as a good sign.

But then I noticed a stony-faced woman sitting in the corner; she looked really scary. She had the hooded eyes of someone who believed everyone in the world was to be treated with suspicion, unless they were a policeman; and even then she had her doubts.

'We are waiting for your lawyer, the legend that is Allegra de Vivo,' said Grimandi. A hint of sarcasm. 'So we are better not to discuss the case until she arrives, or she'll foot fault me for something. But I can ask you how you are. How are you today after your traumas?'

'Is this your boss?' I asked, pointing to the woman in the corner.

By merely drawing attention to her, I'd made him nervous. He attempted to cover it with a smile. 'In a manner of speaking,' he said. 'She is not part of the conversation. She just happens to be sitting here. How are you?'

'I'm staying in a hotel,' I said. 'Between the luxury breakfasts, and the maid to make my bed for me; believe me I am suffering.'

He nodded at this; too serious to laugh, it seemed.

There was a commotion at the far end of the office. A whirlwind was whisking past the desks, stirring up paperwork on its way. Signora de Vivo, my lawyer, was approaching. She was wearing her trademark black clothes and deprived, temporarily, of the opportunity to tap something rhythmically, her head was jiggering on her neck. Before I knew it, she was in a chair beside me shuffling her papers on the detective's desk. She then took out a pen and I thought she was going to write something, but it transpired her sole use for it was to tap rhythmically on a file. She accompanied the tapping with a shake of her knee. So far, so expected.

The funny thing was that when she caught sight of the woman in the corner she became quite still. She looked alarmed.

'What is she doing here?' she asked.

'She isn't here,' said the detective. 'She is just sitting.'

'So, this is why we are not in an interview room,' said my lawyer. 'So that she can be present.' The woman who was the subject of discussion responded by slowly closing her hooded eyes; on the face of it so that she could doze off, but probably so that she could listen more intently.

My lawyer started afresh tapping her file; like her clockwork mechanism had been wound up again.

The detective had some handwritten notes on a pad. I tried to read them upside down. One item said, 'Flesh under suspect's fingernails.' That didn't sound good. Evidently I was the suspect, not the deceased.

The detective opened a file over his notes to prevent my further reading. The file was already alarmingly large. It had a number of post-it notes to flag up various sections.

'First of all,' he said. 'There is our forensic examination of your body. I would like to ask a few questions about it.'

'Sure,' I replied.

'Under your fingernails we found tissue that matched the deceased's skin.'

'Okay.'

'Have you any idea how that happened?' he asked.

'I can only conclude that I scratched him,' I replied. 'Were there scratches on him?'

'He had scratches on his arms, forearms, and the side of his chest,' he replied.

'As I said, perhaps I scratched him. All the signs are that he attacked me, so perhaps I defended myself.'

I was half expecting my lawyer to caution me against talking. I stole a glance in her direction to see what I should do, but she was largely transfixed by the mystery woman in the corner. It was all very odd.

'But do you recall having scratched him?' pressed the detective. 'Do you recall attacking him?'

Attacking him? I was the one covered in bruises.

I tried to stay calm. 'I can honestly say I cannot recall attacking him by scratching him,' I said. Then I was annoyed at how I'd phrased that; I was implying that I was sometimes not honest.

'What *do* you remember?' he asked.

'I remember sitting drinking the wine,' I said. 'But huge amounts of the night are missing from my memory.'

He didn't press me further about my recollections. Why not? Perhaps he was coming back to it.

'The scratches on his body are consistent with you defending yourself. But they weren't deep. According to the pathologist, they hardly drew blood. In fact, he felt it was odd that there wasn't more blood drawn.'

'I am not a pathologist,' I said. I somehow sounded shirty. 'I don't usually have to defend myself against men, so maybe I'm not very good at it,' I tried.

'It's like you didn't defend yourself at all,' he said.

Was he claiming I did attack him, or I didn't attack him? It wasn't clear.

The detective turned to another page in the file. It had a post-it note at the top. Was he going to go through every page with a post-it? There were a lot of them.

'This is more delicate,' he said. 'We have photographs of your genital and anal area,' he said.

'Oh joy!'

The inspector looked at me strangely. I decided to not attempt levity again. Suspected murder was, of course, a serious issue.

He showed me some photographs. They were pretty gruesome. Evidently, they were of me.

'There is tearing in your anal area,' he said. 'And bruising.'

'I have had constipation since I have been in Venice. It has been painful going to the toilet.' I wasn't lying in the slightest. I didn't want to mindlessly blame the deceased for everything; even though I did indeed blame him for everything. Absolutely everything.

The detective placed more photos on the desk.

'Wow, ouch, is that a photo of my back?' I asked. There was a line of nasty bruises down it. They were sometimes circular and sometimes in a line. They were unsettling shades of red and black. They were surprisingly circular, to my eye – well some of them were circular at least; I wondered what the police made of that.

'It looks like someone has been hitting me. Hard,' I said.

'Do you remember being hit?'

'No. I do not recall anyone hitting me.' Again, I was being totally honest.

'And there was sperm in your vagina,' he said.

'Let me guess...'

'I find you quite flippant,' he said.

I wanted this man to think the best of me, even though he had probably done away with the phone evidence; it's odd when you think about it. I replied, 'This has been a really bad experience. I am trying not to let it all get to me. I am trying to not sink.' I breathed in and out as though to calm my nerves. 'I am trying desperately to see the lighter side,' I said. 'I am sorry if that comes over as flippant.'

He studied my face and then looked more sympathetic.

'I understand,' he said. 'The sperm sample matched the deceased; we are awaiting the full report. But there is certainly evidence you had intercourse.'

'There is also the bruising,' I said. 'Around my parts.' I decided to try and get on the front foot. 'What does the audio tell us?'

'The audio?' asked the detective.

'The audio that I taped on my phone,' I said.

'It cuts out unexpectedly,' he said.

'So it does exist?'

'What?'

'The audio on my phone does exist.'

'Of course it exists,' said the detective. 'We listened to it together, you and I.'

'It's not listed in the evidence,' said my lawyer.

'Yes it is.'

The detective searched the file and then showed it to us. It was referred to on one line only, but it was certainly mentioned. It was very likely indeed that my speed-reading lawyer had simply missed it in her haste.

'But I do want to ask you about the audio,' said the detective.

'Yes?'

'Why does it stop when it stops?'

'The deceased spotted my phone and accused me of taping him. So I went through a big show of turning my phone off.'

'Why didn't he then erase the audio?' asked the detective.

'Because he didn't have my PIN? Because he believed me when I said I wasn't taping him?'

'Or because he was dead,' he said. 'And the assault happened after the phone was turned off?'

'He had a violent change of mood. He was suddenly very angry. You heard the tape yourself. You heard him turning angry.'

'I have listened to the tape very carefully,' said the detective. 'And what I can hear is possibly entrapment. You said yourself you were leading him on.'

'Not to beat me black and blue,' I protested. I looked to my lawyer for support.

'I haven't heard the tape,' she said.

Oh great.

'I don't know how to put this decorously...' began the detective. 'But there is another way of looking at all this.'

'Go on.'

'Miss Fisher. You don't appear to have defended yourself. There were just small scratches on him.'

'So?'

36

'So do you indulge in sexual activities that are violent? It would explain why you didn't apparently fight back.'

'No,' I replied.

'Are you into bondage or BDSM. Consensually, I mean,' he pressed. 'I have to ask.'

I again expected my lawyer to offer guidance, but she was now engrossed in looking at my photos.

'It's not my kind of thing,' I said. 'I'm just not a whips'n'handcuffs kind of gal.' This was entirely true. 'I'm not saying I've never had my arse slapped. But that's sex isn't it?'

'It is?' asked the detective.

I looked to the two women for confirmation or denial of my statement. Neither of them helped.

'So you are saying no? Can I put "no" on the record about BDSM?' asked the detective. 'I would point out that the evidence may be against you.'

'Well which is it?' I asked. 'I murdered him, or I didn't touch him at all? You can't have it both ways.'

'I am just trying to get to the bottom of things, Miss Fisher.'

I finally achieved eye contact with Allegra. She nodded her head to imply I should calm down a bit. Or rather she adjusted her already nodding head to imply something or other. There was something 'off' with her, even by her standards. Perhaps she was ashamed she hadn't spotted that the audio was indeed logged as evidence.

'I am literally sitting here thinking through my last couple of boyfriends,' I said. 'And thinking what sort of sex we had. It's not that there's never been any rough as part of the rough and tumble. It is just, as I said to you before, I am not a tie me up and cause me pain kind of girl. So, no, I would not characterise the sex I have as violent.' Except, in truth, with this one person. The person now dead.

He turned to another page in his file.

'Next item,' he said. 'Your urine sample, Miss Fisher.' Should I encourage him to call me Emily? It would probably give out the wrong vibe. He'd said Miss again, not Signora. An allusion to the fact that I am a foreigner. Did that mean something? I was over-thinking. 'There were suspicions,' he said.

'What suspicions?' I asked. I could feel the energy draining from me. Being accused on endless different levels, from endless different angles, is very tiring.

'Suspicions your urine would not be neutral,' he said. 'We have the preliminary tests. Your urine had traces of drugs in it.'

I knew it. I literally knew it.

'What drugs?' I asked. Seriously, what drugs? I am not a total stranger to such things. But it had been my suggestion to test my urine; surely that would count in my favour.

'A date-rape drug commonly known as Rohypnol,' he said. 'Was found in your urine. There was also a trace of something else, but it's not clear. It might be nothing.'

'I had a date rape drug in my body?' I asked.

'In large amounts,' said the detective. 'And the same drug was found in your wine glass.'

'Oh well. That fits with my amnesia,' I said.

'Did you see the man known as 'A' place anything in your drink?' asked the inspector.

'No. But if he was trying to drug me, he would hardly do it in front of me.'

The inspector nodded. He turned to another post-it note.

'We searched the property where the deceased man lived,' he said.

'And?'

'And we found a bottle hidden there with the same drug in it.'

'You found date rape drug at his apartment?'

'His house, yes. He had a bottle hidden behind a dresser. The sample from that matched the drug in your urine. Also, we found a small bottle of the same substance in his trouser pocket. The trousers he took off in your apartment.'

'Wow,' I said.

'There were fingerprints on both the bottles. His fingerprints.'

'So the evidence is that he drugged me. And he might have done this before,' I said.

'We don't know that,' said the detective quickly. 'He is a respectable man.'

Clearly not.

'Can you tell me what actual evidence you have that I may have done a murder?' I asked. It was worth a shot.

At that question, the detective fell into silence. The lady in the corner's eyes were still completely closed, but now it was if she were holding her breath as well. She was definitely interested in this answer. Even my black clad lawyer became motionless.

'We are investigating a puncture wound that we found on his chest above his heart.'

'Okay, but what did he actually die of?' I asked. 'Has he had a post mortem examination?'

The detective didn't need to consult his notes on this, but he did take time to choose his words.

'We haven't got a full toxicology report and so for that, and a few other reasons, the results of the post mortem investigation are not official and final.'

'But?' I asked.

'The deceased had some cocaine in his blood stream and a lot of alcohol. The amount of cocaine was not thought to be at dangerous levels.'

'So no date rape drug for him then?' I asked. Again, it sounded flippant. What is wrong with me? The detective appeared to be being helpful; I should encourage him.

'It appears he had an embolism in the brain,' said the detective. 'His brain function stopped.' he said. 'A massive embolism.' Unexpectedly he added my name. 'Emily Fisher.'

'Yes?'

'You are free to go.'

'I am free to go?'

Quite reasonably, I was stunned.

'We must assume at this time and with the evidence that we have,' continued the detective. 'That the deceased drugged you. Then once you were drugged, he assaulted you physically. That you fought back to a degree, but you were sedated so it was largely ineffectual. Then he assaulted you sexually. Then for medical reasons, unrelated to other events, he died.'

My lawyer instantaneously went from assimilating events to a state of attack.

'We will file charges,' she snapped.

'On what grounds?' asked the detective.

'It was clear all along that my client was the victim of a savage beating and rape and yet you arrested her. The overwhelming forensic, physical and audio evidence was of my client being physically and sexually assaulted and yet because of the identity of the deceased, because of who he was, you somehow managed to find one tiny mark on his chest and spin that into an accusation against the victim; all in a pathetic attempt to rescue the reputation of the dead man and smear my client. And it isn't even plausible! We all know that men get up to a whole sorry pile of perversions, violence and misogyny and dress it up and call it BDSM, but whoever heard of a woman handcuffing herself to a man and murdering him? No one! You're a disgrace!'

The woman in the corner opened her eyes slowly. She cleared her throat. It had the effect of stopping my lawyer in her tracks. She ignored what my lawyer had said, and addressed the detective.

'So,' she asked. 'There will be no charges?' Her voice was a drawl.

'No charges,' confirmed the detective.

'And you are satisfied that you have been investigating the case fully and without any hindrance?' she asked.

'Of course,' replied the detective.

'That you have fully investigated the possibility that there might have been a murder or manslaughter?' she asked.

'Yes.'

'But what of the puncture in the chest?' she asked.

'It was a tiny wound and it left some bruising on the chest surface, so it was of definite interest as a possible cause of death. But the pathologist was not sure it was much more than superficial; it was unclear if any puncture wound got as far as the heart. As I said, the wound itself was tiny in diameter so it was hard to track. And the cause of death was definitely in the brain, so on the balance of evidence it has been deemed an irrelevance.'

The woman considered this; she cupped her knees with her hands and rubbed them in slow circles as she did some thinking.

'And there was something about some missing keys?' she asked.

The detective wasn't expecting that. He consulted his notes and flicked through a few pages.

'According to the initial scene-of-crime forensic team,' prompted the woman.

The detective found the correct section of the file and read it.

'It was noted that we couldn't find the deceased's keys,' he said. 'But that means nothing either way. Some people don't carry keys. Or maybe he left them somewhere.'

'So that's that?' asked the woman.

'That's that.'

On hearing this, the woman rose from her chair. For the first time, it became apparent just how tall she was. She towered over me and I felt instinctively afraid. My lawyer looked on with big coaled eyes; she was stock still. The tapping had gone; it was not clear her heart was even beating.

'In that case,' said the woman. 'Emily Fisher?'

'Yes?' I had kept my nerves largely under control all morning, but now my voice was tight in my throat.

'On behalf of the police force of Venice...' She was going to apologise?

'What?' I squeaked

'I would like to thank you.'

She reached out her hand to shake mine. Then she had a thought, and hugged me instead. She had a very bony ribcage, so it was more than disconcerting.

I was distracted by a chirping rattling noise that I couldn't identify; it was most odd. It turns out that is what it sounds like when my lawyer's giggling.

'So do you want to press charges for wrongful arrest?' the tall woman asked me.

'No,' I replied. 'I want to go home.'

'For that I thank you,' said the woman. 'You have to understand that given the identity of the deceased, given his family and status, we have to be seen to thoroughly investigate the possibility of murder or manslaughter. It cannot look as though we covered anything up. In that, we have to thank you for your forbearance.'

I only really felt truly in the clear when I was in the fresh air outside. I walked for a little with the lawyer just to get some distance between me and the police building.

'Who was that woman?' I asked at last.

'A very high up person,' she answered. She shook her head as she considered events.

'That's a bit vague,' I said.

'A very, very, important, high-up person in the justice system. It doesn't get much higher, at least not in this region. Unless you want the President himself sitting in the corner.'

'I don't want anyone sitting in the corner. I just want it to be over.'

'I suppose I should have guessed, when I was asked to take your case,' said Signora de Vivo.

'Guessed what?'

'That you have friends in high places,' she mused.

'What? I do?' It was total news to me. 'I really don't.'

The lawyer shook her head dismissively.

'Yes Emily, you have friends in high places.'

And with that she disappeared up an alley. She didn't even say goodbye.

PART TWO

THE WORLD ACCORDING TO EMILY

ONE

THREE WEEKS PREVIOUSLY

It started with a woman standing across the street from my office. Just standing. Staring.

Well I say street. The alley – or calle to use its proper local term – that I can see out of my office window is only about two metres wide. My direct view from my desk is of a plastered wall that is intermittently flaked to reveal some brickwork. Like a lot of Venice, the pockmarks and flaking go up to a well-defined line; the highest the damp and its salts can rise up the wall from the water table below. It's a surprisingly high line, especially when you think about the physics involved.

Because the calle is narrow and runs west to east, the sun only illuminates my bit of our view for at most an hour first thing in the morning and an hour in the late afternoon; the rest of the time there isn't much to look at.

If I lean forward, however, there is a little more to see. The alley widens out to the right where there is a small bar/trattoria on the corner beyond, and the owner has lined a few tables and chairs for customers down the alley along the far wall. Venice is not a huge island, but it is crowded, and as a result every square inch is used wherever possible, even in the less touristy areas. Beyond the trattoria there is a stone bridge that leads over a canal to a church beyond. It is 16th century and has a Titian and is famous for its trompe l'oeil effects. Apparently. I have never been in. I am not proud of this.

Our office building is temporary and was previously a workshop for a woodcarving business that died with its owner a year or so previously. We appear to be the only office workers in the area, unless you count the post office staff round the corner on the quayside. Until recent years, Venice had a large insurance presence on the island; in the post-war economic malaise, white collar companies were given financial incentives to move to the island to provide jobs, and as a result one of Italy's largest insurers had offices in St Marks Square no less; but over time, and with the rise and rise of tourism, the various functions of the office moved back to the headquarters in Trieste and the company's presence in the city was reduced to a minimum. Our offices were chosen to allow us to visit specific businesses around Venice that had made insurance claims.

The only problem about our location was that we were on the bottom of the island and I had somehow secured accommodation at the very top, in an area called Cannaregio. It was a lovely neighbourhood but it was about forty minutes' walk away. As a result, I had taken to halving the journey by using the waterbus; a number 2 would take me from the jetty near my office, round the top of the island and back down the Canal Grande to a jetty near the Rialto Bridge. The rest of the walk took in some lovely shops and bridges and views, and made for a perfect reward after a long day gazing at a computer.

So to set the scene, I was working side by side with Adam and Angelo, processing insurance claims.

Angelo, as usual, was keeping his head down and working in silence. His phone made a noise and he squinted at it. He then looked half-heartedly for a cord to recharge it. How could a man who worked in such a stolid fashion not have the wherewithal to keep his phone charged? A depressed man, perhaps. A man lost in thoughts past.

Adam, meanwhile, was his usual restless self; a tragic victim of his gadfly attention span. He was talking generally, just to fill the air.

'The thing that makes me uneasy,' he said. 'Is that when shopkeepers and residents in Venice took out their insurance, I don't think it was made obvious to them that they wouldn't be able to make a claim if there was flooding. What do you think?'

That's his way of trying to get us to talk; he makes a lengthy statement and then asks a question. I was hideously over-worked and trying to concentrate, so the pause he left stretched longer and longer. Ultimately though, it's nice to be nice; so eventually I cracked and replied.

'How do we know that for sure?' I asked. 'How do we know it wasn't made obvious to them?'

Adam leapt back in, enthused that he had a response. 'Because most of them have flood defences in their doorways that were professionally fitted. They were assuming that some flooding was inevitable, and they were prepared for it. If they took out flood insurance they must have felt they were insuring against an extra-high water level that could not be predicted,' he said.

'We don't know that,' I said. I was mindful that our own office had a flood barrier built into its doorway. It was left by management permanently padlocked in place, in case there was flooding at a weekend or evening when the office was unattended. As a result, just to get into the office, you had to lift your leg about two foot in the air and step over the mini wall. It was ridiculous, and kind of incriminating that the company did indeed understand what constituted normal variations in the tide levels.

'What do you think Marco thinks?' asked Adam.

What does our boss and line manager think? He thinks we should be working, not asking asinine questions.

Adam sprang up to go and talk to Marco; his office was a little down the corridor. I reflected that Adam was one of those people who in his own head only really existed if his existence was confirmed by others. Constantly confirmed by others. That, and his unabashed air that he was eager to rise up through the company, made him exhausting company.

Adam returned sometime later and slumped in his chair.

'Marco wasn't in,' he said.

Adam, you can suck up to the bosses all you like, I have been working at this company long enough to know that in fact there isn't a career ladder here, so you might as well chill out.

'What you need to do is apply for a job at a rival company, and then in another two years apply to move back again,' I said. 'Mysteriously our management will reward you with a far better job than if you had stayed here all along and actually helped out.'

'What?' asked Angelo. I had provoked a rare reaction from the care-worn almost-handsome one.

'Nothing,' I replied. 'Just thinking out loud. What do you think about the claims, Angelo?'

Angelo considered my question in his cautious hen-pecked way. He would want to express the company line, but on the other hand he wouldn't want to disagree profoundly with Adam or me. Basically he wanted a quiet life, and a chance to grow some balls.

At length he spoke, 'The total damage to property in Venice spread amongst all the insurance companies might be up to a billion.' He was stating a fact rather than offering an opinion; the diplomat's way out. 'Insurance companies can't be expected to cover all of a sum that large; we would simply cease to exist. And there are the government schemes that have already kicked in. They are generous.'

Adam wasn't listening and didn't apparently care. He spotted a member of management go past our doorway. He bounded off after him to schmooze. Ten minutes later I heard him talking to a further colleague and asking him about his children, and a further ten minutes after that I heard him talking to the receptionist, Eta.

Eta was a woman of unknown age who was forever indulging in beauty treatments; Botox, fillers, chemical peels. As a result we have no clear idea how old she is; she's certainly not twenty, and she's certainly not fifty, but after that all bets are off. She had recently slipped across the border to Slovenia to indulge in some obscure cosmetic treatment not apparently licenced in Italy, or indeed any sane country. Adam feigned an interest in it. To judge by the conversation bouncing off the corridor walls, it was as if Adam wanted to indulge in the treatment himself. 'Five to ten years younger?' he was asking. He was already painfully young. Five to ten years younger would make him a pre-pubescent. Not the way to go, Adam.

He finally settled back down at his desk, and blatantly looked around for a further distraction rather than actually do any work. For all his ambitious desire to rise up through the company; the one tactic he was never going to stoop to, was to do a genuine day's work.

'Adam!'

'Yes Emily?'

'How about some work?'

He considered the idea, and seemingly pleased with the novelty of the suggestion, logged onto his computer. It was some time after that the woman in red appeared.

It was only me who saw her. It had been a windy day with brittle sunshine; the sort of day that wouldn't declare its hand; it could brighten up, or we could get a deluge and be in for a record flood. And that would mean more insurance claims for us to process.

'Did you see that?' I asked Adam.

'See what?' Adam shares my window with me, while Angelo has to lean over two desks to even see natural daylight. Perhaps that's why his skin is so pale.

'There was a woman standing across the alley. She was wearing a bright red dress.'

'No,' replied Adam firmly. He plainly wanted to concentrate on something; so that's a first. I leant over to look at his monitor; to find out what was consuming his attention. He was playing a computer game. A computer game. I should be really telling him off; he was my assistant after all, and we were so snowed under with work.

'She was staring at me,' I said.

'She was staring at you?' asked Angelo; the second time that morning I had piqued his interest. An office record, and a PB for me.

'She's already gone,' I said.

We were interrupted by a tourist who blocked my line of vision. Our office was not close to any of the most famous attractions of Venice, but the city is beyond saturation point with tourists, so inevitably some of them seep through, like damp, to the alley where we work. Mostly I stare at them, but they never seem to find it uncomfortable.

This particular tourist came right up to the window of our office and took a photo of us at work. I smiled and did some jazz hands at him. He didn't see anything strange in that and took more photos. I resisted the temptation to lift up my t shirt and flash at him.

'Oh now she's back,' I said. 'She's holding up a sign.'

I stared at her and she stared at me.

'She's holding up a sign?' asked Adam. He wasn't interested; he was just doing that thing where you are not really listening at all, but just repeat the last sentence you've heard.

'Yes,' I said. 'Oh, now she's gone.'

'What did the sign say?' asked Adam.

'It said Emily.'

'Emily?'

'Yes my name. Emily. In big black letters. She was looking straight at me. She was holding up a sign saying Emily.'

Adam peered briefly out the window. There was nothing to see.

'Weird,' conceded Adam, but he was noncommittal. He was very committal, however, about zapping aliens on his computer screen. I should tell him off. No. I can't get round the fact he is just so good looking. Do good looking people get to behave worse than the rest of us and we don't notice it? Probably.

It was startling. Why would a woman hold up a sign with my name on it? And it wasn't just that. The way she'd stared at me; a hard piercing stare. It was like she'd turned her irises to black just for me. My heart started to pound thinking about it. Oddly enough, a while earlier when I had actually seen her, I hadn't felt alarmed at all; I had taken it in my stride.

I got back to my work. My thoughts were almost back to the dry subject of the small print in insurance documents, when a light flashed in my eyes. A piercing light.

46

I looked up out of the window and there was the woman again; the woman in the red dress. She was holding a sign in one hand and a laser pointer in the other. She was directing the laser pointer around my face to try and get my eyes. Well that's just dangerous. She caught me with the beam once too often and I was left with a flashing zig zag in the centre of my vision. The result was that it was now harder for me to see what was written on her sign. It was no longer 'Emily.'

I blinked a few times and tried to focus. I tried not to look directly at the sign, but tried to read it from the side of my vision. The woman was still staring at me.

The sign said, 'Follow me.'

'Look! Look!' I said.

Adam didn't look up; saving planet Earth from aliens required his full concentration.

I reached left and tapped his wrist. 'Look out there!' I said.

He played his game for an infuriating extra two seconds. By the time he did look up, the woman was gone.

I dashed up from my seat. I didn't take my handbag or shut down my computer.

That was my first and biggest mistake.

I ran past reception, stepped over the wretched flood defence, and out into the alley. I looked left and right. I couldn't see anything. The woman had been across the alley from our office but slightly to the left, so I felt it was reasonable to search on that side; and there was certainly no one on the bridge to the right; but on the other hand, on the left I could see a long way ahead and there was no one there either. Perhaps she had ducked into a side passage.

I proceeded with caution and looked down an alley to my right. I could hear footsteps echoing ahead. I went through the alley and discovered it emerged into a small residential square; paved in stone and surrounded on all sides by houses. The square was empty but there were two alleys leading off it at the far end. I ran across the square to the most obvious alley – the one that geographically had the most chance of going somewhere. It was perhaps ten yards long and was nothing but the brick sides of buildings. At the end it turned right into a much longer, wider alley. There was no one there.

I backtracked and got myself back to the little square.

I tried the other alley.

This one led down to a canal. I walked cautiously forward. At the end of it on the right there was a recessed doorway. The woman in the red dress was just standing in the doorway, stock still and silent.

She smiled at me.

'Emily Fisher?' she asked.

'Yes.'

'I have something of extreme interest to you.'

'What? What have you got?' I asked.

She gave a barely perceptible nod. I realised too late it was directed to someone behind me.

I felt a sack pulled over my head and down over my body.

The other thing that happened, and this is of equal importance; was that it had started to rain.

TWO

Arms wrapped round my chest, trapping my own arms at my side. I wriggled and kicked with everything I had. I assumed the woman in red was still in front of me, so I kicked forwards hard, but I just made contact with the wooden door. I then rammed my heel backwards hoping to catch someone's shin. The sacking smelt of hessian and sawdust. I could see a hazy light through it, but no actual images, and the day had darkened as the rain took hold which didn't help. I felt something grip round my waist, trapping my arms with it. Then it tightened. A belt?

Then I felt myself being lifted up, and carried backwards.

'Help! Help!'

I wriggled and kicked as best I could.

'Be quiet if you know what's good for you.' It was a man's voice.

I had heard that a kidnapper feels the most vulnerable for the first few minutes of the abduction; while they are still out in the open and not on their own pre-prepared territory. This might be my best chance to get help.

I filled my lungs with air.

'Help!' I shouted. I thrashed around as best I could.

'Excuse me Signore?' said someone. A passer-by presumably?

'Help!' I shouted louder.

I was now being carried faster.

'Signore?' continued the man's voice, more distant already. 'Should I call the police?' But I could feel us turning a corner.

'Yes, call the police!' I shouted, or shouted as best I could through the sacking.

One brave passer by; would they actually do anything? He had already been braver than most people would be by calling out, so would he persist? Would he call the police? I doubted it, and even if he did; by the time they arrived we would be long gone.

I filled my lungs for another hefty scream, but my skull banged against something hard. It knocked the wind out of me and jarred my neck. The bone in my scalp was now thundering with pain.

I was being carried down some steps. The rain was obviously heavy now; it was making my sacking sodden; I could feel it on my legs. Then we stopped and I couldn't make out what was happening. And then there was a slow motion sway, rising up and falling left then right; the unsteady swimming feeling you get when you are stepping onto a boat. Then one of the men grunted under my weight. I am not that heavy. Then an uncertainty of motion, followed by a long drawn out swing back; was I being swung ready to be thrown?

'Help! Call the police!' I shouted. I didn't even know if anyone was there to hear me.

I was lowered - with some care to be fair – onto the floor of what I presumed was a boat. Then all the light went as something heavy fell on me; it pressed me down head to toe. Probably a tarpaulin.

I felt defeated. Who would kidnap me? Venice, famously, has a low crime rate. The abductors knew my name, so it wasn't a random crime. It was me they wanted, but why? I have no money. I doubt my employers would stump up cash to bail me out. It had to be something other than a ransom. But what?

There was a rhythmic pounding where the boat was moving at speed through the water. It was faster than a normal boat would move in Venice. Would that draw attention to it? I doubted it. Or rather, it wouldn't draw enough attention for someone to call the authorities. Perhaps I should have counted in seconds how long the trip was. Would that be any use? Anything more than a minute's travel and I could be almost anywhere. After all, Venice is not an island; it is 118 islands.

The boat's action was getting more choppy now and harder going; we were going further out to sea.

I felt with my hands. By some miracle was there something on the decking beneath me that I could use as a weapon? Of course not. And even if there was; there was the sacking between me and it.

Think Emily, think. What could I do to go on the offensive here? Perhaps my next opportunity was when they were forced to move me again. But what could I do? Then a truly frightening thought struck me. What if this wasn't a kidnapping at all? What if they were simply planning to kill me and dump me overboard in the sea?

I scoured my brain for who I might have offended over the years. Quite a few people probably, but no one in Venice, surely? At least, not as far as I knew. Except the work we were doing in general; we had been in the newspapers where businesses and local famous families had grouped together to get publicity for how they had been treated by the insurance companies. My name had been in the papers and on the internet. I had been treated as if I was a spokesman for the company but in fact all I had done was deal with queries as I went along. Was I the public face of the callous insurance companies that hadn't paid out for the Venice flooding? It was entirely possible. But would they murder me for that? Would a disappointed policy holder go to all this trouble to bundle me into a boat and drop me off the side? It seemed very unlikely.

Was there any chance I could wriggle free? In my mind it was a leather belt that was trapping my arms. What if I wriggled my arm round a bit? If I could get an elbow above the belt line, then I might be able to free my whole arm. But then what? Try and tear the sacking over my face? I wriggled. I wriggled again. It was all hypothetical. I was stuck.

The motor of the boat was slowing. The water was more calm. Had we got to our destination, or were we in the middle of the sea? Surely we hadn't gone far enough out? Surely they would want to drop me in the Mediterranean proper, not just the lagoon.

I decided to reassure myself that if they were going to drop me into the sea then they would attach me to something heavy. I promised myself I wouldn't panic until that had occurred; in the absence of a heavy weight being attached to me I would assume it was just a kidnapping. *Just*? *Just* a kidnapping?

I could feel the boat steady as it was moored up, and then an asymmetric lunge as someone stepped off the boat. Okay, so we weren't in the middle of the lagoon.

The tarpaulin was removed. My gauzed light returned. Heavy rain lashed my legs once more.

'One, two, three...'

I was lifted. It was at least two people.

I wriggled my legs and body violently. Solely out of pride.

I was floating through the air.

'Help! Help!'

But the acoustics were duller, and we were now in shadow. There was an odd stillness about the place.

'Careful through the doorway,' said one man. Well that was a pretty hefty clue. We were perhaps indoors already. It felt colder. Perhaps we were in a warehouse or similar. I was then carried perhaps twenty yards.

'Hold her still.'

I stopped wriggling in order to listen.

Nothing to hear, but a clamminess on my legs where we were somewhere colder and danker.

'Hold her. Hold her steady,' said the man down by my legs. I reckon there had only been two of them for some while now; there had been no evidence of the woman in red since they had put the sacking over me.

51

I felt something pulling around my ankles. They were being tied. I tried to kick out to keep my legs free, but they were already trapped.

Then there was another bracing feeling around my ankles which puzzled me at first.

And then I realised something very heavy had just been attached to them.

THREE

My ankles were now completely immobile. I imagined in my head that the weight that was binding them was a concrete block, but it could have been anything. The combined weight of me and the concrete block was now too much for the men to carry; I was sinking in their arms and I could hear them straining.

'We've got to position her forward before we drop her,' said the man near my face.

'This is too heavy. We'll have to swing her.'

I was too weak with fear to protest or scream. And besides, what would be the point? Should I beg instead? There was no obvious tactic that would work.

'You swing the legs and when you let go, I will push the body after,' said the man by my head. They wanted the weight to drop in the water first. What difference would that make? I would drown anyway. I couldn't work it out. And what was the water? I thought we were indoors now?

'One.'

'Two.'

'Three.'

I swung out in mid-air.

I was suspended without dropping for about a second.

Then my legs were yanked straight downwards, and my spine was flicked like a whip.

My ankles hit the bottom first. Then my arse. Then because I couldn't protect myself with my hands, my head fell backwards with a thump. It had already been hurting. Now it hurt some more.

It wasn't water I was in – that was something at least - and I hadn't come to rest on a concrete floor. It was maybe a mattress or some bedding.

It was my ankle and my lower back that did the first complaining. My ankle had been twisted sideways and it sent a pain up my body that was so sharp I felt sick. But my back wasn't far behind; a duller but more profound pain where it was jarred. Then my head started throbbing again. The pain was so severe I was going to faint or be sick or both. Throwing up in the confines of the hessian sack; just great.

There was someone beside me. They were tying me up even more? No, the pressure around my arms was going. Then there was pulling. I was being jostled and shoved. They were taking the sacking off me.

I caught a glimpse of someone's leg; then as I turned my head, I could see a second leg as someone was climbing up and away from me. I was in a pit, like an old-fashioned inspection pit for looking under cars. But there are no cars in Venice. Looking under boats then? Or I was on the mainland now at the docks? I tried to see what I could spot about the kidnappers that would help identify them later, but my movement was constrained and everything was happening fast. Quite formal brown leather shoes. Dark blue trousers that were like the ones you wear with a suit. What else could I see? Nothing. Nothing at all. Because a large lid came down on some hinges.

Everything went black.

Well at least I hadn't drowned. And wow did my ankle hurt. I once rolled the same ankle when I was wearing high heels and I almost passed out with the pain. It was so bad, and took so long to recover, that I have largely been wearing flats since. But enough about the fun times when I used to have a social life and wear heels to parties and then wore flats and wasn't kidnapped in any way; what could I do about my predicament?

Had I seen anything else before they put the covering over the pit? It was only a few seconds and I had concentrated on trying to identify the men, but what else had I seen in the periphery of my vision? I felt sure the pit wasn't bare. I thought I had seen something at the edge of my vision but what? I felt around with my hands. I was definitely on a mattress. Could I remember seeing the mattress? I somehow felt it had stripes, but had I imagined them? It didn't matter either way. What else was here? I was sure that something had registered in my vision. Some sort of clutter.

What could my hands find?

I felt my ankle. It was swollen on the right and my two legs were bound together. It was a metal cord that was wrapped around my ankles a few times; metal laminated in plastic, a lot like the ones you use to chain up a push bike. This cable led, I discovered, not to a concrete block, but to a big round metal weight; the sort that weightlifters use. The way they had fixed it was quite convoluted, so I felt there was a little hope that I could wriggle out of it. And then there was the fact that I couldn't feel a lock. Had it been tied in some way? If it was tied, then it could be untied. As a result, I felt almost positive about my predicament. But the feeling didn't last; I soon felt further along and found they had indeed used a padlock to bind my legs.

I padded my hands around some more. Would my eyes accustom to the dark or was there really no light down here at all?

The place smelled musty; like it regularly got soaking wet. But the mattress was dry, so it must have been placed in here very recently.

As a first step I patted around the periphery of the mattress. It was against the wall at one side and it more or less met the walls at its upper and lower end. But along the other side there was a gap of about a metre; this was cold flooring. I felt it with my palm. I could feel grime and dust, but was the floor made of concrete or was it compacted earth? It wasn't clear. Bricks perhaps. Possibly it was a brick floor.

I tried to be methodical. The wall that was clear of the mattress, was the wall where the man had pulled himself up to escape. It was this area where I felt there might have been some items that my brain somehow registered, but I didn't quite see directly. I positioned my legs at a slightly different angle so that I didn't hurt my ankles even more, and which gave me a little more scope to move.

What could I feel? I think it really was a mechanic's inspection pit; I was becoming more and more convinced it was something like a pit in an old boatbuilding yard to look under the hull of boats.

Another possibility was that it was part of the cistern system. Before Venice had mains water provided in pipes, they had a huge issue with obtaining fresh water; after all, Venice is surrounded by a salt water lagoon and there are no fresh water lakes or wells on the island. As a response to this, every district used to collect rainwater from rooftops and gutters, and it was filtered through sand, and stored in cisterns underground. The cisterns could be as big as a town square or as small as the inspection pit I was now it. There were over 6000 of them and some of them were over a thousand years old. The clean water thus collected was drawn by the residents from a well in the centre of the piazza. A local trusted person, such as a priest, was paid to peer down the well twice a day and check for dead rats and so on. Most have been filled in now, but about 600 remain and the evidence of them is still in abundance in nearly every square you visit in Venice. The reason I knew so much about the cisterns was that we had received an insurance claim where one had collapsed leaving a sinkhole. Either way, I had a feeling I might be in one now.

None of these thoughts helped me, except that if it was an inspection pit created from the edge of a larger cistern then one side may be made of a different material from another where it had been walled off, so it may be easier to break through. It was only an idea, but I was short of useful leads as to how to get out, so I was grateful for it.

I felt the walls. My hands felt dirty just feeling them. Was it oil and axle grease that was on the bricks, or the slime of getting repeatedly wet from canal water? I sniffed my fingers. It was the smell of dirt and river and maybe oil. I padded further along. I knocked something off something else. It made a thunk when it landed. I felt around. There was something like a little table in the corner. No, it was a small crate, like a crate that fruit sometimes comes in, or bottles. I felt down beside it and round the floor. It was a plastic bottle that I had knocked over. I weighed it in my hand; it was heavy where it was full. Probably water, then. I put it back on the crate. Okay so they didn't want me to die of thirst. That was something.

I felt around some more. The crate was on its side with its opening facing me. Inside the crate was a large round tin; like when a restaurant needs a massive amount of cooking oil or tinned tomatoes. It was open and empty. My heart sank. Was I supposed to pee in that? I had a mental image of trying to sit on it to pee while my legs were tied to the iron weight and all the time my ankle was throbbing where I had sprained it. Oh well, at least it was further evidence they expected me to be alive for a while.

Was there food?

I continued padding my palms around in the pit. Nothing. Perhaps even the crate and the empty tin can were just litter and not there by design. But the mattress? Why would a mattress be down here unless it was for me? This is the sort of pit that would flood at high tide; this mattress was dry, so it hadn't been down here long.

I sat for a while trying to think through my options.

What about the roof? Was that the weakest link? Could it be broken? I pulled at the weight at my ankles so that I could stand up. It wasn't quite possible; I could sit up a bit but that was about it. I got the crate and moved it towards me. I then levered my bottom onto it. It gave me a bit of sustainable height. I felt upwards. I could just about feel the ceiling with my fingertips. It felt very solid, but it was hard to tell. I listened. Was there anything to hear? No. The rain had got even more insistent though. I could hear it hammering on the distant roofs.

I hadn't checked under the mattress. There was just a chance that there was litter or debris in this pit before they flung the mattress down; there might be something I could use as a tool.

I got off the crate and lifted up the mattress as best I could and felt around. The more I felt around, the more despondent I got. What was I hoping to find? A spade? A knife? I kept at it nonetheless. I would rather be doing something, than nothing. I had almost covered the whole distance with my hands when I found a bottle top; the metal kind that you get on beer and have to lever off with a bottle opener. That was something at least. Maybe I could scrape between the bricks and loosen one to then use that as a tool; perhaps to batter at the roof. Or I maybe I could use it as a weapon if they return. At least this had the makings of a bit of a plan.

I put my prized bottle top carefully on the crate and felt around the wall with my fingernails. I was very methodical. I started from one end of the pit. Heavens knows I had plenty of time to do this properly. If I couldn't find a brick, was a bottle top enough of a weapon? Could I sharpen it perhaps? If I got close to someone's neck, then I could scratch into it and maybe the element of surprise would count for something. No, the brick idea was better; I would look for a brick I could use.

And then I noticed something.

Not something good.

When I had searched the floor it had been dry. But now it was distinctly wet. And what was worse; it wasn't many minutes ago that it had been dry. I moved my fingers a little to the left and right. It was like a small puddle was forming. It was like there was a little spring under the bricks feeding it.

And then I heard it.

It was vague at first, but then I got my ear in and it was obvious.

The emergency high tide flood sirens were being sounded around Venice. They only set off the sirens if the water was going to be at least ninety four inches – 1.1 metres - higher than the normal high tide. This pit felt as though it was getting flooded every day anyway, let alone when there's an Acqua Alta; a metre or more of water would drown me.

I listened as the siren changed tone. They have a different siren for 1.1 metre, 1.2 metre and so on. For the worst flooding – 1.4 metres and above – the siren goes through four distinct pitches, one after another. I counted each change in pitch of the siren.

One.

Two.

Three pitches. 1.3 metres higher than normal.

At least I think that is the system. Is it different at different parts of the Lagoon? I wasn't sure. Either way, if I didn't do something, I was going to drown.

They sound the sirens about two hours before the high tide – at least, I think they do.

I was stuck in a pit that was going to flood, and I wasn't even able to stand up. I reckoned at most I had an hour to get out.

FOUR

And the trouble was, I had no idea how much time was passing. When you panic, does time go faster or slower? For example, I am quite a nervous flyer, but it is particularly take-off and landing that freak me out and they probably only take a minute but it always feels like forever; particularly for whomever I may be flying with. By the time I have communicated my anxiety by clawing the skin off their upper arm, or systematically crushed the bones in their fingers as I hold their hand ever tighter, no doubt the person I am flying with feels the take-off has taken an hour. So time goes slower in those situations, but what about now, here, alone in the dark?

The water was getting more insistent now. The puddle was spreading across the floor. I placed my finger about a foot from the edge of the puddle and kept it there. I was trying to console myself that perhaps the water would just seep in a little and leave it at that. After all, when I was first thrown into the pit it hadn't felt wet so much as dank; perhaps the pit just leaked a little. Given that it was difficult to gauge time in the all the panic, I nonetheless felt it was minutes rather than hours before my finger started to feel the puddle of water reach it.

Perhaps I could somehow stop up the hole where the water was seeping in? But with what? Could I get some earth from somewhere? Or use my prized bottle top? What about my clothing? Even as I thought them, all these ideas seemed forlorn and helpless.

I leant back against the wall feeling despondent. Of course I felt despondent - I had every right to be – but it wasn't a useful emotion at this time. I needed a fighting spirit. I needed ideas. Why was my brain giving me all the wrong emotions?

My back was damp.

I felt behind me.

Water was coming through the wall and soaking my back.

They were trying to kill me. They didn't want to throw me off the boat; they could easily be spotted doing it. They wanted me to drown due to the flooding. The flooding that our insurance company didn't pay out for. Then why put the mattress in here? And the drinking water? Perhaps they figured it might take a few days before a high tide came that was sufficient to drown me. Perhaps they didn't want me dying of dehydration; they wanted me to stay alive long enough to experience drowning.

The water from the wall behind me was now a jet. It was spraying into my back. I shifted round to stay relatively dry; for the moment at least. If I was going to drown then I was hardly going to stay dry forever.

I pulled my crate over and tried to rearrange my ankles so that I could sit.

Would someone miss me? Who would miss me and raise an alarm? Adam and Angelo had both seen me leave the office but what had they made of it? My brother Pete was due out in a few days to say hello, but what use was that? What use was any of it? Even if they spotted I was missing, they wouldn't know where to find me. They would ring my phone that they would then realise was in my bag in the office, and that would be that. I was so stuffed.

The water was getting in its stride. It was now about my ankles. It wasn't too cold; that was something at least.

Think Emily, think.

Was there some way I could scrape through the wall sideways? If I could loosen up one brick, I could loosen another. Then I could burrow up and outward perhaps? I started trying to check the walls. I just needed one brick that was not as firm as the others. I scraped and pushed at brick after brick, starting as high as I could reach and working down. I could find little by way of encouragement though.

There was one brick where at least I could feel its outline was better delineated; it was perhaps less wedged in or had lost a little of its surrounding cement. I got my bottle top and scraped at the edges.

The water was now up to my calves. I was making some headway scraping a furrow around this one brick, but would it lead to the brick becoming loose? And then what?

I was making best progress in the mortar that was beneath the brick, so I concentrated on that. I managed to get to the depth of the bottle top. I then felt something give; bits of cement were coming out in large pieces. Okay. That was something.

Something bad.

Water was now coming in through the gap I had made. What started as a trickle, became a pour. I had somehow managed to make matters worse.

FIVE

I screamed.

A rat had run straight up my arm and its tail or whatever had flicked my face before jumping off my shoulder.

I was stuck in the dark with a rat. I really do not like rodents. They freak me out, out of all proportion. I had no chance whatever of seeing where it now was, and I certainly wasn't going to pad around with my hands looking for it. I remained very still. There might have been some whimpering. And then some crying.

I am not the sort of person who readily feels sorry for herself, and it was pointless giving in to tears, so I decided I'd allow myself thirty seconds in the darkness to collect my thoughts, and after that I was going to think of something proactive I could do.

The only positive aspect of the rat situation, was that it must have come from somewhere. Was there a little hole in the wall, and if so could I use it?

Another rat scurried over my thigh.

I yelped.

Oh this is just terrifying.

I had heard that in Venice as a whole, one sign that an Acqua Alta was coming was that all the rats were forced up on to the streets. They poured out from the storm drains and basements and dashed across the pavements. I tried to kid myself that all I had felt was the first rat a second time. I didn't allow myself the notion that the pit was slowly filling with panicking rodents. I needed to stay as calm as humanly possible and look for the gap where the rat (singular) had come out. I was going to need to check the walls for some sort of gap in the bricks.

The water was up to my waist now; the pit was filling much faster than before. I had a mental image that the rodent would be sitting on the crate, as the only dry place to sit; so I wouldn't be checking that area of wall as my first priority. I felt sick even thinking about it.

I used two hands to check the periphery; half below the water line and half above. I was halfway along the second wall when I found it. There was a hole about half the width of a brick. Perhaps more. A rat hole; a rat run. It was largely full of water.

If one rat had come through the hole, then there may be others in there. Rats are not loners. There was a plop in the water near arm. Like if a rat dropped into the water. Concentrate Emily. This hole I had found was my best bet; if I could loosen a brick around it, I might be able to dismantle the wall. I did some deep breaths to try and calm myself down. I was going to put my hand into the rat run.

Shivers went down the length of my body while I forced myself to place my fingers in. I then wriggled my palm where it was a bit stuck and I pushed. The tips of my fingers were now beyond the bricks and into the earth behind. It was wet. By turning my palm up, I could claw at the earth a little and remove some by scooping it and dragging it back through the hole. I did this a few times. I tried not to think what it would be like if a rat appeared and pushed against my fingers. They say rodents are more afraid of humans than we are of them; I find that wholly unlikely.

I tried to scoop the earth away in a manner that left a particular brick less supported. I was hoping I would then be able to wobble and lever it. If one brick came out, then others would follow. I smuggled my bottle top into the hole to help with the scraping. The earth was coming away more and more easily by the minute.

Even if I could get a section of the wall away and created a channel, would I be strong enough to pull the metal weight round my ankles up with me to escape? Well, I would just have to.

I finally got enough earth removed that I could feel the whole width and height of one brick. I now tried to pull at it. Nothing moved. It was stuck solid.

The water had risen more by now and the brick in question was completely submerged. Possibly that would help soften the mud behind. I pulled the brick again. No dice. I removed my hand and tried pushing the brick inwards. I have never been a person who frequents the gym, so I don't have especial strength in my arms; just the usual amount that Mother Nature gave me. I really could have done with some strength.

I gave the brick an extra shove inwards, largely powered by frustration and anger.

It gave a little. Not much, but just enough to give me hope. I placed my hand back in the hole and tried to pull the brick outwards again. It moved. I repeated the manoeuvre several times, pushing the brick in, then out. About ten minutes later, and I had the brick out and in my hand.

I was now up to my chest in water, but at least I had some hope that my plan was working to some degree. I was splashing and making as much noise as I could with my excavations to try and keep the rat or rats afraid of me; or keep it so that I couldn't hear them at least. I was now pulling at the bricks around the aperture I had made, to see if I could remove more and create a pathway upwards and outwards. No luck so far, so I placed my hand into the hole and tried my previous trick of removing the earth from behind the bricks. Within a minute or so I could feel two bricks coming loose, then three. I felt with my fingers upwards to see how many layers of bricks were above my hole and that I would need to remove to get free. It was fourteen. Okay, I could do that.

And then I remembered something the locals had kept trying to stress to us in the office. For years, a freak high tide – an Acqua Alta – would subside within only a few hours. But the point about the November floods and the previous disaster in 1966 was that the water level didn't reduce between the two tides each day; it just stayed high. Oh well, it was no good finding yet more ways to panic; I would just have to press on.

I kept scooping the mud out of the hole and wobbling the bricks, and then I started wondering gloomily about the water I was in. Did it have Lyme disease in it? And there is another disease called Lepto-something that you can get from polluted water. And didn't they once have Cholera in Naples? You could get seriously ill from the bacteria in rats pee or whatever. I made a mental to not touch my face, well, ever again basically. Although, just the thought of all the potential germs somehow made me want to instantly mop by brow.

Another brick came away, and then another. This gave me renewed energy. I put my hand back in the hole to scoop out more earth and almost immediately the tips of my fingers scraped against something sharp. In my mind it was a broken piece of glass, but there was no way of knowing. I pulled my hand out and shook it in the, probably disgusting, water to try and clean the cut. I felt gingerly with my other hand; there was a distinct tear on the pad of one finger and probably two others. I felt as if I was bleeding, but it was so dark there was no way to tell.

I heard a noise.

Was it rats?

Were they attracted to my blood? Surely not; they are not piranhas. I needed to calm down; my predicament was bad enough without letting my imagination run away with me. There was a splash where something dropped into the water. Was a rat swimming up to me? I dry heaved with fear.

Then I realised the sounds I had heard were from the outside world, not from in my pit. There was someone above. Should I shout out? I had nothing to lose.

'Help! Help I am drowning! Help!'

I listened to see if there was a response.

I could hear some sort of movement involving the roof of my chamber. The noise had come almost immediately after I shouted, so I felt they were people who knew where I was; my captors. A passer-by would have stopped and listened, whereas the kidnappers had a job to do and would be setting about it.

But then the noise stopped.

Perhaps it was just someone walking through the warehouse.

'Help! Help!'

There was definitely something going on up there. If it was my captors, should I attack them or plead with them? My ankles were bound, so my room for manoeuvre was hopelessly limited. But I did have the element of surprise. I had a brick or ten to hit them with. I could hold a brick in my hand below the water level and then bring it up and smash it over someone's head.

That would only work if there was one person though; I could attack one, but a second one would be able to defend themselves or, worse, simply lock me back in the pit to drown.

Also, was the water clear? I assumed it was cloudy and therefore I could hide my brick; but there was no light and so for all I knew, the water was clear. It seemed unlikely though; as a rule, if you can smell the dirt in the water then it was probably as opaque as gravy.

There was the noise you get when you undo a big padlock. These people had keys, so they were my kidnappers. There was a scraping, and a shaft of light appeared at one side. I was blinded at first. I hunkered down a bit so that the water level was up to my neck. It might make them act faster to save me – if they wanted me alive, that is; I had got it into my head at his stage that the flood sirens had been the motivator for them to check on me.

As the light appeared, four rats – three large ones and one smaller one – scurried up the walls and out. Then just when I thought it was safe to panic, a fifth rat along my shoulders and up to the light. I was so startled I fell backwards into the water.

When I resurfaced, I could make out some feet standing above the pit; they belonged to masked men. The roof had been pulled completely to one side.

I decided to play it calm and speak in measured tones. 'You are going to have to remove me. I am going to die in here. I am going to drown.'

There was silence. I could see better now. There was one person certainly, but I thought I saw a second person further back.

I gripped my brick hard in my right hand keeping it below the water level. Where was my bottle top? I seemed to have lost it. Either way, a brick was better.

If the person got in the pit should I attack him when he was most unawares, or should I wait until he had released my legs? The latter would be best, but it may never happen so I would have to play it by ear.

There was talking. It was definitely two people. One them crouched down to peer at me. I couldn't see his eyes through his sunglasses. He was worried I would be able to describe him to police later. Or recognise him now perhaps? He talked some more to his colleague who was standing. I think they were talking Venetian; so that made them locals. He shifted his legs over the side, so they were dangling down. I could probably reach out and pull him into the pit; it would have the element of surprise, but it wouldn't free my legs.

He talked again to the other man. He said something like, 'She could drown if we don't untie her.'

'Let her drown,' said the other one. 'What's it to us? As long as her body isn't found today. If it's found in a few weeks, it'll be fine.'

'It's slightly better if she's alive.'

It's *slightly* better if I'm alive. It's a *whole* lot better if I'm alive, matey. His legs were still dangling down. I could crack a brick against his shin. And then what? What if one of them had a gun?

Before I could make a decision, the one with his legs dangling took his shoes and socks off. He rolled up each sock and placed them one in each shoe, then placed the shoes somewhere safe out of reach. A meticulous person. Or someone who valued their shoes.

He slipped into the water beside me. The water was as muddy as I imagined. He felt around in the murk for the padlock by my feet. He had the key ready. It took a lot of fussing about, but then I felt my ankles come free. The man was still leaning forward concentrating on my ankles when I got the brick and raised it high above him.

'Look out!' shouted the man above.

I brought the brick crashing onto the man's skull.

SIX

The brick made a sickening thud as it hit the man's skull. He dropped instantly below the water.

The man above shouted, 'What the?' and scrambled forwards to the pit. He had no apparent weapon.

I pushed hard on the man who was with me to keep him below the water line. 'Don't come any nearer or I will drown him,' I said.

He came nearer. He swung his legs over the edge of the pit. He wasn't taking me seriously.

'You're already drowning him,' he said. He had a point. If the man was unconscious below water, it wouldn't be long before he drowned. I took my hands off him by way of panic. I'm not a murderer, I'm just desperate. The body was limp. I didn't know what to do so I prodded it.

I prodded it again.

I've killed a man. I've killed a man. My mind was dazed at the enormity of it.

The man above was equally concerned. He jumped down into the water beside us. He'd left his shoes on.

Before either of us could do anything, the drowning man reared up. He gasped and flailed about and coughed and choked.

I used the distraction as an opportunity to hit the other one with a brick. This strike was less successful. I caught him part on the shoulder and part on his left ear.

He reeled away holding the side of his head, while the one who had almost drowned stood up and swayed about, trying to orientate himself. He was covered head to toe in muddy water and had blood running from his head and down his face.

The other one made himself big.

'Right enough of this,' he said.

He reached into his back pocket and pulled out a knife.

I don't think of myself as brave, but there is a certain power you get from being desperate.

I tested my legs to check they were genuinely free. Then I gauged where I thought the submerged crate was. I bounded onto the crate and sprang up to grab the edge of the wall to pull myself up.

I had one leg up on the workshop floor above, but then I felt a pull on my trailing leg. I looked round and the half-drowned man was gripping my calf. The good news was that he was inadvertently blocking the path of the man with the knife. I wriggled my body around and used my free leg to lash out. I hit the head of the half-drowned man. His sunglasses fell away. It was a miracle they hadn't gone before. The man looked at me straight in the eye. Did I recognise him? No, but I would now be able to remember him.

The next thing we knew I was up and out of the pit.

Could I get the roof back on the pit to trap them? It looked heavy and there was already a hand and then an arm emerging. I decided it was better to run.

But which way?

I was in some sort of repair workshop, perhaps for boats. It didn't look as though much work had gone on here for many a year. There were a few dirty patio chairs and some oil drums. There was a doorway to my right, but it was brighter to my left. If I could just get to somewhere where there were other people, it would be something.

There were footsteps behind me, rapid footsteps; someone was running. I made it to the end of the workshop and tried a door. It was locked or stuck firm. The man running behind me was close now. Far too close. At the far end of the wall there was a staircase. I dashed for it. I have quite a good turn of speed, especially for a woman, but I can't keep it up for long.

I took the stairs two at a time. It took me to a disused office. There was an abandoned desk and an office chair.

It was a dead end. There was no way out.

There was a glass window and shutter beyond.

The man was now up the stairs. He stood in the doorway and held his knife in his right hand and made himself wide. He knew he had me cornered, but he wasn't going to lunge forward in any hurry. He held all the cards.

I picked up the office chair and held it in front of me. It was a bit too heavy to wield with any conviction. At best it was a shield or a delaying tactic.

The man in the balaclava smiled. He was enjoying his moment.

I swung the office chair as best I could left and right, but I was kidding no one.

I then had an idea. I held the chair in front of me and ran as fast as I could at the window.

The glass shattered but the windows and shutters got wedged against each other. I pushed again with the chair. It would have to do. I started climbing out the window.

My head and torso were out in the open air; my legs were still stuck inside. I was maybe six metres above the canal. There was a narrow pavement below; if I plummeted onto it then I would crack my skull. I had to somehow spring forwards and reach the water beyond. But how?

I wriggled some more, but now I could feel the man holding my legs. I kicked and pulled and I don't know how I managed it but I was now outside the building upside down, my face scraping against the wall, being held by one ankle by the man. If he dropped me, it would be hard to protect myself from the flagstones below. I shook my legs nonetheless. I had visions he would get a knife to them, perhaps cut a tendon in the back of my calf.

I wriggled and kicked again, trying desperately to get some sort of purchase on the wall with my fingers. But what was the use? I couldn't possibly stop myself from falling, unless I was properly holding on to something.

I kicked my free foot hard against his hand. I wriggled the entire weight of my body as I did it. This loosened the man's grip on my ankles. I could feel him attempt to grasp me again, but it was just not possible; gravity got the better of both of us.

I slipped from his fingers and I fell.

SEVEN

I plummeted with my hands braced hard above my head. But would that afford any real protection for my skull? Surely my arms will buckle under the weight of my body? I would probably break my wrists, but I would also probably escape.

My hands hit something hard - presumably the stone pavement below. I tried to kick my legs against the wall and arch my back at the same time. An electric pain shot through my right elbow where it glanced something hard. I was flipped on my back now, with no point of contact with anything solid. My next thought was, 'I wonder if I am going to crack my back?' Nothing seemed to happen at all for an eternity and then, wallop. I hit the water. I had done some sort of somersault.

I must have been in a daze because I don't recall what happened next. Then I kind of came to, and I was scrambling deep in murky water. I was trying to work out which way was up. Then my hand scraped against something hard and I realised I could see where it was lighter so that must be the surface, and that I was deep below. I pushed on the bottom of the canal to propel me to the surface. I did a breaststroke motion with my arms and a flipper kick with my legs and was soon making progress upwards. I was not going to die today.

The front of a boat hit me.

A blue hull passed overhead in the water; the front of it had caught my arm. It was perhaps a police launch, or a private motorboat; it knocked me downwards, and as I bobbed back upwards again I could see the propeller spinning in the water and coming towards me. That could chop my fingers off.

I pushed hard against the last bit of hull to push me back down again. My lungs were tight to bursting point; they were begging me to relent and stop holding my breath. I made myself stay below the water for an extra two strokes hoping that I would get out of the main thoroughfare of the canal. I got my head above the water and spluttered and coughed and breathed and breathed again. I couldn't see anything because of the water in my eyes and maybe some sort of slime. Then I realised I was quite near a wall with some ornate brickwork. I swam towards it and realised it was part of the footings of a bridge. It was something to hold onto.

I was safe.

I needed a shower and change of clothes and get to the police – possibly not in that order - but to get into my apartment I would need to go to the office where I had left my keys and purse. That felt like days ago but was actually only a few hours. I pulled myself up onto a walkway and tried to get my bearings. What time was it? And where on earth was I? Was I on the main island of Venice or one of the other islands? Murano perhaps?

A watery sun had come out, but it was obvious where it had been previously raining because I saw tourists ahead who had thin plastic coverings over their clothes and plastic overshoes. The walkway was submerged in water but only by a few inches, so it was easy enough to make progress with a half walk, half wade action. I looked down at myself; I was wearing a pair of trainers, some leggings and a t shirt; all of them were covered with mud and soaked through. My hair was matted into rat's tails. One tourist took a photo of me by holding up an iPad. I grinned and posed for the sheer hell of it. I then picked some pondweed out from between my teeth.

Round the next corner the canal was wider, and the buildings were a bit more modern and regular than I would expect from Venice proper. I was becoming more sure it was the island of Murano; it is more residential than Venice and has a glass blowing industry. I walked along feeling thoroughly sorry for myself, but relieved. I had no money, so how was I supposed to get back home? I would need to find a police station.

And what about my kidnappers? Were they searching for me? I walked back to the corner I had just turned; I peered back along the smaller canal where I had been swimming. I couldn't see anyone; just an old lady with a wicker shopping basket and some wellington boots. What would the kidnappers look like? They could hardly walk around the streets with their balaclavas on, so if I did spot them I would have a chance to see their faces.

No point in lingering. I wasn't far from the workshop where I had been kept prisoner so it made sense to get some distance between me and there. I was pretty sure I was on the other side of the canal to the workshop, so that helped.

I found a café first. It was on a bit of quayside that was above the waterline and was half full of people. Everyone in there was elderly and male; thrown out by their wives every morning where they were cluttering the house. They were all well turned out, mostly wearing jackets, in that way that elderly men do who are from the generation where you took pride in your appearance even when relaxing at home. Most heads turned to look at the bedraggled woman standing in the doorway dripping all over the floor.

A rotund proprietor with a white apron came round the counter to stand in front of me.

'Can I help you, Signora?'

'I have been attacked and pushed into the canal. Where is the nearest police station please?'

He went off and came back with a simple wooden chair. He placed it in the middle of the café for me to sit on.

Then he froze, and his eyes went wider.

'Your hands,' he said. 'What have you done to your hands?'

I looked to where he was looking. My right hand was covered in blood where I had cut the tips of my fingers earlier.

'I will call the police,' he said. 'Do you drink coffee?'

I was taken in a police launch back to the island of Venice and at the police station I had another wait, but this time with a blanket and a second cup of coffee. Eventually I was ushered into an office to meet a detective called Inspector De Sica. He was gangly for an Italian, with a prominent nose and greying skin. He listened attentively to my tale of kidnapping but without making comment.

Unexpectedly, however, he said, 'What brand of water?'

'What?'

'You said there was a bottle of water in the pit with you. What brand was the water?'

'I don't know. It was dark.'

'And what about the crate that was in the pit with you.'

'What about it?'

'Did it have any distinguishing features, like the name of the company who made it, or the goods that would have been in it.'

'Not that I know of. As I said, it was pitch black.'

'But it wasn't dark when they took the roof off the top,' he said. I couldn't believe my ears; he seemed to be giving me a hard time.

'Well by then I had better things to do that check on the brand name of the water bottle,' I replied.

'Hmmm,' he said.

He didn't appear to believe me. I didn't get it. Why wouldn't he believe me?

'These are tiny details,' I said.

'Tiny details can often be very important.'

'Sure.'

'And why were they abducting you?' he asked.

'I don't know.'

'Was there a ransom demand?'

'I haven't a clue.'

'So, no ransom demand as far as you are aware.'

'They didn't sit with me and share in depth information about their plans,' I said.

'Can you identify them?'

'Probably not. Their general build, the clothes they wore. I think they spoke Venetian.'

'Interesting. That is getting more and more rare, particularly with younger people,' he said.

The detective asked me a number of general questions about myself and I appreciated that they had to be asked, but they had the net effect of making me feel not believed but also that I had no real proof for what had happened to me.

'And could you take us back to the workshop where you were held?' he asked.

'Probably.'

'Only probably?'

'There will be a broken window. The window I jumped out of. And we know which café I ended up in, so yes, I think I could find the workshop where I was held.'

'Think?' he queried. Why was he being so difficult?

'I jumped in the canal and then I was hit by a boat and so I was pretty disoriented,' I said.

He considered this and wrote something on his pad.

'Okay and so let's go back to the lady in the red dress,' he said. 'Would you be able to recognise her again?'

'Definitely.' I felt bounced into making my answers more concrete.

'Okay, right so we will get a colleague to take a statement and perhaps we will get someone to make an identity picture of the woman in the red dress.'

He stood and went to leave the room. At the door he turned and said, 'Except. Well, I know who you are.' He nodded to himself and left the room.

He knew who I was? What the hell did that mean?

It wasn't until late afternoon that I was able to get back to the office to retrieve my keys and other belongings. The tide had properly subsided by then but had left the alleys and walls looking dirty and sodden. I couldn't see any massive damage though; perhaps the Acqua Alta hadn't been as high as predicted.

At San Basilio there was just Eta on reception. Everyone else in the office appeared to be out, even though it wasn't five o'clock. I was in no mood to query it.

'What happened to you?' asked Eta.

'More to the point what happened to you?' Eta's eyebrows were covered in angry looking brown scabs.

'I've had my eyebrows microbladed. It will make them look younger and more natural.'

Having them cut a thousand times and dye rubbed into the wounds will make them look natural? Yes that's exactly what young, naturally attractive people look like.

'What happened to you?' she asked in return.

'Oh, I was kidnapped.'

I went off down the corridor to find my handbag. 'I've had a terrible day,' I flung over my shoulder.

Not, it turned out, as bad as the day that then followed.

EIGHT

The next day I overslept, but that felt fair enough after my traumas. I rang work and got through to Marco and explained the situation and that I would be in a couple of hours late. I also explained that I had to go back to the police in the afternoon to help them some more. Marco was quiet on the phone. There was no, 'Wow, you've been kidnapped?' But I didn't think anything of it at the time.

When I finally got into the office my first alarm bell was that no one asked me how I was. Eta and Marco knew for sure what had happened to me and so they were bound to tell other people; but not one person asked me any details about the day before. No one even said hello.

Eta at the front desk had buzzed me in, but then didn't look up or acknowledge me as I entered the building; instead she kind of ducked her head down. Perhaps she'd had yet another cosmetic procedure done overnight, and it had gone so spectacularly wrong that even she was ashamed of the outcome.

I passed Marco's open door and threw a hello in his general direction but there was no response; he only has a tiny office, so it is not as though he was at the far end and couldn't hear me.

When I got to my own office, there was only Adam.

'Good morning Adam!' I tried brightly.

He did a brief nod and got back to his keyboard. He looked sullen. It was truly odd. Er, this is a man I've had sex with. This was the people-pleaser hoping to bounce up through the ranks of the company powered by the spring in his thousand euro Versace shoes; it was like I had done something wrong. I had just been kidnapped for heaven's sake. Wasn't he even curious about what happened?

'Er Adam, do you know what happened to me yesterday?'

He tapped a bit more on the keyboard, sighed, and then looked up. He actually sighed.

'What happened to you yesterday?' he asked, as though humouring me. This wasn't like Adam at all.

'Remember there was a woman in a red dress, and she was out the window and she was holding my name up on a piece of paper?'

'I didn't see that myself, but I remember you saying something,' he said. 'Go on.'

'I followed her down a few alleys and the next thing I knew I was bundled up in some sacking and kidnapped. I phoned Marco about it earlier; did he tell you?'

'Well I heard something,' he said vaguely.

'You don't seem very interested,' I said.

'Um,' he replied. He blew out through his lips. I was disturbing him. 'Yes of course, I am interested,' he said. He pushed his chair back away from his desk to go through the motions of looking interested.

'Then they bundled me into a boat, and they tied a weight around my ankles and threw me into a pit. Then I scraped away at the bricks of the wall; look, I've cut myself.' I showed him my bandaged fingers. The plasters looked a little too fresh and clean to make for a good story, and in fairness they had healed well already; the cuts must have been superficial, even though they bled profusely at the time.

'Then what happened?' he asked. Was it me or was his tone sarcastic? I mean, he should be rivetted. I was giving him the most exciting bit of office gossip he would get this decade. I was giving him the scoop. And he was looking bored. The nearest his own gossip had ever got to excitement was when his mother had her varicose veins done in her legs; it was about a month ago, and they reduced them by injecting them with a chemical. It wasn't a great story and I had trouble eating my lunch straight after.

'Well then, as you know, there was a flood alert yesterday and it turns out I was on Murano and the pit got flooded. The kidnappers must have wanted me alive because this motivated them to get me out of the hole and that's when I attacked them with a brick and got free. I had to go to the police and everything.'

'Quite the day,' he said.

He didn't move. He was waiting for me to give him non-verbal permission to get back to his keyboard. How could he not find this all amazing? And since when did he find work the least bit worthy of his time?

'Oh forget it,' I said. 'Get back to work. Where's Angelo?'

Adam shrugged. 'Dunno.'

'Well when did you last see him?' I asked.

'He left about the same time as you. Yesterday. He hasn't been seen since. That's the problem.'

That's the problem? What did he mean by that?

I let out the longest breath. I tried to clear my head of all this apparent nonsense. I turned on my computer and started work.

I checked emails. Nothing important jumped out at me, so I would check them more thoroughly later and reply then.

Then I brought up my work for the day. The claims I had to process.

I stopped in my tracks.

I couldn't make sense of my computer screen. I couldn't make sense of anything that I was reading.

I have a pretty good system for organising my work. I keep a simple Word document where I list my tasks to be done. When tasks come in, I place them at the bottom of the list; and when I have done a task, I delete it from the top of the list. That way nothing gets forgotten and I address the jobs in the order in which they arrived, not according to some mythical perceived importance.

As a result, on this particular day the first insurance claim that I was supposed to investigate was for a flooding claim. No surprise there. The claim had been brought by a firm that owns a hotel and four restaurants, two of which were sublet. I had started looking at this claim document the previous the day; the day I was kidnapped. But when I looked at my computer this time, I couldn't find the file. Or rather I could find the file, but I couldn't find the open claim. It had, on the face of it, been paid in full. But by whom? It was my job to okay any payment, not anyone else's. So how had the claim got paid?

I looked at the next job on my list. This was a family who owned a number of properties on the island of Venice, but also on Burano. Again, when I looked at the file, the claim had been paid. It made no sense. I brought the policy up and checked its wording vis a vis flood damage. There was nothing unusual there. Our standard policy was that the flooding was a foreseeable hazard and that the business owner should have taken reasonable precautions to protect their property. Why had these claims been agreed?

I looked at the next item on my list of jobs to be done. This was a car showroom on the mainland at Campalto. They had suffered some vandalism where a number of cars had been attacked with paint stripper. I read the police report and the witness statements. It all seemed in order and it seemed entirely fair to pay out the claim. I marked on the case that we would pay, but I found my access was blocked when I tried to proceed.

I found that odd, but assumed it was a technical issue. I wrote on a pad to query the case, but I wanted to crack on with work rather than get waylaid making phone calls. The whole department was behind, and I had just missed a day of working. Perhaps that is why everyone was being odd with me; I had gone missing without explanation when we all knew we were over-worked. Perhaps they thought I was making it all up just to get a day off. If I wanted a day off, I'd invent a migraine, not a whole abduction story.

I looked at the next two insurance cases on my 'to do' list. They were both major flooding claims, and when I looked up the files it turned out they had been paid. But again; by whom? I checked the small print in both cases. According to our official guidelines, there is no way that those claims should have been paid out,

'Have you been working on any of my cases, Adam?' I asked.

Adam was not at his desk. When had he left the office? His jacket was gone, and his computer was logged off. It was like a weird dream. How had I not noticed him leaving?

I got up from my desk and walked along the corridor to find Marco. His door was closed. I went to knock, but Eta at the front desk said, 'You can't go in there.'

'Why not?'

'They are in a meeting. It's private.' I still couldn't see her face. What on earth had she been up to?

'A meeting?' I asked. In the months I had been here, there had never once been a 'private meeting' — it was a very relaxed office where everyone's door was open, and everyone talked to everyone else as they worked.

I went back to my desk and on a whim I rang my brother Pete. I realised I hadn't talked to him since my ordeal yesterday.

'Pete! How's you?'

'Yeah good. I'm coming out to see you tomorrow? Is that still on?'

'Yep. You're going to stay in that hotel I found you? I would have put you up, but I only have one room.'

'No worries,' said Pete. 'You know I love hotels.'

'Yeah. We'll do something touristy on our first night. We'll go to Harry's Bar or something,' I said. 'But look. I have a whole pile of weirdness to report. There was a kidnap and now something odd has happened to my work... oh hold on.'

'Hold on, what?' asked my brother.

There was something going on outside my window. There was a commotion in the trattoria across the alley. It looked like a man had stolen a whole pile of food and a waiter had tackled him. The man stealing the food didn't look especially poor; in fact, he looked middle-aged and well-to-do. He was holding a large plate of pastries and was trying to wriggle from the clasps of an elderly waiter. Now he was free and was running, but shouting over his shoulder. Perhaps the man was drunk or on drugs; although he didn't look the sort. He dashed past my window. I craned my head forward to keep up with events. The man tripped on seemingly nothing, and the plate of pastries went scattering along the ground. He picked himself up and ran off, the elderly waiter shouting after him.

I relayed the events to Pete down the phone as they happened; and I was going to tell him the more important news about what happened to me, when Adam appeared in the doorway.

'The police want to talk to you,' he said.

NINE

I was ushered into Marco's office. It is a small airless room at the best of times, but what little life it ever held within its walls had been sucked out by having a policeman and a detective in it, along with Marco and Adam. They were all looking like I'd just killed someone. The detective showed me his ID.

'Okay boys, is there a problem?' I asked.

'We need to ask you a few questions about yesterday,' said Marco.

There was nowhere for me to sit; all the seats had been taken and an extra one had been brought in for the detective, reducing the floorspace even further. I was left with a small patch of floor to stand on at one corner of Marco's desk.

Usually if you stand when everyone else sits, it gives you authority; somehow it was the opposite today. It was like I had been asked to rise to my feet in court to face my sentence, while the men sat in silence, arms crossed, judging me.

I had been assaulted and kidnapped. I had been hit by a boat and had nearly drowned.

I looked to Adam; I raised my eyebrows and hands to ask what this was all about. His expression back was, 'You've really done it now Emily; there's nothing I can do to help.' He was disappointed with *me*? He was half my age; that's not even possible.

The other men looked to each other to see who was going to do the speaking. Marco cleared his throat.

'Can I run you through a couple of insurance claims?' he asked.

'Okay,' I replied.

He tapped on his keyboard and then turned his monitor around so that I could see the screen. It showed an insurance claim that I had never seen before.

'What do you have to say about this?' he asked.

'Well, I'd have to read it,' I replied. 'I have never knowingly seen this before in my life.'

It was an insurance claim for two and a half million to compensate for flood damage to a number of shops on the main island of Venice. I could well believe it was in my virtual in-tray to be looked at, but I had certainly not got round to reviewing it.

'What of it?' I asked.

'Could you go to the section which shows the history of the pay out?' asked Marco.

I found the relevant section.

'And could you tell us who agreed to the pay out?' said Marco.

I turned to stone.

It was my name on the document.

'Um, well it seems to be me,' I said. My heart was thumping. 'But it wasn't me.'

'What date did you agree to this pay out?' he asked.

'The 25th,' I read.

'Yesterday,' he said.

'Well I can't have done it yesterday. I wasn't even in work yesterday. I was abducted.' As I said the words, they somehow sounded wrong. How often would you ever say, 'Of course, yesterday I was abducted.' It just sounds odd when you say it, even though in this case it was true. I stood my ground. What else could I do?

'It literally could not have been me,' I said. 'I was abducted.'

'Have you got any proof for where you were yesterday morning?' asked the detective.

'Yes. I reported it all to the police. I was abducted and held in a workshop in Murano.'

'But have you got any witnesses to that?' he asked. 'Any proof?'

I stopped to think.

'Well there was the owner of the coffee shop where I went to get help.'

'When was that?' he asked.

'Early afternoon?' I replied. 'I am not sure exactly. But there will be a phone record of when he called the police.'

'Have you got any witness to where you were in the morning before you went to the coffee shop?'

'Yes. The abductors. I was abducted!'

'Someone else?' asked the detective. 'Someone we can talk to?'

Marco seemed the most ameliorative in the room.

'You have to understand,' he began.

'Yes?'

'That you agreed to over twenty claims in a two hour period yesterday.'

'Okay?' I said.

'Okay, as in you agreed you did it?' asked the detective. I was going to have to learn to choose my words more carefully.

'I didn't do it. To be clear. I didn't do it,' I said. 'I was abducted.'

'But you have said yourself, you have no proof for that. What is your proof?' asked the detective.

'The claims total nearly a hundred million between them,' said Marco. 'It's a breathtaking sum.'

'Well stop the money,' I said. 'Stop the pay outs.'

There was silence in the room. This made no sense. It was a massive international insurance company with safeguards and systems. I was not the final arbiter as to whether actual cash was ever sent out.

'We are surely in time enough to make sure no damage is done,' I said. 'Just stop the payments.'

'We can't,' said Marco.

'Why not?'

'There is a mechanism for allowing immediate relief for policy holders when there is an emergency,' he explained.

'Yes,' I said. 'For immediate air travel when you are trapped somewhere and the like. But that is not relevant here,' I said.

'It shouldn't be relevant here,' said Marco. 'But that mechanism has been invoked. It was used for each and every claim. Then finance sent the money out in the afternoon. We were alerted by the end of the day that our claimant accounts have been virtually drained in one day flat.'

'But not by me,' I said. 'I don't have that sort of power. I would have needed a second signatory to achieve that and, as I said, I was kidnapped at the time. So I wasn't even the first signatory.'

The atmosphere in the room was getting even worse than before. It was like everything I said was considered by the room to be a lie; and every time I spoke my lies it was making matters even worse.

'What?' I asked. I meant, what are you all staring at? 'Just get the money back,' I said.

'We have been trying all morning,' said Marco. 'Talking to banks, contacting clients.'

'And?' I asked.

'It was like they were tipped off that they had to move the money somewhere safe almost instantly,' said the detective. 'In some cases, the money has already moved on. In some cases, the claimants have suddenly become difficult to contact.'

'Some claimants have simply been rude to us,' chimed in Marco. 'They said we paid out the claims and that is the end of the matter. See you in court. That kind of thing.'

'I was kidnapped!' I protested. 'You have to believe me. I had nothing to do with this.'

'Well was there like a ransom demanded?' That was Marco. I thought he was the nearest I had to an ally. Obviously not.

'No. Not as far as I am aware. There was no ransom demanded,' I replied.

The air was like a dead weight in the room. The whole thing was like when you are hit by a huge wave. For a while, you don't even know which way to swim, which way is up. I did some deep breathing to help my light headedness. I badly needed to sit, but there was nowhere but the edge of the desk. I perched myself on it, but it looked flippant.

'Okay,' I heard myself say. 'Right. Let's think this through.' But I'd run out of words.

'And?' asked Marco eventually.

'Well who was the second signatory?' I managed. 'Who okayed the payments to be paid so rapidly?'

'Angelo,' said Adam. Oh, he was joining in now.

'Your colleague Angelo,' reiterated the detective. 'Colleague and friend.' Friend? That was unnecessary. And Angelo was about the only person around here I half trusted; he was just too care-worn to be a rogue.

'Well, what does Angelo have to say for himself?' I asked.

'We don't know,' said Marco. 'He has gone missing. He went missing yesterday, about the same time as you. Just after you left the office, he left too.'

'You are going to need to accompany us to the police station,' said the detective. He stood and gestured to the door.

I was loathed to even move. At least the office felt like relatively safe territory.

'Um okay,' I said. 'This is a lot to take in. I am going to need a glass of water. And I will get my bag. And... oh I don't know.'

TEN

Was this actually a crime? I was on a police launch going off to the police station for the second time in two days, and I found myself wondering if any actual crime had been committed. My instinct, of course, was that it was indeed some kind of fraud, but think of it on the front page of a newspaper. 'Insurance company pays out promptly for flood damage and in full.' It didn't have much of a ring to it. Then the article below would read, 'In a shocking development previously unknown in the world of insurance, Society Metropolitan paid policy holders in full and without quibble, to compensate them for the massive damage sustained during the Venice high tides.' It didn't sound like a crime at all. Someone had logged in as me and pretended to be me to process insurance claims; so that was a crime against me certainly; but what was the general crime that had been committed beyond that? Well, no matter. You just know in life when you are in trouble. It was mirrored in the reactions of others. The worst of it was that I had done nothing at all; I had simply been framed.

Well at least I now understood what my abduction was about. It was nothing to do with a ransom or whatever. The idea was to get me out of the way for the day, and then use my computer to agree to a mass of insurance claims.

But that meant that whoever okayed the claims must have sat at my computer in my office. How were they not noticed? Or did they log in as me but from another computer? Either way it would have to be someone in the building. This must mean there was a trail logged on the hard drive to show who used which computer and when. If I could show that the pay outs were agreed from a computer at the office at a time when literally no one saw me at the office, then I would be in the clear. I think. It was all very confusing.

And where the hell was Angelo? I had always had him down as honest. The thing is, among other things, that when you have sex with someone you get to know them well; you certainly see a different side to them. I felt I knew Angelo, and I really didn't think he was a fraudster.

Also, what did I have to gain personally from agreeing to these pay outs? It wasn't as though the policy holders were my friends or relatives. Perhaps, though, they were the friends and relatives of Angelo. How much did I know about him really? Perhaps I was just the foreign stooge brought in to blame for his scam.

The police complex near the station is quite large, but nonetheless I was hoping to see some faces I could recognise. Perhaps the detective I had dealt with the day before, Inspector De Sica. No, I was stuck with the men who had been in Marco's office.

'I have not introduced myself properly,' began the inspector as he settled behind a desk in an interview room.

'My name is Inspector Conte,' he said. 'How are you?' Italian good manners. Well that was something at least.

'I am fine thank you, and you?'

'Fine.' He sat back in his chair. The only other person present was a policeman sitting in the corner. I was intrigued; if they were arresting me on the spot, they would be recording the interview. Or were they allowed to record it without telling me? I had a vague memory from the trial of Amanda Knox all those years ago, that the Italian police recorded her even when she thought she was in private. Perhaps I was wrong, but it was best to be on guard. Oh what am I saying? I hadn't done anything wrong. I needed to start thinking about the whole situation differently; but how?

'I have to tell you Signora Fisher we have had an anonymous tip off about you.'

I thought my spirits couldn't get any lower.

'Okay?' I offered.

'We have been told to look at your bank account.'

'Why?' I asked.

'We do not know,' he said.

'And have you looked at my bank account?' I asked.

'Signora Fisher I am only just getting my head around whether there is even a crime. After all, the people of Venice have been crying out for the insurance companies to play fair with them about the floods. If I arrested the one woman who helped all the poor business owners. Imagine the outcry.'

'Well this is a twist,' I said. 'A bit of sympathy? But I must make it clear I did not okay those claims.'

'But is it a crime if you did?' he asked. What was he saying exactly? These were the very thoughts I'd had myself half an hour earlier, but that was not the point.

'I would like to make it clear that I did not okay those claims,' I said.

'So you say.' He smiled. 'Could I ask if you have internet banking?'

'Yes, I do.'

'Could I ask that I look at your bank account? Just to show that I have followed up on the anonymous tip.'

I had a very bad feeling about this.

The inspector adjusted a cuff on his shirt. It was already immaculate. He was very precisely dressed, but seemingly fair. I wondered if 'precisely dressed' and 'fair' would somehow be contradictory traits. Probably not.

I reluctantly got my phone out of my bag and went online to my bank.

There was the usual rigmarole of passwords and the name of my first cat. Then my stomach lurched. I couldn't believe what I was seeing.

I scrolled down through the items. There were the usual payments to Netflix and my electricity bill. There were multiple items where I had bought stuff from Amazon. There was my rent. Nothing strange in any of this, but all the time my overall balance as shown on the top line was wrong. It was completely wrong.

I scrolled down to find signs of a deposit.

And then I found it.

It was a deposit of 60,000 euros – about 70,000 in US dollars. I stared at it and stared at it.

I looked at the codings next to the deposit; the supposed description of where the money came from. I couldn't make it out. It was just random letters; perhaps shorthand for the name of a bank, but possibly not. Then it said, 'Ref: agreement.'

I was very loath to show the detective my bank details. Was it time to get a lawyer?

'Well?' asked the inspector.

'I think I have a problem,' I said.

'How so?'

'Someone has credited my account with 60,000 euros.' There seemed no point in hiding it. I passed the phone to the inspector. He looked at the screen in silence.

'Can I scroll up and down?' he asked. His politeness was as meticulous as the clothes that he wore.

'Sure,' I said. 'I know it sounds unlikely, but I have nothing to hide.'

He read my bank statements for a bit.

'So usually you do not have much money in your bank account. Maybe a few thousand euros around payday and then by the end of the month it is mostly gone.'

'I am a normal person,' I said. 'It is just me. I don't have a husband. I rely on my own money.'

'Yes, of course. A normal person,' he said. 'Normal person.' It's like he was trying the words out on his tongue; testing them to see if they could possibly be true. Somehow, they tasted wrong to him.

'You know how this looks?' he asked.

'It looks like someone bribed me to agree some payments from my insurance company,' I said. 'Have you found my colleague Angelo yet?'

He grimaced, rather than answered.

'And have you any explanation for the money that has been deposited in your account?'

'None at all,' I replied.

'Okay, well I will write down the letters that are written next to the deposit and we will ask the bank what they mean and where the money came from,' he said. 'But it is one thing for an employee in an insurance company to agree to a claim. It is another that they were bribed to agree to a claim.'

'I can see that.'

'That is definitely a criminal offence,' he said.

ELEVEN

'How did you not notice that someone had put a large sum of money into your bank account?' asked the detective.

'Yesterday I was abducted, and today I have been taken in for questioning,' I said. 'There was no stage where a logical thought was to check my bank balance. And the money was put in only yesterday.'

He looked at the desk in front of him. There were two files. He closed one and opened another.

'Talk me through what happened yesterday,' he said. 'Start at the very beginning.'

At least he didn't say, 'Talk me through what you *claim* happened yesterday. What you *allege* happened to you.'

I talked him through the story.

Eventually he said, 'Would you be able to take me to the workshop in Murano where you were held?'

'Yes, I would have thought so. We were going to do that today anyway.'

The inspector stood.

'What, now?' I asked. 'You want me to show you *now* where I was held captive?'

'Yes. Right now,' he said.

'Can I just go back one topic?' I asked. 'If someone was bribing me, I am hardly going to give my bank details to them. I would want an envelope of cash, or perhaps I would set up a Swiss bank account. I am clearly being framed.'

'Most criminals I have ever met were not very clever,' he replied.

So now he was accusing me of being stupid.

'And when the evidence is against them,' he added. 'A lot of them claim they are being framed.'

Cheers for that.

We took a police launch back to the island of Murano. At first, I was in the launch with just Inspector Conte and the policeman driving the boat, but we took a detour to go round to the St Marks Square side of the island to pick up Inspector De Sica – the detective who was supposed to be investigating my abduction.

St Marks Square was a drab sight where the water level was so high. Tourists were restricted to standing on a line of raised boarding to queue for the Basilica and the Doge's Palace; their garish holiday clothes a contrast to the grey water around them. This didn't deter many of them from taking photos with their selfie sticks, posing with inane grins on their faces; this was their holiday after all, a week they had been looking forward to all winter. I wouldn't begrudge them what little fun they could squeeze out of the rain and gloom, but I had an image in my mind of a beautiful old woman dying in front of strangers, and they were eyeing up the rings on her fingers and posing for photos in front of the corpse. I felt sad for all concerned.

Detective Inspector De Sica joined us on the boat. He and Detective Inspector Conte appeared to be fast friends. They stood side by side sharing office gossip against the wind; one pale and as thin as string, the other short and perfectly turned out; the latter was nodding fervently and laughing at the titbits as they were divulged, both nonchalant to the beauty of the lagoon around them.

'Can we go to the café where I was picked up by the police, so I can get my bearings?' I asked. The two happy detectives looked round at me as if they had forgotten I was there, then De Sica nodded.

'The osteria?' he asked. 'Sure.'

In theory I like the idea of boats; I imagine myself as an impossibly glamourous Elizabeth Debicki or Sophia Loren reclining in a 1950s bathing suit at the back of a speedboat made of shining varnished wood. A bronzed hunk in white shorts powers us across a blue sea to a swanky harbour bar, my silk scarf trailing behind us in the wind. That's the dream, anyway. But if the water gets too choppy and the bow starts bouncing erratically on the waves, the truth is I grip the bench seat like a vice and stare like a laser at what appears to be the only life jacket on the entire vessel, and wonder who I would have to fight for it when, inevitably, we capsize and drown.

The launch was going at quite a speed and although Murano is not far from Venice, we had somehow hit bumpy water. Wouldn't the police, of all people, want to employ a little health and safety, and provide me with a life preserver? Evidently not. The pilot's response to the worsening conditions was to push the throttle harder and make us bounce ever more precariously over the waves. This didn't deter the two detectives from being even more animated – there must be some very juicy office gossip doing the rounds – while I, for my part, made myself into the shape of a human starfish; all four limbs braced to stop me being flung like a slingshot into the high seas, and all the time trying not to throw up.

Murano has far fewer internal waterways than Venice, so it was easy enough for us to find the quayside with the café. Out of pride I tried to make my face look less green; breathing deeply and turning my head away from the men, but then I felt a tap on my shoulder. I smiled as best I could and offered an arm for them to help me from the boat.

'No need to get out,' said Inspector Conte. 'Just point us to where you say you were held captive.'

I directed us forwards and then round the corner to the edge of the bridge where I had surfaced from the water.

'Okay. Stop for a while where I work out where I was swimming, from and to,' I said.

It was only the day before, but somehow everything looked different; very different. Sunnier, for one thing. The previous day I had been flustered and panicked, so I didn't exactly hang around to admire the view or look for landmarks that would be useful at a later time.

'So,' I stalled. 'I was held on the other side of the river. I think. And I broke a window and jumped out of it. So we are looking for a broken window about one floor above the water line, and there was a pavement below but it was more narrow than usual. I was worried I'd crack my head on it.'

The two detectives peered around and, inevitably, none of us could see a broken window on any building whatever. The water level was lower than the previous day, which didn't help, so perhaps I needed to look higher up the buildings than I thought.

'I hadn't done a lengthy swim,' I said. 'So the workshop couldn't be far from where we are.' I don't know who I was reassuring; certainly not myself.

No matter how much I looked there were no apparent broken windows on any building.

'Okay, so perhaps I travelled a bit further than I thought,' I said. 'There must be a bit of a current, and I was hit by the hull of a passing boat.'

We looked at the turgid canal; today the current was so lazy and the water so thick that there was a bird's feather right by me that was lying on, not in, the water; and no matter how long I gazed it, it wasn't going to move.

The two detectives had gone from scrutinizing the quaysides to scrutinizing me.

'I have not gone mad,' I said. No, but I might have made it all up. 'This is the correct place. That was definitely the café where the owner called the police. And this is the bridge where I climbed out of the water.'

Think Emily, think. If I can't support my account of being abducted in any way whatever, then it looks far more likely I spent yesterday morning at a computer ripping off my employers in exchange for a hefty bribe.

'Maybe I am the wrong way round,' I said. 'Maybe I jumped into the water and by the time I had got myself up from the bottom of the canal and been hit by the boat, maybe I was turned 180 degrees.'

'Okay,' said Detective De Sica. 'So what do you suggest?'

'Let's move along the bank a bit left and then if we can't find the place we'll try going right.'

It was possible that in all the confusion I had turned a corner in the canal system; I just needed to check out the options and look round the corners and not panic.

Suddenly I saw a broken window that was about the right height above the water. To be fair, it didn't look exactly the way I remembered it. I felt cautiously relieved.

'There it is!' I cried in a voice that was a lot more certain than I felt. 'There's the broken window, and there is the quayside where they must have carried me into the workshop.'

We moored up and climbed out of the boat.

DI Conte tried the door to the workshop. It was locked. We peered in the windows.

'You're sure this the place?' he asked.

'Yes,' I replied. I was desperate to be on the front foot for once.

'I'll see if I can locate the owner,' he said.

He conferred with his friend and made a phone call back to base to see if they could do a little research about who owned the building.

'We will walk round to the front and see if there is another way in,' he said. But no sooner had he said it when his lankier colleague freed a window that he had been playing with. He hopped into the workshop before anyone could argue. With a bit of a wrestle, he soon had the bolts open to the door and we were walking inside. This struck me as unusual – usually buildings in this part of the world were well secured.

To the left I could see the stairs I had run up which led to the deserted office. There were more steps than I remembered, but generally speaking this felt like the right place.

As a result, I opened my big mouth and announced, 'This is definitely where I was kept.'

'So where is the pit where you say they chained you up?' asked De Sica.

'It's in the middle of the floor, give or take, a bit deeper into the building.'

I sniffed the air. There was a strong smell in the building that I hadn't smelled the day before. I couldn't quite place it; it's a smell you associate with roads.

'Does it smell odd in here?' I asked.

Before anyone could answer, we were disturbed by a man calling to us from the far end of the workshop; the exit to the street. There was a shadow in the doorway.

'Can I help you?' he asked.

He was a well-dressed man in a tailored three-piece suit. He had a long face and a grey well-tended beard.

'Can I ask what you are doing on my property?' he said.

The two detectives looked at him with interest.

'Signor Valdi!' said Inspector Conte. 'How are you sir?'

'I am fine thank you, and you?'

'Just fine. We are investigating the possible abduction of a woman,' said the inspector.

Possible?

'The *actual* abduction,' I corrected.

Despite his solemn face, this Signor Valdi appeared to be genial. 'Well then that is a serious matter,' he said.

'This is the lady in question,' said Conte.

This Signor Valdi tilted his head in concern. 'You poor thing. When did this happen?'

'Yesterday,' I replied.

'Where?'

'Right here in this workshop.'

He looked in turns concerned, and then slightly amused. 'Where?' he asked. 'I hope you don't think I kidnapped you?'

He was the wrong shape and age to be either of my abductors. And he was too genial.

'Show me where,' he said. But it was too pat. He was being too smooth.

'I was placed in a pit, that was like an inspection pit when you examine under a car, but it might have been an old water cistern. And I tried to escape by clawing away at bricks on the side of the wall. So the pit will have about six or ten bricks missing on the wall that is nearest to where we are standing.' I offered my fingers forward to flesh out the story. 'I cut the end of my fingers scraping away the earth to remove the bricks.'

'Well lead on,' said Signor Valdi. He was plainly an important man. It was the way the two detectives already knew him and were being deferential. Presumably he owned the building, but it was more than that; it was like he was local dignitary. Could I simply ask? Why not?

'I am sorry,' I said. 'I do not think I have been introduced. I am Emily Fisher and I work for the insurance company Society Metropolitan.'

'Charmed to meet you,' said Signor Valdi.

'You are the owner?' I asked.

'I own various properties around here. For my sins, I am also a local councillor.'

'And can I ask why you happened to be here?' It seemed very odd to me that a multiple property owner and local councillor would just happen to be entering one of his empty properties at the moment we arrived.

'I was having a coffee nearby and someone said there was someone in the building here. I am not so high and mighty that I cannot investigate a little matter myself.'

The two detectives laughed to acknowledge that he had made a pleasantry. Again, it all felt a little too pat.

'So please,' he continued. 'Show me where you were held captive. This all sounds very serious.'

I moved us deeper into the building. Surely the pit where I was held was not too far from the waterfront where we had entered?

I couldn't see anything. There should be a clear and obvious covering to protect the pit so that no one fell in it. But I couldn't see anything on the ground at all.

I backtracked a little. I looked around.

Surely this was the right place? There had been the broken window, and the stairs up to the office were just where I remembered them. But where was the pit? My heart was pounding now. Something was very wrong. You can't just make a big pit in the ground disappear in a few hours flat.

I examined the floor carefully. I knew I couldn't make any eye contact with the other three. The ground was dusty in that grimy, oily, gritty way that workshops can be. In fact, it was too grimy. But what did that prove? I scrutinised the floor moving forwards and backwards.

Then I realised I was standing on it. I was physically standing where the pit should have been. The ground was gritty, but beneath the grime and dust I could see that the section below my feet was new. It was recently tarred or asphalted – whatever the difference is between tar and asphalt. I bent down and walked a little forwards and backwards. There was a rectangle that was clearly a different colour to the rest of the floor. It was where the pit had been filled in.

'This is it,' I said. I knew I would sound like a fool, but I needed to state the truth. 'It has been filled in.'

'It has been filled in?' asked Inspector De Sica. He looked at his colleague to gauge his reaction. His reaction was hard to read.

'Someone has filled in the hole,' I said. 'Look, this bit of floor is much more new than the rest of the floor.'

Silence from the other three. I had no proof in the first place that I had been abducted, and now this.

'This workshop has been empty for about a year,' said Signor Valdi.

'That wouldn't stop someone filling in a hole,' I said. It sounded so lame. But what else could I possibly say?

Detective Inspector Conte got a phone call. He walked a little away to talk, and then soon returned.

'Good news,' he said. He looked at me. 'Your friend has re-appeared.'

'What friend?'

'Your colleague Angelo.'

TWELVE

Presumably I wouldn't be allowed to talk to Angelo. Presumably we would be kept in separate interview rooms and they would see if our individual stories matched up. They might even try and play us off against each other. Either way there would be a presumption that I had colluded with him and that I was guilty.

But the thing is, I was not guilty. I really didn't take a bribe to rush through a lot of hefty insurance pay outs. I had to think about how to defend myself; given that I couldn't prove I had been abducted. I could easily have logged onto my work computer using a remote connection, agreed to a pile of claims, then jumped in a canal and presented myself in a coffee shop spinning a yarn.

I hadn't even been able to show the police where the pit was where I been held. The owner, Signor Valdi was plainly guilty as hell. He must have organised getting that pit filled with rubble and then covered with tarmac. That was the smell I had smelled when I entered the building a second time with the police; tar. Filling an inspection pit with rubble and tar was hardly the sort of thing your employees or tenants do without asking; so he was definitely involved. He was wholly incurious about the floor in that workshop, and that in itself was suspect, but it is not the sort of thing that would be any use in a court room. I needed evidence in my defence, but what?

We were soon back at the police station and I was placed in a room on my own. I was getting peckish, but at what stage is it reasonable to ask for some food?

Inspector Conte came in on his own and sat down.

'I don't mean to sound rude, but is it wise that I am alone with a detective?' I asked.

He considered this. 'You are free to go at any stage and you are free to not answer questions. You are not under arrest,' he said.

'Are you recording this?' I asked.

'No.'

'Why not?'

Again he paused, this time to remove an imaginary piece of lint from his immaculate jacket.

'There will be time to record events later. There is a lot I want to understand,' he said.

Is this all a trap? Good cop, bad cop. Do stretched police forces even have the manpower for good cop bad cop? It must double up the number of detectives they need to employ. Focus Emily; you are one or two dud answers away from being arrested, and if the detective is to be believed, I am one or two good answers away from my liberty.

'Can I make a suggestion?' I asked.

'Sure.'

'Is it possible to analyse the computer activity yesterday? I get it that someone logged onto the computer as me, but exactly when? And on which device? Did they simply use the computer at my desk? And if so then I am in the clear, because people saw me leave the office.'

'So that is the first thing,' he said.

'What?'

He got his pen ready in anticipation. 'Who saw you leave your office yesterday?'

'Well certainly Adam and Angelo, because I share an office with them. And then Eta at the desk would have seen me leave.'

He wrote that down. 'What time?' he asked.

'About ten.'

He wrote that down.

'The trouble is,' he began. 'Neither Adam nor Eta have confirmed that you left.'

'Well Eta might not have seen me perhaps, but Adam?' Adam didn't confirm when I left?' Each new development was a further blow to the head, and yet the detective had just said I was free to go if I wanted.

'Are they claiming that I sat at my desk at the office all morning?' I asked.

'No, Adam says you left at some stage, but he had a busy day, he was in and out of the office, so he can't testify for sure. Apparently, you left your handbag and your coat. You left your computer on. You didn't close down your computer.'

'So? I didn't realise I was leaving the office,' I said. 'The woman with the red dress held up a piece of card. It had my name on it. Then it said "Follow me" and it was so strange that I dashed out of the office to follow her. I didn't think I was going to get kidnapped. I left my computer on and I left my coat because in my mind I would be back in a minute.'

'It is a very odd thing. The woman in the red dress you claim was holding up a sign with your name on it.'

'Yes, it is odd,' I agreed.

'So it would be hard for a jury to believe.'

Oh great.

'And what about Angelo?' I asked. 'What did he say?'

'We are talking to your colleague Angelo.'

What a nightmare.

'The trouble was,' said the detective. 'You left your computer on. You didn't log off.'

'But I wasn't in the office,' I protested.

'According to whom?'

Think Emily, think. It wasn't enough that Angelo might back me up. The police probably think he was the ringleader who organised the fraud in the first place. And if he was the ringleader then why would he back me up anyway, when he had clearly been the one who framed me?

'Is there anyone in the trattoria opposite the office who remembers the woman with the red dress? They might have seen her holding up her sign. They might have seen me following her,' I suggested.

The detective went back a topic. 'The thing is that whether or not you left the office you left your computer on; so that it could be accessed by remote access. You could have accessed it from anywhere; because you left it on.'

The detective wrote his own thought down. He looked at his writing and nodded.

'And when exactly was my computer used?' I asked.

'We have had a man analysing your computer today. The fraud team of your employers were involved straightaway.'

That felt ominous even though I was innocent, and why didn't he mention that earlier?

'Your computer was accessed remotely with Remote Desktop type software,' he said. He clearly knew more than he had initially divulged. 'Had you previously set up your computer to use remotely?'

'Yes,' I replied.

'Were you allowed to?' he asked.

'I don't know.' I was pretty sure we were not allowed to, but I had done it anyway. 'When I started working at the Venice office,' I said. 'There was so much work to be done and I didn't know anyone in town, so I was doing a bit of work from my apartment. To try and clear the backlog.'

'Your employers said you were not supposed to use remote access to your computer,' he said.

'We do it all the time,' I protested. 'We can be out in the field dealing with a customer. It can be very useful to log into your computer back at the office to check the details in a policy.'

'But that is in your normal office in Corsica. Not here in Venice.'

Indeed. Not here in Venice.

'The problem is,' started the detective. 'You didn't close down your computer when you left the office. It meant you could access it from elsewhere via the internet.' He was really dwelling on this.

'I left in a hurry and I thought I was coming straight back,' I protested. It wasn't looking good for me. 'If Adam was so concerned, perhaps he could have leant over and logged my computer off for me.' I sounded a bit churlish. Adam was my best bet for an alibi. If I could talk to him and jog his memory a bit?

How much evidence would they need for them to arrest me? I thought the huge payment into my bank account was damning enough, but for some reason not in the eyes of the police.

'Does anyone else have the access codes, the passwords, for your Google Remote?' asked the detective.

'No,' I replied. My voice sounded miserable. 'I didn't use Google Remote; I used a similar system. But no.' If I had just closed my computer down when I'd left the office. It is the sort of thing management are forever telling us to do, and we all ignore. But how often does a woman appear outside the window of your office with a sign up saying to follow her?

'I am happy to believe you,' concluded DI Conte. 'But you need to offer me some details we can substantiate.'

And with that, he shuffled his papers and stood up.

Was that it? Was I now going to be arrested?

'Er, what's happening now?' I asked.

'Nothing. You are free to go.'

'Free to go?'

'Yes. Orders,' he said. 'Someone high up says you are free to go. It is an ongoing investigation and I have been told not to arrest you at this time.'

I was totally disconcerted. I felt like a cat that has been campaigning for a door to open, but when it is offered the open door it sniffs and looks suspicious rather than walk through it.

'Oh, one other thing,' he said. 'Your friend Angelo is outside. You might want to say hi.'

THIRTEEN

'You look awful.'

'Thanks.'

'No I mean it. You look dreadful.'

Angelo looked awful.

'You look great,' he said.

'Thanks.'

We took ourselves over a few bridges to get ourselves psychologically away from the police station and found a coffee shop to sit in. Angelo was a young fit man, but where his face used to be slender, it was now hollowed out, and where his frame used to be athletic, it was now wiry and got at. He had obviously been through a lot in the last two days.

I stood and checked my own image in a nearby mirror. Thankfully Angelo was right; I looked great. Somehow. Okay, so I had given my face a trowelling of foundation that morning, and when I refreshed my make-up later, it was less a re-application, more a repointing; but that is a woman's prerogative.

'So what is your story?' I asked.

'I was in the office and it was maybe ten minutes after you had gone,' he said. 'And Adam said to me, "Look there's a woman out the window. She is holding up a sign" and I looked and there she was, just like you said; a woman in a red dress holding a card up with my name on it.'

'Adam said this didn't happen,' I said. 'He just said he remembers us mentioning something, but he didn't see anything himself.'

'I know. But at the time he was saying to me he saw the woman himself, and that now she had a sign with my name on it.'

'So you followed her?'

'Yes. Like an idiot I followed her, and I was attacked. I was taken off in a boat and there was some sort of solvent placed over my face. I woke up and I was chained to a furnace.'

'A furnace?'

'Yes, like something you use to incinerate.'

'And how long were you kept?' I asked.

'Until the following morning. Then out of the blue they put a sack over my head again and unlocked me. I was taken in a boat and dumped quite near my home. They clearly knew where I lived.'

'And in that time, someone used your computer to agree rapid payment of various insurance claims around the city,' I said.

'Yes.'

'And did someone deposit money in your bank account?' I asked.

'The police asked me exactly the same question,' he replied. 'No. No money in my account. Did someone put money in your account?'

'60,000 euros.'

'Do you get to keep it?' Unusually witty for the dour Angelo.

'Have you got any proof that you were abducted?' I asked.

'I am hoping that the sedative they placed over my face might have left some sort of trace in my blood stream,' he said. 'Also I managed to snatch a bit of hair from one of them during a tussle. I kept it in my pocket. The police are analysing it.'

'That was more than I managed to do,' I said. 'I have no proof at all.'

I told him my story. When I got to the part where I took the detectives back to the workshop, we mulled over the fact that the pit had been filled in overnight.

'It wouldn't be that difficult to fill a hole,' he said. 'And if you had left any blood or DNA at the pit it got rid of it. And your prediction that there would be ten or so bricks missing would help corroborate events. And if the mattress had still been there... You can see why they filled in the pit. It totally discredits you. But it is the co-ordinated manner of everything that interests me.'

'In what way?'

'Well there were twenty-four policies that were paid out. That is twenty-four companies and individuals who stood to gain. Were they all involved like a syndicate? That takes a lot of organisation.'

'Apparently you can't get much DNA off a hair sample. You need the cells at the roots,' I said.

'What?'

'Just thinking about what you said earlier. And how did they access your computer?'

'Remote Desktop or whatever it was called,' he replied.

'You had set that up?' I asked.

'No. I hadn't. Not at all.'

I looked at Angelo. I was having uncharitable thoughts. He could be lying to me. He could be fabricating the whole scenario of being kidnapped. He could have simply walked off for the day and sat somewhere at a laptop, first logging in as me using remote access and then logging in as himself; so organising this mass giveaway of money. It was the same thoughts the police no doubt had about me. If he was in league with local businesses, then it suited him that his story mirrored mine so that he also looked like a victim; but he could easily have cooked the whole thing up himself.

'So you think you are being framed, like me?' I tried. 'Why didn't they put money in your account like they did with me?'

'I don't know. Maybe it looked like I already had a motive. Maybe they want my motive to look like I am helping local families because I am a local myself. You are an outsider. You would need to be bribed, otherwise what is in it for you?'

'Why haven't they arrested us?' I asked. 'Why are they encouraging us to talk to each other?'

'I don't know.'

'Is one of us wired to try and trap the other one?'

He laughed at that. I don't know why; I wasn't joking. But the Grey One seemed quite cheerful given all that had happened to him.

He said, 'We're the ones being framed. It doesn't look good for us. Not without some evidence to back us up. Have you got any evidence that you were abducted?'

'None whatever,' I replied.

I slumped back on my chair. There was something about his story that smelled wrong; it was too close in detail to mine. He would know about my story because he had planned it; so it was easy to mimic when telling his tale.

'Okay,' I said. 'But if it wasn't us who did the fraud, who was it?'

'Adam.'

Was he too quick to say it?

'Why Adam?' I asked.

'Who else would be able to access our computers? Who else would be able to install remote access onto my system at the office? It would have to be while I popped out of the office for a few moments and left my computer on. It couldn't be anyone else.'

'You're saying it has to be someone in a position to spot those small windows of opportunity in a day where you were leaving your computer unattended.'

'Yes. It would be much harder for any other colleague.'

'Okay but have you got any actual proof against Adam?' I asked.

'None whatever.'

And that was the thing. We were there in that café across the river from the railway station and Angelo had stated categorically to me that he had no proof against Adam. He didn't pause. He'd clearly just said, 'None whatever.'

Later he changed his story.

Adam as the brains behind the fraud. Eager-to-please - unless it actually involved getting some work done for me - social-climbing Adam.

'Surely he is too, oh I don't know, flimsy and flighty to have organised all this,' I said. 'Too young. Too junior.'

'He's actually very sharp,' said Angelo. 'And he's very ambitious.'

'Then he wouldn't jeopardise his position in the company,' I countered.

'He's not ambitious in the company. He's ambitious to get on in Venice society.'

'Actually,' I said. 'I am going to pop outside for a bit. I need a bit of fresh air and a chance to think on my own.'

I went and sat on a step at the foot of the bridge. I wanted to get my head around everything.

On the face of it, all the evidence was against Angelo. The person who I had taken as care-worn and quiet had shown himself in a completely different light. In the café just now, he had chatted more, and in longer sentences, that at any time since I had known him. How much was I in fact under-estimating about him? How much did I simply not know about him? He could easily have faked being abducted, and then sat somewhere accessing my computer and then his own. He was a local; he could easily be in league with a lot of interested businessmen in Venice.

But on the other hand, I knew that I had been abducted and that I hadn't okayed the claims, and no one seemed to be believing me. Wasn't I treating Angelo exactly the same way that I was being treated? And how could my deep-down belief that Angelo was a bit down-trodden, a bit dull, be so far from the reality?

Another thing that kept puzzling me was that we hadn't been arrested. What was that about?

So what about Adam? If Angelo is telling the truth, then Adam is the one lying his socks off. He knew full well when I left the office and that I never came back, so he had very much put himself in the frame for being a liar. Why on earth would he lie unless he was involved and wanted to discredit me? If he lied about me, then it was very credible that he had indeed pointed out the woman in red to Angelo and then pretended he did nothing of the sort.

He could easily have set up Angelo's computer so that it could be accessed remotely. He just had to wait until Angelo and I had been called into some interminable meeting, or popped off to make tea and coffee. If Angelo had left his computer unattended for just five minutes, that would be enough to set up remote access; three minutes probably. If you knew what you were doing it wouldn't take long, and would leave no obvious trace.

I spotted Angelo looking at me through the window. What was he thinking, I wonder? Then I realised he had his phone to his ear and was talking to someone and was probably just gazing at me for something to do with his eyes. I sighed and stood up. As a working hypothesis I was going to have to trust him. I walked back towards the café and when Angelo saw this, he terminated his phone call. It was probably a coincidence of timing rather than him being furtive, but who knew anything anymore? I sat down opposite him.

'So what shall we do?' I asked.

Our phones rang almost at the same time as each other. Two different policemen were calling us to say they wanted us to return to the police station, or rather go to a different police station on the other side of the Island.

It did strike me as odd that we weren't simply going back to the police station we had just been to, but the last few days had been so bizarre that I just chalked it up as being yet another strange event. Should I have blindly set off to the police station without making a few checks? Probably not. But who would I have checked with? Either way, I stood up and simply followed Angelo.

My head was light, and my legs were spongy, so I was forced to sit down again. I should have eaten something with my coffee, and I would have preferred not to have had to walk; but on an island where there are no cars you can't just hail a taxi.

'You are going to have to help me,' I said. 'I am not feeling well.'

Angelo smiled and pulled me out of my seat and then put an arm around me; half in support, half in comfort. He took us over the bridge towards the train station but then turned us right. As we started to walk, he spotted a kiosk and got me a chocolate bar.

At one stage in the walk I did voice my misgivings, however.

'That was odd,' I said.

'What?'

'Well coming to think of it. The phone call I got from the police telling me to come in. It came through to my private mobile.'

'How do you mean?' asked Angelo.

'Well, like you, I have a work phone and a private phone. And when I went to the police station I gave them my details, but I gave them my work mobile as a contact number. I mean, you don't want to live in fear of your own cell phone ringing. Your work phone, you can turn off when you want to opt out of the world. I figured...'

Angelo thought about this and shrugged.

'Also is this the best way to the police station?' I asked.

Angelo had taken us down some very narrow alleys and then over a bridge, then through a residential area and over a larger bridge. I was losing my sense of direction. One thing was for certain; the alleys were now getting more narrow by the second. At one stage it was so narrow I had to turn sideways and breathe in just to get past a building.

'And I didn't recognise the person on the phone,' I said. But then why would I? It might be a sergeant or whoever does the desk jobs in an Italian police station. Why would I know them? It was just that it was all adding to my sense of unease. 'What about your phone?' I asked.

'What about it?'

'Did they use the number that you gave them?'

'Yes, I think so,' he replied. He sounded evasive though.

'And what about the person who rang you? Did you recognise them?'

Angelo turned us left onto a narrow walkway that ran along the side of a canal. It was totally deserted and not overlooked. With one trip I would end up in the water. One shove from a man bigger than me, and I would end up drowned.

'We could run away together, you and I?' said Angelo. It came out of nowhere.

I stopped and made him stop also. I looked at him. Running away with Angelo. Dour, grey Angelo. No. Yes we had indeed dated, but no.

'I haven't got any money Angelo,' I said. I noticed I didn't say, 'This is crazy' or 'Where would we live?'

'You've got 60,000 in your current account,' he said.

Seriously? And maybe he's got several million from the insurance fraud he'd just organised.

'We could have a holiday together though?' he said.

'Perhaps when this is over.' I chose a tone of voice that was transparently a fob off.

He held my two hands in mine. He squeezed them harder than made sense. 'No now. We could get away now. I've got money.'

A thick set man had appeared ahead of us. By some instinct, I looked back. There was a similar man behind. They weren't tourists.

'Where have you taken us?' I asked Angelo. Seriously, this was not the way to the police station.

Was I imagining it, or did the man ahead have a bulge at his hip that could be a handgun?

I eyed up the canal. Could I just dive in?

'It's against the law to swim in the canals,' said Angelo. Was that a joke? I had obviously telegraphed what I was thinking; it was not like he was a mind reader.

The man ahead of us was walking forwards. His eyes were fixed in me. The man behind was in Angelo's line of vision. Angelo pulled his lips into a line and nodded at the man. It was some sort of acknowledgment.

He addressed me again. 'What do you think Emily? Just you and me? Maybe just a few weeks.'

I was nonplussed. What was this? What did it mean? His face was set in a solid expression; intense and sincere.

He spoke again, he was even more insistent. 'Basically Emily, at this moment in time there are two options, and I want you to think very clearly about what both of them mean...'

The men either side of us were getting closer; step by step.

Angelo gripped my arm.

'What two options?' I asked.

I was horribly afraid.

FOURTEEN

Why would I run off with Angelo? True we had been due to go out on a date the night before. There must have been a cosy trattoria where a table was set for us and we never turned up and the proprietor shrugged and thought 'People eh? Why can't they have the common decency to cancel?' A better question was, how did I end up dating the care-worn Angelo in the first place?

I suppose the answer was that to a degree I had never quite admitted to myself we were dating at all. We'd had that walk after work around the area where we worked, but it wasn't a date; we didn't then go to bed or follow it up.

I had encouraged him to talk and tell me what he knew about Venice; but he never really got chatty per se; it just wasn't his style. He did show me the old boys who run their fishing rods off the corner of a disused marina. And he showed me a church in Zattere which had a funny carving on its outside wall. On the face of it, it was Jesus and he was trying to put his own hand down the front of his pants. He had an angel on each side pulling at his arms trying to stop him. It was baffling and funny at the same time. Then he took me to a small backstreet bar where it was only locals who clearly all knew each other.

I asked him to introduce me to them and he said, 'But I don't know them.'

I said, 'Nonetheless let's talk to them; tell them I'm a crazy English girl who wants to hear about the life of actual locals.'

Angelo agonised about this and then struck up a conversation with two women by the bar and we all thoroughly enjoyed ourselves. I bought us all some cocktails and it was fine. It was companiable. But it wasn't a date, and if he had been bowled over by the evening or my company, it was totally out of proportion to what we actually did. Or so I felt anyway. He was a pleasant man and I had managed to coax him out of his shell a little, that's all. I had made him feel good showing me the area, and getting me talking to a few locals.

Then he rang me one day.

It was a Sunday in late January that should have been drab, but the sun was giving us an unexpected blast; it was acting like a surprised teenager. 'What?' it said. 'I can shine in the winter you know. I just choose not to.'

Like a lot of Venice, my apartment doesn't get direct sunlight through the windows, but I had discovered a spot two blocks away where I could sit on the quay of a boarded-up warehouse. The first floor was converted into industrial chic yuppie apartments – unusual for Venice - so it wasn't totally deserted, but the beauty was that the quay wasn't a thoroughfare; it was blocked off at the end and led nowhere, so there were no tourists. Best of all, it formed a sun trap with a view over the lagoon. I took a blanket to sit on, a book to read, and the internet to browse; I figured I would spend the morning there until my stomach called me to lunch. In truth, the river itself is quite busy at that section; barges of building materials – concrete and joists – drift past, as do the barges that deliver the hotel laundry and boxes of vegetables and fish for restaurants. But on a Sunday, it is largely serene apart from a few locals taking their boats off to the other islands to have lunch with family and friends.

So when my phone rang and it was Angelo, my heart didn't exactly leap. I was settled and enjoying the peace and the view. If anything, I was irked to be disturbed.

'What y'doing?' he asked. He didn't usually speak like that. He didn't usually speak at *all*, unless he was in the mood. I was stunned that dour reticent Angelo was ringing me in the first place; so stunned that at first I didn't even reply.

'How would you like to come to a beach party?' he asked. 'Meet some of my friends?'

Angelo goes to beach parties? Angelo has friends? He struck me as the solitary type. I assumed his weekends revolved around a meal on his lap with his face illuminated by Netflix. His voice was uncharacteristically full of energy; he was sounding very perky indeed. I took far too long to process all this and managed to still not say a word in reply.

'What?' he asked. 'You still there?' He sounded deflated.

'Yeah,' I replied.

'It's just, well you know,' he said. He was a fundamentally shy man who had psyched himself up to make this phone call, and he was losing his confidence fast. 'I just thought you are new here and you don't know many people.' His tone had changed to apologetic. 'I am sorry if I misjudged things. I am so stupid. I should have guessed that you had amazing weekends, off with friends and the like.' His voice drifted off.

I felt I'd done wrong by not being more enthusiastic; I'd certainly done wrong barely speaking.

'I just thought we'd clicked,' he said. He thought we'd clicked?

I tried to heap some smile into my voice. 'It sounds far better than anything I had planned,' I said. It was overly bright. And how to deal with the 'clicked' thing? I couldn't think of any words that didn't sound clumsy. 'Well, thank you for thinking of me,' I concluded.

He picked me up by boat.

'Sorry,' I said. 'You caught me in a funny mood earlier.'

'Really? I didn't notice anything.' Yes you did, and you sounded disappointed. You had planned in your head how we'd have a whole fun day together; you had psyched yourself up to push out of your natural timidity and when you phoned me, I left you hanging.

'You're a good man,' I said. I kissed him briefly on the lips.

I looked for somewhere to sit in the boat that would allow me to look alluring, but also let me grip on for dear life.

'Can we ask that we don't go too fast? I'm not actually that good with boats,' I said.

'No worries,' he said. 'We'll hug the coastline as much as possible. It will be less rocky.'

'Thank you.'

He drove the boat carefully and with consideration. This was a man full of decency, I thought.

We sailed across to Lido in order to drop down and around to Alberoni. At one stage a powerboat cut us up at speed. It was followed some way behind by a police launch trying to catch it up.

'What the hell?' I asked.

'They are illegal clam hunters.'

'What?'

'At night they race around with their powerful engines and churn up the seabed to spin the clams into cages; perhaps the police are trying to arrest them. That's my guess anyway,' he said.

I had been doing well with my seasickness, but the sudden rolling of our boat gave me a lurch of nausea. The thought of eating clams and then raw seafood made it worse. I eyed up the edge of the boat in case I needed to throw up.

'You okay?' he asked.

'Yeah, sure.'

But I must have been green because Angelo said, 'Actually I could do something about that.'

He took the boat on a detour to a little beach house with its own jetty.

'You can stay in the boat,' he said. But he was acting kind of mysterious – particularly for someone I had always marked out as plodding and hen-pecked - so without asking I got out and followed Angelo to the house. He knocked on the door once. Then counted to four under his breath and knocked twice more. All very mysterious.

Eventually the door opened and a lad in his twenties peered at us. He kept mostly out of view, in the shadows of the room behind. He had an emaciated frame, hollow cheeks and ginger hair. I'd have thought he was prematurely aged from too much exposure to the sun, had he not been so pale. A druggy, then. Care-worn Angelo from the office knows a drug dealer? This is massive!

'Who's she?' asked the drug dealer.

'She's a friend. She's good. She's Emily,' said Angelo.

There was some muffled conversation and some money was passed palm to palm. The door closed again and we waited.

'It's just a weekend thing,' said Angelo.

'I'm not judging,' I said. And I wasn't judging. I was too surprised to judge. Angelo the dark horse. Angelo the drug taker. I had not seen this coming.

'It's nice to come bearing gifts to the barbecue,' he explained.

'Yeah no worries.'

The door re-opened and a couple of envelopes were passed out by an unseen hand. There were a few words exchanged followed by a brief laugh from the red-haired druggy. 'I serve you well,' he said, and closed the door.

We walked back to the boat.

'He's called Fat Sam,' said Angelo. 'He's English.'

'He's not very fat,' I reflected.

'And his name's not Sam.'

'And he's not even English,' we said together.

As we set off in the boat again, I tried to square this new drug-taking Angelo with the one I had in my head. He still wore the same staid clothes, and he was the first man I'd sailed with in my time in Venice who actually wore a life jacket; that told you something right there. I wondered what other secrets there were to discover about him.

'You're trying to imagine me taking drugs?' he asked.

'Well...'

'I'm not averse to a little spliff,' he said.

'Sure.'

'I also have sex,' he said with a smile.

'Sure,' I said. It was just so hard to imagine.

The beach at Alberoni was all about the dunes; dunes, pines and deadwood. It faces the Adriatic Sea rather than the Venice Lagoon which added a touch more wild to the waves, and breeze to the air. There were two dogs scampering around the sand and Angelo's friends had a barbecue on the go. They were in their twenties and thirties; cousins, friends, locals and guests; there were Flavios and Lucas, Robertas and Marias. They kindly spoke English as a courtesy if they thought I was interested in their conversations, which I mostly was. Everyone was festive; celebrating a bit of sunshine we'd somehow hoarded into the winter and unwrapped like a gift.

'So Angelo has a girlfriend at last,' said an earnest looking woman, possibly a Sara. She had a feast of silky hair that lapped her face in the wind.

'Does his wife know?' said a pleasant looking lad – a Luca or an Allessandro - who was down to his Speedos and towelling his hair after a swim. When I looked alarmed at his comment, he added, 'No, no, it's good that he's dating.' Did that sound like irony?

Angelo beamed that I was being called his girlfriend; his face was splattered with pride. But when he caught my eye he then looked abashed, and fussed around procuring me a bottle of Moretti.

I wanted to say to everyone, 'I'm not really his girlfriend.' But I'd feel like a heel.

'He's always gone for older women,' said someone behind me. Then whoever said it let out an oomph where I think he was reprimanded by being hit. I was now an age where I was an older woman. And not just as a turn of phrase; someone had been hit for saying it out loud. It didn't feel fair. It's not as though I spend my evenings watching Murder She Wrote, and getting quotes for my upcoming stairlift.

'Still,' said another. 'Better not to tell Gianna.' I swear I could hear stifled giggling. Best not to turn around and see who was talking.

A dog came up to me with a large stick in its mouth. I went to take it from him, but he wanted to show it to me, not give it to me. I found my own stick; we both had one now. I threw mine in the sea. The dog looked eagerly from me to the sea and back again, wagging its tail but not moving. I was going to have to fetch my own stick back again, it seemed.

Angelo had been watching. 'Come on!' he shouted. He started running towards the sea. He had all his clothes on; his shirt, his trousers and his shoes. He grabbed my hand as he passed me. The dog was pleased with the excitement and raced to the sea as well; we were soon all three in the water. Somehow my stick got caught by the waves again and again, so we ended up chest deep, sometimes swimming, sometimes wading. The dog didn't want to give up his first stick so that slowed him up. As a result, Angelo was the first to touch mine, but before he could grab it properly, I pushed him over. I emerged from the sea holding my stick like a trophy, proudly above my head. My dress was now largely see-through from the water and I felt absurdly gratified that the boys were all now staring at the outline of my breasts. The girls slapped the boys with the back of their hands and there was general jollity, especially when they clapped eyes on the drowned rat that was Angelo. His clothes were sodden from head to toe.

He took off his leather shoes one by one and poured out the sea water; it was comical and adorable. Then one of the Marias ran forward with a towel to help cover me up.

'Will you be alright?' she asked.

Why wouldn't I be alright? Why the concern? Because I was older? I decided I was getting paranoid about the age thing and asked her instead what was cooking. Then I was distracted by the look on Angelo's face. He was staring at me. He had big wide eyes and was just staring at me. At first I thought there must be something wrong, but then I realised it was just that he was proud. Proud to call me his.

That evening Angelo dropped me back home by boat.

'I would invite you in for sex,' I said. 'But I'm just not in the mood.'

'I didn't say we had to have sex,' he said.

'No, I did. I've had a lovely day though.'

'We could just hang out,' he said.

'Er. No.'

The look on his face was just awful. But how do you say I'm glad I came, but now I'm pleased to leave?

'But I'll see you in the office tomorrow,' I said. 'And we'll go out another time.'

'Yeah?' he replied, but he didn't sound encouraged.

To sweeten the deal, I held his cheeks in my hands.

'Yeah,' I said. 'I've had a lovely time. We'll go out. We'll make a date.'

And that's how you slip into a relationship with a decent man. I was like a log drifting down a stream, all the time closer to the ocean and further from where you want to be. There was never an obvious time to call a stop to the progress, and he never did anything that a reasonable person would object it. But it was lazy dating. Just going with the flow. And what was the alternative? I barely knew anyone else in Venice.

Sooner or later we ended up having sex. It was unexpectedly great. He was indecently competent for a man who only wore grey. I think it stemmed from the fact he had been married; he knew where everything was, and wasn't afraid to use this information to my advantage.

I suppose the thing is that the first time you do it with someone new, you are kind of getting their set routine. I mean you put it out of your mind that they have done this before in exactly the same manner with someone else, and in the case of a married person they have done it a lot with just one person; but that is absolutely fine. I mean, if you go to a job interview you wear your best jacket, you have your pre-set A game and no one expects otherwise, and you'll do the same thing at the next job interview. I was treated to Angelo's A game and it was a polished performance. No complaints from me.

'Well, I don't need to tell you how good you are at that,' I said afterwards.

'Yes, you do,' he replied. 'Who doesn't want to be told they are good at sex?'

'A Roman Catholic Priest?' I replied. 'Holly Moly. Well I think we've discovered your special talent.' I mimed being electrocuted on an electric chair. 'And your wife left you?' I asked. Way to ruin the moment, Emily.

'I left her,' he corrected. 'Being criticised every day is no way to live.'

'Yeah,' I replied. 'Although I would say that I think you are used to someone who likes vaginal and clitoral stimulation at the same time. Whereas I myself do like both, but not at the same time. They have to be addressed separately.'

Angelo's face froze.

'You are giving me pointers???' he asked.

'Er. I was just saying.'

'No one says things like that,' he said.

'Evidently I do.'

He looked like I'd hit him in the face. He was literally rubbing his cheek in disbelief. He then went on the attack. I didn't see that coming; I'd had him down as a passive person who rarely did more than react to events, but how quickly he turned; he was certainly reacting to events now.

I thought he was going to hit me. Hard.

'You just have to correct people all the time, don't you?' he shouted. 'I notice you do it with Adam at the office. Does it make you feel superior, correcting people all the time?'

He was so angry. And this was so unexpected. He was clearly very sensitized to receiving any criticism. He focussed on a point in the distance to calm himself down. He walked a few steps away from me and then back again. He was more reasonable now, but he still had the look of a man with immense anger below.

'I really don't think I correct people all the time.' I said.

'You know what you are?' he asked.

'No?' Now I was the one who feeling despondent. I really don't know what I am.

'A self-sabotager,' he said.

Self-saboteur. Sabotager isn't a word.

'Okay time out,' I said. I made a T sign with my hands.

'Time out?'

'Yes. I have misjudged the situation and I said something inappropriate and I apologise. You are a good person and I am sorry. Okay?'

He didn't look mollified.

'I've lost some capital with you,' I said. 'I will apologise again. But it goes to show I don't know you very well. When I get to know you better, I will make fewer mistakes.'

'You want to get to know me better?' That had inadvertently perked him up.

'Yes. But having lost some capital with you. I might as well re-iterate the clitoral and vaginal thing. Separate concepts. For me at least. And no doubt a number of other women.'

He stared at me.

And then cracked a smile.

'You're a dark horse,' I said. 'I'm having trouble reading you. You have to give me that.'

But my abiding memory, when I pictured him, was not of the flash of temper I saw that day, or of the hours he would sit in the corner of the office working dourly. The abiding memory I had of him was from the night after the barbecue on the beach; of holding his cheeks and looking at his face. And when I looked at his face, I saw a good man. A good man who was troubled.

What I didn't see coming, however, was how much I had come to mean to him. I was now face to face with him on the edge of a canal, and he was proposing we ran away together. He was proposing it with two heavies either side of us, with guns in holsters on their hips.

PART THREE

THE WORLD ACCORDING TO PETE

ONE

THE NEXT DAY

I was looking forward to seeing my sister Emily in Venice. She had moved there a few months earlier and I am sure this was not her intention, but she had inadvertently taken half my social life away with her. When I got there, however, she had completely gone missing; disappeared off the face of the planet. But I didn't know this at first, so I wasted valuable time.

I arrived by plane, coach and vaporetto – water bus. I had booked myself into a fine boutique hotel in the St Marks area and rang her. No response. This is not unusual with Emily; she usually has a thousand distractions – socialising, more socialising, drinking, Sundays lost with hangovers, more socialising, and the occasional bit of work.

She had given me her address and warned me that it was slightly hard to find her apartment because the address system is a bit vague in Venice, so she had suggested that we meet up at a bar near a well-known landmark. The arrangement was that I would phone when I got to Venice, and we would fix the time and place. Only two days earlier there had been a bad flood where the high tide had swamped St Marks square, so originally in my mind we were going to meet somewhere obvious like that, but now that was probably not the case.

So on my first night I had to content myself with not seeing Emily at all. Instead I had a perfectly pleasant meal at my hotel, but somehow coveted everyone else's meals but my own. I sat in the window of the hotel's restaurant and ate a decent enough ragu, but across the alley there was a restaurant that looked far better than mine. It was called The Aschenbach and I got the idea it was its opening night, because a stream of young and trendy people kept arriving and they were greeted by effusive staff who themselves looked more than pristine. The waitresses were wearing jaunty sailor suits that had clearly been designed by some top international designer, and the waiters and maitre d' were wearing uniforms that riffed on those worn by dashing naval officers; it was all, presumably, to accentuate that it was a fish restaurant.

I strained to see what they were all eating. I even at one stage left my restaurant to stand outside and peer in at their windows.

Bottarga. I saw bottarga.

Bottarga is sometimes called Sicilian caviar. In the summer months the southern Italians harvest the roe from grey mullets, they salt it and press it, and then they leave it to air dry for six months. It used to be thought of as the poor man's sea food feast, but now it is very sought after and served in Michelin-starred restaurants. This must be the fresh crop from the previous summer, available for the first time. I could see it through the window; it was only a metre from me, but we were tragically separated by glass. A solid chunk of eggs, glowing with the yellow and red radiance of a sunset. It was being grated over a small bowl of pasta. Beside it, was placed a thin slice of bottarga upon which they were drizzling olive oil and lemon juice. There were two waiters serving the food, and it was presented with such a deliberate accentuation of manners, commitment and self-respect that I felt strangely moved by it. It was visceral. Did I imagine it, or could I smell its fresh smoky bouquet, rich with the warm salty smells of the sea all the way through the glass of the window?

I was woken from my reverie by a tap on the shoulder.

'Do you have an invitation?' asked a bouncer.

They have bouncers for this restaurant. To keep people like me out, no doubt.

'Er no,' I replied. 'How do I get one? How do I reserve a table?'

The bouncer looked me up and down. He made no attempt to disguise his incredulity. He was looking at my clothes. My haircut. My figure. My age. My everything.

'It's not for you sir,' he said. Oh, but it is.

'I know I look like a tourist, but I can dress up,' I said.

'No sir.'

Well how rude.

I skulked back to my hotel and consoled myself with a drink by the fire.

My hotel was oriental in style and an Aladdin's cave of cosiness. Wood fires are banned in Venice to avoid burning down the city, but the proprietors had got round that by installing a firepit affair in the lounge that ran on gas, and although I am sure it technically conformed to regulations, it didn't exactly look safe; it was basically naked flames in the middle of a room. But on a chilly, cheerless day, when I had been forcibly reminded of my lack of youth and trendiness by a bouncer at a restaurant, glass of brandy in hand, that fire was fine by me.

I periodically tried ringing Emily but to no avail. There was no point in texting her more than once, so I left it for a while, but I had an uneasy feeling even then.

That night I dreamt of a restaurant where the waiters were carrying cake to tables of trendy young men braying over wine. The cakes were on silver platters and the icing was in the style of sailor suits. I stood before the diners pleading to be allowed to join them. I was naked and rubbing the cake over my body in an effort to ingratiate myself with them.

I woke up feeling truly alarmed. Why does the brain come up with images like that?

I decided to go and visit the offices where Emily worked. She still wasn't answering her calls, so it seemed the logical thing to do.

I used Google maps and crossed the Grand Canal via the Ponte dell'Accademia, and five minutes' walk later I had found the branch office of our insurance company. Easy as pie. I have no idea what we did before smartphones. Got lost, presumably.

The offices didn't have a reception as such – they do not see members of the public face to face – but they did have a security camera at the door and a buzzer system and a peculiar flood defence that I had to step over.

I was soon talking to a lady at the desk. It turned out she was called Eta – named, presumably, after the Spanish terrorist organisation. Hopefully her middle name was Isis. She was one of those women who would have been good looking, had it not been for her out of control limp plumping and skin tightening, and tattooing on the eyebrows. Her lips were literally the foremost part of her face; more prominent, even, than the nose. How did she get it into her head that was attractive? I squinted at her nose; I reckoned she'd had a nose job to reduce it, but it just added to the problem of making the lips look too pronounced.

'Hi,' I said. 'My name is Pete De'Ath and my sister works here. Emily Fisher. I wondered if I could see her.'

Well that was odd. Somewhere under the woman's pancake foundation, her skin had turned grey. It was worse than if she'd seen a ghost. If I hadn't known better, I would have thought it was fear; but why would she be afraid of me asking after my sister?

'There is no one here who works by that name,' she said.

'There is no one who works here by the name of Emily?' I repeated. 'No one here called Emily Fisher?' The woman was clearly misinformed, or very new to her job.

'No.'

'Yes there is,' I insisted. 'This is the offices of Society Metropolitan?'

'Yes,' she replied.

'Emily Fisher works here. Right here.'

Time to pull rank. I got a business card from my wallet and handed it over to show who I was.

'I am the senior claims adjuster for Europe for Society Metropolitan,' I said. 'And my sister Emily Fisher is a claims processer. She has been working here for a couple of months. Emily Fisher. About so high. Blonde. Always wears the same dress. Day in, day out. Occasionally black leggings and a t shirt. You wouldn't forget that.'

'There is no one here like that here.' She said it indignantly. She said 'here' twice. She pulled a face and looked restless like I was being a nuisance. But I had only just got here, and all I had done was inquire after Emily, how was I a nuisance?

I got my phone out and I showed her my email that had the address of this office in it.

'Is this the address of this office?'

'Yes Signore.'

I didn't know what to say.

'How long have you worked here?' I asked.

'In Venice? Two years. In these offices, a few months.'

'And you have never seen... hang on I will get you a picture.'

I scrolled through my phone and found a picture of Emily.

'This lady,' I said. 'This lady is working here.'

She shrugged. 'Perhaps in the past. For a few days...'

'No not in the past. No not for a few days. She has been working here recently day after day. She was brought in from Corsica to help handle your flooding claims.'

She shrugged again.

'Is there something else I can help you with?' she asked.

'Who else can I talk to here?' I asked. There was no way I was going to move.

'You can deal with me, Signore.'

'Okay,' I said. 'Emily mentioned some other colleagues. There was an Angelo.'

'There is no one called Angelo here,' she replied.

'Okay.' I tried to search my memory. If not Angelo, what other name was it? I was sure it began with A. Antoine? 'Adam?' I tried.

A shadow crossed the woman's face. She pursed her plumped lips even further forward in irritation.

'There is no Angelo here,' she said.

'There is no Angelo here today? Or there has never been an Angelo? And what about the other names. Antoine? Alonzo? I think it was Adam.'

She wasn't going to answer. We all have a different attitude to lying. I got the impression she was someone who tried not to lie whenever possible, but was happy enough omitting information from an answer as an alternative. It's a tactic my sister employs, so I'm well versed in it.

'I am going with an Adam. I noticed you didn't answer me. What about an Adam?' I asked. 'Is there an Adam here?'

'There is no Adam here.' She was quicker this time, but more shifty.

I tried again. 'I am more senior than you in this company. I am asking you a direct question. Has an Angelo or Adam ever worked here?'

'I am finding you intimidating Signore. I will need to ask you to leave.'

'You are kidding me.'

'I have answered your questions,' she replied. 'Is there anything else I can do for you?'

'Yes, you can get your boss.'

She considered this for an irritatingly long time without speaking. She kept looking at the door, wondering how she could get me back through it. She had totally regretted her earlier decision to buzz me in.

I sat heavily on the carpeted floor.

'I am not moving until I talk to someone,' I said.

TWO

Ten minutes later, I was struggling to lift my bulk off the floor. I had been invited to meet someone called Marco, but my knees had seized up.

I was ushered into his office. He was about forty and looked honest enough.

'How may I help you?' he inquired.

'My sister is Emily Fisher and she was working here in these offices. I am having trouble getting in touch with her. Her phone isn't connecting.'

'Emily Fisher?' asked Marco. He shook his head. 'I can't really talk about employees.'

'You can't or you won't?'

He firmed up his response. 'There is no one working here called Emily Fisher,' he said.

'What about someone called Angelo? Emily mentioned a colleague called Angelo.'

'There is no one here called Angelo.'

'What about an Adam?' I asked.

He looked at me steadily. He wanted me to know his patience was wearing thin.

'I am your superior,' I tried. I hated saying things like that. 'I work for the same company as you,' In truth it was not clear I was his superior – we worked in very different departments and he probably knew it.

He exhaled. He tapped on his computer as if to check a database. He read his screen for a while and looked up.

'There's no Adam,' he said.

I stared at him.

He decided to throw me a crumb. 'We do have someone here called Adzio,' he said. 'He is often called Adam. His second name is Amelio. Ad and Am. Some people call him Adam.'

'Can I talk to him?' I asked.

'Well what is your business?' asked Marco.

'Insurance,' I said bluntly. 'Like yours.'

'But what exactly?'

'I have a specific insurance claim I want to discuss with him,' I lied. 'I think he has made an error.'

'Then you can raise it with me, I'm his line manager,' said Marco. If he was Adam's line manager, why had he needed to prevaricate; pretending to look up something on his computer before suggesting him?

'I feel it is probably a misunderstanding and it is quite technical,' I said. 'So I think it is only fair that he has a chance to clarify it before I make it look like a big deal.'

'You have come all the way from Corsica to check on the "quite technical" details of a claim?'

I loomed over his desk in a manner that made me look fat and wide. I managed to eclipse all natural light from him just through the act of standing, and the net effect was just the right amount of intimidating.

'I thought you said you were looking for your sister?' he asked.

'I am your superior in the organisation,' I tried for a second time. This conversation was deteriorating fast.

Marco's eyes were doing some calculating. What if this problem got escalated; how would that play out? What if it transpired I really was important? (I'm not.)

He relented. 'Sure,' he said. 'I will take you to his office.'

Adam was overly trendy and manicured, in the manner of young men who have money to spend for the first time, from their first job, and spend it all on their appearance; he visited a barber twice a week, his teeth were bleached, and his trousers were cut eccentrically – they were too tight round his calves, a little short to his shoes, and the crotch was about six inches lower than his balls. The general effect was that he had been trying on someone else's trousers and got stuck – the trousers of a child. And they were made of a Burberry style fabric for heaven's sake. They were preposterous. And he was wearing a bow tie; was that even a fashion? He swung on his office chair and greeted me with a raised eyebrow.

'Apparently there is an issue with a claim?' he asked. He held out a hand to shake mine. 'Do sit.'

There were three desks in his office, but the other two were bare of paperwork or personnel.

'Where are your colleagues?' I asked.

'What colleagues?'

'You normally work with a man called Angelo and a woman called Emily. Emily is my sister,' I said.

'I have no colleagues,' he said. He fanned his hands by way of demonstration. 'I have the whole office to myself. As you can see.'

I collected my thoughts. I had made it this far. I wasn't going to be fobbed off.

'Okay,' I started. 'Emily, yesterday, sat at that desk there and was talking to me on her phone. She got distracted and she ended up describing something going on in the street outside. There was a bit of a fracas at the trattoria across the alley. If I move to her desk, I am willing to predict that I will be able to see a trattoria from her window, a little to the right.'

Adam studied me. His face did not register anything that I could discern.

'Well,' he said at last. 'This is all very intriguing. And this woman is called Emily?'

'Emily Fisher.'

He considered this.

'If you don't mind me saying,' he said. 'You would be able to predict the view from that window just by standing outside. You would have seen that trattoria on your way into the office.'

That was a dud note. If he really hadn't heard of Emily, he would be very intrigued by a man turning up claiming his sister worked with him. His instinct wouldn't be to question my evidence.

'Okay,' I said. 'But it was a very specific incident where a man – well-dressed by all accounts - tried to steal a plate of pastries. It was unusual. Emily sat at that desk and described what she saw. And an elderly waiter tackled the thief, and the pastries went flying everywhere. It was very memorable; so you would have remembered it, and it is not something I could have seen just now.'

'I have no recollection of that whatever,' he said.

The office door opened, and Marco re-appeared. 'Everything alright here?' he asked. He had barely waited a minute to disturb us; he just wanted to be able to tick the box that he had left me alone with Adam as requested. Again, I felt this was not normal behaviour. Surely, he would have shrugged at what he'd heard from me earlier and got on with his day? Would he have followed up so quickly? These people were hiding something.

'Look,' said Marco. 'I think we've done everything you have asked of us. We are a busy office and we have work to do.'

The next thing I knew, I was back out on the street.

THREE

I had no idea what to do.

I mean, what do you do if the world suddenly claims your sister doesn't exist? This was going to take some thinking about. I had no idea where to go, or who to report to. I could hardly go to the police. What was the crime exactly? 'I have come across some work colleagues who claim they have never met my sister.' Although I could of course report her as a missing person.

I went for a sit in the trattoria across from the insurance offices to collect my thoughts. They appeared to do coffees for tourists as well as full meals, so it was a logical place to have a coffee and a think, and then probably some lunch if all that thinking reduced my sugar levels.

I sat at a table outside and had some very nice zaeti with my coffee. Zaeti are yellow cookie creations - 'zaeo' means yellow in Venetian dialect – that are in the shape of lips and made with butter, maize flour, milk, sugar and raisins. If I was going to mount a lengthy hunt for Emily, this was just the sorts of fuel I would require; a perfectly proportioned mix of saturated fat, sugar, and empty calories; and totally delicious.

I accosted a passing waiter.

'Do you mind me asking, but was there an incident here yesterday where a man tried to steal a plate of pastries and run off with them?'

He looked at me puzzled and shook his head. He got on with clearing up a table.

'During the morning,' I tried.

'Sorry Signore,' he said.

Perhaps I needed to talk to someone older. Emily had said it was an elderly waiter, after all.

I scrolled around on my phone to get Emily's home address and see if Google maps would like to help me.

The internet presented me with a pretty definitive drop pin for where it thought I should go, so after my coffee and excellent biscuits I set off.

It was about a forty-five minute walk to the other side of the island but walking in Venice is a total delight, so it was hardly a chore. I found Emily's apartment through an iron gate and up a flight of steps, and pressed the buzzer on the door.

Nothing.

I pressed again and knocked.

I was going to turn away when the door opened. An elderly lady stood in front of me holding a cloth and a cleaning spray.

'Hi. Emily Fisher lives here.' I said it as a statement. 'Is she in?'

She shook her head.

I got out my phone and found the address I had been given by Emily. I offered it to the woman.

'Is that this address?' I asked.

She didn't even look at the screen. She just shook her head and said nothing. Did she even speak Italian? I tried English.

'Can I speak to Emily Fisher please?' I asked.

No reply. She sealed her mouth hard in the manner of a toddler refusing food.

'Emily?' I shouted over her shoulder.

I darted my head left and right to see what could be seen in the apartment.

'Excuse me,' said the woman. 'You go!' So she could speak. She went to grip the edges of the door to push it back against me.

'Emily?' I shouted.

I put a foot in the door and pushed. I barged past the woman and inadvertently caught her shoulder. She reeled against the wall.

'You hurt me!' she called from somewhere behind me. I doubt she was lying.

I ploughed forward, but I didn't know the layout of the flat so I was afraid I would take a wrong turn and not progress far. The first room I came across was the kitchen. There was a mop and a bucket where the woman had evidently been cleaning, but no sign of Emily. What about her possessions? There was no sign of those either. Had I got the right address? It was going to be really embarrassing if I hadn't.

I wanted to move back into the corridor to look for a bedroom, but the woman reappeared in a determined fashion in front of me.

'I call the police,' she said.

I ignored her. I barged past her afresh, and this time found a bathroom. I looked in a cupboard. There were a few odds and ends on the counters and shelves. There was a half empty bottle of mouthwash. Emily doesn't use mouthwash. There were some indigestion tablets; again, not the sort of thing Emily uses. These items didn't even particularly denote that a woman had been here, let alone my sister. I looked in a drawer below the sink. Some eyeliner.

Well that was something at least. I looked at the brand. I didn't recognise it. Emily wears Benefit make-up, but probably does use other brands as well. Every woman I have ever known uses one brand for moisturiser, another for foundation, and yet another for lipstick; so basically, I didn't know what I was doing or what I was looking for. I hadn't turned up any evidence; and there was a mounting feeling I was at the wrong address altogether. Clothes would be a better clue; I was in with a chance of recognising Emily's clothes.

I was hit on the head.

'Ow!'

The woman now had a broom in her hand and was attacking me with it. She hit me on the head a second time.

'I call police! I call police!'

'Go on then,' I said. 'Please do!'

She changed tactics. She jabbed me full in the stomach with her broom handle. Hard.

'Stop doing that!' I said.

I grabbed one end of the broom. I held it steady so that she was no longer either prodding me or hitting me. But what she lacked in strength, she made up for in tenacity; we had quite the tug of war going.

'I get landlady!' she shouted.

'You do that. Please. Get the landlady,' I said.

She turned as if she was going to get her phone, but it turned out to be a ruse, because the moment I relaxed my grip on the broom she started hitting me with it about the head and shoulders. I felt cheated. And physically hurt.

'Stop that!' I pleaded.

We held each end of the broom again, which meant we were now at a fixed distance from each other. This allowed her to kick my shins, without me being able to get out of the way.

'Stop it!' I shouted. 'You call the landlady. Please!'

'I will!'

'You call the landlady, and I am keeping the broom.'

'You stay there!' she said.

'Fine. I'll stay here,' I said. 'I am trying to find my sister.'

She pulled her phone out of her apron and the moment she was distracted by it, I dashed into a bedroom.

There was nothing to see in there. I pulled open drawers. Nothing. No clothes, no make-up. No personal effects at all.

There was a wastepaper basket by the side of the bed. It was made of wood. The cleaner had made her phone call and was back again. She was watching me.

She saw which way I was looking and we both made a dash for the wastepaper basket at the same time.

There were various tissues and some pieces of scrap paper in it; they were all scrunched up into balls.

The cleaner now had one side of the bin and I had the other. We pulled it to and fro. Either I was weak, or this woman was freakishly strong.

'You give me basket! You give me basket! This is not yours!'

She was pulling so hard on the bin, that I decided to let go. She went flying backwards. She slipped on the floor and her head shot back against the bed. The contents of the bin went everywhere.

I scurried around picking up the balls of paper and stuffed them in my pockets. It was largely just to spite her.

'Is everything fine here?' asked a voice. Someone had come into the apartment. 'Er, excuse me!' said the voice louder.

I looked round to see an efficient looking woman in a pencil skirt. She looked about fifty.

'Can I help you?' she asked. 'I am the owner of this property.'

Well she came quickly.

'I live on the top floor,' she explained, as if she could read my mind.

I turned to talk to her, and the maid took the chance to kick me in the shins.

'Seriously?' I asked.

She looked resentfully at me. 'He steal stuff from rubbish,' she said.

I addressed the landlady. 'I am looking for my sister. She is called Emily Fisher. This is the apartment where she has been staying for several months. She has now disappeared.'

'There is no Emily Fisher here,' she said firmly.

I recited the address I had been given and the woman confirmed I was at the right place; that was something, at least, and calmed the room a little.

'Can I show you a picture of her?' I asked.

She shrugged her compliance.

I went to reach in my pocket and both women jumped. 'I am getting my phone,' I explained. 'It's not like I have a gun.'

'Gun?' said the maid. Oh, for heaven's sake.

I showed them both a picture of Emily. 'Perhaps you knew her by another name? Or perhaps her employers rented this apartment on her behalf, so it wasn't in her name? Have you seen her?'

'No,' said the landlady.

'He's got papers in his pocket. He stole papers!' said the maid.

'Is this true?' asked the landlady. 'Have you stolen papers?' She said it like stealing litter was a major crime.

'I need to go to the bathroom,' I said. As in, I need to go to the bathroom, lock the door, unfurl the pieces of paper and read them quickly. I clutched my stomach in an implausibly dramatic fashion. 'It is an emergency,' I added.

I ran to the bathroom before they could stop me. I locked myself in.

There was soon a banging on the door.

'Come out. Come out now!' It was the maid. She had been emboldened by the arrival of the landlady; as if she needed further emboldening.

'I call the police!' shouted the maid.

'Do! Please! Please call the police!' I shouted back. 'You keep threatening you will call them, but you never do it. Call them!'

The banging continued on the door, and I got the bits of paper out of my pocket and unfolded them. They were handwritten notes. I got my phone and photographed each of them in turn. I wasn't sure if they were in Emily's handwriting. They appeared to be names and addresses and figures and some codings of some sort. I scrunched up the papers again and put them in my pockets. I then flushed the toilet.

I emerged from the bathroom to find the cleaner had re-armed herself with her broomstick. She held it in both hands like a sword; tense and ready for action. But I couldn't see the landlady anywhere and this emboldened me to walk forward. I raised a stern finger at the maid.

'No hitting,' I said.

'You leave now,' she said.

That just made me want to stay. 'No,' I replied. 'I want to talk to the police.' I went back along the corridor to the bedroom. I looked in a wardrobe and under the bed. I couldn't find anything. If Emily had been here, she had done a good job of clearing out.

I unlocked the latch to an external window. It was very stiff, and I had to jiggle it before it would open. It gave way to reveal a tiny ornamental balustrade and a canal beyond. It was all a bit dank out there, but I didn't learn anything.

I left the bedroom and went back to the kitchen area. The landlady was there, deep in conversation on her phone. When she saw me, she finished up what she was saying with, 'He's here now.' She rang off.

'The police are coming,' she said to me; but she said it mildly, as if she was somehow admitting defeat.

I sat and waited for the police. I didn't have to wait long. A plain clothes man appeared. The landlady had been waiting by the front door. She ushered the man in.

'Good morning. How are you? Can I help you, Signore?' he asked.

I was ready for him.

I showed him my phone.

'This is this address,' I said, showing him an email from Emily on my screen.

'Yes,' he said.

'My sister is called Emily Fisher. She is an English woman and she was living at this address, but she has now gone missing. She works at the offices of Society Metropolitan here in Venice.' I omitted that everyone at those same offices currently claimed they have never heard of her either.

'Okay,' he said.

'I need to report my sister as a missing person,' I said.

'Well that you can do at the police station,' he said. 'Why are you here?'

'Because she lives here,' I said.

'Not according to the Signora,' he said, waving in the direction of the landlady.

'Yes, well something is wrong,' I said.

'In what way?'

I pointed at him. 'Well for example, you are not a policeman.'

'Yes I am.'

'No. You are a detective. The landlady said to me that she would ring the police. So for such a trivial matter as a man making a slight nuisance of himself in an apartment, the dispatch officer would have sent a policeman. You are a detective. And you came very quickly.'

'I don't follow,' he said.

'Oh yes you do.'

'What is more,' I continued. 'The landlady did not look surprised to see you.' The detective looked sullen.

'Would you like to tell me what is going on inspector?' I asked.

'There is nothing going on,' he said. 'What is more, I am told that you have some papers in your pocket. They do not belong to you. Can you hand them over, please.'

I pulled out the crumpled pieces of paper and pressed them into the man's hand.

'Now perhaps you could be so kind as to direct me to the police station so that I can report my sister as missing.'

FOUR

The detective took me himself in a police launch to the police station, and an hour later I had registered Emily as missing.

It was not clear what I could do for the rest of the day. It felt wrong going back to my hotel for a drink, but on the other hand there was no point me wandering around the streets of Venice calling 'Emily!' up at the windows. I felt dispirited by events and inadequate. A proper brother would be designing 'Missing' flyers with Emily's picture on it and pasting them to lampposts; he would be collaring passers-by near her apartment or near her work, asking them if they had seen anyone matching Emily's description. Instead of any of that, I went for an aimless walk.

I was following my nose through the alleyways when I got as far as Sacca San Girolamo. This faces north and across the lagoon, and I was suddenly aware of the Dolomite mountains on the mainland and a sharp wind to match. In a square there were old folk on fold-out chairs sitting in amicable silence. I was drawn to some white fliers attached to the lampposts. They had images of faces on them; 'Missing' posters, I thought. But on closer inspection they were announcing funerals. The first one I read gave the name of a local man and the details where we can go to pay respects. He was 83 and originally came from Trieste. I went from flyer to flyer, partly out of boredom, but also because in some dream-like way I half expected to find a photo and a description of Emily. An old lady in black sat and observed me with kind eyes.

'I am looking for my sister,' I said. 'She is called Emily Fisher. She is an English lady.'

'My daughter was that age when she left us,' said the lady. Left the island, or left the land of the living? And what age? I smiled my thanks.

Because I was at the top of the island, almost as far as I could be from my hotel. I formed a route in my head for how I could meander back, but nothing is straightforward when walking in Venice; no line is perpendicular to another and the main river, the Grand Canal, turns back on itself. I was soon lost.

I tried to backtrack and took one meandering side alley too many and found myself on a narrow quayside with a solitary gondolier. He was a lean looking man with startlingly red hair. He fixed me in the eye and with no attempt at charm or theatre said, 'I take you for a gondola ride?' But his demeanour was too gaunt, too grasping. He was in the wrong part of the island to pick up tourists. It was like if a gondolier had got lost and couldn't find his way back to his territory and food, and was reduced to touting for business from people who wouldn't possibly want his services.

I shook my head, confused. 'My sister is missing,' I said.

'I row you well,' he replied.

I couldn't possibly take a gondola while Emily was missing; it was a too frivolous thing to do; water taxi, maybe, but not a tourist gondola, and certainly not this one.

I turned to go.

'I row you well,' he repeated.

With a renewed sense of determination and some help from my phone, I walked back to the area where Society Metropolitan had its offices. I settled myself at a table at the trattoria opposite. I figured I would keep a beady eye Emily's workplace; I certainly didn't have any other plan.

I rang my own office in Corsica. I got put through to Emily's line manager Isabelle.

'Hi Isabelle, it's Pete De'Ath. I know this is a strange thing to ask. But can you just confirm that Emily, my sister, has been transferred to the Venice office for a while. I have been to the local office here, and they claim they haven't heard of her. Have I got the right office?'

'I would have thought so,' she replied.

'Well is there another office in the city she could be working at?'

'What's the address where you are?' she asked.

I gave her the address. I could hear some tapping on the computer.

'Yeah, that is the address I have on the computer here,' she replied. 'Give me a moment. I will just check a few things.' There was more tapping. 'No, that is the only address I have in Venice. I'll check on Emily's file a second.' Now the pause was very long. So long I thought the phone had gone dead.

'Hello?' I asked. 'Are you still there?'

'Er, I was just checking something. It says here that Emily is on leave at the moment. Is that any help?'

'Well,' I replied. 'I was going to meet her here. It is a holiday for me. I suppose it is possible she booked a few days off to spend with me.'

'No it is more than that. She is off for three weeks according to this.'

'And it doesn't say where she has gone?' I asked.

'No.'

'Okay, well thanks Isabelle. Could you do me a small favour?'

'Sure.'

'Could you ring up your counterpart at the office here in Venice and talk some sense into him. He is called Marco. Explain to them that you know for a fact Emily works here. Perhaps ask to speak to her, and see what they say? Then could you ring me back?'

'Why may I ask?'

'Because on the face of it, Emily has gone missing.'

I have always found Isabelle to be reasonable, so I wasn't too surprised when she said a cheerful, 'Okay.' She hung up.

Cheered that I had at least done something to investigate Emily's disappearance I ordered some food.

I had a cicchetti with an ombra in a bacare – which is a bit like tapas, and roughly translates as 'a bite to eat with a bit of drink in the shade of an eatery.' The 'bit of drink' was an excellent chilled local white wine and the 'bites to eat' were little squares of polenta topped with shredded cooked onions and, variously, baked sardine, spicy sausage and anchovy. It was theoretically possible to eat them in two or three demure bites, but why bother? I ate each one whole. I have never been convinced by polenta; I have always found it slightly pointless and if it is left soft, a bit off-putting, but with the onions and grilled sardine on top it was a pretty enjoyable snack. I was in the act of placing the last one in my mouth when I caught the eye of an elderly waiter – a different waiter than when I had been there earlier.

'Tell me Signore,' I sprayed through a mouth of wet polenta. 'There was an incident here yesterday.' I swallowed the last of my food and put my hand up to apologise. 'A well-dressed man tried to steal a plate of pastries,' I said.

'You know about that?' he laughed.

'So it did happen?' I said.

'Of course, just like you said. We caught him but it was so long until the police came, and then when they did arrive they were not very interested.' He shrugged. Police, eh?

'So the police would have a record of it?' I asked.

'Perhaps.'

'And you would be happy to testify that it happened?' I asked.

'Why would I need to do that?' he asked. I had made him wary.

'Oh nothing. I am being silly,' I replied. After all, the fact that this story about a man stealing some pastries was verified proved in my mind that Emily had worked in the office across the road, but it wouldn't be of interest to anyone else. Still, at least it was something.

A woman caught my eye walking slowly along the alley. She was pushing a baby in a stroller. I reflected that I have spent so much time away from England, that my English is now international English; why else would I have thought to use the word stroller in my head, not buggy or pushchair? She looked as though she had barely got over her recent pregnancy and was struggling a little as she walked. She was immaculately dressed; she had a navy tailored jacket and the loose fitting three-quarter length trousers that all Italian women seemed to be wearing this year.

She stopped to look in at the windows of Society Metropolitan. She wasn't checking her appearance in the reflection of the glass; she was looking into the offices. She looked wistful. She shook her head as if to wake herself up, and moved on.

As she got closer to the trattoria, her eyes fixed on me and didn't deviate. She frowned. She walked a little faster and came right up to me.

'Peter De'Ath?' she asked.

'Yes,' I replied.

I had never met this woman before in my life.

'You are the brother of Emily Fisher, yes?'

'Yes, but how did you know that?'

'I have seen photographs of you,' she said.

'Where?'

'On the internet and stuff.'

'What?'

'Yeah. I have been cyber-stalking your sister,' she said. 'Then I saw she had a brother in the same company. So I read about you too.'

'You know my sister?' I asked. 'You are cyber-stalking my sister?'

'Yes,' she replied. 'I know all about her. You have to understand I have taken quite an interest in her.'

'Why?'

'Because she has run off with my husband.'

FIVE

I was totally floored.

'You'll have to excuse me,' I said. 'This is a lot of information.'

'Your sister,' she said slowly.

'Yes.'

'Is Emily Fisher.' She said this even slower.

'Yes,' I replied.

'She is colleagues with my husband Angelo.' She waited for me to register that I had understood.

I nodded.

'They work together in that office there.' She pointed across the road. 'And they were having an affair.'

'Okay.'

'And now they have run off together.'

The woman's name was Gianna and she was plainly a bit uncomfortable on her feet, so I hurried to offer her my chair. The waiter found me a chair of my own, so we were soon sitting side by side facing forward into the narrow alley.

'What's that smell?' I asked. I had just caught a strong whiff of surgical alcohol.

'Hand sanitiser,' replied Gianna. 'People have started using it a lot.'

'Why? I find the smell most off-putting.'

She shrugged. 'Yeah it's very irritating.' Gianna had an air of a woman who got irritated very easily.

'Why are they using it?' I asked. I could see a waiter, but also a customer by the doorway rubbing their hands in it.

'They are trying to stave off the inevitable,' she replied.

'Which is?'

'Which is not important. Your sister has run off with my husband.' She was sounding very shirty, possibly with me.

I tried to deflect her mood to increase the chance of getting some clear facts. 'I have been into that office.' I pointed across the street. 'And they told me to my face that they had never even heard of my sister.'

This had the desired effect; Gianna looked surprised. 'But she works in there with my husband,' she said. 'For sure.'

'Yes!' I said. 'Thank you.'

'Well, what on earth are they trying to do? Why would they say that?' she asked.

'I don't know. I don't get it. The receptionist, everyone in there, told me to my face that Emily did not exist.'

'Eta, the receptionist, said that? Well that is just weird,' she replied. 'What did they say about Angelo?'

'They were opaque,' I replied. 'I had less cause to question them about Angelo, because he is not a relative.'

She considered this. 'My understanding is that they both told their bosses they were taking three weeks off,' she said. 'So now it is suddenly like they don't even exist, you say.'

'When did you last see your husband?' I asked.

'Two days ago. I kissed him goodbye when he went to work. It was a normal day.'

'Have you reported him as missing to the police?' I asked.

'He's not missing. He's run off with your sister.'

She looked distressed even thinking about it, and it was like her anxiety had spread to the baby who stirred and made a warning noise that it would soon want attention.

'A boy or a girl?' I asked.

'A boy. Look, he's dressed in... oh no worry.' She flicked a finger in my direction implying she was talking to a man and therefore there is no point in explaining basics to me. 'It's a shame he's a boy. I look at him and I think I could hate all men forever after this.' She was angry.

The baby was stirring more now and would plainly need attention. I was keen to get any information I could from Gianna before she became too distracted by childcare. 'Why would Society Metropolitan pretend they had never heard of Angelo and Emily?' I asked. 'They were colleagues.'

'And lovers,' she corrected helpfully.

'We don't know...' I began. I felt that as I was not in full possession of the facts, I should defend Emily. 'I just feel...' I started. But whatever I was planning with that sentence it was stopped by a glare from Gianna.

Emily was not one who would necessarily share the details of her love life with me, but on the other hand, I reflected, she was not the sort who would run off with a married man whose wife had just given birth. No sooner had I had those thoughts however, when my brain provided quite a few examples of Emily's dubious behaviour over the years. I decided on another tack.

'If I may ask... how do you know they were having an affair?' I tried. 'I am just getting my bearings you understand,' I added hurriedly.

'I caught them in bed together.' Well that is pretty conclusive.

I paused to think.

Gianna took my pause as a sign I wasn't supporting her. 'Look if you don't believe me, I can describe her bedroom. I followed him one morning to her apartment.'

'You followed him to her apartment?'

'He ran off to work one morning and left some important papers behind. I ran after him into the street and he was walking the wrong way. He wasn't walking towards his office at all. I already had my suspicions by then. I followed him at a distance, and he went to your sister's house. He let himself in. He had a key.'

'He had a key to Emily's?'

Every time I attempted a clarification, Gianna just got more cross. 'Well there was a key hidden in a hanging pot of flowers,' she said dismissively. 'Like a hanging terracotta pot?'

I recalled just such a pot when I visited Emily's earlier. Was that earlier today? It had been a very long day already.

'So he let himself in,' she continued. 'I then dithered. I hung about. But he had put the key back in the terracotta pot, so I thought what the hell and just let myself in and crept through the apartment.'

'That was brave,' I said.

'I found him in bed. He was lying waiting under the covers, face down. He had certain bits and pieces laid out ready.'

I was loath to ask, but ask I did; 'Bits and pieces?'

'You know, sexual stuff.' She barked this. By getting her to recount the details she was now properly angry. 'You know what I mean.' She stressed 'know'.

I didn't know, and I was not sure I wanted to; we were talking about my sister's sexual predilections here.

'And he's from a good family!' she protested. 'A very posh well-connected family!'

How was that the least bit relevant?

'So I confronted him,' she continued. 'He was waiting in bed under the covers, silent and still; waiting for her to creep into the room. It gave him the shock of his life when it was me.'

'Hang on,' I said. 'So Emily wasn't actually there?'

'What difference does it make? It was her bed. Maybe she'd popped out to get them breakfast goods or something.'

'But she wasn't there?' I was clutching at straws, but it gave me a way of defending my sister.

Gianna started shouting at me. Shouting. 'Look, I recognised the sort of sex they were up to! When you are married you know your husband's taste in sex even if you don't let them indulge in it. Well your sister was going for it, and then some, I can tell you.'

The baby had been more or less settled, but on that he gave a start. Then there was a pause. Then just when we thought it was going to be okay, he started bawling his lungs out. At least that forced the angry Gianna to do something other than shout at me. She fiddled with the baby's straps so she could lift him up and comfort him.

It gave me a chance to think. Was that like Emily? Did she get up to specialist sex? It was certainly clear over the years that Emily found sex a lot of fun – and she was very confident in that department - but kinky stuff? No one wants to think of their sister having sex; I had been just about to order some more bites to eat, but now I had quite gone off the idea.

'Look I can describe her apartment,' said Gianna. Gianna then, unbidden, described Emily's apartment. She had certainly been there. Just as importantly, I had certainly been there; this was, after all, a point of some debate only a few hours earlier.

My face was blank from trying to take so much in. Gianna took this the wrong way.

'Look, if you don't believe me,' she said. 'He sent me a text by accident. It was meant for her.' She reached in her handbag for her phone. 'Do you want to see it?'

'Er, no, that's okay.'

'I want to show it to you. I want you to see what your sister is like.'

'Okay. I feel you are getting angry with me about something my sister has done,' I said.

Mercifully the baby, who had calmed down readily, was now making a lot more noise again. In his world view, he had been very patient all morning – why, at one stage he had gone a whole thirty minutes without any discernible food or entertainment. The same thing happened to me once; I felt his pain. Gianna sniffed his bottom and pulled a non-committal face. 'I may have to change his diaper,' she said.

There was a baby changing bag that was integral to the design of the buggy; she undid its flap to retrieve a changing mat. This all had the effect of making Gianna a little calmer. I saw this as my chance to reason with her.

'You will have to help me,' I said.

'How so?'

'Well this just doesn't quite seem like what my sister gets up to.'

'That's what people say about Angelo too,' she spat. 'Because he is quiet, because he is shy, people think he could not possibly be like this. But, I mean, he's done this before. He hangs out with those friends of his on Lido by the beach, and gets up to all sorts of stuff.'

We were distracted by the door opening of Society Metropolitan offices. It was Adam leaving the building.

I saw him first, but Gianna was alerted by my expression and soon saw him too.

'Adam!' shouted Gianna.

Well this will be interesting. Will Adam acknowledge to Angelo's wife that Angelo exists? And in front of me?

It was hard to tell for sure whether Adam had even heard his name; when Gianna called him, he almost started to look round, but then seemed to think better of it and hurried away.

'Adam!' she called again, louder.

This time Adam didn't look round at all. But he did hurry more. Had he heard us and was deliberately ignoring his name? I would say yes, but I had no proof.

'Run after him,' said Gianna. 'Stop him! I'll catch you up.' How? How was she going to catch me up with a baby?

Adam looked as though he would be no stranger to a morning run. I on the other hand, have a washboard paunch and legs so short they barely touch the ground when I am sitting on a standard chair; my body was categorically not designed for running; it was designed for eating.

I had no hope of catching Adam if he didn't want to be caught, but purely to avoid yet more wrath from the ever-angry Gianna, I lumbered into action.

SIX

Adam was ten yards ahead of me. He was walking at a speed that would just about pass for innocent. It was nonetheless fast, so I was forced into a canter just to be in with a chance of closing the gap with him. He was soon over two bridges and off towards the quayside.

A large family of tourists with trundle luggage came out of a side alley; they were swirling in the same manner that water circles a plughole; they were plainly lost and oblivious to how much they were going to impede the rest of us. Didn't they know that you aren't even allowed to wheel your trundle luggage in Venice? It is literally against the law – although it doesn't seemed to be enforced at all - but quite right that it is against the law; it makes such a ghastly racket. One day all cities will pass this law, and wonder why they hadn't done it before.

The quayside was quite crowded where people were pouring off a water bus. I could see Adam's head bobbing, about fifteen people ahead of me. He had a striped linen jacket; a garish look that only the young and the senile would imagine they could pull off. It made him very easy to spot.

I was distracted by a man with a large backpack. He turned without checking if it was safe to do so and hit me with his backpack on my shoulder. Why do people who wear backpacks not realise what a liability they are, and look carefully before turning around? I had no sooner had this thought when a woman carrying her dog – a common sight in Venice – unexpectedly stopped and got in my way. The next thing I knew, I had lost sight of Adam.

'He's gone to the left!' It was Gianna shouting from behind. Just how slow was I, that a woman holding a new-born baby had almost caught me up? Another few paces and she would be overtaking me.

'To the left!' she called again, employing her trademark anger.

I turned down an alley that led back inland, but Adam had totally disappeared. I showed willing by making it to the end and looked ostentatiously left and right; but it was just to put on a show to Gianna. Adam had given us the slip.

Gianna and I re-grouped and went back to the trattoria, but this time we took a table inside by a window. That way we could keep an eye on the offices of

Society Metropolitan but not be noticeable. It also allowed her to go off to change the baby in the toilets.

Both Gianna and the baby looked more at one when they returned.

'Oh I forgot,' I said.

'What?' inquired Gianna.

'The weirdness about claiming my sister doesn't exist goes further than just the office.'

'How so?'

'I went to my sister's apartment and I was told by the cleaner and by the landlady that my sister didn't live there. That they had not even heard of her.'

'Why is this happening?' asked Gianna. 'What does this mean?'

'I have no idea, but there was some litter in a bin in her bedroom. Some scrunched up papers. I photographed them with my phone.'

'And?' she asked.

I got my phone and found the photos.

'It could be my sister's handwriting, but I don't think it is.'

'Could be?'

'Well how often do people write to each other these days? You send a WhatsApp or even an email, but a letter? I mean we see each other most weeks; we don't even exchange birthday cards, so I am not sure about her writing.'

'What does it say?'

'It might possibly be the names of companies and some policy numbers of insurance claims. I wouldn't swear to it, though. But I do feel it lends credence to the idea that Emily was there.'

'Well I know she was there; she was fucking my husband.' She was angry again. Of course, she was.

'Gianna I understand you have had a terrible time, but there is no point in being angry with me personally.'

'I'm not angry!' she barked, louder than before. 'Not the least bit angry. I'm frustrated.'

I breathed in through my nose and out through my mouth. I smiled. A smile of consolation for what she had been through.

'Don't you smile at me,' she snapped.

Gianna set about feeding the baby. I thought for a terrifying moment she was going to breastfeed at the table.

Now, I don't have a problem with women breastfeeding in public – quite the contrary – but when you are also supposed to be having a committed conversation with the woman whose breasts have just appeared, it is hard to know where to look. My tactic is usually to maintain eye contact with the mother and refuse to look away from their face. The trouble is, it has the air of a staring match; I end up looking like a psychopath whose eyes are stinging from never blinking.

It turned out that Gianna was bottle-feeding. My sigh of relief was so audible that Gianna laughed. A laugh! Well that was something at least.

While she was feeding the baby, I got a pen and a napkin off a waiter and jotted down the details I had found on the screwed-up bits of paper in Emily's flat. I then Googled the firms listed. They were all companies in Venice. I then rang my office in Bastia. It was soon confirmed that the numbers and letters on the bits of paper were indeed policy numbers for insurance policies. It wasn't much, but if I was going to play detective, I was going to need to follow up any scrap of a clue that comes my way.

I relayed my findings to Gianna.

'Okay, but what does that prove?' she asked. This woman was very hard work.

'It proves I've been lied to,' I said. 'It is something. It is easy to think you are going mad in a case like this.'

She conceded this. 'Don't I know it.'

The waiter came to take our lunch order. Gianna ordered a pizza with anchovies, capers and black olives.

'But you mustn't,' I protested.

'Why can't I order a pizza?' she asked.

'Because in Venice they have banned wood fires, so the pizza is just from an electric oven. A pizza should come from a wood burning pizza oven. Pizza is the one thing you don't order in Venice.'

Gianna surveyed me with disdain.

'It's just food,' she said.

Just food? Just food?? What kind of a concept is that? She plainly had no idea who she was talking to.

I was suddenly aware of Gianna's stomach; it was probably just the way she was sitting, but was it possible she was pregnant again? It was the way she placed her hand on her stomach. I remembered that earlier she had been walking with what appeared to be a little difficulty; but surely the baby was only four or five months at most, so even if she was pregnant she couldn't be heavily pregnant? And later, when we saw Adam, she had been running quite fast. It was quite confusing.

'You are a foodie?' she asked. She was trying to be pleasant. 'It just so happens I have been eating very salty food all through my pregnancy and beyond. Anchovies, olives... pizza dough is full of salt also. It didn't stop when I gave birth.'

Yes, but a Venetian would wait until she was on one of the other islands to eat pizza, surely? Perhaps I was over-thinking.

I deliberately ordered a salty dish myself to show her how it is done. I have no idea why I felt the need to go into competition with a possibly pregnant woman about how to imbibe as much salt as possible in the most elegantly gastronomic manner available, but there it is.

I ordered bigoli in salsa. Bigoli is thick handmade spaghetti made from wholemeal flour and the sauce was onion, anchovy, a dash of tuna, a glass of white wine and some olive oil. It is a local dish as old as Venice itself and with a final sprinkle of fresh parsley is a meal fit for kings and paupers alike.

'This is how to get your blood pressure up with a serious salt spike!' I announced as the waiter brought our food. Gianni's pizza looked satisfyingly anaemic in comparison. I curled the spaghetti in a spoon and tasted it. Gianna was totally indifferent, so I refrained from saying, 'I win!' I am a master of self-restraint.

I looked around to find out what the locals were treating themselves to by way of fluid. There was a young couple at the next table each with a fluorescent orange drink; presumably spritz - prosecco, fizzy water and Aperol. I have never liked them myself and am constantly amazed at how popular they are; in my short time in Venice I had seen people drinking them at ten in the morning, but also at midnight. I don't get it; to me, they taste like a childhood vitamin supplement. I decided on a glass of prosecco instead. After all, it was a wine made only forty miles inland from Venice; it is – relatively speaking – local, and it certainly gives Champagne a run for its money; it would be insulting to the locals not to order some. But then I remembered that Emily was missing. I had better stay sober. I ordered a glass of fizzy water. My sister. It was not the first time I have made major sacrifices for that woman, and it won't be the last.

'Look!' said Gianna. 'He's back. Adam is back. Collar him.'

But I had barely started eating my delicious food.

I looked at my plate of bigoli and sighed, then I was up and off from the table and out the door.

Adam had already buzzed the door of his office to be allowed in. I heard the click as the door mechanism was released; he now needed to lift his legs one by one over the flood defence barrier. I threw myself forward and just managed to get my foot across Adam's before he made it inside.

'Adam, we need a word,' I said.

'We?' He looked up and down the alley.

'Just thirty seconds of your time.' I did my best to look insistent. I held firmly on the door until his shoulders slumped. I shepherded him back to the trattoria.

'Hello Gianna,' said Adam. 'How are you?' He hadn't even looked directly at her. He knew she was there.

'You know who Gianna is, then?' I asked.

'Of course, he knows me,' said Gianna. 'I am the wife of his colleague Angelo. We have met many times.' Somehow her anger, yet again, was directed at me. What on earth had I done wrong?

Adam didn't deny he knew Gianna. He stood about a metre from us. He looked as though he was hoping to keep any interaction short and then escape.

'Adam, where is Angelo?' asked Gianna.

'Angelo?' He was playing for time.

'I need to know where my husband is.'

Adam's eyes were darting around the room. What was he afraid of? *Who* was he afraid of? Gianna's hand moved to her stomach. Just how pregnant was she? If indeed she was pregnant. Perhaps the baby in the buggy was older than I thought; I hadn't actually asked its age, he could be seven or eight months I suppose. I was no judge of such things. I realised Gianna had widened her eyes at me to ask me to take up the reins with Adam.

'I don't understand what is happening,' I said. 'But this pretending that my sister doesn't exist won't wash. I work for the same company as you and I have had it confirmed today that this is exactly the office where she has been working. This lady is looking for her husband, and my sister is missing. Now are you going to tell us what is going on, or not? Are you going to help us?'

Adam took a step back as if he was going to suddenly run. This was all preposterous, but I didn't know quite how to handle it. What exactly could I say to him?

Gianna barked at him, 'Adam!'

'What?'

'If Angelo has run off with Emily it is not for you to keep their secrets,' she said.

'It isn't that,' he said.

'Then what is it?'

'We have been...' he started. But then someone new came into the trattoria and it made him go quiet again.

He then apparently steeled himself to act - to offer us something so that he could get away from us. He walked towards Gianna and whispered, 'Look. Meet you at San Zaccaria. You know? Tonight at seven.' He then turned on his heel and disappeared before we could argue.

I looked to Gianna. 'Do you know where that is?' I asked.

She nodded.

I hurriedly ate my pasta before anyone could stop me. Gianna's eyes grew wide, so I looked up to wonder what fresh problem she had noticed. It turned out that she was simply appalled at all the slurping and hoovering noises I was making.

'It was close to going cold!' I protested.

'It's disgusting. That's what it is.'

You're so graceless and bad tempered; no wonder Angelo left you. Is not what I said. But I could have done.

'So what shall we do with our afternoon?' I asked. 'It is a long time until 7pm.'

'I need to get the baby sorted out. Change his clothes. Get fresh diapers. We have got off lightly with him.' She pointed to the baby. 'I don't want to push my luck. Give me your phone number. I'll send you the details of where Adam says we should meet up.'

SEVEN

That evening I was waiting in a trattoria in a tiny square. It wasn't the eatery in the same square as the church of San Zaccaria, but in a smaller square down an alley further away. I was there at the dot of 7pm, but neither Gianna nor Adam appeared, so I double checked I was in the place Gianna had told me before settling down fully.

I wondered if it was breaking some sort of protocol to order some food. I had tried ringing Emily a few times in the afternoon, but still no answer. I Googled who this Angelo person was, just to get a picture of him in my mind. He was presentable rather than good-looking; nothing special. I couldn't imagine Emily going for his sort, and certainly not for a married man; it was too big a commitment for a woman who gets lots of offers from men. Emily, as a rule, could barely commit to regularly watering a houseplant – she certainly wouldn't run off with someone - but who knows; the magic of Venice, the loneliness of being away. Emily is not good on her own; she always needs to be in the company of someone, she always needs to be doing something. Or someone. But why was everyone denying she even existed? It made no sense.

I thought I saw Adam.

I had been watching two little lads through the window kicking a ball around further up the street, and I realised there was a man just beyond them on the other side of a stone bridge. He was about the size and shape of Adam but when I scrutinised him, he turned away and out of sight, so I wasn't sure.

Then there was another movement to my right. It was also a man. Again, not dissimilar to Adam's shape and size. He was just hanging around. It was like he was waiting for his dog to do something, but there was no dog. I squinted into the half-light. Maybe there was a dog after all; it was hard to say. I had a bad feeling just sitting at this restaurant table. A feeling I was being watched and I was exposed and vulnerable. The feeling was deep in my stomach. Upon reflection, it was probably hunger.

I studied the menu. They had a handmade ravioli made with sea bass, tossed with fresh asparagus that had been griddled. It sounded great.

Someone was standing over me. Somehow Gianna had sneaked up on me while I was distracted. She looked great. She was wearing a burgundy coloured evening dress and she had combed her hair out.

'You look dead glam,' I said. 'No baby tonight?'

'I left him with my mother-in-law,' she replied. 'It strikes me as the least she could do, given how her son behaved.' She stopped herself and changed her tone. 'No, actually, I am going to be positive tonight. It's a meal out without the baby, with my new friend Pete.' If this is how she treats her friends – shouting at them, haranguing them – how does she treat her enemies?

'Are you up for a drink?' I asked.

'Of course. A drink, a nice meal and hopefully we will get some information out of Adam and it will be an evening well spent.'

I wasn't sure of the exact format of the evening. Was Adam joining us? But I needed no persuasion to have a decent meal with a glamorous woman. I ordered the ravioli I had seen on the menu and Gianna ordered a pasta with mushrooms.

Italy is a country of mushroom lovers; in the autumn they pour into the woods in their thousands looking for porcini and chiodini – chiodini are a rich browny-orange colour and are sometimes called honey mushrooms - and the Italians know what they are doing when they cook them. The more I thought about it, the more I felt I should have gone for the same as Gianna. I asked Gianna if she would like to share some prosecco.

'Sure, why not,' she replied. 'This is the first evening I've had out since I've had the baby. How sad is that?'

'Not sad at all,' I said. 'Every stage of your life has pros and cons. There will be plenty of years of meals out ahead. But I've never had a child. It is something amazing I have never done.'

'You're very kind,' she said.

Gianna's phone got a text.

'Walk towards the church but take the first left.'

'What?' I asked.

'This text is telling us to go down that calle,' she said. She pointed through the window in the direction of some tourist shops. Someone who looked like a student was wandering along carrying some books and talking apparently to himself. We used to think that was a sign of madness, but now we assume they have a headset and are making a phone call. There was no one else in our line of vision.

'Why?' I asked. 'Can't he meet us here?'

I was loath to move from somewhere where we were surrounded by people, to some unlit alley.

'Text him back,' I said. 'Ask him to come to us.'

Gianna texted back. After a while she said, 'There's no reply.'

'No little dots. No "Adam is typing" or similar?'

We both craned our heads around rather than move.

'But what about the food?' I asked. 'We've ordered a cracking meal, and we are supposed to abandon it?' If I had said something as flippant as that at lunchtime Gianna would have been cross; but she was in a profoundly better mood this evening. 'And now the waiter is coming,' I added. He was carrying a silver bucket of ice and the fizzy wine.

I addressed the waiter, 'Can you pour it, and we'll be right back?' He was a portly man with a thick white apron. I love it when the waiters have white aprons. I don't know why.

'Come on then,' I said, rising. 'Let's walk down that alley.'

Gianna stood but then refused to move. 'I've got a bad feeling about this.'

So did I. I heard myself say, 'We'll link arms.'

'What?'

'In this post #MeToo era where there is no such thing as appropriate touching, I'm suggesting we link arms,' I said. 'Moral support for each other.'

It made her laugh at least. 'Sure,' she said.

We linked arms and walked out the restaurant and down the alley into an area where there was no lighting.

Ahead of us, a little boy in a red raincoat ran out of a doorway and onwards to a path that lay beside a canal. He went up to two people – a man and a woman - and addressed them. They talked for a bit. Gianna and I had both spotted it and instinctively stopped.

The little boy ran from the men to us. He looked about eight. He spoke in Italian to us, but in a manner I didn't quite catch – a lot of local children use the Venetian dialect.

I think he said, 'I have come with a message for you, what are your names please? Are you Gianna and Peter?' He was grinning with the fun of his job.

'Yes,' replied Gianna. 'We are Gianna and Peter.'

'You give me money,' said the child.

'Seriously? Why would we give you money?'

'And I will give you instructions,' said the boy.

Gianna looked to me.

I looked in my wallet. I only had twenties. I looked at the twenties and I looked at the boy. In any currency – dollars, pounds, euros – a twenty is a twenty. Gianna was making no move towards her own purse. If I said to her, 'But I only have twenties' I would look like a cheapskate. But it was a twenty, and he was an eight-year-old boy. I handed him the money. Just to look good in front of a woman. A grumpy woman at that. God, I'm pathetic.

The eight-year-old looked very pleased with his twenty euro note – as well he might. He stuffed it into his trouser pocket using a deep ramming action.

'Over that bridge take the right,' he said. 'Then the next left and walk to the end.'

'The first right over the bridge and then left?' asked Gianna.

The child looked unsure. He put his hands up to reassure himself which was left and which was right. 'Well I think…' he began.

'No. Not I think. We need to be sure,' I said. I was twenty euros down, after all.

The boy went to run away. I shot my arm out and grabbed him.

'I don't want to sound cheap but for a twenty I think I deserve more than a vague set of directions and a see you later,' I said. 'You can show us.'

The boy wrestled his arm to try and free himself. He looked around to see who was watching; he was wondering whether to cry for help. He relented.

The three of us walked over the bridge and took the first alley on the right. It was dark so I got my phone and turned on its torch. It was a narrow alley with pockmarked orange brickwork. We proceeded with caution and soon found a second alley that led off to the left. This was longer, and – as if this was even possible – even darker than before. People could easily follow us into the alley and have us cornered. I gripped the boy tighter. He might be useful as collateral. Or a human shield.

'Let's get out of here Gianna. This can't be good,' I said.

We backtracked. I tried to move us with some pace. I didn't want to let on how much I was afraid – after all, I am a man. *Supposed* to be a man.

There was now someone in our way.

It was Adam.

Instantly, the child put his hand out to ask for more money. Adam gave him a note. I bet it wasn't a twenty.

'You get paid twice?' I asked the child.

He grinned and scampered off.

'So Adam, what is this all about?' whispered Gianna. 'Where is my husband?'

'Your husband is fine,' said Adam. He kept a discreet distance from us and was constantly looking up and down the alley as if half expecting someone would appear. 'At least, as far as I know, he is fine,' he said.

'Why are we whispering then?' I asked.

'Trust no one,' he said. 'I mean no one.' Well that was melodramatic.

'Just tell us what is going on,' I said.

'Okay,' he started. 'There is a group of businessmen and they were aggrieved that the insurance companies were not paying out for the flood damage last year. Angelo is... well he is from a traditional family here; well-connected. They needed two signatories if they were to pull off a scam where they quickly got money paid out on policies. Angelo is one. He is helping them, but then they needed to get your sister's virtual signature as well. She claims she was kidnapped on the day this all happened. Abducted and held captive for a whole day. But when challenged she could offer no proof. What is for sure is that she was away from the office and during that time her computer was accessed remotely and used to agree to a lot of pay outs. Then she received a large sum of money into her bank account. 60 or 80 thousand I heard.'

'Well that is simple then. The people who got the money are behind the scam,' I said.

'No.'

'No?'

'No,' said Adam. 'They deliberately agreed pay outs to twenty-four policies. Twenty-four represents the original twenty-four families who ruled Venice for centuries, although obviously they are not the same twenty-four who had policies; it's a symbolic thing. Anyway, maybe only maybe half of the actual policy holders are involved in the fraud; maybe fewer. The others are decoys.'

'What's in it for Angelo?' asked Gianna.

'He looks like the victim. He says he was also abducted that day, like Emily. But he is a hero in the eyes of many; helping the families who have been hit so hard. No doubt, in time, he will be offered a good job with one of the families. No doubt he will get some money. His own family probably stood to gain massively one way or another. I mean, Gianna, you know his family.'

'But he's run off with Pete's sister Emily?' asked Gianna.

Adam looked around again – ostensibly to see if anyone had entered the calle - but in fact I think he was just stalling for time; it was a sensitive topic.

'Has he run off with Emily?' asked Gianna again.

'They were either in it together, or perhaps that was a later complication,' he said. 'It depends who you listen to. Some say they were in it together all along. Some say she was indeed abducted and Angelo accessed her computer. But certainly, and you will have to excuse me Gianna, he was having an affair with Emily. So it makes sense she ran off with him. Maybe she even thinks he's innocent.' He paused, and darkened his voice. 'Some even say that he has abducted her. That he seems like a decent man, but he became obsessed with her...'

'How do you know these things?' I asked.

'I'm just telling you what I hear.' He was more restless now. 'Look, I need to go.' He now addressed Gianna hard in the eyes. 'Look, I have to warn you. You have to be very careful. You are dealing with serious people here. Some of them are affronted businessmen, sure, but some of them are gangsters and smugglers and worse; we are talking major organised crime. These are people who think nothing of killing. If you keep poking around, they will come for you. Mark my words. Take this seriously. Just asking questions could get you killed. They are protecting their own, and their own currently includes Emily.'

'But, how do you know these things?' I asked. I felt he had dodged my previous question; he said he was just telling us what he heard, but from whom?

'My family is also one of the twenty-four,' he replied. 'There was talk of this happening some weeks ago. Our family was approached. I was approached. But I would have nothing to do with it.'

'Do you have proof?' I asked.

'It is hearsay and conversations that I cannot prove. But be careful. Be very careful; if you keep making inquiries they will get you.' He made to go.

Gianna pulled him by the jacket. 'I need to see my husband,' she said.

There was a noise. There was a movement at the far end of the alley, but it was so difficult to see down there that it was hard to know. I flashed my phone-torch ahead of me. A man was standing there. A tall athletic looking man. Adam was visibly shaken. I think he had been planning to walk that way, but on seeing the man he made to go backwards.

'I need to see my husband,' said Gianna. 'Where is he?'

'And why are people pretending they don't exist?' I asked.

'I'll text you if I find something out,' said Adam. He grabbed Gianna's wrists and removed them from his jacket.

He was gone.

The man at the end of the alley started walking towards us. He was moving far too purposefully for it to be coincidence. We scuttled after Adam as best we could.

We were soon back by the canal and then we kept going forward down the alley to the little square with the restaurant.

'We'll be safer here,' I said. 'Other diners as a witness, and so on.'

And we'll be so close to the food and prosecco, that we might actually get to eat it.

EIGHT

'Is your husband capable of organising a fraud?' I asked Gianna. 'Is he the sort who would carry out such a big crime?'

'Is your sister?'

'No.' Except she did indeed carry out a massive fraud in Corsica two years back in a scam involving a corpse. But somehow my instincts told me this was different. Claiming she was kidnapped, but defrauding the very company she worked for? The finger of suspicion would start with her on day one, so she would have found another way of going about it. Would she lie about being abducted? Again, I would say no; but she had comprehensively lied at length to me in a previous scam. She did that for a quarter of a million; what price would she expect to endanger her job or even risk prison? And surely she would have had far more sense than just take a large bribe straight into her bank account. No. In my view, Emily was not directly involved. But did she then run off with Angelo?

'My husband is a mouse of a man,' reflected Gianna. 'A meek little mouse.'

And yet you are angry at losing him.

'Angelo doesn't have the spine to organise a major fraud,' said Gianna.

And yet you married him.

'He just didn't have the balls,' she continued.

And yet he gave you children.

'Why are they pretending Emily and your husband don't exist?' I asked Gianna, not for the first time. She was picking at her food; clearly too traumatised to eat. Her pasta looked simply delicious. There is a trick to cooking with mushrooms. They are 80% to 90% water, so if you can evaporate the liquid out of them, perhaps by frying, and then combine them with some dried mushrooms that have been soaked just enough to release their flavour, or ground in their dried state into a powder; you get a symbiosis where the fresh mushrooms take up the concentrated flavour of the dried mushrooms. And it wasn't just that; mushrooms are a natural source of the much-maligned monosodium glutamate. It's a flavour enhancer, and astonishingly it is also found in high levels in parmesan cheese; Gianna had put parmesan on top of her pasta. Well anyway, Gianna's food looked and smelled delicious and she was barely touching it.

I had already finished my ravioli. I wondered if it would be poor protocol to offer to eat her food for her. Probably. She pushed the plate away. Tantalisingly, it now sat six inches from my left hand. It was taunting me. It was all I could see on the table.

'I don't know. It makes no sense,' she said. 'If they were wanted by the police then it would be the other way around, surely? The police and everyone would be quizzing us about where we thought they could be.'

'What are you going to do?' I asked.

'Bring up a baby on my own, apparently. I mean that's the stereotype, right? Man moves on; woman left holding the baby.'

I wondered where Emily and Angelo could have gone together. Emily would have no connections in Italy and no money, so it would have been all down to Angelo. Or perhaps, as Adam said, she had been abducted.

'You and I are going to have to play detective,' I said.

'How so?' I noticed that despite her lack of appetite she was still knocking back the wine. She beckoned the waiter over and ordered a classy bottle of local pinot grigio. I wondered if I was paying for this, perhaps on the grounds that my sister was getting the blame for stealing her husband. On the other hand, her husband was probably guilty of dragging Emily into a major fraud that could land her in prison, so what is the social protocol here? Go Dutch? Also, all this wine drinking kind of blew a hole in my theory that she was pregnant.

'We are going to have to find Angelo and Emily ourselves,' I said.

'Yes,' she replied.

The fresh wine arrived, and she was halfway down a glass of it before I had even had a chance to draw breath. And still her untouched mushroom pasta sat on the table calling me by name. I surreptitiously moved my fork towards it, but at the exact same moment the waiter came over. 'Shall I take it away?' he asked.

'No!' I cried involuntarily.

'It's just that I thought the Signora had finished.'

'She has,' I said. I suppose. I watched reluctantly as the plate of food was carried off the kitchens.

'They can't hide out forever,' said Gianna. 'He will want to see his child, surely? If not me, he would want to see his child.'

Gianna was sounding forlorn rather than angry which made a pleasant change – for me at least. 'He's...' she began, then she paused to reflect, apparently, on the qualities that made her husband the man he was.

'He's a good man,' she nodded to herself, somehow reassuring herself, puzzling it out. Evidently not. What with the fraud, and the Fifty Shades of sex going on with my sister.

'Angelo mentioned he was well-connected. Or he comes from a big family,' I said. 'We could start there with our logic when trying to find him?'

'What do you mean?' she asked.

'Well who in his family would be the king pin? If this is a fraud organised by the big families of the island, who would be the person in his family who would pull the strings and make things happen?'

'His uncle Julio,' she said. She hadn't needed any time to think about it. 'We'll go there tomorrow.' Gianna then stopped speaking and went into a trance. I waited, but she seemed farther and farther away with each second. And then seconds turned to minutes. What was the protocol here? Just walk away, go home, and leave her staring into space? Sit reading a novel across the table? Reluctantly, I tapped her wrist.

'What?' she asked.

'Is there anything you want to talk about?'

'Yes. Men!'

I knew I would regret asking. She launched into an angry diatribe about Angelo that went on, and on, and on. And then every time I thought she had run out of things to say, she went on some more.

Gianna was one angry woman.

We arranged to meet again the following day. It was in roughly the same neighbourhood where Emily had rented her apartment – Cannaregio. Gianna suggested we meet by the bridge Ponte delle Guglie. As is often the way with winter in Venice, a fog had set in. Despite this, and the fact that the bridge led to a residential neighbourhood, the crowds of sightseers were already abundant; although what they were going to see in the fog was – literally – unclear. This was a district where normal people were trying to live and bring up their children, but one group of tourists in particular were hampering the locals even more than usual by forming a confused shoal at the foot of the bridge. Those that weren't gazing at an upside down map, were frowning at their phones, but not one of them thought to pull the group to one side so that people could get on with their day.

Between the fog and the crowds, it was going to be difficult to spot Gianna, so I wondered if I should walk around a little to look for her or stay put and let her do the looking. I had visions that if we both moved around, we would endlessly elude each other.

I needn't have worried. Like so many of the bridges in Venice, the Ponte delle Guglie has stone steps up and down. Gianna had her baby in a buggy and was struggling with both the holidaymakers and the steps; she was taking no prisoners with either. The distance between the front and back wheels was just the wrong length for the size of the steps; if she got the back wheels successfully down a level, the front wheels then fell off the step in front. This necessitated that she had to use the buggy arms for leverage and half carry the whole affair – the seat in one arm and a handle in another - to take the weight off the wheels. Not one tourist offered to help, or indeed even noticed her; would they have behaved like this in their own countries? I moved forward to help her, but by the time I had negotiated a way through the crowds she only had one step to go. I ostentatiously lifted my end of the buggy anyway, and she ostentatiously snarled me. It was going to be another fun day with Gianna and her temper.

'You could have done that before,' she said.

We were distracted by a refuse man from the city council; he had a fluorescent tabard on that said, 'Keep Venice Clean.' In English, not Italian. We needed to get out of his way. He had a large custom designed handcart that had tiny wheels at one end and large wheels at the other. It had been crafted to allow him to lug it up stone steps and down narrow alleys far more adroitly than the much lighter and smaller baby buggy.

'So where are we going today?' I asked Gianna.

'Change of plan,' she said. 'I have just this second had word from Adam. He is going to help us. He texted me and I phoned him. He is going to hook us up with a Signor Turturro. Adam said he has been asking around, and this Signor Turturro will know a lot of the things we want to understand.'

'So we are not going to see this Uncle Julio at all?' I asked.

Gianna looked puzzled at my question, then the mists seemed to clear and she said a simple no.

'But information from two different people; this Signor Turturro and also Angelo's uncle? We should talk to both?' I asked.

Gianna sighed impatiently. 'No!' she barked.

'And Adam said that making inquiries was dangerous. Has he changed his tune?'

'Oh, he was just exaggerating.' She now was just one notch below shouting. I have never met someone who gets so angry so easily, and for so long.

'So where do we have to go?' I asked. I used a soothing tone; the sort you use on household pets who look jumpy.

'Well that's just the problem. We have to meet him in secret. It has to be somewhere where no one can overhear us or know that we have met.'

I imagined a darkened room where the disembodied voice of this Signor Turturro talked to us, then I imagined being blindfolded and taken to a secret location. It turned out the reality was far worse.

'We have to go to Poveglia,' said Gianna.

'Oh that it not good. That is really not good,' I said. 'Poveglia?'

'I know.'

'But it's illegal to go there.'

'I know,' she replied.

NINE

It has been illegal to go to Poveglia since, I think, the 1960s. Beyond that fact, I knew little. Gianna furnished me with further details over coffee.

'Legend has it that 160,000 people have died there and are buried in its soil. A journalist once calculated that as a result half the soil now consists of dead bodies.'

'Why?' I asked.

'It was a quarantine island for years, where ships coming from a long way off could be vetted – in fact it is the island that gave us the word "quarantine" because you had to stay there forty days. Before that, it was called "Trentino" but it turned out thirty days was not long enough; two ships brought the plague to Venice, and as a result it became the island where Venice took it's infected relatives and dumped them there to die. And then later in history it was the home of an infamous mental hospital.'

'That's interesting.' I said.

'I can be interesting,' she replied. 'I'm not always Angry Lady, you know.'

Not always. Most of the time.

'I don't feel very well,' she said.

She looked dreadful. I ordered her more coffee.

'Have you got a hangover?' I asked.

'No, why?' she replied.

Because you drank a couple of bottles of wine last night while barking me through your entire relationship with Angelo? I was actually very bored and desperate to get away by the end – it is supposed to be my holiday after all - but you just wouldn't stop for breath?

'No reason,' I said.

'Actually, I think it might be fear,' she said. 'The police could do us for going to the island, but if we are stuck there and something goes wrong, there is no way to run for help. What a nightmare this whole thing is.'

She pointed to the baby.

'Cute,' I said.

'No. I don't usually let him have a nap in the morning otherwise he doesn't sleep at night, so he is going to be difficult. I just... well I am all over the place. I am not coping very well.'

'Can we get a water taxi to Poveglia?' I asked.

'No! No one will take us,' she sounded quite wretched. 'They will report us. I have borrowed a boat. Can you pilot a boat?'

'Sort of,' I said. 'It depends on the boat.'

The boat that Gianna had borrowed was a Brube.

'You teenager,' I said.

'How so?'

'These are the motorboats that the youth all use.'

'Are you saying I'm not young?' I think she was joking, but I didn't know her well enough to be sure.

Basically, a Brube is a solid but speedy motorboat. On the face of it, they are not especially suited to transporting mothers with babies and all the paraphernalia of feeding bottles and changing mats. But Venetians are boat people - hardly any of them own a car - they spend their lives hopping in and out of boats. As a result, although my instinct was that I should offer my services to Gianna, before I knew it she had bounded aboard and secured the buggy in the boat with the baby contentedly sleeping. It was me who was left on the quayside wondering how to ease myself onboard without any help.

'Can you cast off?' asked Gianna. As in, can I untie a boat, push it away from the quay and then hop adroitly back onboard before it sails out of reach, all without tipping it, its contents, or myself into the water on account of my unwieldy bulk and general lack of fitness?

'Sure,' I said.

I tripped at the first hurdle. I was struggling to even undo the mooring rope.

Gianna was graceful about this, and abandoned the helm to help me out. She untangled the knotted mooring rope with a flick so nonchalant it shamed me, and then she steadied her footing at the edge of the boat and offered me a hand to get onboard. I would have dearly loved to say the words, 'No, no, there's no need.' But I took her hand gratefully.

The baby decided that now was the time to wake. And cry. It was like something had stung it. Gianna seemed oblivious to the child's needs though; she let out the throttle of the boat and we were off.

The speed limit on the smaller waterways is little more than walking pace – 5km/hour – and that rises to 11km/hour on the bigger waterways and 20km/hour in the lagoon as a whole. However, the fog was impenetrably thick and represented a major problem. It was so thick you could bite chunks out of it and feel full for a week.

'Should we be out at all in this?' I asked, trying to get myself heard over the combined noise of the wailing child beside me, and the Mercury motor behind.

'No,' she replied. 'The large passenger boats have radar, but the small boats shouldn't be out at all. It is very dangerous.' She accelerated, as if somehow this proved her point. I gripped the edge of my seat, as if somehow this proved mine. Did she not think we were a small boat? What little I knew about Gianna was based on the, in turns, angry and mournful woman I'd met yesterday; a woman disoriented by being abandoned by her husband. I was now seeing another Gianna – a can-do nautical Gianna – a woman at one with the sea.

'Well this is going to be something,' she shouted into the fog. 'We could die!' She sounded enthralled at the prospect.

Even the baby fell silent at that.

The island of Poveglia is about three miles south of Venice but less than a mile from Lido. Gianna seemed very sure of how to get there, despite a total lack of landmarks to go on and the lack of visibility.

A sturdy metal boat emerged from the fog and then was swallowed up just as quickly. It left us reeling and rocking in its wake. Gianna responded to the incident by speeding up. Of course she did.

'We don't want to hit a cruise ship,' she shouted. 'So we'll cross the main channel as quickly as possible and get to Lido and drop down.'

On cue a cruise ship loomed out of the gloom; it was the size of a football stadium and probably contained as many people. A lesser man would have panicked. I am a lesser man. I tensed my knuckles around my seating and scrunched up my eyes. Gianna swung the boat sharply to our right and we all keeled sideways. I belatedly put an arm out to make sure the baby was secure. It is not clear how that was going to help; if the cruise ship hit us, it would be like swotting a tiny moth; we'd turn to powder. The cruise ship wouldn't even know it had hit us.

Gianna laughed against the wind. She corrected our course which made us rock even more precariously and then settled again on a path to Lido, buffeting the boat up and down on the waves. I was mute with fear.

At length, and having used up eight of our nine lives, a building and quayside loomed up in front of us. It looked as though we had reached Poveglia. If I hadn't felt so rattled by the journey, I'd have been impressed.

'How did you find it?' I asked. 'I can barely see my hand in front of my face.'

Gianna laughed. 'I have been sailing on this lagoon since before I could walk. I know where everything is.'

We moored up near what appeared to be a large mansion or perhaps a barracks. Gianna hopped off the boat and I passed her up the baby and the buggy.

'The asylum is round the back,' she called.

'Okay?'

'Apparently, it is haunted.' She said it like she was sweetening the deal.

'What time are we meeting this Signor Turturro?' I asked.

She looked at her phone. 'Another twenty minutes. I know the spot,' she said. 'I'll show you round.'

There was some scaffolding on the building, but it was unsafe and in disrepair; a long-abandoned project. Gianna took us forwards along the quay and a tall clocktower appeared.

'In 1922,' began Gianna. 'They opened a mental hospital here. Legend has it that the doctor in charge tortured the patients and killed many of them. He butchered them horribly. They say he went mad and threw himself off the bell tower to his death. Some say he was carried up to the top by the patients, kicking and screaming and was thrown off.'

The story did nothing to calm my nerves. This place was batshit scary.

'Over there is the plague field. Where thousands of Venetians are buried. If they got the signs of the plague they were stolen in the night by men in hoods and taken out here and abandoned to die. They say that at night the wind still carries their cries across the water to Venice.'

'I'll rest sounder tonight knowing that,' I said.

We walked along the canal and then between the buildings - Gianna nonchalant as if she were simply taking her baby for a stroll – me, trying to avoid fallen fence work and broken glass. For an island where people weren't allowed by the authorities, there was a lot graffiti and vandalism on show.

'Who is this Signor Turturro anyway, and why are we having to meet him in secret?' I asked.

'He is from one of the old families,' she replied. 'A big businessman. He owns a lot of property and some industry on the mainland. He is a politician and given what we now know...'

I presumed she was referring to the massive scandal about the flood defences. There had been 35 arrests, including the mayor himself, on charges that 20 million euros had been misappropriated or used as bribes; money that was supposed to go to building the barriers that would have saved Venice from the very floods that were the cause of all this conflict; the scandal was very high up and didn't involve 'the little people' at all.

'One irony was that the inquiry into the corruption and the change in its management actually slowed up the building of it. It might have been finished by now otherwise,' said Gianna.

'I had heard,' I said.

'Anyway, if I was of a suspicious nature – and I am – it would be easy to believe that Signor Turturro is one of the ring leaders behind this fraud. He is well-connected and in the thick of it. A bridge between the old money in Venice and the more modern criminal elements out at the port; the people involved with smuggling.'

'Smuggling?'

'Drugs. Immigrants who want to settle in Europe. Caviar.'

'Caviar?' I asked.

'Sturgeon is a protected species and there are quotas for how much that can be harvested and exported. Anyway, it is thought he is involved in caviar smuggling. But that is not important to this. What is important is that Adam has a cousin and she is married into his family and he has agreed to meet us. But no one must know.'

'Okay now this is just spooky and macabre,' I said.

Gianna had taken us round to the front of the asylum building and was negotiating the baby and buggy in through the door. We were in a large hallway with an elaborate staircase that spiralled up. The balustrades were ornately curved metal in a 1920s style. There were leaves and branches littering the floor where some roof had collapsed, and the large wooden doors had long since given way. Gianna was exploring as if it were a house she were half planning to purchase; pushing through to the next room and then the next, all the while turning her head left and right.

'We used to come here for parties as teens, but I haven't been back. We sat around a fire drinking and telling ghost stories. There was one night when a girl was crying inconsolably from a spooky story I told. She was sitting just there sobbing.' She pointed to the spot.

'Fun times,' I said.

She had stopped us in a room with a number of old bedframes in it; solid metal enamelled bedsteads and wrought iron cabinets that perhaps once held medicines. They were partly covered in ivy that had grown in through the broken windows. It was beyond creepy, but it was the most Gianna had enjoyed herself since I'd met her, so I wasn't going to put her off.

We heard a gunshot. Both of us stopped.

'Did you hear that?' I asked.

'It was probably nothing,' she replied.

Probably nothing? A gunshot?

Whatever it was, it made Gianna change tack. 'I need to feed the baby before we meet the man himself,' she said.

The baby. Had she even mentioned the baby's name? Had she told me and I had forgotten?

'There is a bridge that goes to the second island,' she said. 'That would make a good place to settle for a while.'

She turned the buggy round on its back wheels to point us back out. We came out of the building to face a church. The mist was a lot less dense on the island, but it still lingered in patches and you couldn't always see far. As well as being foggy, it was dark; like it should start to rain but it somehow hadn't.

We pressed on through the overgrown gardens and got to a curved wooden bridge with upright logs forming a support at each end. Gianna had been right; this was a better place to stop and feed a baby and change it; less broken glass and ivy, fewer ghosts of mistreated mental patients. While she warmed the bottle and laid out the changing mat, I asked her about herself.

'My family were originally from the mainland. They were farmers. We moved here in my childhood. We only moved thirty kilometres, but somehow we were treated as if we weren't local at all. Mind you we didn't even speak the language at first. The local language is a bit like Spanish. Or rather it is a bit like Catalan mixed with Italian and French. But I soon picked it up from other kids at school.'

The baby was enjoying its bottle, and Gianna was enjoying the baby. They rocked together contentedly, and a cormorant flew down and perched on the opposing bank to survey the water for fish.

There was another gunshot. Louder this time. Much louder.

I ducked my head low. Gianna raised hers up, to look around.

Then there was another shot. This time the mud on the opposing bank flew up. Someone was definitely shooting at us.

Even Gianna ducked down after that.

TEN

We had to protect ourselves and we had to protect the baby.

The shot had come from behind us – the part of the island we had just visited and where our boat was moored. That meant that the only shelter available to us was the underside of the bridge.

Gianna crouched forward; her instinct was to protect the baby with her back. I did the same thing; evidently my instinct was to protect my paunch. We then tried to scuttle forwards using our bums and legs, towards the canal and the footings of the bridge.

Another shot hit the ground behind us. This had the effect of making us less cautious. We both raised ourselves a little on our legs in order to move faster. I instinctively let Gianna get to safety first. I mention this because historically I have a lamentable track record of saving my own skin above all others'; my unexpected chivalry came as a surprise even to myself.

The moment we got to the foot of the bridge we realised we had a problem. Or rather an even bigger problem. The ledge underneath it, above the waterline, was too narrow to take a human. Gianna's tactic was to sit on the edge and let her feet dangle over the water. She then shimmied her bum along sideways.

Another shot.

This one hit the bridge itself. Wood splintered about two feet away from my head. I considered Gianna's tactic for myself, but I am a man who hasn't had a waist since the late 1990s and I have an arse like a badly stuffed sofa; it just wasn't feasible that I could fit my bulk under the bridge. I dropped fully into the water instead.

It was freezing. It was so cold it sent pains across my chest as my circulation constricted – it was winter, after all. I couldn't find the bottom of the canal, so I grasped the bank as best I could.

'Do you think they are in the clocktower?' asked Gianna.

'I have no idea.'

There was another shot; like the first one, it hit the bank beyond.

'The clocktower is some distance away. The church perhaps? That is closer,' I said. 'If it is the clocktower, then to get to our boat we will have to go past him.'

'Or her,' she corrected. I was armpit-deep in some very slimy water, I was shivering with cold, and yet she felt the need to insist on non-sexist language.

'Why are they shooting at us?' I asked.

'No idea.'

'If we stay protected by the bank of the canal, I don't think they are perched high enough to get to us,' I said.

'But how do we move away from here?' she asked. 'I can't drop into the water with the baby. And I can't move sideways along the bank because there is no ledge beyond the bit I am sitting on.'

I didn't want to give in to despair. Or to be precise, I didn't want it obvious I had given in to despair in front of a woman. My own situation wasn't much better than Gianna's; it would be hard for me to get sideways along the canal, stay low to avoid the bullets, and find enough to grip onto along the canal bank as I moved.

'We could phone for help?' I said. It was only then that I realised my phone was in my trouser pocket along with my wallet. It was getting a good soaking. I reached into my pocket and retrieved it and my wallet and placed them on the bank. I half remembered from somewhere that you mustn't then try to use the phone; it will just short circuit in all manner of destructive ways. 'I think I am supposed to take the battery out,' I said, largely to myself. I turned my phone in my right hand. It was a well-built smart phone that had cost me several hundred to buy. I had always been pleased with it, but I had no idea whatever how to get the back open or the battery out.

'Have you got your phone? I asked.

'It's in my bag along with everything else; it's on the stroller,' she said.

I peered as much as my nerves allowed, raising my eyeline an inch but not much more. The stroller was hopelessly out of reach and an open target for the gunman.

'If I crawl on my stomach, and pull it by the wheel towards us?' I suggested.

The idea got no enthusiasm from Gianna, and even less enthusiasm from me, but what else could we do? At least it would get me out of the freezing water. Into the cold air.

I raised myself a few inches.

I was met with four shots, one after another.

In my panic, I let go of the edge of the canal. My head plummeted below water level. I emerged with a particularly oily bit of weed draped on my hair. The baby chuckled. It was probably a coincidence. No time to hate the baby now.

'Okay. You stay here,' I said. 'I will see if I can get round the island to the boat. Then bring it back round to here and you can get on the boat.' I'd like to pretend

I sounded manly and heroic saying this; so I will. In truth, my voice came out in a squeak.

'There is a slight problem with that,' said Gianna.

'Just one?'

'The key to the boat is also in my bag. In the stroller.'

Sometimes in life, you do have to actually be brave. I lifted one leg and then the other out of the canal and I lay sideways on the ground waiting for the panic in my chest to subside. It didn't.

'In the movies, they kind of attract the fire by creating a little diversion,' I said.

'Like if I got topless?' she said. How could she joke at a time like this? She was even grinning. She caught the look on my face. 'I think it's nerves,' she said, by way of explanation. 'I'm getting a bit hysterical.'

I suddenly found myself lunging up and forward. I did it before my brain could stop me. I grabbed the nearest wheel of the buggy and pulled it hard towards the river. It responded by falling straight in the water. Well at least I wasn't shot in the process.

I figured that if I could rescue Gianna's bag quickly enough then it wouldn't get soaked through and her phone would still be usable. I splashed and flailed in a half-swim half-flounder manoeuvre that I have perfected over the years for just such situations. The aim, of course, was to retrieve the fast-sinking buggy; the effect, however, was to make Gianna so concerned about my welfare that she starting taking off a layer and placed the baby somewhere safe in preparation of jumping in and rescuing me.

Before she could come to my assistance, I unexpectedly stood up on a rock. I was now only waist deep in the water and was so pleased with myself I quite forgot about the sniper.

'Don't just stand there, you'll get shot!' hissed Gianna.

Mercifully, the gunman didn't choose that moment to take a pot shot at me.

I gathered Gianna's bag and the baby's buggy and got them safely to the bank. The floor of the canal was ridiculously uneven.

'Where do you think the other person is moored?' I wondered. 'Is there a chance his boat is easier to get to than ours?'

It turned out that the reason the sniper hadn't shot for a while was that they had probably been moving position. I knew this because a fresh shot hit the opposite bank, and for the first time it was under the bridge. He - or she - was getting far closer to us, and was edging round our position.

'I think that means he's behind and to the west of us,' I said. 'But from the angle he got his shot, he is really close.'

'Then we are going to have to dash for it while we can,' she said.

'Well if we really run, they can't kill all three of us, I suppose.' Although in fact I bet they could.

'We'll go to the east of the island, sticking with the trees, and work our way round to the boat,' she said.

But what if our boat is gone? If they had any sense, they would have disabled it in some way. 'It's as good a plan as any,' I said.

Gianna took her handbag and I took the baby's bag and my wallet and phone, and on the count of three we lifted ourselves up and ran.

ELEVEN

We kept in line with the canal but hugged the trees as much as possible.

There was one shot and then a second.

I slipped on something so slithery my imagination ran wild – a snake? A wet rotting human corpse? – but out of pride I wanted to keep up with Gianna who had somehow got well ahead of me despite the fact she had a baby to carry.

We were soon at the other side of the island and we could see the hotels of Lido across the lagoon. It was only then that I realised how much the fog had cleared; being shot at had reduced my inclination to observe the changes in the weather and admire my surroundings. Funny, that.

We dropped down to walking pace (Gianna) and gasping pace (me) and were just about to feel good about our progress when we heard a motorboat.

We crouched down behind a tree.

Gianna tried her phone. She looked at her blank screen for a long time. 'I don't think it's working,' she murmured.

The noise of the motor launch was getting closer. It then lowered its engine to a phut phut noise. It was clear that whoever it was, they were searching for us and they felt we were nearby.

'We are going to need to go inland a little,' whispered Gianna.

I scanned the woodland to see if there was an obvious but safe path – it needed to be an improbable combination of both impenetrable in terms of us being seen, and clear in terms of us running through it.

We froze. The boat had stopped, and two people were talking. 'They are in there,' said one. 'You moor the boat and then you sweep round that way. We'll trap them in the middle.'

The middle of what? They weren't exactly whispering which struck me as odd, but it might have been over-confidence; they felt we were defenceless, and they didn't need to take precautions. They were probably right.

'Do you think there are three men in total?' I asked. 'The sniper was in the clocktower, perhaps, and then perhaps the same person came round from the west, and these two came in a boat from the east. I don't think there was time for the sniper to get round and into the boat.'

'Three of them. Why the hell do they want us dead?' she asked.

We heard the cracking of twigs. Someone was walking towards us through the undergrowth. The island just wasn't large enough to stay hidden for long. They would soon find us.

'It's now or never,' I said. 'Let's run inwards and round towards the boat.'

We both took a deep breath and ran.

There might have been running behind us, and there might have been shouting, I wasn't sure; it was all I could do to concentrate on finding a safe course forward. Gianna showed a good turn of speed but with one hand clutching her baby to her chest, she was finding it hard to clear the bushes and branches using her only free arm.

There was a shot. This one was a shotgun cartridge. It pockmarked the trunk of a tree nearby. If I had been two metres to the right that would have been my chest.

My foot caught a metal peg and I stumbled. I fell forwards onto a tarpaulin that was stretched out over the ground; as I fell onto it, it collapsed under my weight. I tried to right myself but my foot slipped and the edge of the tarpaulin gave way. I was now in a pit of brown mud. Stuck on my side. Caught on a ribcage. A human ribcage. The individual bones of the ribcage were wrapped over my chest. I put my hand out to push myself up on something solid. The something solid was a human leg bone, slimy where it was coated with clay-like mud. Then there were skulls – four, five human skulls. Then leg bones, endless leg bones. And arm bones.

An arm came down towards me. It was Gianna. I managed to stand but the sea of bones was extraordinary slippery, and their macabre nature was totally disorientating. The walls of the pit were mercifully regular however – a neatly cut trench wall about two feet high – so despite my ineptitude I was soon out.

As I ran, I ran my sleeve over my face; my cheeks were covered in bone juice.

'I guess historians are doing some excavating here,' said Gianna.

We came to an unexpected clearing. It was near a large octagonal fortification that formed an island in its own right.

'The boat is to the right,' she said.

It meant us running along the bare quayside for fifty yards with no cover whatever. We were sitting ducks. The other option would be to go into the buildings and try and work our way through them internally. If we went inside we could easily be cornered; if we ran along the quay, we could easily be shot. Without conferring, we chose to run along the quay.

There was a gun shot, but I couldn't work out where it was.

There was Gianna calling something, but I couldn't hear her over my own laboured breathing.

Then somehow, in all the confusion, we were clambering into the boat.

I had visions that this would be the part where our luck finally ran out; we would get stuck, the boat would not want to start, and we would be easily picked off by the men with guns. Our bodies would be dragged off to join the plague victims in the shallow grave nearby; after all, this was the island where the Venetians disposed of their dead.

I crouched in the boat, waiting in my mind to be shot. In the stillness, I raised my head a fraction to get my bearings.

The nearest I got to an injury was whiplash where Gianna shot the boat forward without any warning.

We instinctively kept our heads down, but we were soon well clear of the island. I was frozen, I was soaking wet, but I was alive. I reflected on the nature of the mud and slime that was on my skin and face after I'd fallen into that mass grave. I could scrub, but I'd never feel clean.

'The trouble is,' shouted Gianna. 'Whoever wants us dead, they aren't going to stop at their first attempt.'

TWELVE

Gianna re-joined me that evening at my hotel bar. Like the previous night, she had no baby. Unlike the previous night, she was looking nervous.

'We need to talk to Adam again,' I said. 'He literally sent us to our deaths.'

'I've been putting that off,' she said.

'And we should go to the police,' I said.

'Why?'

'Someone's trying to kill us.'

'What use will they be?' she asked. 'They have been no help about Angelo and Emily.'

'We need to keep them in the loop, at least.'

'But it is illegal to go Poveglia. That might be the thing they pick up on. The idea that we were shot at; we have no proof that even happened,' she said.

'The fact is, we were shot at. You left your stroller there. There will be bullets lodged in the bridge.'

'I have a plan, and sure we can go to the police,' she said. 'But I want a bit more information first. I think we should drop in on Signor Turturro. On his home territory.'

'And do what?'

'Find out what he knows. If we go to the police, we will have their attention at first. The more tangible information we can lay out to them while we have their attention, the better. There is a conspiracy, where top people have organised a fraud to get those insurance pay outs paid. They are trying to stop us from uncovering it. If we get some information on them then the police will investigate and we will not be the problem anymore, the police will.'

'Maybe,' I said.

'By the way, I have shown admirable self-restraint not asking before, but what the hell are you wearing?' asked Gianna.

'Ah.' I had been to the shops, and also the barbers.

'What do you mean ah?' replied Gianna. 'You look like you've been arrested by the Fashion Police, thrown in the back of one of their vans, and beaten with the Trendy Stick. I mean that jacket; how do we describe that? Rainbow, paisley, plaid? Help me out here. Words are wholly inadequate to the task of describing the offence that my eyes behold.'

'Yeah okay.'

'And your neck ties,' continued Gianna. 'Plural. Ties. Is that, like, made of vermicelli? Florescent, green, vermicelli. It's made of pasta, right?'

'No?' I replied uncertainly.

'And your hair cut.'

'Yes.'

'What have you done?' she asked.

'I just thought I would freshen up my appearance,' I protested.

Gianna followed my gaze to the restaurant across the road.

'Oh no, don't tell me,' she said. 'You were hoping that if you dressed young and trendy they would let you have a reservation at that new fish restaurant you keep mooning over.'

'No,' I protested. Well, yes actually. She was 100% correct.

'Peter I thought you were sensible.' Whatever gave her that idea? 'And is that make up you're wearing?'

'No, it's not. It's the light.'

'Maybe moisturiser that's got tint in it?'

'No?' I answered.

'There's no fool like an old fool.'

'Thank you for that, Gianna.'

She was right; I looked ridiculous.

'Well now you mention it,' I said. 'How *do* I get into the restaurant across the alley there?'

'The Aschenbach? You can't,' she replied.

'I can't?'

'No. There is a four month waiting list and you have to know people, and you have to be a billionaire, or a movie star, or genuinely young and genuinely trendy. And you are not even one of those things.'

'Cheers.'

She shrugged. 'Just telling it like it is.'

I looked forlornly across the restaurant in question. As if to taunt me, I could see a waitress in her designer sailor suit deliver the most delicious looking fish dish I had ever seen. It was a tall thin cylinder shape of what looked like saffron-infused kedgeree; a tower of curried rice and herb with different kinds of shellfish and freshwater fish. Just thinking about it, made my stomach rumble audibly.

'Oh cheer up,' said Gianna. 'By the time they finally deign to let you have a table, the restaurant will already be out of fashion. Or bankrupt. Nothing dates faster than Trendy.'

She was probably right, but it was still all I desired in all the world.

'Come on greedy-guts,' said Gianna. 'You go up to your room and change into something more sensible. I know a perfectly good restaurant just a couple of streets away. You'll love it, and we won't have to mortgage the house to afford a meal there. Oh, and ruffle up your hair or something, you look like a 1930s transexual.'

Gianna got us to a good eatery in a genial enough fashion; she even managed a bit of small talk about food and eating out – she obviously knew about restaurants and cuisine. In fact, for all her anger and misandry I quite enjoyed her company, and I got the idea she enjoyed mine too.

But I was forced to conclude that she was a woman who didn't in fact even like feeling calm; because suddenly out of nowhere, she erupted again. It was like she'd temporarily forgotten herself and what role she was supposed to be playing in life; before we knew it she was worked up afresh on the subject of how we were being treated. Instead of sitting, she was pacing the floorspace between the restaurant tables.

'And how dare they lure us to that island and shoot at us!' She shouted this at the face of a diner who was foolish enough to look in her direction to see what the noise was.

'What do you think Adam will have to say for himself?' I asked. I made some lowering motions with my hands to see if she would take the hint.

'Don't you tell me to calm down!'

'I just...'

'How about you ring him for a change? See what you make of him?' Things were, as usual, my fault.

'My phone doesn't work. I take it yours does, even though it got wet?' I asked. 'So you say you haven't contacted him yet?'

'I didn't quite know how to play it,' she said.

Gianna picked up her phone and scrolled to find Adam's number.

Adam had lured us to Poveglia to be shot at. What was the best way of confronting him about this? Anger? Reasoning? I needed to think, but Gianna was so distracting buzzing left and right in front of me. I got the restaurant's oversized menu and held it up to block my view of her. And then I got distracted reading the menu. They'd got Ribollita. You usually find this in Tuscany. It is a beautifully thick stew made with lots of white beans, dark greens, vegetables, olive oil, all with day-old bread soaking into the juice. Gianna thrust her phone into my face.

'Pronto. Adzio,' said Adam.

'Hi, it's Pete. Emily's brother.'

'How are you?'

'Fun fact. I nearly died today.' It turns out I was feeling sarcastic. 'We went to the island of Poveglia as you suggested to meet Signor Turturro and we were shot at. I was within two inches of losing my life.' More like two metres, but he wasn't to know that.

'I never told you to go to Poveglia,' he said. 'It isn't even legal to go to Poveglia.' He sounded genuinely puzzled.

'You said we should meet Signor Torturro there and that he had information for us.'

'I said no such thing.'

I put out a hand to stop Gianna on one of her fly pasts.

'Did Adam - Adzio – tell us to go to that island today?'

'Definitely,' she replied.

'He's saying not.'

She took my phone off me. 'Now listen to me you stinking little bag of shit. I taped that phone call.' A pause her end. 'Yes.' Another pause. 'Okay well what story are you giving me now?' She rattled off a pile of invectives in Italian that would make a stripper blush and then handed the phone back to me.

'He will make more sense now,' she said.

'Okay,' said Adam. His tone was more careful now – more respectful. 'I will see what I can do.'

'See what you can do about what?'

'I will see where Signor Turturro is. I cannot promise that he will be able to help you though. This is largely Gianna's logic.'

I didn't know what to do. This was a man who had probably colluded in trying to get us killed, but also we had no leads whatever and he was offering us a fragile route to possibly finding out some information.

'But to clarify,' I said. 'Did you send us to Poveglia or not?'

'No,' he replied.

No?

I made my voice sound more angry. 'Well either way, phone us back with something within the hour, or we will go to the police,' I snapped. I tried to then turn the phone off with a flourish, but somehow the 'End Call' button on the screen was not responding. I stabbed at it several times with my finger, then swiped it up. I could hear Adam talking on the other end. In desperation, I turned the phone off as a whole. It is hard to be a diva with these modern technologies.

The idea of getting him to ring in an hour was my only triumph and – I am almost ashamed to admit – driven by the desire to get through an entire meal undisturbed for once.

Now the phone call was dealt with, was Gianna going to settle down? The waiting staff had been tolerant thus far, but one of the waiters was consulting with a manager and kept looking in our direction.

'Five years of marriage,' I heard her say. 'I know he was a grey little man, but he was *my* grey little man.' Her ranting had moved away from Adam and us nearly dying that afternoon, and back to the errant Angelo. 'What's she like your sister?' she asked suddenly. 'I mean really like?'

'Sit down and I will tell you,' I tried.

'Would you leave a pregnant woman?' she asked.

'You're pregnant?' I asked.

That did the trick. She sat down at the restaurant table in front of me, defeated.

'Yes, I'm pregnant,' she said.

'When are you due?' I asked.

'August.'

Her switch had flicked again from agitated to bereft. She swigged from her wine and must have seen a shadow cross my face.

'Italian women drink while they're pregnant,' she said firmly.

'Fine,' I replied. I wasn't going to pick a fight. Not with Gianna. I looked it up later though, and according to one study 50% to 60% of Italian women drink while pregnant; the highest percentage amongst comparable nations. But that doesn't mean they drank as heavily as Gianna, surely? Just the odd sip of wine here and there.

'And did you really record Adam's phone call to you?' I asked.

'Of course not,' she said.

That was a shame. It could have been useful.

THIRTEEN

I got up early the next morning to go online, using remote access to my office in Corsica. I was trying to get as many details as possible about the alleged fraud that had taken place here in Venice. I soon ended up with a list of people and companies who had gained; I felt I had some leads to go on. Soothed by the idea I already had some achievements under my belt, I went down to breakfast.

Ah, the worldwide phenomenon that is the Hotel Buffet Breakfast Bar. Where else, or when else, would you pile a plate high with soggy half-cooked bacon and a cinnamon whirl, and some pancakes and syrup, a yoghurt and some cubed mango, slices of three different kinds of cheese, slices of salami, melon, pickled herring, a pink wafer biscuit, miso soup, sushi, macaroons, black forest gateau, a croissant, an apple and mini baguette to eat later – all of which I have encountered on my travels at hotel breakfast buffets, and none of which so much as raise an eyebrow if you pile them on the same plate as a medley – or 'The Breakfast Taster Menu' as I prefer to call it. The reason you need an apple and mini baguette to eat later, incidentally, is that curiously no matter how much you eat at the buffet breakfast you will still end up feeling hungry mid-morning.

Sometimes, sitting alongside the buffet, there is a bottle of Champagne in an ice bucket. I have never understood this. Are we allowed to open it and have a glass? Does a member of staff shoot out of the shadows the moment you touch it and say 'Excuse me sir, you have crossed a line; that is purely for decoration.' Or have we been missing a trick all along, and we could have been having free champers with breakfast every day of our holidays at no extra charge?

And then there is the machine that warms slices of bread by placing them on a conveyor belt. I won't dignify the apparatus with the term 'toaster' – it knows what it's done. If you put a slice of bread in it once for its magic journey, about five interminable minutes later it plops out the other end, not toasted in any way, but stale; the bread has been artificially staled by warming it on both sides leaving no discernible colour on its surface. If you put the same slice back through the system a second time, however, it comes out burnt. There is no known in-between stage. Sometimes it catches on fire. I have wrestled with these contraptions for nearly twenty years of my adult life, and have now given up the unequal struggle and avoid the machines altogether.

A happier fascination that I have is with the big block of scrambled egg available in the heated silver server with the hinged lid. On a good day, the scrambled egg is so solid it can be cut with a knife into slices or outsized cubes. It's so wrong, it's right. Add some sliced hotdog sausages and some ketchup and I am one happy tourist. Nothing says 'Holiday' like inappropriate hotdog sausage for breakfast. Bliss.

Fortified with my buffet breakfast feast, I then made a few phone calls. I was interested in what the recipients of the pay outs then did with the money. A few had evidently given the money back or at least placed it in escrow while the lawyers haggled; I could place those families and companies further down the list of suspects, at least in the short term. The number who had spirited away the money with a knowing haste included the Valdi and Turturro families – two names that kept cropping up - and these were the two policies with the single biggest pay outs. It made sense to investigate them as much as possible, therefore.

Another matter of interest was what, if anything, was known by the company about Emily's whereabouts. On this topic, my local line manager Daniel, back in Bastia, had made some inquiries and was eager to share them. He, like me, had had no joy from our colleagues here in Venice, but he knew someone who knew someone who knew about the matter, and although no one seemed to know where Emily was or why people were suddenly claiming she didn't exist, he had found out a lot about the events leading up to her disappearance. He recounted at length the story of how she claimed she was kidnapped and placed in a pit, and when she took the police back there, the pit had been filled in. It felt like a John Buchan novel and was more than intriguing.

It was daytime and so Gianna had the baby with her again. This seemed to be the pattern; she could readily find childcare in the evenings, but the days were just her and the baby with nothing to keep them warm but the anger she felt in her heart towards all men. Imagine a man who had this same level of hatred of women and who then vented all day on the subject; how long would it be tolerated?

'What's worse,' she said. 'I've had to go all the way to Marghera to buy a new stroller. Because this city is now a theme park for tourists, there are no shops at all for the people who actually live here. I lost my entire morning.'

In point of fact, as she said this we were sitting opposite a shop called a Polleria which specifically sold various cuts, sizes, breeds and ages of chicken and little else; it was hard to see how it was aimed in any way at tourists; but I did understand what she was saying.

I turned my attention to the new stroller Gianna had bought on the mainland. It was even bigger than the one she left behind in Poveglia; it had huge outsized wheels and various storage areas; it was the SUV of strollers and so high tech that if you took your hands off the controls it could probably reverse itself into a parking space. It showed no sign whatever that it could be folded up, was clearly punishingly expensive, and was just – well – impractical on every level. How did baby buggies get like this, and why?

I shrugged and moved on with my thoughts. Adam had provided directions for how we could find Signor Turturro and a vague promise that 'He is usually at home in the morning.' We decided to go and visit him without an appointment; at the very least it would deprive him of the opportunity to book a couple of highly trained assassins in advance of any meeting.

The Turturro family home was literally palatial, and overlooked the Grand Canal. Such palaces were originally designed to be entered via stone steps from the waterside, but for obvious reasons we approached it from the street behind. The door was a dark ornate wooden affair with panels of carved lions and dragon-like serpents, plus there was a whole coat of arms thing going on. It was so grand I felt intimidated even knocking on it.

'I'm guessing these people are rich,' I said. No one had responded to my first knock and I was too chicken to then knock louder. Instead I waited. Something would no doubt happen in time; perhaps the time it would take me to grow a spine.

Gianna kicked the door with a free foot.

'These people owe me an effing explanation,' she said. For all her habitual anger, she was not one to swear. 'I had to buy a new stroller because of them.'

They nearly killed us, and the stroller was the problem?

A man opened the door wearing a well-fitting Prada suit. It followed the contour of his muscles. I wish I fitted a suit as well as that. And had muscles.

'Can I help you?' he asked.

'We are here to see Signor Turturro,' said Gianna.

'Do you have an appointment?'

'He's expecting us.' Good one. If he's not expecting us, he should be, after what he's done.

'One moment,' he said. He took our names and with a waft of the hand he gestured that we should enter. We were taken across a small courtyard and up some steps beyond and through a further door.

There is something incongruous about manoeuvring the wheels of a baby buggy up the steps and over the threshold of a 17th century palace; even if the buggy in question was a state of the art Italian affair with a Gucci baby changing bag draped over its handles. Just how much money did Gianna have? Surely her husband's position at the firm was no better than Emily's? I know there had been a lot of talk about his family being wealthy but... I was distracted by the interior of the palace.

We were in a hallway with a sweeping staircase ahead of us. It was decorated in the style of 'stinking rich'.

We were shown to some cream coloured velvet chairs while the man in Prada went off to make inquiries.

'Look at the chandelier,' I hissed.

Although we were grown adults, I felt guilty leaving the chair I had been told to sit in. But I couldn't resist checking out the chandelier. It was suspended from the roof at the top of the stairwell which was three floors up. Each floor of the palace had a high ceiling; so the chandelier rose fifty feet or more illuminating each floor as it fell.

'The sheer weight of it,' I marvelled.

'It's magnificent isn't it?' called a woman's voice from somewhere beyond. I looked round to see Melania Trump walking towards us. It was quite a shock. Well, okay, it wasn't actually Melania Trump; it was a tall woman who was beautifully dressed whose face, figure and clothes all screamed 'I used to be a supermodel and then I found a billionaire to marry'.

'Wow!' I said.

'Did you just say wow?' spat Gianna.

'Sorry, I was just looking. Admiring the chandelier.' I pointed up the stairwell, but I was fooling no one.

'You said wow because you saw a beautiful woman?' whispered Gianna. 'Well, that's just pathetic.'

'Sorry,' I said again.

'Why on earth would you apologise?' asked the Melania lookalike. 'We live in a city of wonders where tourists spend more time marvelling at their hotel breakfast than a Titian in a nearby church. They think a Bellini is a cocktail, not a painting by one of our most celebrated artists.' Well steady on lady; if you say Bellini to me, my first thought is indeed of a refreshing mix of Champagne and peach puree. I'm only human. 'The point is,' she continued. 'It is alright to go wow.'

'You are very kind making me feel good about snooping round your home,' I said. And overlooking the fact that I'd actually gasped when I clapped eyes on your amazing figure. 'I am assuming this is your home?'

'My name is Sophia Turturro, by the way,' she said. 'I am the wife of Roberto Turturro. How can I help you?'

'We were hoping to talk to your husband,' said Gianna. 'We thought we had a meeting planned with him yesterday, but he did not attend. And then we were attacked.'

'He had no such meeting in his diary yesterday. There must be some mistake. You are?' asked Sophia Turturro.

'I am Gianna Totti. Wife of Angelo Vincenzi. My husband is missing along with the sister of my friend here, Peter De'Ath. Her name is Emily Fisher.'

Sophia Turturro looked perplexed and then smiled. 'But I am being rude. Please let me take you somewhere where you can tell me all about it,' she said. 'Somewhere with a view and some fresh air.'

We were walked down a lavish corridor full of an incongruous mix of old masters, art deco furniture and garish contemporary art. We were soon in a sitting room overlooking the Grand Canal. Upon entering the room, a male servant flung open the windows without being asked.

'Venice is all about the light,' said Sophia. 'The dazzle on the canals, the darting refractions on the underside of a bridge; the sunsets like a blood orange behind the palazzi. And it's about the sounds; the church bells, the slap of water against the quayside, the echoing chatter of schoolchildren down a calle. This palace has stood here for three hundred and fifty years, and the light is still the same and the sounds are still the same. It is the pleasure of centuries.'

Well that was very fluent.

Signora Turturro flicked her wrist to signify we should admire the room. A huge ornate mirror was on the far wall reflecting the view of a white-stoned chiesa on the other side of the water. I turned my attention to the window; the view was simply magnificent, and so bright and so vibrant; the rich even get better light than the rest of us. Even the air was fresher here. It was hard not to be in awe. Gianna managed it somehow.

'Where is my husband?' she barked.

'Why would I know?' replied Sophia. She considered Gianna's anger with polite interest. She had an air that she knew things, but perhaps that was just her manner.

'There has been a fraud committed whereby my husband has been implicated in releasing funds from insurance companies that he shouldn't.'

'And what has that got to do with us?' she asked.

'Your family is one of the recipients of the money,' I said.

Sophia shrugged. Even her shrug was elegant; like silk sliding over porcelain. 'That is probably the case,' she said. 'We claimed on our insurance policy for damage done by the acqua alta, but there is nothing strange in that.'

'Can we speak with your husband?' asked Gianna.

'There is no need. Everything he knows, I know.'

'My sister was abducted and held prisoner on a property owned by colleagues of yours,' I tried.

'What colleagues?'

'The Valdis,' I said.

'We occasionally do business with the Valdis, but they are not colleagues,' she replied. 'But whoever did that should certainly be brought to justice.'

'When she returned with the police, the pit where she was held had been filled in,' I said. 'Your colleague Signor Valdi was present as the police arrived. It seemed quite the coincidence given that he doesn't live there. Why would he be in Murano?' I was gabbling. I was miles from where I wanted to be conversation-wise; why would she know about the actions of Signor Valdi? What was odd was that she wasn't pulling me up on this.

'I do know something about this,' said Sophia Turturro. She did? She must have seen some surprise in my face because she added, 'I am trying to be helpful Mr De'Ath.'

'Can we speak to your husband please?' asked Gianna.

'Gianna!' I remonstrated. 'She's being helpful.' And Gianna, of all people, was being sexist; why shouldn't we deal with this woman in front of us?

The baby was restless, so Gianna started pushing the over-sized buggy forwards and backwards trying to placate it. She somehow did this and also hissed in my ear. 'Just because she is attractive, it doesn't mean she is helping us. Stop thinking with your cock. Bloody men.' It seemed to me that because she was attractive – or rather a woman who led with her looks - Gianna didn't want to deal with her at all.

I smiled at Sophia, as if Gianna wasn't in the room. 'What is it that you know?' I asked.

'I happen to know your sister was mistaken,' she said.

'How so?'

'Either she took the police to the wrong place, or her story was wrong.'

'And you know this how?'

'I am well-connected.' That phrase again. Well-connected.

'She's lying,' said Gianna.

'Gianna, that is just rude,' I said.

'We have been shot at,' snarled Gianna. 'Your sister was kidnapped and is now being accused of lying about it. This woman is wrapping you round her finger because she can afford Botox and fillers on a daily basis, and you are accusing me of being rude? Other people are out there shooting at us and kidnapping people, and you are having a go at *me*?'

Sophia Turturro greeted this with the impassive but positive face we came to expect from Melania Trump when her husband was speaking at a rally. She was class. I wondered how old she was; it was literally impossible to tell. I was distracted by her hair; it was so glossy it shone with its own light; when she turned her head it appeared to swing in slow motion, just like in the movies. How do you get hair like that?

'Can I make a suggestion?' she said. 'A possible explanation?'

'Sure,' I replied.

There was the sound of spitting behind me. It could have been the baby rather than Gianna, but I doubted it.

'There has been a lot of work in Murano filling in the old water cisterns, to make them safe. It is possible that is what your sister saw.'

'Who said it was Murano?' asked Gianna. 'We never mentioned Murano.' Er, yes we did.

'I have my ear to the ground,' replied the fragrant Sophia. 'I know the business of these islands. This case is not news to me.'

Gianna snorted loudly, and seemingly to back her up, the baby made a loud wet noise in his nappy.

'What specifically can I do for you?' asked Sophia. 'Your husband is Angelo Vincenzi? The Vincenzi family; I know them.' Gianna was having none of it; she turned to look sullenly out the window. Sophia took this with a good heart and addressed me instead. She took on the air of explaining things to an outsider. 'Venice is very egalitarian,' she said. 'We do not have cars; we all have to walk the streets or use the boats. Rich or poor, kings or tradesmen we pass each other on the street every day, we use the same local shops. We know each other by sight; we know each other's family history. Each year there are fewer of us living here, so that just concentrates us even more.'

I didn't know what to say to that; it was after all just a platitude. Sophia took my temporary silence as her cue that she had talked enough. She blessed us with a benevolent smile.

'Sit here a while and I will see what I can do,' she said. 'You want to see your sister? You want to see your husband? I want that too. Let me help. The families of Venice should stick together. I will make some phone calls.'

Sophia wafted from the room. I sat back into a luxurious armchair; its bizarrely soft cushions lapped and stroked my senses. Gianna remained fuming at the window with one arm rocking the buggy behind her. Then she had an idea. She found a small silver tray and held it out to me.

'What's that for?' I asked.

'For you to put your balls on a platter for her.'

'Oh you are so funny.'

'She blatantly knows whole piles of information and is feeding us a few scraps just to look helpful,' said Gianna. 'The sheer fact she knows who we are. The way she knew about the cistern in Murano.'

'What do you want me to do? Torture the intel out of her?'

'If you did, she wouldn't even pull a face as you did it; she's had so much Botox and filler.'

'How old do you reckon she is?' I asked. 'Forty? Fifty? Sixty?'

'Oh, I do know this one,' replied Gianna. 'She's sixty. And her breasts are thirty.'

'Well, we'll see if she turns anything up before we judge her,' I said.

'Why would a woman this important be helpful unless she is guilty in some way?'

'Because of the egalitarian society?' I ventured. Big mistake.

'Egalitarian be damned. Do I live in a palace like this? Our apartment is so dingy we don't even get direct sunlight into our windows, and the canal smells of effluent where most houses in our area still haven't got septic tanks and flush their toilets straight into the water. Well I say "our" apartment, but it's just me, isn't it? Since he ran off.'

'Look, I am sure there is some explanation for your husband's apparent disappearance along with my sister.'

'Yes there's an explanation. He's a philandering shit who can't keep his penis in his pants.'

'Yeah. Sorry,' I said. I had no idea what I was apologising for.

'It's not as though he's perfect. He takes off his clothes at night and flings them near the laundry sack. Not in the laundry sack. Near the laundry sack. After dinner he picks up his dirty plate and places it near the dishwasher. Not in the dishwasher.'

This struck me as small fry compared to the accusation that he had organised a major insurance fraud worth a hundred million and arranged to have my sister abducted and implicated in the crime then somehow seduced her in the process, or was holding her against her will. What was Gianna going to mention next? That he placed toilet rolls in the holder with the free end facing the wall, while she preferred the free end facing outwards?

'He went to the dry cleaners last week.' She was getting more shrill now. 'And he picked up his dry cleaning. Not *our* dry cleaning. *His* dry cleaning.'

Okay, well fair enough; that did sound pretty irritating.

'I had had a whole day doing childcare and he had specifically said that...'

Mercifully, Gianna was interrupted by Sophia Turturro re-entering the room.

'I have made some phone calls,' she said. 'But although it seems everyone has heard of this story, no one can agree on where your, er, relatives, are. One person said they have gone to Rome, one said they are on the mainland in Mestre. Another says they are hiding here on the island. But one source said they would be willing to speak to you. It is a police source who would be willing to talk to you anonymously. I have pulled some strings for you. I have arranged a meet up. You don't look pleased.'

We both looked at Gianna. Her brain was still in full rant, it seemed, about Angelo not getting his dirty socks as far as the laundry sack. Even Sophia was alarmed by the look on her face.

'I would still like to talk to your husband,' said Gianna at last. Why? She seemed pretty set on speaking to him rather than his wife; I wondered what she knew.

The Prada man from earlier came into the room and stood in the corner. He made the faintest of nods to Sophia. Seemingly as a reply, she held out a piece of paper to me with some writing on it; she must have been holding it all along. Why had she waited to offer it?

'This is the address you need to go to,' she said. 'You need to be there in forty minutes.'

I took the piece of paper from her hand and she held her lips tight together in a particularly firm smile that was meant to signify that the meeting was at an end. We had to go.

Gianna was torn between being dismissive, and wanting to see what was written on the card. She tilted her torso towards it and read it out the corner of her eyes.

'I know where that is,' she mumbled.

On the pavement, Gianna said, 'What a liar that woman was. These people are worth billions, they have business interests from fashion to car factories to wine; filling a little hole in the ground in Murano would not make their daily conversation unless it was important to them.'

Gianna's anger had been freshly re-charged by her encounter with Sophia Turturro. So much so, that she was way ahead of me already, muscling her unwieldy buggy up and down flights of stone steps and navigating bridges with a turn of speed that left me wondering if I would lose her altogether. I ran to catch up.

'And who is this secret source in the police?' she asked.

'Is there any chance we can sit down? I have been on my feet all day.'

'No!' she barked. 'We'll find this address.'

'Okay,' I said meekly.

'It's not as though you are in my good books.'

'What have I done?'

'Fawning all over little Miss Boob Job back at the palace. Ridiculous.'

Gianna stuck her own chest out and talked in a baby voice. 'Oh Peter do you take me seriously now?'

'She didn't speak like that.'

'Oh Peter, perhaps if I pull the end of my hair sideways through my teeth, you'll find me sexy...'

'Look Gianna, if you're going to be angry about everything you come across, all the time, it's no wonder...' It just slipped out.

'No wonder what?' She stopped and pushed her face into mine.

No wonder your man left you.

'No wonder you get so upset,' I tried. It was the best I could manage.

'You're pathetic,' she spat. And this is how she treats people who actually help her. She stormed forward again, her Gucci changing bag swaying behind her.

'And I want to know what you have found out,' shouted Gianna into the wind. 'You have obviously done some fact finding this morning and not filled me in.'

'*Yet*,' I gasped. 'I haven't filled you in *yet*.'

'Well?' she asked, not slowing in the slightest.

'Of the twenty-four recipients from the insurance pay outs, eight spirited away the money almost instantly. They have rather self-selected themselves as chief suspects. The eight include the Valdis and the Turturros, but they also include a claim from a member of Angelo's family, and also someone from Adam's family to be fair.' I figured she was already angry so I might as well tell her what I'd discovered about the Angelo connection now.

In the event, this new information had the effect of calming her down a little; she needed to process it.

'How close a relative to Angelo?' she asked.

'His uncle's family,' I replied.

She did some calculating. 'It's hardly a smoking gun,' she said.

'No, I agree. It would be nice to get him in the clear, though.'

The address we had been given was right at the top of the island, but not that far from where we were. We passed through the old Jewish quarter on the way. For all Gianna's indignation, she hadn't lost the desire to tell me about her city. 'The Venice Ghetto was the one that gave English the word ghetto in the first place, the Jews were compelled by law to live here.' We were struggling up the stone steps of a footbridge at the time; I was lifting one end of the buggy while she lifted the other. 'They were locked in every night and had to pay for their own security to ensure that no Jews left the area during curfew.'

'Like Trump trying to get the Mexicans to pay for their own wall,' I offered.

'Not the same at all,' she said. So that's that, then. 'Under Christianity at the time,' she continued. 'The Venetians were forbidden to lend money while charging interest, but the Jews weren't restricted by their religion, so they became bankers lending money to the Christians to finance their various trading ventures even though they wouldn't allow the Jews to work in their trade guilds. It was all pretty messed up.'

As if on cue, two smartly dressed men with big black hats and wispy beards walked past us deep in conversation. Another thing we saw were soldiers in green combat camouflage with pistols on their belts. To be truly camouflaged in Venice you would need to wear a fabric that looked like a crumbling red brick wall, or perhaps a Titian painting. Just saying. Beyond that, stood two guards dressed in blue, also with pistols. These were Guardia di Finanza. The Guardia di Finanza are specialist arms police who deal with the illegal drugs trade. I had no idea what they were all doing here.

'Welcome to the ghetto,' said Gianna.

I got the impression that our route was forming a bit of a dog leg, but I had to rely on Gianna's sense of direction. Nonetheless I felt the need to query our progress.

'You're right,' she conceded.

'And?' I asked.

'I think we are being followed,' said Gianna. 'So I have taken us on a round trip.'

'Followed?' I couldn't help looking round.

'Don't look round,' I said. I looked round again. I am incapable of not looking round when told not to. Gianna kicked me in the shin to help concentrate my mind.

Happily, being hit in the shin gave me an excuse to sit on the pavement and rub it. In so doing, I could legitimately sit and gaze in the direction of our alleged shadow.

'Which one is he?'

'She. It's a woman. Dark hair. Attractive. Summer dress. In winter. Big brown leather bag.'

FOURTEEN

The woman in question was about ten yards behind us, pretending to be preoccupied with her phone.

'Just wait until we move,' said Gianna.

We walked forward across the main courtyard of the ghetto and across a bridge on the north side. The woman was definitely following us, but was also talking on her phone to someone and studying us as she spoke.

'If the woman is in collusion with the Turturros then she would know where we were going, so why bother to follow us?' I said. 'I don't think she's related to them.'

We pressed forward along a towpath and then down a further alley and over another bridge beyond. Gianna then took us down alleys that were more and more obscure; sometimes darting left, sometimes darting right. No matter what we did and what decision we made, we could still hear the echoing footsteps of a woman behind us wearing heels.

'It could still be the Turturros. Sophia could have rustled up someone when she made her phone calls. She then kept us waiting and occupied for a bit while they arrived,' whispered Gianna. She stopped with the buggy and got her phone out. 'Actually, I've got an idea,' she said.

The footsteps behind us stopped, but I couldn't see the woman. How did she know to stop? Surely they couldn't track us in some way? What if they had put some sort of tracker in the baby buggy while we were at their palace? It seemed too far-fetched. More likely she could hear our footsteps down the alleyway and just had to follow the noise.

'What if we took our shoes off?' I asked.

'What?' asked Gianna; she was looking at maps on her phone.

'Never mind.'

'There are lots of abandoned houses in Venice waiting to be restored. A thousand or so,' she said.

'Okay?'

She was talking absently while checking something. 'They would cost a lot to restore so only really a hotel chain has the kind of money needed, but there is currently a ban on more hotels in Venice itself and we need affordable housing, so they are left in limbo. They are mostly safely boarded up but... found one!'

'What?'

'There is one coming up which we could nip through and out the other side. I knew it was around here, but I just wasn't 100% sure where it was. Come on, let's give her a run for her money.'

And with that she dashed forward.

We ran. Gianna showed enormous agility, sometimes half lifting the buggy to get it over a stone step, sometimes just using its impressive bulk to get momentum. It was like it was some sort of Olympic event - a bizarre event granted - but no more bizarre than that sport where the cyclists go round in circles following a little motorbike, or the one where they ski down a mountain then shoot something with a rifle, then ski on again. I found my own legs were unusually spritely, by my standards, and we had covered a lot of distance in no time, switching between alleys as we went. Finally, Gianna dropped to normal walking pace. She was about four yards ahead of me, then in the time it took me to check my footing on a flagstone, she was gone.

Like a magic trick.

It felt like a trap. I was in a deserted alley. I didn't know where I was, and I was alone.

I proceeded very slowly, one careful footstep at a time.

A hand reached out and pulled me sideways.

'Get in here!' hissed Gianna.

She dragged me into a broken-down doorway. We picked up the buggy between us and hid behind an internal wall beyond. There were bricks and litter on the floor and empty bottles where local youth obviously hung out. Particularly annoying were the little shiny empty bottles of laughing gas. It's not that nitrous oxide is the most terrible drug – dentists have been using it on children for centuries – it is the litter that I find particularly irritating; can't the youth take their rubbish home with them in a bag? I prised myself away from my heartfelt - if middle-aged - thoughts and listened carefully.

We could hear the footsteps of the woman in heels. The echoes got louder as she walked down the alley and then seemed to diminish again. Gianna's plan had appeared to work.

We stood in silence and tried to keep our breathing shallow.

Silence.

A jolt as a bird flapped off somewhere in the joists above.

Then the footsteps returned. Click clack. Faint at first and then more resolute.

'Surely we'd shaken her off?' I whispered.

Gianna put her finger to her lips for me to be quiet. She was angry with me. Of course she was.

The footsteps stopped.

Total silence.

Surely the woman following us wasn't armed? And there were two of us and only one of her; that would count for something especially as one of us was Gianna.

There was a crackling, like when someone is walking slowly and steps on a dried twig. The woman was trying to be silent and we were trying to be silent. So who was afraid of whom? Oh, who am I kidding? I was afraid. Of everything.

Another crunch under foot. Then silence. Then the clank of the tiny silver bottles being disturbed on the ground.

Then the baby stirred. It was just possible that only we heard it, because we were attuned.

We waited. There was possibly the sound of a breath.

Then the baby cried. It wasn't much, but it was enough. There was no mistaking it.

Gianna dashed forward. There was a room beyond, and then more light beyond that, so it seemed the direction to go in. A floorboard creaked loudly and there was a chinking of bottles behind us.

It was unlikely we could outrun the woman; especially given we had a baby to push.

I decided I would try something brave.

As Gianna went on ahead, I waited behind a wall. The moment the woman appeared in my line of vision, I put a leg out to trip her up. Irritatingly, she didn't fall; she lurched to her right. I bundled forward, stomach first. The woman was not quite on her feet; she was reaching out with a hand to steady herself. I pressed my advantage – i.e. my stomach – home. I kind of bounced her against a wall.

'Ow!' she protested.

I have heard that in self-defence you have to use the other person's weight against them. I have no idea what that means. I am about 280 pounds. She was maybe a 100 pounds. Why use her weight against her, when I've got all of mine to use? I literally sat on her. I planted my ample arse on her torso then bounced up and down for good measure. Her legs and arms started kicking and flailing. I did an extra bounce for the hell of it and then reached up to some sort of shelving above us, to haul myself up.

Before I knew it, I was out the back of the building. I could no longer see Gianna, so I hurried in a random manner down the calle and over a footbridge.

I had the address of where we were supposed to go, and Gianna claimed she knew where it was, so I wasn't too worried; we could meet up there.

In fact, I was feeling quite pleased with myself and how well I'd effected my escape when I realised there was a man in front of me blocking my path. And a man behind me blocking my path.

And they both had a knife.

FIFTEEN

Why knives? They are such an unpleasant, spiteful, weapon of choice. Most people care what other people think of them. Anyone who brandishes a knife is deliberately asking to be thought of as a nasty piece of work. These were among my many unhelpful thoughts I had when facing my two assailants. I often find when under extreme stress my thoughts are the opposite of helpful; instead of asking how best to defend myself, instead of feeling for keys in my pocket as a potential weapon, or thinking of something amazing to say that would stop them in their tracks, my brain just prevaricates and pontificates. It is amazing I have lived as many years as I have.

Both men looked very Italian; particularly the one in front of me. Top button of shirt undone? Check. Blue tight-fitting jacket and trousers? Check. Dark designer sunglasses? Check. Close-cropped black curly hair. Blade now swishing through the air, left then right, as he stepped determinedly towards me. Check.

I had no idea in my head what I could possibly do.

Beg?

'Guys! What exactly is it that you want from me? Why kill me when I would be much more useful to you alive.' I had no idea what I was talking about. What possessed me to go down such a narrow, deserted alley in the first place? I should have gone to the main tourist areas so that the crowds would at least witness anything that happened; that might have curtailed their actions a little, or I could even have shielded behind a passing tourist. For heaven's sake Pete, the whole problem with Venice is that it is overcrowded with tourists, why would I choose seemingly the one place in the entire city where there is not a soul to be found?

I took myself backwards.

After two backwards steps I felt a knife in my kidneys.

So this is how I was going to die. Alone in an alley, unlamented and unloved. And unfed. I hadn't even had lunch.

'Is it money you want? I can give you my wallet.' But I knew it wasn't money they wanted.

'You're Peter De'Ath?' asked the one in front of me.

'No?' I tried. A better answer would have been 'Who?' or 'What do you mean?' Almost any answer but 'No' asked as a question. If I was going to be this stupid, I might as well take the knife off the nice young man and plunge it in my own chest; it would save time and heartache, and spare getting any blood on the man's freshly-laundered designer shirt. Coming to think of it, why were they wearing such posh clothes? You'd think hoodlums would wear something more practical for murder-related activities, then change afterwards into something more formal for their evening of flanking the boss and looking menacing.

The man's head flicked up and back – whiplash style. Then his whole body flicked back.

Gianna had driven her baby buggy into the back of his legs.

On an instinct I stuck my arse back firmly to see if it would knock over the man who was behind me. He half fell over. I pushed my arse backwards again. Somehow the ruse had worked. Or twerked.

'That way!' shouted Gianna.

We ploughed backwards through the alley. I literally stood on the hand of one of the men and in the same breath Gianna somehow got the buggy and baby up and over him. We dashed like our lives depended on it – which of course they did – and were soon in the next street.

'Let's find somewhere full of crowds,' I called. But this caused us to dither whether to go left or right, when in fact almost any choice in Venice would get us back to the tourists eventually.

We turned left.

Our pause had allowed our attackers a crucial few seconds to get their bearings and catch up. I could glimpse them behind us, running forward.

We ran down a short alley and were confronted with a crossroads; we could go forwards, left or right. We chose right, the footsteps of the two men echoing in our ears.

We were a few yards into the new alley when we realised the woman who had been following us before – the woman in the summer dress - was standing square in front of us.

She reached into her leather bag and brought out a handgun. She held it firmly in both hands and pointed it directly at us.

'Don't move,' she said.

I instinctively flinched.

'Don't move or I will shoot.'

SIXTEEN

'Now, do you two mind telling me what you're doing?' asked the woman.

What?

There was no longer the sound of running behind us. Were the two men now standing still, blocking our retreat? I turned my head slowly – I didn't want the woman with the gun to misconstrue it as a 'movement' but I couldn't see them.

The woman with the gun started towards us. I backed backwards one step, and then another, out of instinct; sometimes our instincts aren't helpful. We were still near the crossroads. We were only a couple of steps away from being able to dart sideways and back into another alley; the men behind us might not have every option covered. We were in with the slightest of chances.

'Are you stupid or something?' asked the woman. 'Don't move.'

'Yeah, don't move Pete,' said Gianna. I could hear her mind whirring; running through our possible options.

'Lay down your weapons,' said the woman.

'Why would we have weapons?' I asked.

'We have had a report of threatening behaviour,' she said.

'Sorry, who are you?' I asked.

'Detective Antonioni,' she said. 'Police.'

Detective Giulia Antonioni took us for a walk south and off to the police station in the San Lorenzo area.

'Didn't Commissario Brunetti work at this police station?' I asked.

'The detective in the Donna Leon books?'' she replied. 'We get asked that a lot by tourists. Are you a tourist?' It was an accusation so sharp no one in their right mind would say yes; not even if, at the time, they were taking photographs with an oversized camera while holding postcards and a guide book, and following a woman with a pink umbrella. 'You do know that Commissario Brunetti is fictional?' she added.

'Yeah, but this police station clearly isn't,' I replied.

'Let's not annoy the nice lady detective who saved our arses from the men with knives,' said Gianna.

We were buzzed into the building and taken to an office.

'Who has claimed we have been engaging in threatening behaviour?' asked Gianna. 'Also, where can I change the baby and feed him?'

'We had a phone call from the Turturro residence,' said the detective.

'But you were following us almost straightaway,' I said. I had got to the stage where I trusted no one.

'I happened to be in the area,' she said.

I found that exceedingly unlikely; that she had nothing better to do than wander the streets of Venice on the off chance that one of the old rich families, who employed actual security staff of their own, felt intimidated by a lamentably unfit insurance investigator and a pregnant woman pushing an unwieldy stroller.

'What threat were we?' I asked.

'You barged into their house making accusations that they were somehow involved in a fraud.'

'You can't barge into their house, as you say. It is literally a fortified palace. And it has guards. And Sophia Turturro herself walked us through the palace to sit in a drawing room with her,' said Gianna, who was combining the tasks of getting the baby unstrapped with working up a steam of indignation.

'Sophia Turturro was even helpful,' I said. 'She phoned the police and made an appointment to meet up with a detective at this address.' I fished out the piece of paper with the address on it. 'She wrote this out herself.'

The detective looked at it.

'That is not a woman's handwriting,' she said.

'What?'

'That is clearly a man's handwriting.' She virtually threw the paper back at me. 'But you are right, she did phone the police. In order to make a complaint about you. That address on that paper. Even if she did write it, perhaps it was just to get you out of the house. Fob you off.'

I slumped in my chair. We were no closer to finding Emily and we seemed to just be hacking people off. Worse; they were closing ranks against us.

'If you don't tell me where I can change a baby, I will change him on your desk,' said Gianna.

'Okay,' I said. 'But we were attacked. I was confronted in a calle by two men wielding knives.' I tried a bit of general flattery. 'It is my understanding that violent crime is vanishingly rare in Venice, thanks no doubt in part to the excellent work of your good selves. So to be the victim of knife crime is something to investigate.'

The detective nodded. 'What did these two men actually do?'

'What do you mean?' asked Gianna. In the absence of being told where she could change the baby, she got her arm and dramatically swept papers across the detective's desk to clear it. She kept eye contact with the detective throughout – staring at her. It was unbelievably provocative. 'What do you mean?' she repeated louder.

Why didn't the detective just tell Gianna where the toilets were?

The changing mat was placed on the detective's desktop and soon the baby was half naked on top of it. Why didn't the detective tell Gianna off? How could this possibly be acceptable behaviour? On some level though, I did find it quite amusing.

The detective addressed me over the top of the baby. 'What did the men with knives actually do?' she asked. 'Did they harm you in any way? Did they steal anything? Did they threaten you?'

'No. None of those things, but surely you don't want people going around with knives?' I replied.

'I don't want a thousand tourists a day reporting to us that they have lost their phones or thought they'd had their wallets stolen, but in fact left them at a restaurant when drunk; but we can't have everything we want Mr De'Ath.'

'So you are not going to help us?' I asked.

We were all distracted by an overpowering stench from the contents of the baby's opened nappy.

'Shall we go to my office?' asked the detective.

'This isn't your desk?' I asked.

'No it is the duty sergeant's,' replied the detective. 'He's not going to be happy when he pops back. My office is up another flight of stairs; we rarely let the public up there.'

Gianna, who thought she had thus far struck a moral victory for mums with babies, looked quickly round the office; wondering, no doubt, how big this 'desk sergeant' was and whether he had a temper on him. She started wiping the baby's arse with much more urgency.

'You did that because I was a woman,' said Giulia Antonioni.

'What?' asked Gianna. She knew what.

'Cleared the desk to change the baby. You felt you could get away with it because I am a woman.' She was probably right.

'You just had to tell me where the toilets were,' retorted Gianna. 'You need to have some empathy with a fellow woman who is trying to bring up a family and find her husband.'

'And you need to show some empathy with an over-worked detective who also has children at home, but it never occurred to you to wonder if I had a family also, but who nonetheless raced after you jokers who kept trying to hide from me and would rather be confronted down an alleyway by knife-wielding thugs.'

The two women seemed to be squaring up for a fight. Was it some sort of volatile Italian thing? It seemed more than that. Or perhaps it was just a Gianna thing.

'Calm down Gianna,' I said. 'And respectfully Detective perhaps you could also…' Her glare was so severe it physically stopped any more words coming out of my mouth. Instead I turned my attention back to Gianna. 'And perhaps you could sit down? You're making me nervous.'

Gianna finished with the baby and sat down as a concession. She added a resentful sigh out of pride. It made her sound like a teenager.

The detective surveyed us both and decided we should go upstairs anyway.

In her office she became more thoughtful.

'I want to know more about you two,' she said. 'What is this about a missing sister?'

The detective listened with interest as we explained what had happened to Emily and Angelo, and to Gianna and me. I explained about the insurance frauds. She made occasional notes, mostly of the names involved. I then took a chance and told her about the events on the plague island when we were shot at.

'You are not supposed to go there,' she said.

'I didn't know that,' I lied.

'Yes, but she should know that,' said the detective. Detective Antonioni turned to address Gianna. She asked her a question in the Venetian dialect.

Gianna shrugged.

The detective then muttered a question in standard Italian – possibly the same question – and this time Gianna replied, 'Not really.'

'Interesting,' said the detective, mostly to herself. I didn't follow anything that was said, so I was none the wiser.

'What do you think the men with knives were trying to achieve?' asked the detective.

'They were trying to stop us from investigating the disappearance of Emily and Angelo,' I said. 'Something absolutely astonishing has happened and we are meeting a massive brick wall of the authorities, the police, the moneyed families who seem to run this island, their colleagues; even Emily's landlady. They are not just stonewalling; they are aggressively trying to stop us get any information.'

'They are trying to kill us!' complained Gianna.

'Yes, just that,' I said.

Gianna seemed to have re-charged herself for a fresh round of indignation. Doesn't it get tiring being angry all the time? I know it was tiring to me.

'Are you only going to take an interest if we are killed?' she spat.

'And do you feel the people who confronted you in the alley are the same people who shot at you on Poveglia?'

'Yes!'

'We don't know,' I conceded.

'Yes!' repeated Gianna.

'Okay, I will file a report,' said Giulia Antonioni.

'Oh you'll file a report. What good is that?' asked Gianna. 'When I am dead. When the baby is dead and lying face down floating in a canal, I will have the comfort of knowing that there is a thin cardboard folder sitting in your filing cabinet with our names on! A report!'

'It's probably all on a computer these days,' I said. 'Rather than a paper file.'

'Pedant!'

Fair comment.

The detective had suddenly had enough of Gianna's attitude. She pulled herself up to confront her.

Gianna made matters worse by shouting, 'What?' Right in her face.

Gianna really was a truly awful human being. I had tried repeatedly to tell myself that she was the wronged party and was no doubt driven to desperation, but being under stress reveals your true character – all of us can be charming when things are going our way – and her true character was vile.

To the detective's credit, she couldn't be bothered with a confrontation. She wafted the back of her hand in Gianna's face as though trying to get rid of a smell.

'I want you to keep me informed if there are any further developments,' she said. She offered me her card and selected a look of disappointment to offer Gianna. 'You can ring direct.'

Gianna physically walked back a step. Even she wasn't going to pick an actual fight with a policewoman in an actual police station.

'You are issuing us with a death sentence,' said Gianna quietly. A little dramatic, but not entirely without foundation.

We were soon out on the street.

And it could have been the fact that we felt deflated with our lack of progress, and it could have been that we were exhausted, and it could have been that I hadn't had any lunch yet; but whatever the reason, the very next decision we made was to prove to be our worst.

THE WORLD ACCORDING TO EMILY

ONE

I am imprisoned. I suppose I should be grateful that my hands are free at least. But I have no phone, no internet, and no key to get out; I cannot even get exercise or breathe some fresh air. In every respect, I am in a prison.

I am imprisoned because I didn't agree to running away with Angelo. I didn't agree to the love on the run that he suggested. The alternative is this. I am fed and I can watch TV. Have you seen Italian TV? When it isn't dull, it is just plain bizarre. There was one quiz show where there were women in bikinis and garter belts in a studio, and they were forming themselves into shapes to make a kind of human Tetris. And there was another show where women dressed as mermaids had to solve puzzles underwater, while a ten year old boy ate cooked calf brain. The most interesting thing about it was that the calf brain was prepared with capers; part quiz show, part cookery lesson. The fact that I dwelt on the calf brain at all, made me realise I was now thinking like Pete; out of boredom all my waking thoughts led to food. I am going out of my mind.

I have my clothes at least, and all my belongings. They were moved en masse from my apartment to here.

I have Angelo. I have as much of Angelo as I want. Lucky me. But I am imprisoned here and the only flames burning in my heart are flames of resentment.

I am not much of a book reader. I read a Harry Potter book once on a beach; I quite enjoyed it, but I found it a bit far-fetched, and I have read my share of thrillers, but I am not the sort who can pass endless days just reading. So what was I supposed to do all day? Have sex with Angelo? It was like Beauty and the Beast. Only the beast is dressed head to toe in grey, and there's no talking teapot.

I found myself dwelling on the principle players in the drama. If Angelo was the wronged party, as he claimed, then Adam was the front runner as the person behind everything. If Adam was innocent, then my suspicions went back to Angelo. The grey man, or the young man with the designer clothes and no discernible attention span; they both seemed unlikely villains in their different ways.

I lay awake in my room with bars at the window. The canal outside takes on its own light at night; the lanterns illuminating far off walkways make musty reflections through the fog, a moon flits behind the scurrying clouds, the foam from a passing boat glints and settles. It is still and mysterious out there; the lights of Venice at night. It's the best part of being stuck here.

As well as Angelo and Adam, Pete kept popping into my mind. Had he come out to Venice as planned? And when he had found me missing, what did he do? He'd always helped me before; would he come through for me this time? I knew instinctively he would; he had bailed me out of bigger trouble than this, he once even helped me shoplift, so why not this?

It was my first January at my first ever job. This was before the company was even called Society Metropolitan. Twenty years ago, fifteen years ago, you could leave school and get a good job without going to university. It was great. And besides, what would I do at university? I know I wouldn't read the books and write the assignments. I would just be short of money and sleep a lot. So after a couple of nonsense jobs, I followed my brother into insurance. But I had no money. This is true most years of my life, but it was particularly true then.

So I found myself in a supermarket and I was hungry. I was really hungry. I had nothing in the house to eat. It was wet. It was cold. I pushed a supermarket trolley around the supermarket, and I filled it with everything I wanted. I got bread. I got milk. I got lager. I got a pack of strange alcohol 'shots' in bright colours in bright plastic shot glasses; lurid red, lurid orange, lurid green, lurid yellow. It was on offer. 'Driving down the cost of those everyday items.' Alcohol shots in bright plastic shot glasses. Why did it matter if it was 'on offer'? I was hardly going to pay for them.

I walked the trolley to the end of the supermarket, and I pushed it past the last empty check out. I then walked with it and placed it against the wall, but behind a till where a woman was working. I then left the trolley and I went to the toilets. Five minutes later I left the toilets, I found my trolley and I acted as if I had paid for its contents previously. I pushed it to the door of the supermarket and then I walked it to my car. I am a genius.

A security man appeared.

'Have you paid for those items?' he inquired. It was a fair question, but clearly he had already decided on the answer.

I elected to say nothing.

'You will need to accompany me back to the shop,' said the security man.

I focussed on him. His name was Daryl. It said so on a badge. Daryl the security man. Probably born in the 1980s. Probably named after Daryl Hall and John Oates. A less likely option was that he was named after Daryl Hannah, Tom Hanks' mermaid girlfriend in Splash.

I eyed up my car and I wondered how much time it would take me to run to my car, get in it, and drive away. The problem was that I did not have my keys in my hand; I would need time to get them out of my bag, and my bag was overstuffed so I would probably struggle to find them. No. There was no way I could escape in my car before the man stopped me. Then he would call the police. Next time I did this I would keep my keys in my hand ready. I was already assuming there was a next time.

Could I flirt with him? He looked pale and angry. Too many computer games, too much pizza, not enough girlfriend. He had a sad suit that was shiny where it was worn, and the trousers were creased under his stomach. He looked sexless but he may be exactly the sort who spends all day watching internet porn. Despite the porn thing, I decided flirting was not the solution.

'Okay fine,' I said.

I turned the trolley towards the supermarket.

He started talking in his radio that was on his jacket collar.

'Janet, assistance. Code ten, by the main doors.'

I didn't like the sound of a code ten, or of Janet: no flirting opportunities there. She would probably believe every word Daryl had to say. Bitch. I hated her already. Guilty until I was proven guilty. Probably because I was indeed guilty. Bloody Janet.

We got back to the shop doorway. It had a vestibule, before a second set of doors took us into the shop proper. No sign of this 'Janet' yet.

'I need something,' I said. I moved my handbag off my shoulder and opened it to look for my car keys. I would find the keys and run.

I was distracted by a very loud voice.

'There you are!'

I focussed on the source of the voice; a large young man coming my way. He was smiling a big effortless smile. He put his hands forwards towards me.

'I thought I had lost you!'

It was Pete.

'Where were you? One minute you were with me, and then I lost you.'

I didn't reply.

Pete looked at the guard.

'When she is stressed, she doesn't speak,' he said.

Pete started moving his fingers across his other hand. He was tapping his palm and his other fingers. He was pretending it use sign language.

'You... must... wait... for... me,' he said. 'You... know... you... must... wait... for... me.'

Pete turned to the guard.

'She knows she must wait for me. Sometimes she just runs off. She gets into all sorts of trouble. Recently I lost her for two days,' he said.

'But she did speak!' protested Daryl.

'What?' asked Pete.

'She did speak. I heard her speak,' said the guard.

'That's a good sign,' said Pete.

Pete turned to me. 'Well done!' he said. He emphasised his point with sign language and patted me three times on the shoulder.

'I heard her speak,' reiterated the guard.

'But did she hear *you* speak?' asked Pete. 'Did you use sign language?'

The guard had seen it all before, and wasn't going to let it go; but you could see from his eyes that a little uncertainty had nonetheless crept in.

'I think you need to accompany me to the manager's office,' said Daryl. We only have his badge to say he was called Daryl. He might be called anything.

Pete pretended he had not heard the man. He just pushed the trolley back into the store and off to a checkout. He started putting the items on the conveyor belt.

I held the handle of the trolley and I rocked a bit forwards and backwards. I added some hooded eyelids where I could obviously only look down. I was not sure what precise disability I was trying to capture. 'Backward' should cover it.

Sometimes you've got to love Pete.

I love you Pete. I fall so you can catch me.

But will he catch me now?

TWO

My realisation that Adam and I wouldn't work came in two stages. One was when a bill came in a restaurant, the other was when we had sex.

We were in the office at the end of the day and Adam was standing up and tidying his desk.

'How about a drink?' he asked. He said it in a, it's-been-a-hot-day-the-sun-is-still-up kind of way. Why would we want to go home to our dank apartments and sit on our own? Except it hadn't been a hot day; it had been a cold day and the work was mind-numbing and a bit of 'me' time at home would actually be quite nice. I said yes, because I had twice said no before; which is actually no reason to do anything.

We ended outside an osteria; it was the nearest, local choice; good value, cosy; decent food without denting my monthly budget. Except Adam was having none of it. By getting me to agree to come out with him he clearly felt he now had permission to dictate events.

'I know a better place than this,' he said. He guided my shoulder with his hand. No, he cupped my shoulder. Like when you guide a child to tell her it is now safe to cross the road. It was not a massive violation of my personal space, but it was memorable; we were colleagues – in fact he was my assistant - and I couldn't recall him touching me even once before that moment.

Then the restaurant he chose was too posh. It was part of a grand hotel; all ornate high ceilings and gilded mirrors. I felt under-dressed and washed out after a long day at work. It was the sort of restaurant where you feel self-conscious talking above a whisper; where waiters line the walls judging you. Could they not play some music at least? Preferably from this century, but last century would do. I looked at the menu. The prices were astronomical. Maybe if I'd been prepared... maybe if it was someone's birthday...

Adam ordered some Champagne. It was bonkers expensive.

'Have you come into some money or something?' I asked.

'I'm not poor.'

'You're not poor?' I asked. 'I didn't say you were poor.' It came out clumsy.

'My family are loaded,' he said. 'I have an allowance.' Then why do you work in our crumby little office, pouring over paperwork? At least it explained the endless designer clothes he can somehow afford; and the posh holidays in the Alps with people called things like Tabatha and Rowena.

'Why do you work?' I couldn't think of a way to nuance it, so I left the sentence unadorned.

'Well my family don't want me at home doing nothing. No one likes to hear about a rich young man who has never had a job. Pride maybe?'

But insurance? I tried to think of other options here in Venice. I suppose it made no sense for him to be a waiter.

He addressed the maitre d' by name. They asked about each other's family.

'The lobster here is great,' he said.

I needed to pause and breathe. It was too much. It was too try-hard. Or was it just that it was unexpected; that this was actually his natural environment and wasn't try-hard at all?

'This is just...' I said.

He apprised me.

'Maybe I haven't made myself clear,' he replied. He leant forward and kissed me.

He was so much younger than me, and yes I had all along fancied the idea of copping off with him. I mentally shrugged and decided to relax into it. A posh weekday meal; what was my problem?

The problem was when the bill arrived on the little silver tray.

Adam's hand instinctively reached out for it and it just felt wrong. Adam was little over half my age and he was paying for me in one of the most expensive restaurants in Italy. It's not something you could do repeatedly. It was awkward doing it once.

And then there was the sex.

I did my thing, but I'm used to my thing; it is someone else's thing that interests me. We're all adults here, not teenagers in our bedrooms after school, grateful for any fumblings that we're given.

Adam is from the generation who watch too much internet porn, so his performance was very acrobatic and done with much confidence; but he was comfortable with being extreme. I'm from the generation that read too much Cosmopolitan: Thirty Sex Tips That Will Make Your Man Beg For More! Putting the OMG Back in Your Orgasm! (Orgasm spelled with the OMG in fluorescent orange.) So the result between us was technically proficient, if a little demeaning; there was a fair amount of slapping involved. I filed it under 'What I did last night,' not 'The first day of the rest of my life.'

But the sex wasn't the problem. It was only our first effort, and we could have tweaked it; I could have given him notes (which I'm sure he would have welcomed). It was after the sex that was the problem.

I went to make some conversation.

'You know, I was out at the shopping mall in Marghera yesterday,' I started.

'Oh really. It's something isn't it?' He nodded and reached for his phone. He didn't wait for more. Surely, he didn't think that was the whole anecdote; that I went to a shopping centre?

I let the silence stretch between us. I waited for him to say, 'Go on.' But he was now plainly engrossed on the internet or whatever. He didn't care whether it was the whole anecdote or not; he had already bounded on to his next thoughts.

I went to the shopping mall yesterday on the mainland and they were selling facemasks and they had run out of hand sanitiser. It was because of the reports from China that there was a health scare called Covid-19. The virus has got as far as the Alps and may get to us soon. That was the story.

I hugged my bare knees and looked out at the view. What was I doing with this man?

Venice's one and only female gondolier was outside. Or was that gondoliere? Either way she was working late. She had two tourists as passengers, both women. What if the two women were married? How modern that 11th century boat would be.

'Oh look! What a rare sighting! The famous woman gondolier,' I said, pleased to have something to say that wasn't as banal as 'I went to a shopping mall'.

Nothing from Adam.

I leant forward to look at his screen; I always seemed to be doing that, to find out what he was thinking. He had better not be WhatsApping some group that he'd had sex.

No, it was worse than that.

He was playing a computer game.

'What's that?' I asked.

'It's Subway Surfers.' When I didn't reply, he explained, 'It is the most played smartphone game on the planet.' He might as well have added, 'Grandma' to the end of that sentence. I felt really thrown by this. I hugged my knees tighter and rocked. Then I felt the need to put on my clothes and dash. I was puzzling why I felt so thrown by his behaviour. But then it hit me. It wasn't that he was playing a computer game. It wasn't that he was ignoring me. What threw me was that he was a full generation below me. A generation where I had no bearings. Where I had no idea whether his behaviour was poor or not.

I now had my clothes on and regarded him from the doorway. I was reminded of a story a friend of mine tells. She has a teenage son who sits in his room all day playing computer games. She despairs that he never goes out, never interacts with real humans, and never gets any vitamin D. 'Can you come down for a meal at least?' she asked. 'Can you at least change out of your pyjamas?' No answer. 'Well can we at least open your curtains?' she asked. Finally, the teenage son let out a sigh of deep despair and paused his game. He looked at his mum and then at his curtains. 'Well, you can open them if you like,' he said. 'But we'll just have to close them later.' That was Adam. And I was the mum.

'Well, I'll be off then,' I said. To no one present.

I later sent him a text saying I thought what we'd done was a mistake. I was his boss, and all. I regretted it. I should have done it face to face to gauge his reaction. He never did reply.

Best to stick to my own kind, I figured. At least that way if I caught a man playing computer games rather than congratulating me on my sexual prowess it would be Candy Crush; a game I'd actually heard of.

But was Adam gutted? Had he not seen it coming? Or did he date other women that weekend and it was all of no consequence at all? I had no idea, and no way of knowing.

THREE

'We could have avoided this,' said Angelo. 'We could have avoided all this pain.' He was gazing at what little view we had from the window; the edge of a building that never got the sun, its plaster peeling, its tiny wooden jetty unused and rotten, and a bit of canal beyond. It was a view that looked good at night, but contrived to look drab by day.

I nodded. I felt weak. In my sleep I was alone and free; my evaporated dreams had been sun-blessed and balmed. Awake, I lived with someone I wasn't that keen on; and I was literally imprisoned.

I lay staring at the ceiling.

I tried to imagine my future. I tried to imagine the simplest of days back in Corsica, days I had taken for granted; seeing Mum, walking through the streets of Bastia to the office, sitting in a bar by the harbour after work. It seemed impossible I would ever get back there.

'We could have been in Nice, living like two young marrieds in love. Or Bordeaux. I really like Bordeaux; it's got soul, you know?' said Angelo.

'I know.'

'It's not a rich person's playground like the south of France,' he continued. 'Real people live there. It would have been cheaper too.' Please stop talking.

He looked at his watch. He looked at it again, like he'd forgotten why he'd looked at it the first time.

'It's nine o'clock,' said Angelo. 'You know what that means.'

'I'll need to go to the bathroom and put some clothes on and have a shower,' I said. 'But not in that order.'

We listened for the knock on the door.

Nothing.

'I suppose it was unlikely that they would be punctual,' I said.

I really wanted to go back to sleep. Narcoleptics have the right idea. An ideal response to stress is just to sleep. Whatever the problem, just sleep through it and wake up when it's gone.

Somehow my legs both swung round and onto the floor without being told to do so by my brain. I seemed to be standing now. I kissed Angelo on the cheek to reassure him; he was all I had, so no point in alienating him. I moved to the tiny corridor.

The duty policeman in the kitchen nodded a good morning to me.

Life in a safe house. Paranoid and claustrophobic.

An hour and a half later and the detectives arrived. They knocked on the main door and identified themselves by recognising each other's voices. There was a short one and an even shorter one. Or maybe I just felt huge and lumbering today. Note to self; must date larger men from now on, to make me feel petite. Perhaps that's why posh middle-aged women drive those enormous four by four cars; to make them look slight by comparison.

'Is this house arrest absolutely necessary?' I asked.

'It's not house arrest, it is witness protection,' said the smallest detective. He looked as if he was preparing to do most of the talking. 'These are dangerous people. If you testify against them they have the sort of connections, er, they know people who could do away with you. So firstly, I need to have a conversation with you, that by making statements to us you are fully aware that you may be placing yourself in danger.'

'Yes,' I said. We were sitting in the kitchen. I had a general feeling of defeat. In this mood, I would agree to pretty much anything. Angelo was standing, like standing and pacing helped his thought process; but if that were true, the company's management would have removed the chairs and desks from the office years ago.

'So the background of the case,' began the detective. 'Is that for reasons we will not go into, we were already taking an interest in Adzio Icardi, the man known to you as Adam.'

'Okay,' I said.

'We were taping his calls, monitoring his emails and things like that. And we noticed he appeared to be organising a fraud at your work. A massive fraud. He appeared to be hugely ambitious. He was trying to curry favour with certain important people around Venice. They were businessmen in the main, but also local families who were influential. We alerted your senior management. As a result, your senior management allowed us to monitor his activities on his computer.'

'But they didn't tell the more junior management?' I asked.

'No. We didn't know who we could trust.' Well that explained why Marco wasn't very sympathetic.

'Go on,' I said.

'And then in fact,' continued the detective. 'We did not then find anything strange going on. We wanted to prevent fraud, you understand, but we hadn't found any.'

'Do sit down Angelo, you are making me nervous,' I said.

Angelo considered this. 'Actually my wife used to buzz around when she was anxious. It was very irritating. I will sit.' He then didn't sit. He was too distracted by events to remember what he'd said even a second ago. So this was how a grey man responds to stress.

'Sit!' I barked.

He sat. Perhaps there were good reasons he became nagged so much by his wife.

'And then we had the kidnappings,' continued the detective. 'Where both of you were abducted separately and held for the day. And during that day your computers were used to make those big payments. We didn't see it coming. We had assumed all along that Adam would use his own computer. Looking back, it was a facile assumption. After all, if he used his own computer, he would have to go into hiding forever.'

The other detective piped up unexpectedly. 'They are dangerous people. They have been attacking your brother,' he said.

'My brother?' I asked. This was alarming news. Up until now I had seen this problem being all about me.

'Yes Mr Peter De'Ath is your brother? He has been asking about you. Just for asking questions he has been shot at and he was set upon by men wielding knives. Anyone who gets involved with talking about this case is making themselves vulnerable. If people even divulged information about you or the fraud or Adam, they were getting threatened. This is why we told everyone to give no information to anyone at all. If asked, they were welcome to deny even knowing you. It would put out a clear message to the organised criminal gang that their intimidation was having the desired effect, and they need threaten no one anymore.'

'Your employers, your landlady, even the police,' said the first detective. 'We told them to say they have never heard of you. And the strategy also helps keep you secure here in the safe house.'

Why not just say we'd disappeared though? It occurred to me that the reason was that the police didn't 100% trust some of their own colleagues. If I had disappeared, then did I in fact go to a safe house? Once a bent policeman wondered that, they might start checking the safe houses to see if we were here. Frankly, they might start doing that anyway. I now felt vulnerable. But if a safe house isn't safe then what is? Perhaps I should have run away with Angelo like he suggested. Perhaps he'd had the same thoughts himself.

I imagined Pete gamely trying to investigate my disappearance and being met with stonewalling; but then attacked, shot at? You literally can't go around the island of Venice shooting people, it is sort of not built for it; you would have to lure them somewhere. Poor Pete.

'And your wife also,' said the other detective. 'Gianna.'

'Gianna?' asked Angelo. He looked surprised or perhaps thrown. 'Gianna is involved? Heaven help us.' He shook his head as he considered this. 'Oh well,' he shrugged. 'I suppose.' He supposed what? He then looked at me furtively to gauge my reaction. It was not even a conscious gesture. I guessed we wouldn't be hearing from him for a while, while he had a long hard think. And wife? I thought it was ex-wife.

'Which brings us to the matter in hand,' said the detective. 'Our own evidence against Adam Icardi is very circumstantial. We need as strong a case as possible to overcome such powerful families; people with top lawyers and lots of money. I understand you feel you can identify one of your abductors as Adam Icardi?' This was directed at Angelo, but he was lost in thought.

'Angelo?' I asked. 'You feel you can identify one of the abductors as being Adam? Is that right?'

'Yeah. Yeah it was him. He had like a tracksuit on and his face was mostly covered but it was definitely him,' he said.

'You'd swear to that?' asked the detective.

'Yes, I'd swear to that,' he said. No hesitation.

It was the opposite of what he had said previously to me.

I said nothing. I decided to see how it played out.

'And there is more,' he said. 'He was taking an interest in my computer. I caught him at my terminal once. He made some lame excuse, but when I checked the history of the computer, he had been having a good old look around.'

'You left your computer unattended?' I asked, largely to make me feel better.

'I was called into a meeting. You know how it is,' he said.

I reflected that I would have no idea how to check on my own computer what it had been up to recently. Maybe that is boy stuff.

'I've got a few stories along those lines,' said Angelo. 'It'll slot together nicely as evidence.'

The detective looked pleased. He was doing a nodding motion with his head. His colleague flexed his neck back and looked at the ceiling; he might have been thinking, or he might have just been tired.

I thought, what if a policeman in his position was in the pay of these rich families? He has just heard something he was going to have to report to them; that Angelo is offering strong testimony against Adam. He was wondering what their reactions might be. His attention went back from the ceiling to Angelo and myself. He smiled. This could all mean anything, but I couldn't help feeling we were sitting ducks.

'And what about you?' the lead detective asked. He was addressing me.

'I have nothing so concrete, I'm afraid,' I said. 'I can give you an account of my abduction, obviously, but I don't think either of my abductors was Adam. They had the wrong build.'

'And you dated him?' asked the detective. How did he know that? And why did it matter?

'Just one proper date,' I said. 'It was nothing. It was over before it began.'

'Is it possible you meant more to him than you realise?' he asked.

'I doubt it.'

'You had sex with him?' he asked. Now it was my turn to furtively look at Angelo to check his reaction. But he looked like he was still thinking about Gianna. What was the deal there? An ex-wife. Why was she so interested in finding him? They hadn't seen each other for... actually, I now realised I had no idea when they had last seen each other; for all I knew they lived together. I had never been to his house. And if he was lying about that, then what else was he lying about?

I realise I hadn't spoken. 'It was just one of those things,' I said. 'You know, like when you sleep with someone at the office party.' I had no idea if sleeping with people at the office party happened in Italy. Presumably it did.

The detective nodded and made a note. A note of what? 'It is possible,' he said. 'That he had sex with you and you dismissed it, but in fact it was a big thing to him. Who ended it?'

'I did,' I said.

'What was his reaction? What if he was resentful and wanted to get his revenge on you?' asked the detective.

'I don't think he was resentful,' I replied. Was he resentful? I tried the idea out in my head. Possibly.

'You are good looking,' said Angelo.

'What does that mean?' I asked. I didn't feel good looking. I didn't feel good in any way at all.

'Men fall in love with you,' he persisted. 'You are the sort of woman that men fall in love with.'

I am? It was a big statement. It's impossible to see yourself the way that others see you. I am the sort of woman that men fall in love with. I thought briefly about my past. Yes, I suppose there were instances of that.

'And when men fall in love, they make crazy decisions.'

What crazy decisions have you made Angelo?

'I've seen the way Adam looks at you,' he continued. 'I think he's got a thing for you. Adam has a thing for you.'

And you, Angelo, seem very keen to build a case against Adam. Perhaps you were jealous of him because I slept with him once. What if, in fact, you were the guilty one; responsible for the fraud? After all, you have changed your story about your abduction; suddenly Adam was involved. Still, the police say they have other evidence against Adam, so maybe I should forget any suspicions I had about the Grey One. But what if the police were also in the pay of the crime syndicate and were bluffing about what they claim they heard on Adam's phone calls? The crime syndicate had big money. The risk of being shot walking home one night, versus a tidy sum of money in a brown envelope; what policeman would refuse? And why were the envelopes always brown in these scenarios?

I thought back to when we made the decision to come into the safe house.

Angelo standing by the canal side. He held my two hands in mine. He squeezed them harder than made sense.

'We could get away,' he said. 'I've got money.'

And the thick set man appeared ahead of us, and the similar one behind, and I realised they both had a gun at their hips.

'Where have you taken us?' I asked Angelo. 'This is not the way to the police station.'

I eyed up the canal. Could I dive in, and get away that way?

He spoke again, this time he was more insistent. 'Basically Emily, at this moment in time there are two options. These men are from the police and they believe our version of events. They think that Adam is behind the fraud and they want to take us to a safe house to give them statements and prepare us to testify against the syndicate who are behind this. But we will live in fear of our lives. People get shot for less by the Mafia. Maybe not straightaway, but we will spend the rest of our lives looking over our shoulders. These police don't even trust the police we were previously talking to; that's how few people we can trust.'

The policemen either side of us were nearly within touching distance.

'They can't make us go with them,' he said. 'We will have to agree to it.'

'If we're witnesses to a crime then we might have to testify regardless,' I said.

'Not if we don't want to, not if they can't find us.'

But we have not really even been dating. Surely?

'Angelo. It was great, but it was not life-on-the-run-having-sex-in-motels-and-holding-hands-as-we-jump-off-a-cliff-together great.' Somehow, I had said this out loud. You're the grey man I drifted into a relationship with. I felt a complete and utter arsehole saying these things, or even thinking them, but these were the facts.

'We are going to have to testify,' I said.

'The safe house is right by here.' He said it in a tone where he already knew this would be my choice; a grey man like him doesn't get a girl like me. His shoulders slumped, but he didn't say anything. We turned to walk with the police.

'Adam finds you attractive. You should see the way he looks at you,' said Angelo. It turns out I had zoned out and we were still in the kitchen of the safe house and everyone was trying to talk to me.

'What if he was so riled at being dumped by you, that he dragged you in as an act of revenge?' asked the detective.

'You've said this before,' I said; this wasn't our first conversation with these detectives. 'I think we can all agree it is a group of companies and families who were aggrieved at not being compensated for the floods and they cooked up the plot. They didn't cook this up as a way of getting their own back on me in particular.'

'But prosecutions are about people,' said the detective. 'We have to present the jury with a human face, and they need to understand that this particular person did wrong and they have to understand why.'

He just kept his gaze on me, like I had all the answers. But I didn't.

'I suppose there was that one time,' I began.

There was one time really early on. I was new to the office. Adam was doing some jobs for me as my assistant. My *assistant*, for heaven's sake, of course he had access to my computer; of course, he knew all about my business.

I said, 'Look, I don't want to sound desperate or lonely, but I am new in town. I know I am in Venice, but I'm not going to traipse around dusty old churches. What can I do with my weekend?'

Adam surveyed me. 'Leave it with me,' he said.

He hopped into my chair and took charge of my computer. He was tapping and bringing up booking systems and images of boats and the sea.

'You should see the lagoon,' he said. 'People think of us as a city of canals, but if you are a child here, it is an island in a lagoon. You need to get out. Visit the islands, have lunch in a harbour, have a cocktail as the sun sets over the water. You have sunglasses I presume?'

'I have sunglasses,' I replied

'And a swimsuit?'

'I have a swimsuit.'

'And a big summer hat?'

'I could buy one,' I said.

'What's the number on the back of your credit card that ends 6252?'

'What?'

In the time it had taken to chat to me, he had sourced a powerboat I could hire for the weekend and he had culled my credit card details from another website or paid for the boat through a website I had previously used. It was the nonchalance of it that struck me. The speed of it.

He hovered his finger theatrically over the 'pay' icon on the screen.

'Do you want a great weekend or not?' he said. 'It's going to be sunny. A rare sunny weekend in the winter.'

'Go for it,' I said.

'Now what you need is a man for your weekend. An experienced local guide. Someone who's fun and knows the best places to eat...'

I had been thrown at Adam's skill with the computer and with my credit card details, so I was slow to respond.

He rephrased the question. 'Would you like me to show you round the lagoon this weekend?' he asked.

'Yes please,' I replied.

'And did you have sex?' This was the detective asking me. Why did it always come down to me having sex? The question was a bit prurient for my taste.

'No,' I replied. 'This is before the other time. It was the first time we spent time out of the office.'

I became over-aware that I was in a room with three men. Four if you count the policeman on guard texting his girlfriend in the corner. Or reporting us to the criminals we were discussing. The guards were on rotation; could we trust all of them? Perhaps they were the weak link.

'And what was the weekend like?' asked the detective.

'Great. Really great.'

'Did it mean more to him than you?' That again.

'No!' I insisted.

'And does that apply to...' started Angelo. Does that apply to the sex I had with Angelo?

I felt weary. I mean, young men want sex. Surely that's the deal. Why was I being made to feel such a heel about this?

'The point,' I said. 'The entire point of that story was that Adam was very adept at finding stuff on my computer and using it. He did it at high speed and it felt sneaky.'

'That's not enough to convict someone,' said the detective. I was evidently pleasing no one. No one at all. And yet I was stuck here.

I took myself to the kitchen window. It had a slightly better view than my bedroom. It was busy out there. A woman was putting washing out to dry. She was putting it on a line that ran on pulleys from her balcony across the canal.

There was a garbage barge collecting refuse from a household. They were doing a three point turn to try and turn round. I watched as the three point turn became four points, then five points. Then a boat went by, steered by a man who had placed the rudder arm between his buttocks. Beyond that, I could just about see a bridge. It was busy with locals and tourists ascending and descending its stone steps. There were crowds of people out there. I watched them milling for a while, and everyone in the room let me. Who are these unknown criminals and business owners who wanted to know where we were kept in secret? Which of those people walking along that bridge was dwelling on how to kill us? Which of them is biding their time, but one day will get the nod from their bosses and follow me home and knife me in an alley?

I jumped a mile.

Someone had knocked on our door. Now someone was buzzing a buzzer. Were we expecting more police? A delivery of food perhaps? I realised how on edge I was. There were muffled voices through the door.

'I'll need to phone for authorisation,' I heard our policeman say. 'Give me two minutes.'

We all craned our heads, but there was nothing to see. It had the effect of stopping the police interview, or the pre-interview; I had lost track of time over the days we had been here. Either way, we still hadn't got to the stage where formal statements were taken. It was more of a prep to ascertain what we might say. Was that even legal? Prepping the witnesses?

Eventually our door opened. A baby's buggy had appeared in the hallway. Of all things; a baby's buggy.

And then behind the buggy I could see a flustered looking woman with thick dark hair and an angry manner; she was pushing the buggy towards us.

And then behind her, I could see Pete.

THE WORLD ACCORDING TO PETE

ONE

We had let our guards down. Gianna and I had emerged from the police station and our natural inclination was to stop and discuss events.

We were just setting off again, and had walked perhaps thirty yards, when a man came out of the doors behind us to have a word. Or rather we assumed he had come out of the police station. He scurried to catch up with us

'Are you Signora Totti and Signor De'Ath?' he gasped. It was like he'd been running a long time to catch us up; perhaps down through the stairs of the building?

He was a modest man. He had the look of an office assistant. Again, this was lulling us. We trusted him too readily.

'I've been asked to protect you,' he said. 'Where are you staying?'

'At a hotel to the west of St Marks,' I replied.

'I really am out of breath,' he gasped. Again, this detail made me trust him. 'I'll take you there,' he said. 'Hotel name?'

I told him my hotel.

He beckoned for us to follow him.

'Do you want to come with me?' I asked Gianna as she jostled the wheels of the buggy first round an intransigent lamppost, and then an intransigent tourist.

'I have no plans, I have no husband, I have no life...' Please don't start, Gianna. She must have caught a look on my face. She stopped listing what she didn't have. Or rather, she kept going, but under her breath. 'I've lost my dignity. I've lost my sanity...'

I suppose one reason I was off my guard was that feisty Gianna was so trusting in this man. She was a local with a local's instincts and in every situation so far she had been the first to turn against whomever we were dealing with; so when she just followed the man without questioning, I did too.

'It's quicker by boat,' he said. 'And safer.' Was it though?

The boat he took us to looked like any other boat. But then, a boat is a boat; it was a seemingly sturdy launch with an integral motor, rather than an outboard.

We headed north along the canal system, which might have made sense, but I wasn't sure. Because the speed limit in the lagoon is nearly twice the speed limit in Venice proper, the most direct route is not always the fastest. Once we were out on the lagoon, he raised our speed and headed north east.

It was Gianna who objected first.

'Excuse me!' she shouted. But she also had to worry about the safety of the baby.

Our captain, who I now realised had not even told us his name, added more throttle; he appeared not to hear Gianna at all.

Gianna tapped me, then before I had time to respond, she hit my arm with a fist.

'Ow!'

'Well do something!'

'About what?' I asked.

'He's taking us the wrong way.' What adult punches another adult just to get their attention?

'I would thank you not to punch me Gianna,' I said.

She hit me again. Harder.

Seriously?

'Do something about him. He is taking us the wrong way,' she said.

I tried to get forward out of my seat, but at the exact same moment the man powered the boat faster. I was thrown back against the arm of my seat; it speared my side and winded me.

The man then drove the boat faster still; it was impossible that this was within the speed limit or that this way would take us to my hotel. As if to prove me wrong about the speed, two motorboats with youth in them went storming across our path. They were blaring out loud music from ghetto blasters. There was a hunky lad at the helm of one of them with a bottle of beer held in his teeth and both hands on the wheel, setting the boat in an arc that buffeted our own. This is all by way of excuse as to why I lost my footing on my second attempt to talk to our captain.

Finally however, I was standing beside him, gripping the dashboard for safety.

'I said west of St Marks. I am staying west of St Marks,' I shouted.

'Yes, yes,' he shouted back dismissively.

'This isn't the way,' I protested.

'It is the way.'

I have never known what to do when people are this adamant when lying. If a person taps a white piece of paper and declares, 'That is black!' I literally don't have a response.

'I demand you take us to my hotel,' I shouted.

'I am taking you to your hotel.'

I wondered if I could overpower him. I bet Gianna could. Rage was like a super power with her. Knowing that Gianna could show me up for the spineless wuss that I am, I made to grip the wheel of the boat.

'What are you doing?' demanded the man.

'I am taking us back.'

The man was smaller than me, but more agile.

'This is the way! I keep telling you.'

He brushed me aside with a sideways swipe of his elbow, but this had a far bigger effect than it should have done. He had locked his foot behind my ankle without me knowing, so the effect of his elbow was to send me back on my heel and sideways. The sudden lurch of my weight caused the boat to keel alarmingly. This in turn caused the pushchair and baby to lift up. Despite its bulk, the stroller was top heavy and a freak wind somehow caught it; before we knew it, it had turned on its side in mid-air and was threatening to fly off the boat. I put an arm out to try and grab it. I was partially successful; it dropped onto one wheel and pirouetted away from my grasp. I recall the baby's eyes somehow fixing on mine; they opened wide in alarm. I got a foot out and up, and it just about managed to trap the buggy against the decking, but it was all very precarious.

But then the captain hit me.

Square in the face.

Both my feet gave way.

I was now on my arse.

The boat, meanwhile, was doing a sharp circle, where no one was at the helm. The man steadied us up, but that in itself caused a lurch and we all realised at the same time that we were powering towards a boat that was much bigger than us. Bigger than us, and much more solid.

Gianna had her hand on the buggy now. The man lashed at her. In response she brought a foot up to kick the back of the man's head. She kicked him so hard, his face ricocheted off the wooden dashboard. Now I saw blood on a switch, along with a fingerful of flesh.

'Look what you made me do!' she shouted at him.

The boat in front loomed above us.

I seized the wheel and turned us sharp to the left, but our boat had no real distance in which to respond so we hit the larger boat full square. A horn went off from the bigger boat. A liner of some sort? But what was the point of the horn? We smacked the side of their hull. This caused the baby and buggy to now spin backwards.

Gianna dived back in an attempt to save the baby, and the man was now up again. He had blood obscuring one eye but was now re-energised by anger. He was above us, using the back of a seat as a springboard. He jumped down onto Gianna. Was it because she had kicked him that he went for her not me? I now had the boat a little more under control; we were in open water but still rocking precariously from the clash with the bigger boat.

This was all suddenly unimportant, however.

It was unimportant because now, for the first time, I realised our real problem.

During all the confusion, another boat had come to join us. The people in the other boat had weapons. There was a man at the helm and then there were two men behind him; one with a handgun and one with an automatic weapon. They were pulling their boat around and matching our speed. These men were not police. They all had black face coverings. These men were out to get us.

We had been taken out to the lagoon to be slaughtered.

TWO

The man in our boat was still angry at Gianna and trying to grapple her. They were both oblivious to the other boat; the one with the gunmen. It left me with the ridiculous task of trying to stop Gianna and the man fighting, in order to explain to them that we had bigger things to worry about.

'Er, excuse me,' I said.

Gianna clawed at the man's face with a fistful of fingernails.

'Er, guys, you need to stop this,' I tried.

The man attempted a kidney punch. But he had little room to swing his fist. It still met with an oomph! from Gianna. To retaliate, she kneed him in the groin.

'Guys there are men here with guns!' I tried. 'Er, hello?'

One of the men was steadying their boat against ours. I smiled at him by way of apology; sorry we're not taking your automatic weapons more seriously.

'Gianna!' I shouted. 'Seriously!' They were now pulling each other's hair, like a couple of schoolgirls in a playground brawl.

The man with the machine gun was now in our boat. I shrugged him a 'What can you do?'

He knew what to do. He pressed the muzzle of his gun firmly into the side of Gianna's neck.

'Oi!' she called. She was angry. Of course she was angry; it's her default emotion.

'Get up!' shouted the man with the gun. The second gunman was now in our boat. He was keeping a distance from us but had his gun braced in both hands. He was a man who'd had training with firearms. He wasn't a chancer.

Could I destabilise the boat? If I rocked it would anyone fall over? Should I simply jump overboard? The two men with guns looked as if they knew what they were doing; they would shoot me if I tried to jump.

The man who had sailed us out to this empty part of the lagoon was now dusting himself off. He moved forward in our boat and took the keys out of the ignition.

'Hand over your phones,' he said.

I paused, but only because I was in shock.

'Common on fatso, hand over your phone,' he said. Well there was no reason to be rude; I didn't call him Gym Bunny Fashion Victim. Not least because it's not as insulting as Fatso. What else could I call him? And why was I worrying about it?

'And you, Wolverine Lady. Hand over your phone.'

They were stranding us in the middle of the lagoon with no key to the boat and no way of calling for help. Why?

Gianna reached for her handbag. It made the man with the machine gun stiffen up.

'I'm reaching for my phone, you moron,' she said.

'Go on then.'

'Well thank you for your permission.'

She stomped a foot towards him just to make him jump. There's bravado, and there's anger, and there's good old-fashioned stupidity; Gianna had gone for the latter. These were plainly men who had killed before. There would be no witnesses. They could dump our bodies in the lagoon. When would we be missed? I was on holiday; I wouldn't be missed. Certainly not today. Gianna? Perhaps Gianna would be missed. Anyone who shares their life with her would surely soon notice the silence, where the angry lady was no longer shouting. But we were not going to be missed in the next five minutes, or even the next five hours. Basically, we were on our own; up a lagoon without a paddle.

Gianna handed over her phone and I handed over mine. Even though I knew it didn't work, it felt like a defeat handing it over. It occurred to me this gave me a glimmer of hope. If they were going to kill us, why take our phones? We could hardly call the police if we were dead.

The three men got back into their boat.

'Do something!' Gianna shouted. At me. What was I supposed to do? Reason with them? Attack them with the baby's changing bag?

'In case you're wondering,' said the man with the machine gun. 'You are going to die.' Not just a contract killer, a clairvoyant as well; he'd read my mind and predicted my next question. 'But we'll dump your phones somewhere random, so the police won't know where to look. I just thought you'd like to know.' A clairvoyant prone to sarcasm; just great.

They cast off and started their engine, then cut it again so they were about five metres away from us.

The two armed men braced their guns ready to shoot us.

I threw myself flat on the decking. Gianna made a lunge for the baby and tried to get the buggy behind her as she lay on the deck herself. It was possibly the wrong decision; perhaps we should have dived into the water instead. But what about the baby? How could we stop him from drowning? If he was kept above water, he would be shot at; if we pushed him under, he would drown. You can hardly tell a baby to hold its breath.

The men opened fire in unison. Bullet after bullet hit the hull of the boat. They were shooting just below the water line. They were being systematic; they were starting at the front and moving back. I could see the hull splintering below the water line about four feet above my head. Then the bullet holes started getting closer.

I shrunk my head into my body. Could I shimmy down the boat a little? That would only buy me a little time; if they were shooting the length of the hull, they would shoot me eventually anyway. Gianna was behind me, and the baby was behind her, so there was a faint chance the bullets wouldn't go through me to her. I would accidentally die a hero, shielding a mother and baby. I imagined the praise I would get at my funeral. It was so not worth it. And anyway, the baby buggy was so large it probably meant the baby wasn't fully positioned to be shielded by us both. It was all so hopeless.

The bullets were getting closer to my head.

I tried to scrabble more towards the back of the boat.

'We'll need to jump out!' shouted Gianna.

'Off the side, or off the back?'

The side would be easier. The back would be unexpected, but in the time it would take to stand up and grapple our way over the back they would see us and shoot us.

'The side it is,' I said. 'You are nearest, so you first.'

A bullet missed me by inches.

'Go! Now!' I shouted.

'The buggy is stuck!' she shouted back. 'There's a wheel stuck or a strap.' That buggy had been a breathtakingly poor choice on so many levels.

The baby was crying. Had it been crying all along? The bullets were so loud. I couldn't climb over Gianna and the baby to get to the sea beyond – it would be a flagrant act of cowardice. But in my defence, I didn't want to die; so I might have to do it.

I shrank further down the boat. I squatted my legs up. Gianna was now no longer covered by me – she was wrestling sideways with the buggy. I had bought myself at most ten extra seconds; they were being very methodical about shooting the hull in a steady line of fire. Water was already flooding into the boat.

Then they stopped.

The bullets just stopped.

They were shouting something at each other, but I couldn't hear; my ears were ringing.

215

Then there was another shot. Had they run out of ammunition? Did they think we were dead? Perhaps the idea was to drown us, not shoot us.

'They will sink,' I heard one of them say.

Their boat revved up. I was aware of my asthmatic breathing and nothing else. Did I have an inhaler? I hadn't had much trouble with my asthma since I'd moved to the Med, so I didn't always carry it.

There was more and more water in the boat. It took precedent over my health issues. The hull was already a foot deep in water. We were going to sink.

I knelt up to get my bearings. I could vaguely see land in the distance. It was a mile away. Perhaps two.

Gianna was standing now.

'Are there any life jackets?' I asked.

She was too busy trying to get the baby unstrapped.

I looked around. I couldn't see anything. Was there a pump perhaps, or a way of scooping out the water, or plugging the holes? But they weren't holes. They had shot a line out of the hull; it was a more or less continuous line, and we were shipping water at a rate than no one could bail out.

I sat down defeated.

'Oh typical!' spat Gianna. 'That's a great use.'

It was typical that given everything, it was me who Gianna was angry with. Wow was she irritating.

It struck me as a shame that my last thoughts on planet Earth would be all about my hate for the unbelievably irritating and irrationally angry Gianna Totti-Vincenzi.

But such is life.

THREE

I looked for storage areas on the boat. Perhaps I could find some life jackets. The last time I was stuck like this it was in a Bayliner halfway between Corsica and France. My biggest recollection of that night was that I had panicked too early; I did have a solution to the problem staring me in the face, but I had been too flustered to spot it. I vowed to myself that this time I'd be more systematic.

'Perhaps I can find a flare!' I shouted, trying to wrest some moral high ground from Gianna.

Gianna, for her part had her baby in one arm and was fiddling with the baby's changing bag.

'Could you help me with this?' she barked. Unbelievable. We were going to drown, and she wanted to change a nappy.

'Is the nappy soggy?' I asked, with what I judged to be just the right amount of sarcasm. 'Because it's going to be completely soggy when we all drown.'

I got forward to try some lockers at the front. The weight of my ample frame made the decking creak alarmingly; I was at the end of the boat where the hull was shredded. The first locker I opened was empty. I went to try the second one, but it was nearer the shot-out section of the hull; I would need to tread carefully. I could make the tear in the hull worse, or get my foot stuck as it pushed through.

'Help me with this bag, you moron!' she shouted.

I'm the moron?

'Perhaps if we find a spare fuel tank and empty it, we could use it as a flotation device?' I shouted back. I couldn't see a spare fuel tank, but it least I was having some ideas. What was her idea? Getting a baby's feeding bottle and using that as a buoy?

No, it turns out her idea was to get a mobile phone out of the baby's bag.

'You have a second mobile phone?' I asked.

'Yes, see if you can plug the water coming through, while I ring the emergency services.'

'Why have you got a second phone?' I asked.

'Why are you complaining?'

As Gianna shouted at the emergency services - because shouting is her well-established way of getting the best out of people - I got the baby's bedding and tried to wedge it into the more dramatic gashes in the boat's hull. The effect was cosmetic at best. The only tangible result would be that if by some miracle we were rescued, the baby no longer had any dry bedding.

The boat was now largely full of water; we were up to our knees.

Gianna rang the emergency services again to give them an extra shouting. Perhaps this was just her way of passing the time. The dispatcher on the phone told Gianna that in order for the emergency services to find her she should come off the line but hold her phone in front of her and do a figure-of-eight motion to help the satellite tracking be more accurate. I think she was just trying to get the angry lady off the phone and distract her with a minor task. After a minute of turning her phone in her wrist Gianna tried to delegate the job to me.

'No I'm good thanks,' I replied.

A police launch came to find us, followed soon after by some sort of coastguard vessel. I have never been so grateful to see some fellow human beings in my life.

They tied our boat up to theirs and placed an electric pump in it. We were given blankets and taken back to port. We didn't need the blankets, but I liked the look it gave us of heroic victims. It was particularly effective when we disembarked at the quayside; we looked like we'd been rescued from some major warzone. A group of tourists nudged each other and stopped to take our photos.

'Where's the stroller?' asked Gianna. She was suddenly very animated. 'Where's the stroller gone?'

'It's all sodden,' I said.

'No. The bedding is sodden, or gone, because you used it to try and plug a hole in the boat.' She added a particularly violent stare to that sentence. 'But the frame is fine. I can't get a third stroller in two days. This is ridiculous. They are expensive. And did you know they aren't covered on insurance? Not my insurance anyway. You're in insurance! You're happy enough to take the premiums I notice.' So basically, it was all my fault again.

'Here's the stroller,' said a policewoman. It had been placed under a bit of tarpaulin for safekeeping. Granted Gianna was angry most of the time, but I couldn't help noticing that her anger about possibly losing the buggy had a different quality about it; it was more about panic. I thought little of it at the time, though.

We were taken to the police station we had been in earlier.

'I demand that we see Commissario Antonioni!' shouted Gianna at a helpless policeman. The policeman cowered on cue; he had not expected the lady in the blanket with the Bride of Frankenstein hair to be this angry. I, meanwhile, wondered at the grammar of it. Given that Giulia Antonioni was a woman, should it be Commissaria rather than Commissario? Sadly my knowledge of Italian was too sparse to help me, and also wasn't she a lower rank than that?

Either way, it turned out that the staffing of the police station was too sparse to get us help in any reasonable timespan.

'I haven't eaten,' I said. This comment could go either way with Gianna. I braced myself for a sharp 'How can you think of food at a time like this?' But nothing occurred.

'We need to feed the baby and get some clothing and we need to eat,' she said. 'I also need to make a few phones calls.' Thought had replaced anger for a while. It was like Rock Paper Scissors, but in her case it was Anger, Maternal Instinct and Thought; sometimes, unexpectedly, Thought won out over Anger, though usually the thought in question was 'All men are awful', which is a close cousin to anger anyway.

'Are we actually under arrest here?' I asked a passing policeman; there was a lot of paperwork and wondering exactly what to do with us going on.

'No,' shrugged the lady. 'If you were under arrest it would be made clear to you.'

'Okay, in that case, we are going to take an hour to get the some dry bedding, and get the baby fed,' said Gianna. And most importantly, get me fed.

'But we're coming back,' threatened Gianna. 'Don't think we're finished!'

If I was them, I would be in two minds about buzzing us back in when we returned.

I found us a nice simple eatery and watched the departing frame of Gianna strop off to get supplies. When she came back, she indulged in another quick fume about how difficult it was to buy basic supplies in Venice 'because of all the tourists.' It was as wearying as ever. 'Oh there were fifteen different shops selling lace and festival masks. They aren't even made in Venice! We used to have a lace industry here, but no, the work is all farmed out to the far east and then even the woman who owns the shop selling the lace sublets it to a poor Chinese couple who are being charged far too much in rent...'

'You seem to have found some baby clothes somehow,' I interjected.

'Somehow,' she spat.

The baby in question had found its own chubby foot and was holding it. That was more than enough entertainment for him for the next ten minutes.

Gianna was distracted by a large plate of bites to eat. It was in fact a second plate – I had eaten the first and had its evidence removed by a waiter – but she didn't need to know that.

'I got you some food,' I said. There was some dried cod, some smoked mackerel fillets, and some grilled shrimp, all on little crisp sections of polenta. Best of all was the branzino – a kind of Mediterranean bass – cooked with caper butter. The silence from Gianna worried me. Was she just about to snarl that she was vegan and how had I not noticed? I was sure I had seen her eat fish.

'I'm really hungry,' she announced. 'Thank you. Life saver.'

'I refrained from ordering a drink for you,' I said. I was annoyed at how relieved I had sounded that she was not cross. This woman was tying me in knots. She should be the one apologising for being so profoundly bad tempered all the time; it has a permanent effect on anyone who shares her life. It is very draining.

I wondered if a glass of wine would be in order for me, but thought better of the idea. I try not to succumb to day drinking when I can; I have enough trouble with night drinking.

'Also, can I suggest the French fries?' said Gianna.

'What?'

'Well you like food. I thought I would suggest something.' She was being considerate; well this was a new development. But French fries?

We ordered a bowl of French fries, and when they arrived it turned out Gianna was onto something. They were an unusual shape. The potato had been cut into long U shapes, like gutters at the edge of a roof. It allowed for enough thickness of potato to give a crunchy outside and a soft inside, but extra surface area for the fat to work its magic and respond well to the balsamic vinegar I then sprinkled over them. Bliss. What an innovation. The only mistake we made was only ordering one bowl.

We finally hooked up with Detective Giulia Antonioni at around four o'clock; she brought a male colleague with her into the interview room.

We recounted our tale.

'Why do you have two phones?' asked the male detective.

'One for work and one for personal use. You're a man; surely you have one for work and one for surfing porn?'

'I'm a detective,' he replied.

'So that's a yes.'

'Gianna, stop antagonising everyone,' I said. 'They are trying to help us.'

'Are they though?' she replied. 'They keep asking us questions, but I don't see them offering any solutions. Three times now we have had our lives threatened. We should be dead by now, and yet somehow we are being treated with suspicion.

'You feel they were shooting the boat rather than you?' asked Giulia Antonioni.

'I am not sure,' I said. 'The side of the boat offered some protection from their bullets, so perhaps they thought they couldn't be sure of killing us with a bullet, but they could drown us if they sank the boat.'

'But they weren't aiming at you,' she persisted.

'They were working their way along the hull with their bullets,' said Gianna. 'They ran out of bullets, otherwise we would now be dead. Does it matter?'

'Yes,' replied the detective. 'It does matter.'

'Our lives are in danger. We thought we were safe in your hands, but we had barely left this police station this morning and...'

Detective Giulia Antonioni had heard enough.

'Could you leave the room please?' she said to her colleague.

The colleague looked surprised but shrugged and left. 'Do you want me to come back at all. I mean, it's four o'clock,' he asked. It was brazen; he fancied knocking off at four o'clock and was not worried if his colleague knew it. Coming to think of it, that's the sort of thing I do at the office.

When we were alone with Giulia Antonioni, she leant forwards to us. She whispered as if the room could be bugged, or someone could be watching through a one-way mirror.

'I have been making inquiries,' she began. 'It was all most hush hush which puzzled me. No one would talk to me at first, which just made me persist more; I had to escalate my enquiries up and up. It turns out your sister and your husband are alive and well and they are in a police safe house at a secret address.'

'Great!' I replied. At least I think the news was great.

'They are testifying against some of the most powerful families in the whole Metropolitan City of Venezia. I have explained to my superiors that your lives are also in danger. I had to stress again and again that you could be killed; that you had been attacked a number of times. But for some reason they were very reluctant to help you. I said, but these people could also testify to help your court case.'

She paused to let that sink in. She then opened a laptop and brought up a picture. It was a photograph of Adzio Amelio Icardi – Adam.

'Is this one of the men with guns, or the man piloting the boat or one of the men with a knife this morning?' asked the detective.

It had never crossed my mind that one of the masked men in the boat was Adam. I tried to recall the features of the men involved; their build, their gait, the shape of their facial features. I felt the detective, Giulia Antonioni, was trying to trade our safety for a commitment that we could drum up some evidence against Adam. It didn't feel right, but before I could form an opinion, Gianna piped up.

'Yes!' she cried. 'The one with the handgun. The pistol. It was Adam!'

'Would you swear to it?'

'Yes, I would swear to it.'

'Would you be willing to testify to that effect?' asked the detective.

'Yes,' said Gianna. 'Definitely. I don't know why I didn't realise this before.'

But Gianna was making this up. None of the men in the boat had the same build as Adam. I was sure of it. It was plain to me that Gianna was lying. But why?

FOUR

'How are you so sure it was Adam?' I asked. 'He was covered up.'

'I know him,' replied Gianna. 'I have known him for a number of years. You know when you recognise someone.'

I felt it should have been the detective pressing Gianna, not me. Instead, the detective listened without comment.

'But,' I persevered. 'He was completely covered up. In a witness box, if you give testimony, a defence lawyer could rip you to shreds.'

'No,' she replied. 'I'd rip him to shreds. He wasn't there. He didn't see what I saw. I know it was him.'

I didn't doubt that Gianna could rip a lawyer to shreds. The detective surprised us with a laugh; perhaps she was thinking the same thing. Even if Gianna wasn't lying, it still felt slim to me in terms of evidence; but perhaps if the police had more evidence up their sleeves? I wondered what Angelo and Emily were offering by way of testimony.

'So anyway,' said the detective. 'In the short term we are taking you to the safe house. You will be re-united with your husband. Pete, you will see your sister. What a holiday in Venice you are having!'

'Can we go there by gondola, at least?' I asked.

'I don't think that would help,' said the detective. She didn't realise I was joking.

We actually ended holed up somewhere else overnight. The police stressed time and again that we must not let slip any clues at all about what we were up to and where we were going. I, in reply, stressed time and again that I was happy to testify to everything I had seen and experienced – indeed it is my job and duty as an insurance fraud investigator – but I also needed regular decent food, and they should consider what wines they were going to lay on while we were in hiding. I believe in life you should always get your demands in early. I was largely joking, but they were surprisingly earnest as they listened; they were short of witnesses and evidence, it seemed, and they needed me.

News of our voluntary incarceration sent Gianna into a flood of fraught looking phone calls which we couldn't hear, but we could see through a glass door. She was pacing about and gesticulating; usually we would assume that a person on one end of the phone wouldn't be able to see or feel the gesticulations of the person on the other end, but somehow by sheer force of personality I felt Gianna was the exception to that rule.

'You alright?' I asked when she returned.

'People!' she said slumping down next to me.

'Where's the baby?' I asked.

She sprung up like she'd been stung. She'd left the baby in the other room.

That night, ludicrously, we spent in a very high-end hotel at police expense; although the experience was tarnished somewhat by not being allowed to leave our (luxury) rooms. I have no idea what the hold up was for us to go to the safe house; I can only imagine that they had to get the okay from someone in authority who worked 9 to 5.

I didn't sleep that night. Not so much through nerves; more through indigestion. We were allowed to order anything at all from the menu of the restaurant downstairs and it would be delivered to our rooms. Inevitably I ordered a seven course tasting menu. With cheese. It was partly out of boredom, but largely because I am childish and couldn't resist testing to destruction the edict that I could 'just order anything.' One course available on the menu was frogs legs stuffed with Italian sausage meat - which meant spicy garlicky pork – and herbs. It was suddenly all I wanted. It didn't strike me as a particularly Italian dish - but don't say I'm not tolerant of the whims of a nation's top chefs - and even if it turned out to be gross, I had the other six courses to fall back on. Plus cheese.

I spent the night lying on my back groaning and holding my stomach that had now swollen to the size and tension of a medicine ball. I couldn't move for the pain. That frog, whose legs I had eaten, certainly had the last laugh.

In the morning, detective Antonioni asked me how I was.

'Just fine thank you,' I replied.

The detective clearly had doubts and looked over my face with concern, then shrugged.

'Oh well, you're off to the safe house in an hour,' she said.

'You?' I asked. 'You said you not we. Are you not coming?'

'Apparently I am not trusted,' said the detective, laughing. 'They don't want anyone to know where the safe house is, who doesn't already know. Some specialist police will walk you there.'

'In that case, thank you for what you've done.' I said.

'And please, yet again,' she said. 'I need to stress you must not tell anyone who you are or where you are going.'

'It is pretty difficult. I no longer have a phone,' I replied. Or any idea where I even was.

When it was time to move, we were given baseball caps and dark glasses, and a police officer in civilian clothes – a female - took the baby and buggy and led the way. We were to follow about ten metres behind the buggy, and there was another plainclothes policeman about ten metres behind us. The two police had guns.

I have never felt so nervous in my life.

There was a woman with an odd-looking rucksack who somehow joined our convey for a while. She looked Arabic and what concerned me was that the rucksack looked full but was evidently very light. I couldn't make it out. The policeman behind us started to whistle a tune, and I think this was the cue for the policewoman ahead to move unexpectedly down a side alley. We all tensed up to see if the lady with the rucksack turned right also, but she just kept going forward and out of sight.

The policewoman with the baby then took us round the block to get back on course but comically she took us down a calle that got more and more narrow until the buggy got stuck. Even though Gianna was behind me, I could feel her tense up.

'The buggy?' I asked over my shoulder. 'You're worried she'll damage it?' I turned and caught Gianna mid eye-roll. At least she wasn't shouting.

'It's the idiocy I can't forgive,' she replied. 'Everyone knows you can't go this way; it's too narrow.'

We had to reverse back down the alley as a convoy, and somehow make it look as if we had all made this decision independently, and we weren't in the least bit related to one another.

Once out of the narrow alley I was now aware of two men in their thirties who seemed to be keeping pace with us as we arced back to our original course. I seemed to be the only one who had spotted them. When we slowed to allow for some school children, they slowed. When we turned left, they turned left. In fairness, they were quite some way back, but given the echoing nature of the calle I felt that if I mentioned it to anyone the men might hear, so I kept my thoughts to myself.

I stretched my neck up and round as if I was trying to resolve some muscle stiffness; it afforded me a good look at them. One had a black leather jacket and the other wore a trendy Puffa. They could easily be concealing weapons. The street we were in was narrow again. If they shot at us, they would hit the policeman at the rear. Then next in the line of fire would be Gianna, and then it would be me. Should I warn Gianna? I resolved that the moment there was any sign of a drawn weapon I would reach out for her and pull her to the ground. She would be angry of course, but it might save her life.

The two men pulled back a little. Perhaps it was all my imagination. The policeman at the rear was certainly keeping his eyes and ears out and seemed unperturbed; so perhaps everything was fine. The man in the Puffa pulled out his phone and dialled someone. Was he talking about us? Would more men now appear ahead of us in the alley and block our way? Probably not.

Or rather, we will never know because suddenly we were at the safe house.

There was a man sat on a low wall outside the safe house door. He looked seemingly unconnected to events, but our policewoman – the one with the baby buggy - walked straight up to him and they conferred. From time to time they looked our way. The man who was sitting, stood and nodded briskly. He knocked on a door.

The policewoman was all set to take the baby in herself, but Gianna stepped forward.

'Fine. I'll take it from here,' she said. 'I'll take the stroller.' Our two police escorts shrugged to each other and departed.

I could see it from Gianna's point of view. She wanted the father of her child to see that she was painstakingly looking after the baby while he had been running off with a floozy. I remembered with a jolt that the floozy in question was my sister.

Okay, now this will be interesting. How will Emily react to seeing Gianna? How will Angelo act? Will he be shamefaced, or will he brazen it out? Will he freeze out Emily or freeze out his wife, Gianna? Was Gianna going to turn on Emily?

It turned out it was none of the above.

Gianna got into the hallway of the safe house and noticed something about the baby that demanded her attention. She bent down to release him from his bedding.

As a result, although I was the second to enter the building, I was the first to get through to the kitchen area and greet Emily.

'How is your holiday going? How do you like Venice so far?' she asked. Funny.

'Action packed,' I replied. 'This must be Angelo?'

Emily nodded and then introduced the two detectives and the police guard beyond. I shook their hands in turn.

'So this must be Gianna,' said Emily pointing down the corridor.

I turned to catch Angelo's expression to see how he'd react to Gianna. He was blank. He drew an uneasy breath and half rose out of his chair.

'That's not Gianna,' he said.

He backed back a little, but his chair largely impeded his movement.

'That's not Gianna,' he repeated louder. He was alarmed.

The woman who I knew as Gianna had finished with the baby. From underneath his bedding she had pulled out a gun.

A solid looking handgun with a silencer.

The sort professionals use.

FIVE

Emily was the most alert. It was like she'd seen more movies than me and knew what to do; which is odd, because I thought no one had seen more movies than me. She got both hands and upended the kitchen table. It formed a shield between us and the hallway, and we instinctively dived behind it. I think the two detectives dived to one side, leaving Angelo, Emily and myself behind the shield of the table and the detectives to our right, deeper in the kitchen.

But now what?

There was a shot. A soft-sounding shot, so it was probably Gianna – or rather the erstwhile Gianna - shooting us; she was the one with the silencer.

'You can't shoot me,' she shouted. 'I have a baby in front of me.' Was she crouching behind the baby buggy and using it as a shield?

Where was the police guard in all of this? Had he drawn his weapons and there was a Mexican stand-off? Did the two detectives have guns?

'There's no need for any heroics,' shouted Gianna. 'I just want Angelo.'

I looked across at Angelo. She wanted him dead. The star witness. We could hardly just hand him over. Even in this 'He's Spartacus!' era, we weren't going to sacrifice him. Absurdly, I looked to Emily for some sort of lead.

'Where are the detectives?' I mouthed.

She shrugged.

A gun went off. A loud one. A police gun.

Within a second there was a muffled shot from the corridor; Gianna's gun with the silencer.

'Well now he's dead!' lamented Gianna. 'I told you it was stupid to act the hero. He took a pot shot at me.' She was sounding outraged – incandescent – this was the 'Gianna' I knew; so her temper wasn't all an act, at least. 'That's exactly what I didn't want to do,' she shouted. 'And now he's dead.'

'The windows have bars,' whispered Emily. 'We can't get out of this apartment. Not without going past her.'

There was a banging on the door. The policeman outside was shouting. My ears were ringing from the gunfire in the safe house, so I was probably hearing some things but not others. The banging on the door got louder. Someone was shouting to be let in. Someone was shouting that he was calling for back-up.

'She's edging the stroller forward.' That was Angelo. I think there was a mirror on a wall on his side that allowed him a bit of a view.

Shielding behind a baby. Genius. But whose baby? If she wasn't Angelo's wife then presumably it also wasn't Angelo's baby.

And where were the other two policemen?

'I'm warning you!' shouted Gianna.

She shot again. Something heavy fell against something else heavy and knocked it over.

'Next time, it won't be your ankle,' she said. 'Now take out your weapons slowly and skim them across the floor.'

A pause.

'Easy now,' she said. 'I will take great pleasure at aiming at your balls. Then you'll no longer be a tosser.'

She'd fired two more shots. I vaguely remembered that you should count the number of bullets an assailant fires; there was a chance she would run out of ammunition and then we could rush her. There was also a chance she was a highly trained hitman who knew how to reload a gun.

The banging at the door got louder still. The policeman outside was trying to knock the door down. Was it possible we could stall 'Gianna' until the police reinforcements came? Could we bargain with her? Appeal to her better side. Oh, what was I thinking? 'Gianna' had no better side.

There was a shot further away; it must have been outside the door. The banging on the door abruptly stopped. I realised in that moment what had happened. The two men who had been trailing us on the way to the safe house weren't out to get me and 'Gianna' at all, they were *with* 'Gianna'. And now they knew where the safe house was and they had shot the guard outside.

The whole thing was now falling into place in my head. All the attacks on us – the gunmen on Poveglia, the men with knives who cornered us in an alley, the men who shot our boat out at sea - it was never their intention to kill us at all. It was all a put-up job to make it look as if we desperately needed protection; to get us into the safe house; to get us united with Angelo so they could kill the star witness.

I thought it was odd at the time that I managed to overpower a man with a knife just by twerking; now I knew why. It wasn't just that we had been blind; it was more the scale of the forces reined against us - their organisation, their determination, their ruthless efficiency; the sheer number of them. It wasn't a case of not seeing the wood for the trees; the whole bloody forest was against us. They were outside the door, they were waiting in unknown numbers at unknown locations throughout the city. Even if we somehow prevailed against this one woman with a gun, she would be replaced; and sooner or later they would win.

'Right,' said Gianna. 'Now you three behind the table are going to need to stand up.'

We looked at each other, frozen with indecision.

'I just want Angelo,' she said. 'No one needs to be a hero.'

Did that make it cowardice for me and Emily to stand up? I motioned with my hand for us all to stay down.

'I'll shoot through the table if you don't stand up,' she said. 'I will shoot indiscriminately.'

If we stood, then we would sacrifice Angelo, but if we stayed sheltered and showed unity with Angelo then we would all die; we would die, and no one would even know our story, they wouldn't even know we'd been brave. I hated myself for even having that thought; but it was the thought that I had.

There was a scuffle.

Had one of the policemen made a lunge for Gianna?

A muffled shot went off.

'I told you, you would regret that,' she said. 'Did I get your thigh, or did I get your balls?'

There was an involuntary whimpering by way of response.

There was some movement and we ducked down, tense. I have no idea why we imagined that tensing our backs would protect us from bullets.

It turned out that 'Gianna' had got the detective and the policeman in abeyance enough that she could go to the front door to let her accomplices in.

We heard rapid footsteps towards us. Men's footsteps. They conferred in whispers then 'Gianna' said, 'Okay, I've done my bit. I'm off.'

There were more footsteps.

'Shall we rush them?' asked Emily.

Before I could reply, a man with a gun appeared over the top of our table edge. He had a balaclava on his head.

He addressed Emily.

'Which one of these is Angelo?' he asked.

Emily refused to answer.

'I asked, which one of these is Angelo?'.

He looked from Angelo to me and back again. He made a decision.

He placed his gun firmly on my forehead.

The gunman stared hard at Emily.

He pressed the muzzle deeper into my skull.

'I will ask you one more time, lady. And then I will shoot. Which one is Angelo? Three. Two, One.'

SIX

The man pulled the trigger back. It was just loud enough for us to hear.

Angelo gasped.

'That one,' said Emily. She flicked her head in the direction of Angelo.

The man swung his gun round and shot Angelo clean through the head.

It transpires - to the credit of Emily and myself - that our next reaction was to see if there was any chance at all we could save Angelo's life and also somehow wrest some control. Without conferring, we both sprung up. I won't claim massive bravery in this; the gunmen had made it pretty clear that they were only after Angelo and after shooting him, he had disappeared from our vision.

When we stood, however, we could see that the gunman was in fact aiming his gun at the injured policeman on the floor. He was going to kill him.

Emily was galvanised. She sprang up on a chair and over the upturned table. The gunman looked surprised but was too slow to react. Before he knew it, she had charged into him at waist height. He keeled backwards and shot his gun into the ceiling.

But Emily also lost her balance and reeled against the wall.

The next thing we knew, the gunman had got to his feet and disappeared out the door.

There was nothing we could do for Angelo – the bullet had gone clean through his brain and out the other side.

I turned to survey the scene. There was a dead policeman the other side of the upturned table. Again, it was clear he was dead; the woman calling herself Gianna was a deadly shot. To our side there was the second detective and the policeman. The policeman had a kitchen wiping-up cloth and was pushing it hard against his inner thigh. He was a dreadful colour grey, but he was probably going to survive. The plain clothes detective was clutching the end of his foot with his hand and doing rhythmic breathing; he was obviously in a lot of pain, but would also pull through.

We had all forgotten about the baby until, in the silence, he tried an exploratory cry to see if he could summon any adults.

'If this baby didn't belong to that woman then who does it belong to? I mean, you just don't leave a baby if it's yours,' I asked.

No one answered.

The detective on the ground was trying to say something.

'You saved my life,' he whispered. 'Emily, you saved my life.'

We discovered who the baby was the next day. We were being debriefed by Giulia Antonioni at the police station.

'How many detectives have there been?' I asked.

'What?' she replied. She didn't understand the question.

'Well Emily and I have been comparing notes. There were detectives who Emily went to when she was abducted. There were detectives I talked to when I thought Emily was missing. There were detectives looking into the fraud at the insurance company and then another bunch who were interviewing Emily at the safe house.'

'So?'

'So, it is one case,' I said.

'It didn't seem one case at first,' she said. 'And there are different departments.'

'No,' I said. 'It strikes me that some of the detectives and some of the police are more trusted than some others. When the gunman came into the safe house, they only wanted to kill Angelo. He was the only one who was offering decent quality evidence against Adam and the rest. Somehow they knew that. So there must have been a leak.'

'Really?'

'One of the detectives or police escorts had been monitoring progress of the talks and they had leaked it.'

'We don't know that,' said Giulia Antonioni.

'The detectives were the same each day in the safe house,' said Emily. 'And the gunmen wanted them dead too. But the police guard changed a lot,' said Emily. 'It would just take one of them to be on the bad side...'

And how could we be sure that Giulia Antonioni wasn't on the bad side also? When we went to the Turturro residence it was suspect that she was somehow available and on the scene to 'help' us. She had then pretended to listen to our tales of being attacked, and 'Gianna' had insisted we see her again. It was Giulia Antonioni who had begged and pleaded that we be allowed into the safe house; her bosses had been against the idea. She said herself her bosses didn't trust her.

'So who was the baby?' asked Emily.

The detective smiled, grateful to be onto a more positive topic.

'It turns out that the woman pretending to be Gianna had applied to be a nanny for a young working couple here in Venice,' explained the detective. 'It was her actual job to look after the baby from 8am to 6pm. It was the perfect cover.'

'So, that's why she didn't have the baby in the evenings,' I said.

'And the one evening she did keep the baby she made up a whopping lie that she was on the mainland and had got caught out by the train times. She told the couple she and the baby would stay overnight in Treviso.'

'I remember her making the calls,' I said.

'But when the nanny and baby didn't re-appear the following evening their suspicions were raised and they ended up reporting the baby as missing. They were out of their minds with worry. Funnily enough, it didn't occur to us at first that we had the baby ourselves. That's what comes of having too many detectives on the case!' She looked pleased with herself, that she had found a way to make light of my earlier questioning.

'So, she was what?' I asked. 'A professional assassin?'

There were non-committal nods from the detective.

'We can only assume,' she said. 'I did wonder about her. She claimed she was Venetian but when I spoke to her in the Venetian dialect she bluffed. She didn't understand me.' The detective was placing space between herself and 'Gianna'.

'Gianna was bloody convincing otherwise,' I said. 'All the details about her supposed life with Angelo. Her pretend pregnancy, her anger, her soul-searching; she really had me fooled. I suppose to a degree she was tapping into a stereotype I was willing to swallow - the stereotype of the angry wronged wife - and she'd certainly done her homework. Where is she now?'

'She has disappeared,' said the detective. 'It is not clear she was a hitman per se. It was her job to get access to the safe house. There is evidence she didn't want to kill anyone herself. We have checked databases for a female hitman. But no one like her appears.'

'She knew a lot about Venice,' I offered.

'Well that hardly narrows it down. Presumably the story she spun about Angelo having an affair with Emily was a ruse to keep Pete tight with her so she would get to the safe house with him.'

'I did feel I kind of owed her something on behalf of Emily,' I said. 'And me and her together had more credibility when we talked about being attacked and so forth; more credibility than just one of us spinning a yarn.' I had a thought. I addressed the detective. 'If you had suspicions about fake Gianna because she didn't understand Venetian and so on, why didn't you check the baby's stroller carefully for weapons?'

'I thought we had,' said the detective. When? At what stage?

'And "Gianna" kept insisting we dealt with you, not other detectives,' I said.

Giulia Antonioni shrugged at that, but she wouldn't meet my eye. Gianna had put on a great show about arguing with the detective; changing the baby on her desk and so on, but they could easily have been in league.

'It turned out the weapon was in a hollowed out section of the baby's mattress,' said the detective, half changing the subject.

'Okay, well what about us?' asked Emily. 'Should I be in fear of my life? Am I still to testify? Have you arrested Adam?'

'We don't have enough proof against Adam,' replied the detective.

'What?' Emily was incredulous.

'But Adam kept directing us to go to places like Poveglia to put us in danger,' I ventured. 'He was guilty as sin.'

'No,' said the detective. 'I have been listening carefully to your account, and in each case it was "Gianna" *claiming* that Adam had told her where you should go. In fact she could have been making it up.'

'Okay,' I said. 'But he was the one who vouched that Gianna was Gianna. That shows they were in league.'

'We have interviewed him at length,' said the detective. 'We asked him why he vouched for Gianna. He says that she introduced herself as being Angelo's wife and he had no reason to disbelieve her, so he introduced her as Gianna to you. He says it was an honest mistake.'

'But then you didn't check her identity,' I said. Further proof that the detective was involved.

'Neither did you,' she replied. 'You took her at face value as well.'

'But I'm not a detective.' We were rapidly falling out with Giulia Antonioni. 'Surely it is bread and butter for the police to ask for identity documents when dealing with such cases.'

Emily snorted in agreement.

'When you think about,' countered the detective. 'The most proof of who did the crime is pointing at Emily here. She still has no evidence she was abducted that time. It was her computer that okayed the claims.'

'Oh great!' said Emily.

'Anyway, you will be alright,' said the detective.

'How so?' asked Emily.

'You saved the detective's life. Saving the life of a policeman from the gunman has made you a legend round here. Every policeman in Venice will want to step up and protect you. They are hardly going to go out of their way to gather evidence on you, and convict you now.'

'Sort of,' said Emily.

But it was true. Emily had been a hero and had saved a life.

'So,' said Emily. 'To recap, I have to go to work and play nice and sit next to Adam at the office, just like nothing has happened?'

'Just arrest him!' I said. 'See what happens. There is his wonky testimony about what happened in the office when the woman in red turned up, there is...' I realised there was little or no proof against Adam, it was just that it seemed like he was the only person who could have done it.

'The trouble is,' said the detective. 'The actual proof is stacked against Angelo, not Adam. It was his computer that okayed the claims, after all.'

'What about the tapes that the police have, that incriminated Adam in the first place? His phone conversations?'

The detective shrugged. 'They are not conclusive. They talk in code, they talk about getting the job done and generalities like that. It wouldn't be enough on its own to convict him.'

The police really had been relying on the testimony of Angelo. And even that, according to Emily, might have been fabricated. Their other 'witness' was Gianna; and she had pretended she would testify against Adam just to get into the safe house.

Emily considered all this and slumped. She turned to me.

'Don't leave me,' she said. 'Stay in Venice.'

PART FOUR

THE WORLD ACCORDING TO EMILY

ONE

I don't get it. I have to sit at work, side by side with Adam? And we are all going to Angelo's funeral when the inquest is over. It's obscene. And I have to make light conversation and get on with work like nothing happened?

And am I even safe? Why was I kept alive? It would have been perfectly easy to shoot me along with Angelo. Are they keeping me as an option to blame the fraud on?

'It seems wrong using his desk,' said Adam.

On my first day back, he came in to work nearly an hour late. I thought he wasn't coming at all. He was still technically my assistant, although I kissed goodbye to any semblance of that dynamic when we slept together. And he arranged for my kidnapping. And he framed me for a major crime. And had Angelo shot. Nonetheless I tried a, 'You're late.'

'I had a meeting with Marco,' he replied.

'What do you mean, it seems wrong using his desk?' I asked. Because you had him killed?

'Well, he's only just died.'

He sat at his own desk. It hadn't moved, but it now seemed far closer to mine than before.

'But why would you use his desk?' I asked.

'Because I've been promoted to his job,' he replied.

Should I get up straightaway and have a word with Marco? They had promoted Adam? Why? It made no sense. The police were only the previous week claiming he was behind the entire multi-million euro fraud. They have promoted him? Bewilderment and defeat left me rooted to my chair.

I realised I hadn't done anything for twenty minutes or so. I hadn't even tapped on my keyboard pretending to work. Had Adam noticed? He certainly hadn't said anything.

I brought up a blank Word document.

I typed, 'I will kill Adam.' I pressed return and on the next line I wrote, 'I will kill Adam.' On the following line I typed, 'Adam must die' just for the variation. It gave me the appearance of doing work and the tiniest amount of catharsis.

'Do you want coffee?' asked Adam. He was standing behind me. Right behind me. Was he looking at my screen? Did I even care?

I looked up at him. I properly looked at him for the first time since he had entered the office. He was looking out the window. He was not focussed on anything, certainly not on my computer screen. He was daydreaming. Daydreaming about killing? About fraud? About what this fraud will get him from the grateful families of Venice? About what he wants for lunch? At least he wasn't springing around and buzzing off to schmooze with colleagues; that was something at least.

Do I want coffee?

'No, I'm good,' I replied, about a minute after he'd asked.

I deleted the Word document and felt guilty. But why should I feel guilty?

Five minutes later I made myself a cup of coffee and returned with it. That'll teach him.

'You had one after all,' he said. He smiled. The sort of smile you use on people with dementia. Like I had cognitive impairment. Cognitive impairment that this lad half my age and wearing eye-wateringly trendy designer clothes was some sort of criminal mastermind.

How many weeks more did I have to work here before I could go back home? Every day would feel like a year. I couldn't believe they'd promoted him.

I walked down the corridor and knocked on Marco's door.

He looked flustered when he saw me.

'You've promoted Adam?' I asked. I planted my hands on his desk and bent down to bring my eyes in line with his.

'He is the obvious man at short notice,' replied Marco. Notice he said man. 'He knows the cases. We are snowed under. There is no obvious alternative.'

'He conspired to defraud this company of millions of euros, and you promote him?'

Marco's eyes darted left and right. He looked confused. He actually looked confused. 'I'm finding you intimidating,' he said. Not confused then; afraid. Afraid of me.

I raised my hands up in disbelief.

'And that's even more intimidating,' he said.

'I don't believe I'm hearing this.'

'No,' he said. 'Let's get this straight. You are the one who appeared to defraud the company of millions of euros, but for some reason the senior management are not pressing charges and neither are the police.'

What? My incomprehension stopped me speaking. It was like discovering the whole world was the opposite of everything I thought. It was like being told that left was now right, and up was now down; and when you look round the room for corroboration, everyone just nods along with the guy talking.

'Adam has been very gracious about the allegations you made about him,' continued Marco. 'Allegations that have no foundation whatever.'

'What?'

'This is what I've been told,' said Marco.

By whom? Where was he getting this from?

'I want you to undertake to not cause any more trouble until this matter has been fully resolved. I would put you on gardening leave, but we are so short staffed. I think you should know I have asked for you to be replaced.'

'But Adam is the one who did it!'

'And you are not to repeat anything like that to anyone whatever.'

What?

'Are you a local?' I asked.

'What's that got to do with anything?'

It's got everything to do with everything.

'Adam is a highly respected colleague from a highly respected local family,' said Marco. 'A family whose ties in Venice go back centuries.'

'Highly respected? By whom?'

'You would be wise to not utter a word of slander about him. Not a single word. They are a very important family.'

I stormed out the office. I would have slammed his door, but no doubt it would have been deemed aggressive. And they would probably be right.

I went for a walk round Venice. A random walk, just following my nose and enjoying the sights like I should have been doing all along. I bought myself a little tub of gelato. I ate it with a purple plastic spoon which I then licked and put in my pocket to save the dolphins.

I rang Pete and arranged coffee.

'I'll be twenty minutes. I'm on Lido having a walk along the beach,' he said. 'I'll take a water taxi.'

We arranged to meet at a bar. To kill the time until Pete turned up, I kept walking. I was so agitated.

I was being followed.

I was sure of it.

I took a winding route to St Marks Square. I walked right to the middle of it. It drew the man behind me out into the open. Short hair. Obviously Italian. Leather jacket. None of the ambling or confusion of a tourist. When I had got him right in the open, I spun on my heel and walked fast towards him. I accelerated. He stopped in his tracks. He appeared to neither see me nor not see me. I walked straight at him, and at the last minute I swerved. I was soon in a side street again.

At the café bar Pete was already seated. He had an espresso on the go.

'I'm being followed,' I said.

I looked around for the man in the leather jacket. I couldn't see him.

I told Pete all about my talk in Marco's office. He considered what I said.

'But we know this,' he said. 'The detectives in the safe house and the woman detective Giulia; they were the ones who were so adamant that they had evidence against Adam. The evidence, such as it is, has probably been kept hush hush and high up. The detectives in the safe house dealt with people higher up in our company, not the likes of Marco. Dealing with these top Venetian families is a sensitive topic. The lower down detectives probably still assume you are involved, and there is no evidence against Adam.'

'Yeah, okay, but that leaves me dangling,' I replied. 'It puts me in a terrible position.'

'I'll ring the detective. Giulia Antonioni,' said Pete. 'I'll see what she can suggest.'

'Well I don't trust her,' I said.

'Well we don't trust anyone,' he countered. 'But at least she keeps us in the loop.'

'Look, there is the man who is following me,' I hissed. 'Over my left shoulder. Pretending to look at lace in a shop window.'

Pete took his photo, then put a call through to the detective. They had a brief but useful conversation. He then forwarded the picture of the man who was following me. He soon got a text in return.

'Apparently he is a policeman. He is protecting you,' he said.

'Or tracking my every move.' I didn't know how I felt. Either my life was in danger, or I was still a potential suspect; neither option was good.

I ordered some coffee.

'Tell them to stop following me,' I said. 'I'll take my chances.'

Pete shrugged and texted the detective.

'I was forced by that gunman to choose whether he shot you or Angelo!' I said. 'I keep having flashbacks. I have never been so traumatised in my life. I dream about it. I keep imagining I can see Angelo's face just before he was shot.

But in fact, I don't think I was looking at him at the time; I've kind of painted the memory in. It all happened so fast.'

'If you hadn't have said which of us was Angelo then the man would have shot both of us,' said Pete. 'It wasn't your fault. You didn't shoot the gun.'

'It felt like I did.'

Pete got his hands and held my hands; an intimacy neither my brother nor I were used to.

'You saved my life,' he said. 'And you saved the policeman's life. I had a gun to my head. Believe me when I tell you I am very grateful that you identified Angelo as Angelo. Even if I burn in hell for saying it. I am grateful to be alive. You are my sister. You did the right thing.'

'Thank you for that. I did want to pay you back for helping with the shoplifting all those years ago. And, well, other stuff.'

'When they make a movie of this, you will be played by Meryl Streep,' he said.

'What?' I protested. 'Not someone younger?' Oh, who am I kidding? This whole saga has aged me horribly.

'I was referring to the movie Sophie's Choice.'

'Yeah I know. But Rachel McAdams, at least. Rosamund Pike? I could channel Rosamund Pike.'

'So now you're playing yourself in this movie.'

'It'll be my breakthrough role.'

Pete changed his demeanour; in that way you do when you want someone to understand there is some bad news to break.

'What?' I asked.

'The thing is,' he said. 'There's only so long I can hang around Venice. I do have a job.'

'When are you going?' I asked.

'A couple of days. Three, four. Will you be alright?'

I was jolted by a text.

It was from Adam.

'I've got a text from Adam!' I said. I couldn't believe my eyes.

'What does it say?'

It said, 'Management have been asking where you are. I have covered for you as best I can, but best come back to office.'

Wow.

I slumped in my chair. I felt so powerless. So helpless.

TWO

Covid-19 was getting a foothold in Europe and there were rumours in the media that we may end up confined to our houses. The public were busy learning new words and abbreviations; self-isolating, social distancing, PPE, and the governments were busy passing laws.

In 1975 the Italian government had passed a law that you couldn't wear a mask over your face in public; it was to help prevent bank raids, terrorism and the like. Now they were busy unpicking the law in case we had to wear surgical masks in shops. At about the same time, we had a missive from our management that if we weren't allowed into the office then we would have to use remote computer access to do our work from home. Oh the irony. I couldn't wait; working from home had to be better than sitting next to Adam every day.

I tried to work. I really tried to work. But the absurdity of the situation had totally got to me. I made discreet inquiries about what on earth people thought had gone on in the safe house. It turns out, the way everyone saw it, Angelo and I had been taken in by the police for lengthy questioning and then there had been a shoot out. With Angelo dead, and not much evidence against me, the police had reluctantly released me. As a result, at the office I was tolerated, at best; I was the one walking the fine line, not Adam. I was the one who was lucky not to be charged with major crimes.

And all the while Adam was chatting loudly in the corridors with colleagues, giggling over office gossip, and flirting with the female temps. He'd even bought yet more clothes. Who buys new clothes and shows them off when a colleague has just been murdered? Who shows no remorse or regret for his crimes? A sociopath. A psychopath.

When Adam wasn't giggling with the temps and showing off his new Gucci waistcoat, he'd sit to my left tapping on his computer. Somehow the tapping on his keyboard was now much louder.

He had the sense, at least, not to make mindless conversation with me; but because of his restless brain, instead of talking he had taken to humming. Sometimes he'd hum tunes I didn't know - young people's music - but often he'd hum show tunes, usually from A Star is Born. Coming to think of it, A Star is Born is about an underling who usurps the older mentor. The older person then kills themselves. Was that the point? Was that why Adam was humming those tunes? If I hadn't been in chronic shock, I would have found that funny.

One afternoon Adam tried to make small talk.

'Do you know what today is?' he asked.

Silence from me. This was taken by Adam as an invitation to keep talking.

'Today is the first day of the Carnevale!' he said. 'The Venice carnival. The masked balls...'

'No it's not,' I protested.

'Ha! I knew I could get you to speak,' he replied. 'Indeed, the Carnevale started on Saturday. There was a musical acrobatic thing on the water near St Marks Square. Did you see it?'

My silence felt churlish. But he was the one who should feel guilty every second of every day, not me. 'No,' I said at last.

'Well, that is for the tourists and the very rich,' said Adam. 'The real fun starts tonight. I have an invitation to a masked party tomorrow. Everyone of importance will be there. Want to come?'

So, not small talk at all. An invitation. An invitation!

'What, like a date?' I asked. The brass balls of the man.

He slid his chair closer to mine. I could feel a breath of concern on my bare arm. This twenty something who barely needed to shave was pretending to be concerned for *me*?

'You've suffered a big trauma. I can only imagine what you went through,' he said. 'You might find getting out helps. It's better than being at home drinking alone.'

Patronising shit.

'I don't drink alone.' I replied. I drink with Pete. Then I go home and drink alone. Then when Pete leaves Venice, I'll skip the bit where I go out first.

'So how about it?' he asked.

Adam was asking me out. How do I respond to that?

'Where do you get off on this?' I asked. 'Seriously. Sit there.' I motioned to his desk and his chair. I placed pencils in a line down the surface of my desk to define my territory. It felt childish, but good.

'Okay!' He put his hands up in a mock gesture of defeat; apparently when he puts his hands up, it's not aggressive. 'Just trying to help,' he said.

You were complicit in having Angelo murdered because he was going to testify against you. You forced me to choose between having my own brother shot or Angelo shot. And you say are trying to help? Just sack me, or arrest me for a crime I didn't commit; anything has to be better than this.

I stood up and walked back to Marco's office.

'Can't I be transferred now?' I asked.

'On what grounds?'

'On the grounds that I have to share an office with a man who has framed me for a multi-million euro fraud.'

'Seriously Emily!'

'What?'

'Do not repeat that allegation,' he said. Well he didn't say it, he whispered it so no one could overhear. What was he afraid of? 'Anyway, haven't they taken your passport away?'

They had taken my passport away. I was under suspicion. Wow. He was right. The man who had been following me, the plain clothes policeman, hadn't been there to protect me at all; he was tracking my movements. I still reckoned I glimpsed him from time to time. I had been in too much of a daze to realise the basics.

Marco set his face in an expression of, 'You can say anything you like; I will not utter another word.' It was the parental disapproval look that characterised my childhood; you've let us down so many times, there is nothing more to say. Don't you hate parents when they try that kind of crap?

I went off to the toilets and rang Pete.

'What are you doing?' I asked.

He took it as a criticism; it must have been my tone of voice. I was just trying to get my mind off things; connect with my one sane ally.

'I'm on a sun recliner on the terrace of my hotel with a blanket over my legs reading a book?' he replied. For a man who hates Australian inflection – making a question out of a statement? – he indulged in a lot of it.

'What book?'

'Does it matter? I'm allowed to read a book,' he said.

'I'm just making conversation.'

'Well you're sounding angry, like you've taken tips from Gianna.'

'How do I get back to Corsica?' I asked.

'Just go! They'll replace you.'

'I haven't got a passport.'

'You could take a train and a ferry.'

'I've rented out my apartment in Airbnb.'

'You could stay at mine?'

My head was now full of images of Pete's place. Unmade beds with dirty sheets. Dirty wine glasses and encrusted saucepans piled up in the sink. My stomach gave an involuntary lurch.

'Can you get a maid or something? A cleaner?' I asked.

'What?'

'And he asked me out!'

'Who asked you out?'

'Adam! He's asked me on a date to go to a masked ball tomorrow.'

'Why?' asked Pete.

'I think he's trying to act like he's totally innocent and trying to help. Or maybe he can't resist returning to the scene of the crime.'

'You're the scene of the crime in that metaphor.'

'Precisely,' I said. 'Or he's just a psychopath sadist. He wants to torture me.'

'There is another possibility,' said Pete.

'There is?'

'Yeah. I've been thinking. Why kill Angelo, but not kill you also? You also were going to testify against Adam. So why not kill you?'

'I don't know,' I replied.

'What if Angelo had done the crime after all?'

'How do you get that?'

'Perhaps he was the stooge who did the donkey work of the fraud; and once the money had been paid out, the organised crime syndicate had no further use for him. He knew everything. What if they thought he was sitting in that safe house spilling the beans against the syndicate? What if no detective or guard in the safe house snitched at all, and the syndicate simply assumed Angelo was testifying against them?'

'But the police said they had their suspicions about Adam,' I countered.

'Two police said that. The others still seem to think you may be involved and therefore also Angelo. Or perhaps the original plan that was spun to Angelo was that a few police in the pay of the syndicate would drum up a case against Adam and he should do the same. The trouble was, Adam is also well-connected and his family was also involved, so they were hardly going to let him go down for the fraud.'

I tried to think this possibility through. It made sense of why Angelo had changed his tune about Adam and started saying he could identify him as a kidnapper.

'Also,' continued Pete. 'It makes sense of why Adam is acting so innocent. In this scenario, he really is innocent.'

'If Angelo was the perpetrator, why shoot the detective in the safe house?'

'He was involved in the ruse to frame Adam. When an assassin turned up to kill Angelo, then the detective assumed he was next. So he opened fire on Gianna, and Gianna had to take him out.'

My head was spinning. 'It still seems to me that...' Actually I had no idea how it seemed to me. 'I still think it is Adam. I know he is young and irritating, but I reckon he's the villain of the piece. Adam is guilty and Giulia Antonioni was the bent copper who helped get fake Gianna into the safe house. That's my instinct.'

'So go,' said Pete.

'Go where?'

'Go to the ball with him,' said Pete. 'Get to know him. He is full of youthful exuberance. Get him drunk, get him talking. You might be able to get evidence on him. Certainly, you will be able to settle in your own mind if it was really Adam or Angelo.'

'It's Adam,' I said. If I kept saying it, I might convince myself.

'Then gather your proof,' said Pete. 'No one else seems to be bothering. It's down to us. Gather your proof, or settle your mind. If you do come to realise it was Angelo, then you are going to feel a lot better about telling the gunman which one he was; it turned out he had you abducted and holed up with rats.'

I sat on the staff toilet with my head in my hands and my phone against my ear. I closed my eyes. I didn't have any other plan. And it did seem like a plan. I certainly couldn't go on the way I was.

'Can I come?' asked Pete.

'What?'

'Moral support. And I've never been to a masked ball. I could be your excuse to leave at any time. I am your guest here in Venice after all.'

'Seriously?'

'What's the dress code?' asked Pete.

'Anything interesting, apparently.'

'Oh, and boy parts.'

'What?'

'The book I am reading is Boy Parts, by Eliza Clark. You asked me what book I was reading.'

'I've heard it's disgusting; sexual and depraved.'

'Yeah, I love it. It's inspiring me to write something similar. Something similar but from the opposite, male, perspective. Harvey Weinstein; My View of Events.'

'Good luck with that,' I said.

THREE

'Adam?'

'Your coffee's gone cold.'

'Yeah. Look I realise I have been a bit of a dick. I have found recent events so traumatising. I keep lashing out. It's bringing out the worst in me. I'm sorry.'

I hate it when we girls apologise when we've done nothing wrong. 'Sorry you bumped into me.' 'Sorry to interrupt you in a meeting.' 'Sorry I made you so angry that you hit my face.' The 'girl sorry' is one of my all-time biggest peeves, but it has its uses; it throws men off their guard. It lulls them into thinking they're superior. It certainly worked on Adam.

'Oh that's okay,' he said. 'You've been through a lot.'

He put his hand around me. He was going to give me a hug. I tried not to stiffen from head to toe; but the body does its own thing. It didn't stop him hugging me. How dare he hug me.

Should I call him out on this? If I complained that a co-worker comforted me after I was involved in a shooting, I'd look like a complete bitch. And Pete was right; we were at a dead end. The police had apparently dropped the case against Adam. Angelo and a detective were dead because of him, and we were the last ones interested. If he was going to get his comeuppance, it was down to us. That's assuming he was guilty.

Adam moved his arm up my back slightly and I jolted like I'd been electrocuted. He must have felt that surely.

I squeezed him back, as a means of then extricating myself; I put my hands on his upper arms and pushed back as if to survey his face.

'Thank you,' I nodded.

I changed my body language to wilt slightly. I got my index finger and played with my lower lip. I tugged my hair across my face and flirted through it.

'Can you do me a little favour?' I asked. 'Can my brother Pete also come to the ball?'

I had become the sort of woman I hate. The sort who does mock flirting to get what she wants. I disgusted myself. It had better all be worth it.

'So you are coming?' he asked. He looked absolutely thrilled. 'This is amazing news.'

'Okay?'

'Oh I am so pleased.' He was buzzing. He was pleased out of all proportion. I didn't get it. Perhaps he gets a thrill from a woman stiffening while he embraces her. Or perhaps he really was innocent and I really had meant more to him that I realised, and he was thrilled to be dating me again.

'You're really pleased, aren't you?' I said.

'I just said I was.'

'I'm just surprised that's all.'

'Why?' he asked.

'Well, I supposed because you are so enthusiastic about everything all the time; your new clothes, your cup of coffee, talking to Eta on reception. You're a bit indiscriminate with your enthusiasms.'

'Well that's harsh,' he said. But he didn't look the least bit offended. 'Let me make this plain.'

'Okay.'

'I really like you. And when you dumped me, I was gutted.'

Or you had Angelo murdered and you got away scot free and you are enjoying the spoils of having me as a victory prize. Or by dating me it makes you look innocent. Or you're a psychopath. I felt tired just thinking about it.

To be fair, I quite enjoyed sorting out a costume for the masked ball. After all, it's the sort of event you quite fancy going to once in your lifetime.

They have shops in Venice whose sole and extensive function is so you can dress up to go to balls. Of course, they do. A city that has surrendered so much to tourism – a city where I have seen for sale both a bottle of wine shaped like a gondolier and a plastic Pope in a snowstorm - is hardly going to stop at selling mere souvenirs.

I looked hot as Marie Antoinette. Seriously hot. I tried on an emerald green, then a burgundy red 18th century rococo dress; I looked great in both, but the skirt was wider than a doorway. I imagined having to do a run for it if it all went wrong with Adam. I imagined crouching behind an upturned kitchen table shielding from bullets while wearing it. Hot or not, it was not the way to go.

There is no actual reason why Venice masked balls should only be associated with the late 18th century; after all, that was literally when the whole edifice collapsed and the Venetians lost their empire. It is odd that we tend to celebrate the eras where debauchery was to lull a civilisation into its undoing; but perhaps this was the very idea I was tapping into when gathering evidence on Adam. Lull him with decadence and debauchery.

Oddly, it came as second nature to phone Adam when I was wracked with indecision about what to wear; despite everything he felt like a friend.

I was standing in the costume shop at the time, dressed as Little Bo Peep – or to be precise, the comedy milkmaid garb that Marie Antoinette used to wear when she played at being a shepherdess on her mock farm; milking the geese and riding the sheep, while her courtiers praised her efforts.

'What are you wearing?' I asked Adam

He pretended I was flirting.

'Jeans. But underneath I'm commando,' he said.

'It's just I don't want to come to the ball as one thing and you as another,' I said. 'We ought to kind of match?'

'Like a couple,' he said. If we seem like a couple and then Adam is indeed found guilty of the fraud, then won't that also incriminate me?

'Like a couple,' I said.

'How about go leftfield?' he suggested. 'Dress like Prince did in the 1980s. You know, Purple Rain and all that but with a baroque edge.' That was actually a very good idea. 'It would suit your figure,' he said. Perv. He wants to screw a female Prince? It was a dark day when I slept with him.

'We don't have to match,' he said.

I asked the lady in the shop if she could do anything along the lines of Prince. She didn't blink.

'Well that was easy,' I said as I admired myself in the mirror and struck up a chorus of Raspberry Beret.

'We get asked for Prince a lot,' said the assistant. 'We don't just do Carnevale costumes. Our most popular costume is Fat Elvis; the Vegas years.'

'Second most popular?'

'Second most popular is Thin Elvis,' she replied.

'Even for women?' I asked.

'For women, the most popular choice is Jessie the Cowgirl, from Toy Story.'

'Toy Story 2,' I corrected her. Evidently, I am indeed the pedant Angelo claimed I was. I get it from hanging out with Pete.

Talking of Pete; I wondered what he was going to wear. I imagined him in different costumes – though mostly as Fat Elvis – the visual image pleased me. It was the most jolly I had felt in days.

FOUR

The Venice Carnevale had been going every day, but with all the turmoil it had simply not registered on my consciousness. Now it was all I could see, everywhere I looked.

A boat of men and women dressed head to toe in gold drifted past me. Their elaborate masks of butterflies and devils were calculated to be both opulent and sinister. A husband and wife squeezed past me down a narrow calle dressed as 18th century big cats – him with a lion mask, her as a jaguar; the end of her tail was elaborately frayed and attached to a gold cane. She held it up to form a mask over her eyes. In a local store I was in the queue behind a couple who had enormous peacock headdresses in shades of black and turquoise; they were buying a bottle of wine to take to a party. I was beginning to feel underdressed. Only at the Venice Carnevale would Prince have looked as though he hadn't made an effort with his clothes.

The Palazzo where our ball was held was like something out of Romeo and Juliet. Ornate stone staircases led up from stone internal courtyards; unexpected balconies appeared high up on the walls. It was decorated for the night in fairy lights and huge white flower petals; they led us in a path up a stone staircase that got more narrow and more twisting with every step, then just when it seemed like a dead end, released us into a massive ballroom on the second floor – high and dry above the floodwater and commoners.

'Who have you come as?' I asked Adam.

'I have come as a libertine and lover.'

'The Marquis de Sade?'

'Casanova,' he replied. Of course. Except he sort of had, and he sort of hadn't. Instead of a mask, he had paid for a top-notch bit of elaborate face painting. He had an eye and a nose painted on his right temple so that as a trompe l'oeil effect he appeared to have two faces; his own, and one on the side of his face that incorporated his own right eye. One of the faces was loving, and one of them was cruel; it was mesmerising and very effective. It also felt like he was flaunting a metaphor.

As for his costume; it was a dashing 18th century affair that gave him the appearance of the sort of lover who would seduce you then dash your arse with a leather belt. Cruel with a dash of dandy; resplendent in creams and golds.

He walked us to a specific grouping for me to meet some people. How did he know who everyone was? The masks were impenetrable. The man he was now introducing me to was short and squat, but the woman next to him whom I presumed was his wife, was tall and had the posture of a younger person.

'This is Signor and Signora Turturro,' said Adam. 'They are very good friends of mine.'

Signor Turturro was dressed as a plague doctor, and his wife was dressed like a sexy witch or Maleficent; they were clearly bonkers rich.

It was disconcerting observing people interact when they had masks on. Did this rich couple despise Adam and at best tolerate him? Or was he in fact a prince; the young energetic horseman of the kingdom being groomed for power and greatness? I couldn't tell from their faces, and I couldn't even tell from their body language; everyone's costumes were so elaborate that they were held stiff and upright. I could barely even tell from their voices; they were muffled behind their masks. I had to rely on the words they spoke and nothing else. But I had my phone set to 'record' and had placed it in my breast pocket in case Adam betrayed himself; so the words – if they could be heard over the noise and the music – would in any case be the only evidence that counted.

'This lady,' announced Adam putting a hand round my shoulder. 'Is the woman who saved the day for us all.'

The plague doctor and Maleficent bowed their heads as best they could, to acknowledge me.

'She was the one who okayed those massive insurance claims for the flooding.'

My face was painted opaque white, and the mask I held over my eyes riffed on the Prince symbol in gold; as a result the Turturros could not see the shock on my face. I didn't okay the insurance claims; I was abducted and the claims were fraudulently processed in my name. Adam knew that was my position, so what was his game? Was the new narrative, that I was happy to take the blame for the fraud?

'We have you to thank for so much,' said Signor Turturro. 'Venice suffered so much from the Acqua Alta. It was superb that at least one insurance company came through for us.'

But he and his wife knew I had been abducted. Pete had questioned them about it. Focus Emily. Now is not the time to feel resentful.

'But Adam,' I tried. 'Adzio, tell them of your part in the proceedings. Don't give me the all the credit.' It was clumsy as a trap, but what could I do? I had to get something on tape.

Adam considered what to say. It was plain he wanted this couple to think the best of him. How much credit would he take?

'When I say things will happen,' he said. 'They will happen. And I told you this would happen. That you would get those pay outs.'

Signor Turturro said nothing.

His wife stepped into the silence. 'We thank you for your contribution,' she said.

The Turturros then didn't further the conversation. Was this because they in fact had no time for Adam? Or was it like when you deal with famous people; you have to think of the conversation for yourself when talking to them, or no conversation may occur at all. There was literally no way of knowing. The Turturros were one of the twenty-four families who gained from the fraud; if they were hand in glove with Adam, then it wasn't clear.

Adam was a little discouraged by this encounter, but his spring-heeled Jack energy was soon taking us off to meet more people at the ball. I wondered where Pete was. He said he'd meet us here, but I couldn't see him. But then how would I know? Everyone was dressed so elaborately that I could barely tell the men from the women, let alone which one was Pete.

I was addressed by a fop. That is to say, an enormously ornate man with a candy floss wig and a white mask adorned with rouge. He held a small stick with red lips against his mouth.

'You are Emily Fisher. No?' asked the man.

'How did you know that?'

'Signor Icardi said you were going to be dressed as Prince,' he replied.

'Then you have the advantage over me,' I said. I looked round for Adam, but he had apparently deserted me. 'Who are you?'

'Let me introduce myself. I am Stefano Muccino,' he said. 'I am very important.'

Well that was smug, and it could mean anything. If you are indeed very important then you would never need to say so, surely. 'I am the prime minister, I am very important.' 'I am the King, I am very important.' But then, this masked ball was so disconcerting. I could be talking to a chancer or a multi-billionaire.

'And who are you tonight Signor Muccino?' I asked.

'I am Philippe Duke of Orleans, the brother of the Sun King, coming to visit the Venetian court,' he said.

'What an honour,' I said. I bowed. Should I keep addressing him as Philippe? The conversation would be a trifle limited. What the hell did I know about Louis

XIV and the like? 'And who were you yesterday, and who will you be tomorrow?' I tried.

I was rescued by Adam who had brought a glass of prosecco for me.

'Signor Muccino is the head of *the* Muccino family,' he said. It was the sort of clarification that made nothing clearer at all.

'Wow!' I went. It seemed called for. 'Pleased to meet you.'

'They provide a lot of the precision engineering behind sports cars and racing cars for Formula One.'

'You flatter me. We just play our humble part,' he said. But he was clearly pleased to have his importance confirmed by Adam rather than have to say again he was important for himself. I was finding him quite irritating. 'We are most indebted to you, Signora.'

'How so?' I asked.

'We lost a lot of days' work with the winter floods and your company was most generous.'

Oh. Now I knew who this man was. He had lodged the most ridiculous bogus insurance claim; one of the worst I had to wade through. It wasn't as though car parts would dissolve in the flooding; there was barely a loss at all, but this man's company was trying to claim millions. Of all the claims that had been paid out in the fraud, this one was the most heinous. The wine I was drinking got stuck in my throat. You don't expect that with top wine.

'You will have to excuse me uncle,' said Adam but I have a lot of people I need to introduce Emily to.'

Uncle? So this was the top family that Adam belonged to, the Muccinos. I had already discovered that Adam's own surname, Icardi, was highly exalted, but he was also a Muccino? Adam was obviously welcomed and liked by his uncle, and paradoxically that made Adam less interested in his company; he was much more interested in the people who *didn't* hold him in such esteem.

'Emily, meet Signor Facchinetti,' said Adam. He pointed to a man who wore a trendy black suit, a high white starched collar, and white swept-back hair. He had evidently come as Fashion Victim Dracula, or Karl Lagerfeld.

'Delighted to meet you,' said the man.

'This is my colleague Emily, who helped facilitate the recent insurance pay outs to your firm.'

This was firming up my theory that I was being paraded around as the nice lady who committed the fraud to help all these people.

Fashion Victim Dracula shook hands warmly with Adam.

'I never got the chance to thank you in person,' he said.

'It was nothing,' replied Adam. This was more like it. I didn't feel Adam would be able to pass up some praise for his involvement in the fraud.

'Well don't be modest Adam, tell Signor Facchinetti of your part in the operation,' I tried.

'I do what I can,' said Adam. 'That is all.' Was he on to me already? Possibly.

A woman with an alarming headdress and even more alarming cleavage moved into view. The hips of her dress were the width of a small car. She came up to Adam and slapped him on the back.

'Here's the man!' she said. 'You have transformed our balance sheet this year.'

Surely such flattery would help loosen Adam's lips?

'But you must thank Emily here,' said Adam. 'She is the one who made it happen.' Adam pointed to our empty glasses and signed that he would get us more prosecco; he departed with Fashion Victim Dracula to talk elsewhere. It left me alone with the woman. I had no idea who she was. or how old she was, or indeed anything about her. I was beginning to hate masked balls.

'Ah Adzio,' said the woman. 'It is a curse to care that much about what people think of you.'

'You know him well?' I asked.

'Since he was born. I am like an aunt. My family and his family are very close. You are dating him?'

'Well,' I replied, stalling.

'He says he is dating a posh English girl. He is thrilled about it. He adores you, you know, Presumably, you are the posh English girl he means?'

'I had no idea,' I said.

'What do you mean by that?'

Well now I was confused as to what to say.

Adam reappeared with a bottle, renewed enthusiasm, and a further guest.

'It is Emily you need to thank for your reversal of fortune,' he said.

He continually made this sound like praise. What had happened was a crime. Was this the Italian way? That if you weren't actually convicted of anything then your reputation was clean; if you weren't actually in prison for the crime, then the crime didn't matter? Or were the locals so aggrieved when they thought the insurance companies wouldn't pay out, that I was a genuine hero in their eyes? And where was Pete?

It turned out he was right by me.

'What have you come as, Aladdin?' I asked. He had a kind of twirly turban whose fabric swept down to completely cover his face. Happily, I had recognised him by his stomach.

'I was channelling Casanova,' he said. Oh great; two Casanovas in my life. Pete sounded a bit drunk. 'Have you tried the cocktails?' he asked.

'No, but when you've tried each and every one of them Pete, you can recommend your favourite,' I said. 'If you're still conscious.'

Adam's aunt introduced herself to Pete, and Adam bounded off again to schmooze with yet another person who had fallen into his line of vision.

'When you say it is a curse to care that much about what people think of you?' I asked the aunt.

'It has always been Adam's weakness,' she replied. 'He does everything all day to be seen to be the best; the cleanest, the brightest, the most loyal to the family, the most likely to succeed. He lives and dies on what others think of him. So much so, it backfires and looks insecure and tawdry. But I love the boy. And so good-looking.'

You've got to love an incestuous aunt.

'Wouldn't you agree?' she asked.

'Oh heavens yes, the boy's good-looking,' I said.

'A word of friendly advice though,' she said.

'Yes?'

'Don't get too attached to him.'

'No?'

'He is always jumping off to some fresh enthusiasm, if you know what I mean?' she said.

'I thought you just said he adored me?'

'He does,' she shrugged.

I whisked Pete to one side.

'I am having a frustrating time,' I said. 'Adam is enjoying that people feel he is a mover and shaker; but when it comes down to specifics, he is mostly putting me in the frame for events without actually saying anything incriminating about himself.'

'I have been getting people talking,' shrugged Pete. 'And I think he is the brother who didn't go to university. He is the one who has got a chip on his shoulder that he has something to prove; thus the way he over-dresses, thus the scam. In reality though, he's the one the family apologise for and he knows it; a person that everyone notices but no one takes seriously.'

Music struck up. A baroque orchestra of musicians with purple eye masks and harlequin diamonds on their faces were playing a staccato dance tune.

Yet another problem with masks is that you can't eat or drink with them in place. Unlike me though, Pete had thought about this in advance; he just had to unwrap one edge of his gold cloth and his mouth was instantly available.

'You chose that costume so that you could eat and drink, didn't you?' I asked.

'Why deny it?' he replied.

I spotted a waitress holding a platter of food; she was dressed in a skin-tight court jester outfit. She had a silver silk scarf tied over her eyes; she was totally blindfolded.

'She's handing out the most gorgeous teriyaki meatballs,' said Pete.

He waved to her. He then beckoned her with a crooked finger.

'Er, she's blindfolded?' I said.

She smiled at Pete – the sort of smile a restaurateur reserves for their best customer. She glided towards us.

'It's the same material that knife throwers use in circus acts when they are blindfolded,' explained Pete. 'She can see really. She was explaining it to me earlier.'

'I might have guessed you had made friends with the caterers,' I said. 'To think, I'd imagined I'd lost you. I just had to follow the smell of the food and there you'd be.'

'Shut up and try the meatballs,' he said. 'And make sure to get plenty of the spring onion at the same time.' If only food were a religion, my brother would be Pope.

He addressed the woman who was standing erect; a silent flagpole pretending to be sightless. 'Have you got more of those cheese pastry olive wrap things? The ones with the rosemary? Oh and also there was a dill and salmon thing?'

'I'll see what I can do.' She smirked and drifted off, but not before Pete had balanced half a plateful of food on my palm.

'How am I supposed to eat these if my hands are already full?' I protested. 'I'll look like a horse eating from a nosebag.'

Pete looked confused. 'They're for me,' he said. He popped two in his mouth by way of demonstration.

'I need to get Adam saying more. I need to get him drunk and bragging,' I said.

Adam was standing right next to me. How long had he been standing there? It was noisy in the room, so perhaps he hadn't heard me?

'We were discussing office politics in Bastia,' I lied to Adam. 'Our boss is a nightmare, but he has a thing for me, so we were hatching a plan.'

'You appear to be holding a large number of hors d'oeuvres,' he said.

'Put out your hands Pete,' I said. He put out his hands. I tipped the food into them. 'Bon appetite!'

I took Adam's arm.

'Introduce me to people,' I said. 'Show off to me how well-connected you are.'

'Well I don't know about that,' he said. But he was being self-deprecating.

'This is Signor Valdi and his wife,' said Adam.

Fear hit my stomach. The man in whose workshop I had been imprisoned. The man who had filled the pit in overnight to help destroy my alibi. They were dressed as a king and queen. Of course, they were. At least this might make for good evidence if I could record it.

'Can I have the pleasure of presenting my girlfriend Emily?' asked Adam. It's girlfriend now, is it?

'Pleased to meet you,' said Signor Valdi. Did he know who I was? I kept my mask hard against my face.

'We are the duo who made everything happen,' said Adam. This was nearer to an admission. He paused for what he assumed would be praise.

'I don't understand,' said Signor Valdi.

'The massive insurance pay out that you had problems with. We are the team that got the payment through.' Adam paused again for acknowledgement.

'I have no idea what you are talking about,' said Signor Valdi. He was being far more cautious than the other people we had talked to. 'We put in a fair claim and it was agreed. Nothing strange in that.'

'But my involvement...' said Adam.

'You weren't involved at all,' said Signor Valdi. 'No matter what you keep implying to anyone who'll listen.'

Adam, judging by the expression on at least one of his faces, was absolutely gutted. He wasn't getting the credit he felt he deserved.

'B... b... b... but.' He actually stammered.

'Now if you will excuse me, I must circulate,' said Signor Valdi.

Signor Valdi, I knew for certain, was up to his neck in the fraud, so what to make of his attitude to Adam? Was he simply trying to stop Adam bragging? Or did he realise who I was, despite my mask?

Before I could take stock of the Valdi encounter a little lady came shooting up. She was dressed like the Queen of Hearts. She was so short that when she hugged me, her head was in my chest. Why was she hugging me?

She started crying.

'You saved my life,' she said.

'How did I save your life?' I found myself stroking her hair to comfort her.

'Until you paid out our insurance, we were ruined. Ruined! Our whole life was over. I owe you my life.'

I winced at Pete over her head.

When I listened back to my recordings later, the only thing I could make out from the entire evening was this woman talking into my bra.

FIVE

As the days went by, my plan to tape Adam confessing to the fraud was proving less than successful. Just like at the ball, he would often allude to events and his involvement, but would never say quite the right words in the right order, and I could hardly keep egging him on over the subject until he did.

The dating itself was problematic. I needed to spend time with him – how else could I get him to confess and tape him? – but I didn't want to leave myself vulnerable. I had it in my mind that despite all his energy and youth, underneath it all he was probably some sort of psychopath who could turn on me unexpectedly; so as a result I didn't want to be totally alone with him and I certainly didn't want sex with him. But he was young; how long would he date me if sex was not on the table?

In terms of Adam's demeanour though, it was like he'd had a reset. He twigged I was a little wary of him or affected by events, so he was much more like when we first met; solicitous and eager-to-please.

He took me to the opera, La Fenice. He said it was, 'The greatest opera house in the world.' It was hard to disagree; largely because throughout our date he was continuously in my face checking my reaction to events. How was I enjoying my wine? How was I enjoying my pasta? How was I enjoying the opera? He was doing such a good job of appearing innocent that even I was wondering if it might indeed be the case after all.

In fairness, the experience was amazing. The opera house had been completely burnt out in 1996 and they worked twenty-four hours a day, seven days a week, rebuilding it to its former glory. Eight years later it reopened. Literally everywhere you looked the decorations are covered in gold leaf; the whole place shining and shimmering with gold. It was truly astonishing. And the opera was good too; La Traviata. La Traviata 'the fallen woman' at La Fenice 'the phoenix'; all that falling and rising and putting up with Adam; it's amazing the contents of my stomach didn't lurch out of my mouth.

'Napoleon stood up there,' said Adam pointing to the royal box.

In an affront to romance, I clutched his arm and smiled into his eyes.

We met some of his friends.

'This is my girlfriend Emily,' he said. I tried to look girlfriendy. It involved clutching him round the waist and simpering at his friends' jokes.

'How did you two meet?' asked a girl with a lot of hair.

'We did a crime together, apparently,' I said. This just made Adam look at me fondly.

What if he was recording me, and I was getting this all the wrong way round?

We walked a romantic way back to my apartment. He favoured moonlit bridges and gondolas creaking in their moorings. In terms of gathering evidence I felt very frustrated. I decided to try something bold.

'What if I wanted in?' I asked.

'In?'

'Well I have met so many interesting people these last few days, thanks to you. And I love it here in Venice. You've all been so welcoming. How do I get in on things?'

'How do you get in on things?' he asked.

The city of Venice is quiet at night; apart from where the students hang out, it is not a town for nightlife, so my phone would have no trouble picking up audio as we walked.

'How do I go native?' I asked. 'Get an entré into Venice society?'

'Well you just stick with me, I guess.'

And that was it. Topic closed.

'You think you're smart don't you?' he asked one day.

I jumped. We were in a bookshop at the time, just browsing. The shop had suffered so many floods that the owner had made a feature of it; all the books were in bathtubs and buckets, to protect them from water.

'How so?' I asked. 'How do I think I'm smart?' The trouble with feeling guilty all the time is that your nerves give you away. Had he noticed me jump? Did my voice change tone? Had he spotted me forever pressing 'record' on my phone?

'You think you are going to catch me out,' he said. 'But you won't.'

And it was the look he gave me at that moment. He was the winner, and I had to suck it up. I was never going to catch him out. I was right about him and he wanted me to know it, without ever saying it.

'Maybe you just don't understand me,' I said. I didn't know where I was going with that.

'What do you mean?' he asked.

'I have done some truly awful stuff in my time. I have committed major frauds. I have been a party to murder.' Keep it vague Emily; he might be recording this, he might be using this against me.

'Murder?' he asked. He was at least intrigued.

'I like to think I'm moral,' I said. 'But, well I guess I've got flexi-morals.'

'Ah they're the best kind,' he replied. He was softening his tone now.

'I just want to get on,' I said. 'I don't want to be stuck in a little office doing paperwork forever. What happened to me with the safe house and the kidnapping was horrible, so of course I dwell on it and of course I want to understand fully what happened; but I also want to move on and up. I don't want to live in the past. I think maybe you can help me with that. Maybe we could be a team.'

He was distracted by my tits. I mean, for heaven's sake. We were talking murder, fraud, kidnapping and betrayal, here; and he was staring at my tits. Okay, so we all knew that after my recent weight gain the twins were in fine form, but *really*. And when you are a woman it is a constant irritant that some men don't even *pretend* to look at your face when you are talking to them. Wow. There was literally nothing I could say at that moment, to this man in particular, holding a book about Machiavelli, that would stop him looking at my tits.

'Yeah,' he said, dismissing with a hand what I had been saying. 'I think we might need to call it a day.'

What?

He was dumping me?

He went straight from fixated by my chest, to dumping me?

It was just like his aunt said; he will inevitably spring on to some fresh enthusiasm. He had enjoyed conquering the woman who blamed him for Angelo's death, but he was already bored of the feeling and was moving on. Or perhaps I was just too transparent with trying to entrap him.

I needed to do something bold. He was turning to go. I had only a second to try some fresh tactic.

'Let's have sex,' I said. I just blurted it out.

'What now?' he asked. At least he'd stopped in his tracks.

'Yeah, sure now. You know, a cheeky quicky in the afternoon,' I said. 'But also plan a date.'

'Plan a date?'

'Yeah. You know where I dress up in something special. Sort out some lingerie.'

Oh Dear Lord he really was a juvenile. I could see he was horny. I mean, I could literally *see* he was horny. He had said the actual words needed to dump me, and because I was offering sex, he was doing a handbrake turn and had seemingly forgotten what he had said only seconds before.

'This Sunday night,' I said. 'I've got whole piles of things I need to do tomorrow. But Sunday night. Let's make a special occasion of it. Come round to my place. Bring some wine. As I said, I'll dress up.'

'Sure,' he said.

So I hung on in there by offering sex. I even had to put up with a quickie that afternoon. All in the vain hope I would get some evidence on him.

I really hated myself that day.

SIX

'Pete.'

'Uh huh?' I had been phoning him several times a day since he'd gone back to Bastia.

'You know how you always come through for me in my hour of need?'

There was a predictable silence on the other end of the phone.

'I don't like the sound of this,' he said eventually.

'Well you do come through for me, and I am grateful,' I said.

'Keep going,' said Pete.

'I can't do this on my own,' I said. 'You need to come back to Venice. I just can't do this on my own. I can't cope.'

I could hear him sigh, but he probably didn't think I'd heard him, so we both let it pass.

'Okay sure. I'll see what I can do,' he said.

'Perfect. Thank you, Pete. You're a lifesaver. Can you come out now? This weekend?'

'I really can't,' he replied.

'I just feel...'

'I know.'

'Is there a particular plan?' he asked. 'Something I can help you with?'

'Maybe.'

'Because you can't go on like this forever,' he said.

'I know.'

But then he didn't come out. Not the next day, not the day after. Not for weeks. It wasn't his fault. He had too much work to do his end, he was short of annual leave.

But it left me wretched. At the office, the company had managed to get some of the fraudulent money back but mostly it was lost. I was still treated with suspicion by everyone I dealt with, and the only person who had Adam down as the culprit was me. I was the only one on his case, and I was making no progress. I was despondent. And despondency drains you of energy. It makes for bad decisions. But I made myself press on anyway. I pressed on with my plan, such as it was.

I travelled out to Lido to visit Fat Sam. There was a faint chance I was still being shadowed by the police, though I thought not; but I didn't want to take any chances so I used a water bus then changed to a water taxi to check I wasn't being followed. Now it was just me, I was more paranoid, not less. I hadn't done drugs for about fifteen years – since a chaotic patch in my early twenties - but now it was all I needed and wanted. Despondency and loneliness make for bad decisions.

The great thing about drugs dealers is they don't ask questions. They also don't haggle over price. I like that; although what I wanted was cheap as chips anyway. He did say one thing though.

'You don't need a needle with that,' he said. 'It'll work without the syringe.'

'I know.' I do know how to do drugs. 'I'll have one anyway.'

'Okay it's just a few drops for a kick, for a bit of confidence. Any more is...'

I grimaced at him. I do know how to do drugs. And I do know my way around the body. And I didn't want to be slowed up by this drug dealer, because I had other places to go and other things to buy.

I paid Fat Sam, and thanked him, and left.

'I serve you well,' he finished.

Is that, like, his catchphrase?

I tried to make my apartment look Come Hither. This basically involved a bit of a quick tidy and clean; dirty plates in the sink and tangled clothes on the floor are hardly alluring. But it's not as though I bought a red scarf to throw over the lampshade. My day's purchases did include, among other things, a new pair of knickers though, and the ingredients for some cocktails.

Adam arrived at my door holding two bottles of wine. One red, one white.

'We don't need to go out,' he said.

'Whoever said we were going out?' Perhaps he was alluding to getting fed. No chance of that mister; I wanted you drunk.

'I don't recall if you preferred red or white wine,' he said. If he dreamt of me at night, he would know.

'I'm making margaritas,' I said. 'And as for wine. Either is good. But usually white wine in the summer and red wine in the winter.'

If a man came into your bedroom set to overpower you, does he mean to kill you or have sex with you? Is there really such a difference? Either way you lay yourself bare.

Okay my mind was tripping.

The margaritas gave me something to do with my hands and brain. I didn't want to sit beside him looking nervous.

'Do you have salt on the rim?'

'Is that a sexual term?' he replied.

If I hadn't been on edge, I'd have found that funny.

'That's very forward,' I said.

'I'm feeling forward. I can't tell you how thrilled I am to be dating you again. You dumped me the first time before I knew it. You didn't have a chance to get to know me first. I'm quite a catch you know.' Yeah but it was the sex that sealed the deal. You went cold on me. You literally said the words to dump me. But your fatal flaw was you couldn't resist the sex. Was that because you were so young, or just because you were a male?

I'd taken a little something earlier and it was making me swimmy. Drugs had seemed like a good idea at the time. Not so much now. I wasn't used to them these days, and I'd probably taken too much.

I raised a glass to him and he wiped away the salt from the nearest part of his glass. If I loved him, I would have remembered if he'd said salt or no salt.

Before I knew it, he had opened the red wine. I helped him find glasses.

'Actually, to be contrary, I'll drink white,' I said.

He lifted an amused eyebrow and got me a glass of white and sat down. When he poured the wine, he was out of my sight.

'I want to know what you did, and how you did it?' I asked. 'Yes, you're right about that.' Part of my endless attempt to get him to confess. If he didn't let his guard down when sex and booze was involved, when would he?

He stiffened. And not in a good way.

'I love how everyone thinks I did the crime,' he said. 'I mean I actually love it. I am being treated like royalty in this city. People have always known who I am, but it is like they are seeing me for the first time. It's a blast. But, you know, let's change the subject.'

But I can't go on like this; giving more and more of myself in the hope he will say enough for me to move on. And what else have I got to give? I am clinging on by my fingernails at best.

'I suppose the question that keeps going through my mind. The reason I can't let the matter drop,' I said.

'Yes?'

'Was in the safe house. Why did they shoot Angelo, but not me also?'

'And if I answer that, we can get on with the date?' he asked.

Yes. Yes, that might be enough.

'I suppose so,' I said. 'It keeps swinging round to that in my brain. I almost lost my life. It is inevitable I am obsessed by it.'

When Adam then answered it was in a jokey manner; it was possible to believe he was telling the truth, but also possible he was being sarcastic.

'The reason they shot Angelo,' he said. 'Was that Angelo was making up some phoney nonsense against me. The reason they spared you, is that I loved you. But since you've been dating me again all you've done is spend your time trying to entrap me.'

He said loved, not love. He used to love me, and that kept me alive. Now he no longer loves me, would he keep me alive?

'What wine is this?' I asked. 'It is a slightly odd flavour.'

He shrugged. 'I can get the bottle over?'

'No it's okay. I often find the first sip of white wine odd and then I get used to it, and then I enjoy it.'

'So I answered your question,' he said. 'We can get on with the date.'

He knew what happened in the safe house. He knew which way Adam's testimony was going. It wasn't a confession. But it confirmed what I felt about him. And now as payment I had to suffer whatever he was planning for this evening.

I tried to turn the subject to the future. In part to check if I had a future.

'What shall we do this week?' I asked.

'What?'

'What do young couples do round here when they are dating?' I tried.

'Go to parties, go skiing in the Dolomites. Sailing,' he replied. 'What are you going to do with the 60,000 euros you got given?' Interesting. It was he who had gravitated back to discussing the crime.

'I suppose I should have a party. Was it your idea I should get the money?'

'How would it be my idea?' he answered.

Perhaps I would never get any killer lines from him, just lots of stray words that don't quite add up. Resign yourself that that's enough, Emily, and you could throw him out now, no harm done.

There was like a snap noise in my brain. The room went purple. Then black. Then back to normal colours, albeit far away. Drugs. Drugs make for bad decisions. Despondency makes for bad decisions.

'Drink up!' he said.

We drank and drank again. I kept sneaking some glasses of water into the mix, but it doesn't actually reduce the amount of alcohol or drug in your system; it just fills out the bladder. And that was the problem the next day.

The evening continued with him repeatedly claiming he wanted to leave the subject of the fraud, but he was also the one to return to it. He enjoyed being near the thrill of it; near to its warm fires.

There was a cat and mouse with the drinks. I wanted him as drunk as possible – if things turned nasty it is always easier to overpower someone who is almost passing out with booze – if he was as drunk as possible, some secret may blurt out. I got a second bottle of red opened for him, then a third, and I poured a few half glasses of my own wine down the sink; I was already fuddled without getting totally plastered on top. But the fact remained, there were repeated instances when he was out of sight pouring the wine out, and – to be fair - a few times when I was out of sight pouring his wine too. The first glass of the second bottle of white wine tasted particularly strange, but that can happen when you go from one white wine to another, so I thought little of it at the time.

Finally, I felt he was as drunk as he could be.

'Any more booze and you'll be incoherent,' I said. Which would be no good for my recordings.

But showing no remorse for his crimes. Expecting to still be loved. These were the hallmarks of a psychopath. I knew this. I had thought it a hundred times. Was I really going to be alone with a psychopath? Wake up Emily, I was already alone with a psychopath.

He hooked a finger into my skirt and pulled me towards the bedroom.

'Enough of this chit chat. Let's do it,' he said.

Lamb to a slaughter, we went through to the bedroom. My heart was in my boots.

He unexpectedly found energy, as men do when sex is in view. He was suddenly dominating; alive with lust and the aggression he'd shown when we'd had sex before.

I tried to respond in kind. I went to undress him, matching his fevered manner, but I was fingers and thumbs and his buttons refused to give. He put a finger up to stop me. Time out. He wanted his smartphone safely out of his pocket and on the bedside table, he wanted to unbutton his own shirt without damage, he wanted his designer trousers carefully folded; he wanted to fold them himself. Not eager to please. Eager to rise. And not so drunk, he couldn't fold his clothes neatly.

'Eager to rise up the ranks.'

'What?' he asked.

I had spoken my thoughts. When will I learn not to take drugs? When will I learn not to drink with them?

'Let's get those underpants off you,' I said.

We tumbled onto the bed and there was the first urgent kissing. He was unbuttoning my everything and flinging clothes wherever they would land.

Then I wondered whether his head reeled a bit. The booze kicking back in, or something else? His expression had changed completely. He was sitting astride me. His cock was literally resting on my stomach. I was pinned down. But his face was far away and a little to the side. His mood had turned badly dark.

'It's just one long attempt to get me to confess to it all,' he said. 'That's what it is. Even if it takes sex. You've got such a nerve.'

'No. No,' I soothed. 'It's not that at all.' It's really not that at all.

'Your phone is over there. Are you recording us, even in the bedroom?'

It was true my phone was in the bedroom when I usually put it in the kitchen at night.

He was angry with me. Properly angry. He gripped my shoulders to confront me.

'If I really am the psychopath you claim,' he said. 'And you are the only person on my case, doesn't it make sense if I kill you now?'

'No, you have to listen,' I pleaded. But to what? I had no words. Words refused to come out. The room was spinning and breathing in time with my breathing. The blood rushing in my ears was deafening me.

'I am so angry with you,' he said.

I made loud thumping noises on the bedding. Four loud thumps; a sign I wanted him to release me. But apart from my arms I could barely move; although Adam was slight for a man, he was still a man and much heavier than me. I wondered if I could reach for something to use as a weapon. Could I overpower him? He had me pinned down.

Unexpectedly he slumped down on the bed beside me. Now he was the one who was despondent. He searched the ceiling for answers and an appropriate mood. Perhaps the worst of his anger had gone.

I leant over and turned off my phone.

'See, I turned it off,' I said.

He tilted his head up to study me. He seemed much more awash with drink now, but he clearly wanted to puzzle things out.

'And what's that?' he asked.

'What's what?'

He pointed to my stretchmarks.

SEVEN

I am not saying that because he pointed out my stretchmarks he had to die. Although he was hardly helping his cause. It was that I couldn't go on the way I was. I had to end things. I had set up the opportunity to kill him and it was now or never. I had been imprisoned with rats. I had thought I was going to drown. I had to choose between Pete being shot or Angelo. Angelo had had his brains blown out. A detective had been shot dead. Two of his colleagues had been injured. And this man, Adam, was running round enjoying the credit; this man, Adam, had used my computer to frame me. This man, Adam, was largely behind the plan; this man, Adam, had the temerity to want to date me, to parade me round like the spoils of war. This man, Adam, had reduced me to a shell.

'Just chill out,' I said. It sounded lame, but in his drunken way he took my words at face value and lay back on the bed. Or perhaps he was passing out. I breathed in and out to clear my own head as best I could.

I ran my fingers over his chest. He had a fine chest. Bone and muscle and not much else. I ran my fingers over his ribs. I felt up about five ribs from his stomach area and probed the gap between them. I straddled his stomach.

'Hmmm. What'ya doin?' He spoke lazily. He was almost asleep.

'Shhh.'

At the head of the bed between the mattress and the headboard, I had a syringe. It was the large hypodermic syringe that I'd got from Fat Sam. I had filled it full of air.

I didn't jab him with it. I chose my place carefully between his ribs; the place which I prayed was just over his heart. I pushed the needle gently and firmly into him. I pushed deeper; through the skin, through the pleural layers.

He jolted. His eyes shot open and his hand came shooting up.

Now he was fighting me. I fought back. I had to somehow hold him at bay. I gripped him with my thighs as best I could. I pushed and scraped with my spare hand. I only had to fend him off for one or two seconds to inject the air into him. The needle was up to its hilt now, but I still had to push the plunger in. But his right hand was now pulling at my hair, clawing at my face. His left hand was pushing at my body.

The plunger was half in.

Now his whole body was convulsing, trying to throw me off. He was lashing at me. Writhing. Clawing.

All in.

The plunger was all in.

But he was still fighting me. He was stronger than ever. Now he was trying to sit up. His eyes fixed on mine.

Now he was disbelieving, pleading. His mouth went to shape a word. Surely the air embolism would only take a few seconds to kill him? It just had to lodge somewhere and stop the flow of blood in his body; perhaps stop the blood to his heart or his brain. But what if I'd missed the heart altogether and just pumped some air into his lung? It would be painful, sure, but it wouldn't kill him. Lungs are used to air, after all.

Still he was fighting me. Now he was deranged. Manic. Frantic. He was scrabbling against my body, against the bed; he was trying to reach the wall for leverage. Endless time was passing but nothing was changing.

Then nothing.

He went limp. Just like that; he went limp. But was he actually dead?

I pulled out the syringe.

As I pulled it out, his eyes opened wide. He addressed me. He addressed me right in the eyes.

'I didn't do it,' he said.

The words were in his breath. His last breath. His lungs could function no more.

Then nothing.

But you did. You did do it. You just wanted me to think the best of you. And me to feel the worst of myself.

I waited. I lay on my back, staring at the ceiling, Listening to my breathing. Listening to the creaks in the house. A splash in the water outside.

I tried to find his pulse to check it. I couldn't take any more surprises.

I checked the time. It was twenty-five to eleven.

The trick now was to not panic. The handcuffs had to be the very last job; once they were on, it was no good me realising I'd forgotten something.

I went off to get my bottle of Rohypnol; another purchase from Fat Sam. I had taken a few drops earlier in the evening to steady my nerves along with a bit of a tablet, but that left nearly all of it. I shared it between two plastic bottles, one larger than the other. The smallest, I half emptied into my wine. I then wiped the bottle, and holding it in a tissue, took it over to Adam. I squeezed his fingers over it. I pressed his fingers round the lid. His fingers were warm and supple, but his arm was heavy. I placed the small bottle in the pocket of his neatly folded trousers and removed his house keys, then set about working on the larger bottle; once I had Adam's fingerprints on that, I placed it in a plastic bag. Twenty to eleven.

I put on a tracksuit bottom and a hoodie. I took the syringe, the bottle of Rohypnol and Adam's keys, and let myself out of my apartment. Adam's place is about ten minutes from mine; I clung to the shadows and took back alleys and let myself in. I 'hid' the bottle of Rohypnol so that it could easily be found by the police. I locked his place back up and when I was a few streets away I flung his keys into a canal. I figured if his keys were found in my apartment there was a chance someone would conclude I could have framed him. Another canal later and I threw away the syringe. Sorry Venice; this is just the sort of littering I hate.

Back in my apartment I took off my clothes.

Now to bruise myself.

I tried hitting myself with my fists, but it is very hard to assault yourself with any conviction; your survival instinct kicks in. I went to the door. I stole myself, then banged my face hard against the edge of the door frame. I think I drew blood, but I couldn't make myself do it a second time. I felt quite demoralised at my lack of ability to self-harm. But my plan couldn't flounder on this.

I had an idea. I went off to find the vacuum cleaner and took off the nozzle. I held it hard against my skin and turned it on. With a bit of practice, I made some pretty convincing bruises. The only problem was that they were far too circular and precise. I practiced with a slow continuous movement, sometimes in ovals, sometimes in streaks. I was making progress. What a macabre new skill to learn. Whatever I tried, however, the bruises on my back were resolutely circular; a giveaway if someone knew what they were looking for. It would have to do.

I had kept a condom from my previous quickie with Adam. I squeezed the contents out and smeared them all around my nether regions front and back. I dabbed some of it onto his cock for good measure.

Finally, I got my handcuffs — another recent purchase, this time from the mainland - and I threw the keys and the condom out of the window into the canal. By chaining myself to you I will take away the one thing you craved; your reputation. Your reputation will be trashed forever. In the eyes of the world you drugged me, you assaulted me, you indulged in the vilest of kinky sex with me. All you ever cared about was what people thought of you; well what will they think of you now? I'll play it coy at first, pretending to the detectives I don't want it to get out, but one will tell another and they will tell a third... and then there'll be an inquest...

I drank my wine laced with Rohypnol, leaving some in the glass for the police to analyse in the morning. I prayed I hadn't drunk so much it would kill me.

I lay next to Adam and handcuffed myself to him. Ten past eleven. I had got it into my head I wanted this all sorted by eleven; I don't know why. Ten past eleven was fine.

I had two thoughts before I passed out. The first was, did the hypodermic leave a mark? I craned my head up to look, but it was now dark in the room. I would have to check in the morning, maybe wipe away any surface blood. It was a thin enough needle; it shouldn't leave a mark. The detective had said repeatedly that I would have to do something very stupid to be arrested by the police; I had saved the life of a detective, after all. But was this so stupid that they would have to arrest me anyway? And if they did arrest me, would the world really believe that a woman would commit a murder like this? It's just not what a woman would do. Either way, only time would tell.

The other thought I had before I passed out was of Angelo. He was a slight man, but a decent one. I pictured his face when I held it in my hands. I pictured him sodden head to toe, laughing on the beach. I pictured his beaming pride when he called me his girlfriend. I may not have loved him. I may even have been just about to break up with him. But he was a good man, a decent man. And sometimes good people have to stick together.

POSTSCRIPT

THE WORLD ACCORDING TO PETE

Italy had recovered from the first wave of Covid-19 and was largely reopen. I took the chance to visit Emily once more. Face masks and hand gel and keeping our distance were now the new normal, and when we watched old movies and TV programmes the actors all seemed too close together. Sometimes they even embraced.

Some things had changed for the better, though. On the plane out, there was no one squashed into the seat next to me, and there was no longer a scrum to get on board – we were embarked onto the aircraft a few rows at a time, starting at the back. How civilised.

One thing that had got worse, however, was the breakfast arrangements at my hotel. The breakfast buffet was still available in all its variety and splendour, but we were no longer allowed to even go near it.

'Guests must NOT help themselves,' read the sign. Well how rude. Instead a lady in black stood behind a barrier and held an empty plate expectantly. She asked me what I would like. She was right to wear black; to be mourning the death of an institution.

'If you could slice some scrambled egg in a sort of rectangular slab, that would be great,' I said.

'Scrambled egg?' she confirmed. She got a scoop of the wettest possible scrambled egg and slopped it onto my plate; it had water running off it at the edges. 'Anything else?'

'Some sliced hotdog sausages?'

She placed four tiny pieces of hotdog next to the egg, in the tepid water.

'A mini baguette?' she suggested.

'Yes please.'

And then she handed the plate to me. She simply handed it across. In her opinion the transaction was now complete. What, no cinnamon roll? No chocolate croissant? No granola and yoghurt, no slices of cheese or cold meat? No wholly inappropriate black forest gateau?

'Next!' she said to the man behind me.

I looked at my plate. But I had barely started ordering. How was a grown man supposed to survive on this?

I didn't move.

The waitress looked round me to further address the man behind.

This is the end of hotel life as we know it. There had been many casualties in our war against Covid, but this? It was a wholly disproportionate reaction to events.

I grabbed a yoghurt from the chiller display, and ran like a bag snatcher.

'Hey!' called the woman.

When I settled at my table, I discovered to my dismay that I hadn't stolen a yoghurt at all. I had stolen some super fat-free pot of nonsense with added bacteria and pro-biotic microbes. It was 'original' flavour; like that would somehow sell it to me. It was originally disgusting, and it was still disgusting.

Oh well. I was booked in that evening for a major Michelin-starred meal in the restaurant of my dreams. The whole of modern civilisation had not surrendered to the virus yet; there were still pockets of resistance holding out, and I was ready to join the rebel alliance.

'So you are sixty grand up?' I asked Emily over the phone.

My sister, over the years, has a habit of landing on her feet.

'Uh huh,' she confirmed. 'We don't know where the money came from, and no one has asked for it back.'

'Did you remind the police about it?'

'Not in the slightest,' she replied. 'I figure I'll let it rest in my account and see what happens.'

'And then what will you do with it?'

'I am looking into cosmetic surgery,' she replied.

'What?' I was shocked. This didn't sound like Emily at all.

'Yeah. I am looking into what I can do to reduce the appearance of stretchmarks.'

'You have stretchmarks?'

'I am totally obsessed by them. Also, I have some wrinkles,' she said. 'I figure, seeing as I have the money...'

'But...'

'When did I get so old?' asked Emily. 'It's just terrible. I mean. Why me?'

'You're not old. You're just a little less young.'

'Oh, you're no help,' she said.

Indeed.

'Oh well,' I said. 'You can tell me all about it this evening.'

273

I had spent the day walking around Venice.

With the lack of tourists and fewer people going to work, the city had taken on a completely different air. Literally. I swear the air was cleaner and smelled better. There were no cruise ships dominating the skylines; swans and cormorants had returned to the canals for the first time in decades, and the fish were evident in the water wherever you looked. Local residents sat on chairs outside their front doors, basking in the sun and the lack of bother from the holiday makers.

Best of all, with bookings down, I was finally able to have a meal in the restaurant I had been trying to get into since I first came to Venice; the fish restaurant where the waitresses wore designer sailor outfits and the waiters looked like naval officers, The Aschenbach.

I was sitting at the restaurant table with my favourite - well okay, my only - sister, and was enjoying a glass of a local cocktail called a cinico; prosecco, lime, mint and cinnamon liqueur. I was, as the youth say these days, living my best life. The cocktail tasted odd though, which was a slight disappointment. I had it taken off to be 'analysed' at the bar, but when the waiter returned he said, 'No the cinico seems to be in order Signore. Would you like a different drink?'

'No, it's alright,' I said. I tasted the drink again. Oh well.

I perused the menu. It had an exotic risotto with monkfish and black cod in miso; I quite fancied it. For a starter, I thought I would have the bottarga that I had previously coveted; back in the bad old days when coming to this restaurant was nothing but a hopeless dream.

'How did you manage to finally get a table here?' asked Emily.

'I was contacted out of the blue by the restaurant,' I replied. 'I didn't even know they had my details. Perhaps I left my number after I'd had a few drinks and forgotten I'd done it.'

'Before we get lost in the food,' said Emily.

'Yes?' Emily looked very serious about something.

'I have spent a lot of time thinking about Adam.'

'Well that's only natural,' I said. 'What happened was huge.'

'Sure,' she said. 'But what if Adam wasn't behind the whole fraud? What if it was someone else and it was simply that social-climbing, eager-to-be-liked, Adam couldn't resist taking the credit?'

'Really?' I asked. Why was she dwelling on this? He had assaulted her, after all.

'I can't get over the way the Valdis treated Adam at the masked ball. They were dismissive of him. And the fact that despite everything, there was no real proof.'

'They were just keeping their distance from a mouthy member of the team,' I reasoned.

'But Adam was so young,' said Emily. 'He was barely twenty. How would he have it in him to have done all that? Murder after all.' She had leant forward and whispered the word murder. 'I just feel with the benefit of hindsight I might have done something really, really wrong because I was in such a bad place at the time.'

Guilt; a new emotion for Emily. She was plainly confused by the feeling. But what on earth had she done wrong?

I was alarmed. I leant forward. 'Emily, what exactly have you done?'

'Oh it's just,' she began. She went to speak further, but then dismissed her thoughts with a hand. 'It's all too much I suppose.'

She needed reassurance. 'He was a posh boy with a sense of entitlement,' I said. 'He was arrogant and cynical. He habitually took cocaine. He never did a stitch of work for you, and yet he was looking for promotion; he *got* promotion for heaven's sake.'

'You're right about that, but it's just that there was no proper proof it was him. Perhaps I was just jumping to conclusions.' Emily sounded quite wretched. This was really not like her; come what may, she usually dusted herself off and moved on.

'Okay,' I said.

'Okay?'

'I've been thinking back through everything, and there was proof,' I said. 'It's just not the sort of proof that would be enough for a court. But there was proof.'

'Which was?'

'Adam and fake Gianna knew each other.'

'Okay?'

'When she said to me that they had known each other a long time, Adam didn't dispute it. At one stage, he mentioned a rough location to meet up at San Zaccaria, but he wasn't specific, and Gianna knew exactly which restaurant he meant, and it wasn't near the church at all. And then there was the fact she knew the layout of your apartment; she must have got that from Adam. We may never know exactly how the fraud was carried out, but we do know for sure that Adam abetted getting Gianna into the safe house to allow the murder. He caused Angelo's death. And then he had the temerity to expect you to date him. He was guilty, and that's that. My suspicion is that Angelo could see that too, and that is why such an apparently staid and honest man was willing to fake his testimony against him.'

Emily considered this for a while and sank backwards into her chair. She was only partially mollified.

'There has long been proof he was involved with fake Gianna,' she said. 'But no matter what he said and no matter what he implied, there was never a shred of evidence that he was involved in the original fraud.'

We were disturbed by the waiter. He came over carrying a silver bucket of ice and bottle of Bollinger.

'We didn't order Champagne,' I queried.

'No indeed sir,' said the man in the naval captain's uniform. It was beginning to look a bit jaded round the collar.

'So, we perhaps should have been consulted before bringing Champagne?' I said. Was it some sort of scam to get us to spend more money?

'It is complementary Signore,' said the waiter.

'Complementary? From whom?'

'From the person who booked your table for you,' explained the man. 'Your meal, and the Champagne has being paid for.'

'By?'

'By a woman who called herself Gianna.'

'Gianna is paying for a meal?' I asked.

'And she has even asked me to pass on a message,' said the waiter.

'Gianna has got us into this restaurant and has paid for the meal and has asked you to pass on a message?'

'Yes Signore,' he said. He got out a card from his breast pocket and then some put on some reading glasses. 'And the message is, "Sorry I pretended to be so angry."' With that, the waiter went away.

Well I never.

'Well that puts a different perspective on the evening,' said Emily. 'Let's bleed the bitch dry. Let's run up the biggest bill we can.' She looked at the menu with animal interest.

'There's only one problem.' I said.

'What?' asked Emily. 'Morality? Taking a meal from a woman who organised Angelo's death?'

'Well that,' I said.

We were disturbed a second time.

There was a cough from a female diner at the table behind me. A dry Covid-style cough. We were now very sensitized to such things.

'Well,' said this unseen woman. Perhaps it wasn't a cough. Perhaps she was just clearing her throat to get attention. 'I can reassure you Emily.'

Who was this talking? I turned to look.

The woman was rising from her table but not looking round. I couldn't see her face.

'I can put your mind at ease,' she said. 'Feel no guilt about anything you did. As your brother said, Adam was guilty as sin, and completely up to his neck in it right from the beginning.'

Gianna. Or rather the fake Gianna.

She still didn't turn towards us.

'And yes, what the hell,' she said. 'Bleed the bitch dry. You probably deserve it.'

The woman moved to the door. She had different hair from the 'Gianna' I knew, but she had her voice and build.

Emily sprang to her feet. She went to apprehend her, but a waiter got in her way. There was a hesitant dance where Emily had not allowed the waiter enough social distance. Gianna was already out on the street. By the time Emily got outside also, she had lost sight of her. After a bit of fruitless searching, Emily came back to the table.

'My days of chasing women down dark alleys are over,' she said.

'Even if they hold a card up with your name on it?'

'Oh well, let's enjoy our meal,' said Emily. 'I have to say I am really looking forward to this.'

She paused. She could sense there was a problem. She looked at me.

'What?' she asked.

'There is a problem,' I confirmed.

'Which is?'

'I seem to have lost my sense of taste,' I replied. 'I literally can't taste or smell anything. I can't taste the food or the cocktail, the Champagne; nothing. It all tastes either wrong, or nothing at all.'

Emily sat back in her seat. She edged her chair backwards to be two metres away from me.

'And you had that dry cough earlier,' she said.

She reached into her bag and pulled out a face mask.

'You're going to try and force down the food anyway, aren't you?' she said.

'No?' I said. 'Maybe?'

'You do know the responsible thing to do is to now leave the restaurant?' said Emily.

'Yes?'

Perhaps I could get a doggy bag?

A NOTE FROM THE AUTHOR

Thank you for reading De'Ath in Venice. I hope you enjoyed it. In keeping with the other De'Ath books I wanted to write a larger-than-life pacey thriller with memorable characters, some good twists, and a few laughs; I also wanted to celebrate the island of Venice; its food, culture and beauty.

I don't know about you, but I thought this particular plot was really quite stressful. When I dreamt up the story, I felt quite sorry for Emily who is really put through the ringer, although that didn't excuse what she then did, and by the time I had made sure Pete was fed, the book more or less wrote itself. Perhaps for the next book I will make things just a tiny bit more relaxed, if only for my nerves.

I have a small favour to ask. If you enjoyed this book, please do consider writing a review on Amazon and Goodreads, or just a star rating would be great. Although the De'Ath books have been well received and have sold well, there can be glitches in the system where reviews and star ratings get lost, and when a book is as new as this one, such losses can have a profound effect. Prospective readers are only human; why buy a book that seemingly no one at all is endorsing? As a result, I would be pitifully grateful, as always, for any help you could offer.

Thank you

Paul Humber

EXTRACT FROM DE'ATH IN CORSICA by PAUL HUMBER. Now available.

THE WORLD ACCORDING TO PETE

It was Friday evening and there was a knock on the door and there was Little Sarah from the office. I didn't realise she even knew where I lived.

'Okay now don't freak out,' she asked.

'Why would I freak out?'

'Promise me you won't freak out?' It was the sort of thing a young person says to their parents. Just how old did she think I was? How depressing.

'Okay.' She took a deep breath.

I looked forward over her, to see if the explanation for her arrival somehow lay in the street beyond. It didn't.

'Okay well the thing is, it looks like I've done a murder. But I haven't done a murder.'

And with that handful of words my entire weekend was comprehensively buggered up.

Normally I have near-perfect Friday evenings. I live on my own. If I want to watch a film or a box set – Game of Thrones, Mad Men, Love Island, Casablanca, Earth Girls Are Easy – I have a wide and varied taste - I can just choose it and watch it and drink a glass of wine, and what the hell a second glass of wine, and I can pause it whenever I like and make a bacon sandwich or get, what the hell, a third and fourth glass of wine; one in each hand.

The point is I don't have to think about whether someone else is enjoying themselves, or indeed what someone else makes of my alcohol consumption or the fact that I am only wearing my underpants. I don't have to worry that someone else is sitting alone in a room gazing at a paused film while I fry the bacon and get distracted by the internet. Also, to be clear, I wouldn't just wear underpants - I was being figurative - even in a hot country I find my feet get cold easily, so I would also at the very least wear socks as well. The point is, because I live on my own, I can just be myself.

And it is bliss.

Let me just take a moment to stress this.

It is bliss.

I live somewhere amazing – Corsica - one of the most beautiful islands in the world. If I want something, I can have it. If I want to walk from my sun-scorched house down the coastal path to the sea; if I want to sit at a café table on the old quayside and watch the boats come and go; if I want to go sailing or walk in the mountains or visit Paris or Nice or Tuscany for the weekend, I can do it.

Some people's lives are a desperate flight from loneliness. Mine is a desperate flight from getting involved. I love my own company and I love the company of others. And that makes me the luckiest man alive.

Little Sarah's real name is Sarah-Jayne, but largely goes by the name of Sarah which - to confuse matters further - she pronounces as Sara. If someone calls her Sarah she gets really shirty which is totally unreasonable – how are people supposed to know Sarah is not pronounced Sarah? Broadly speaking, she is likeable though; she's a young Tigger of a thing who joined our office about six months ago, increasing the English contingent in the building by exactly 50%. My initial reaction when I saw her, therefore, was that her problem was somehow related to work.

Our business is insurance, and our office is a tiny backwater branch of a huge multinational insurance empire. Our area shows a slightly high level of claims for boating accidents and life assurance generally, but the latter is due to the fact that Corsica routinely has the highest murder rate per capita of any French territory – you've got to be good at something, it might as well be murder - so there has been repeated interest in the high pay out level for deaths from head office, which is irritating. On the other hand, we have below average statistics for burglary, fire, and car theft and so the figures balance out. It is the way of management, however, that you never get praise for the figures that look good, you just get earache about the figures that look bad.

I am digressing as usual.

Sarah was wearing a flimsy summer dress and some plastic sandals. In fact, coming to think of it, this is probably the first important fact about the murder: the clothes Sarah was wearing. If you were going to plan a murder, you would wear something practical like leggings or a pair of jeans. Sarah was wearing a mid-length spotty cotton dress that was white and blue. It had a slight puff at the skirt and it would have left her upper back and shoulders completely bare, were it not for what she was wearing underneath which was – as far as I could see - a black nylon halter neck body stocking with a lacy pattern to it. It was meant to look racy as in, 'Look I am wearing sexy underwear under my dress,' but the effect didn't work. Apart from the fact that the underwear looked cheap and didn't match the dress, it showed off too much of her back and shoulders which were doughy pale and dotted with a distracting number of black moles. The point is – and I am repeating myself on purpose – these were not the clothes of a murderer. These were not even the clothes of a skilled seductress. You could see she was going for a 'game girlfriend' look, but instead of looking flirty, it just looked forlorn.

I appreciate this is not amazing evidence either way, but consider the opposite: when the case got to court, if she had been wearing black leggings and a mask and somehow it was caught on camera, then the prosecutors would have had no trouble saying 'Does this look like the sort of clothes you wear on a date?' If you allow one line of logic, then you have to allow the other.

So anyway.

Sarah stood there and she said, 'I don't know where to begin.'

Oh and she was a dreadful colour. She wasn't just pale; she was Uma Thurman Pulp Fiction pale.

'I suppose,' she began. 'I suppose that you're the only English person I know here. Well there's your sister Emily, but you know what I mean. You know, here in Corsica, I've only been here a few months and I don't really know anyone. I certainly really don't know what to do in a situation like this. I mean what do you do? Well what could you do? The answer is I don't know what to do.'

I tried to look patient - it is the social protocol in such situations to look patient - but I was well within my rights to just look irritated: it was the weekend, and she owed me an explanation.

'It looks like you've killed someone?' I repeated. 'And you don't think you did it. But you're not sure.'

'I didn't kill him, but it looks like I did,' she repeated.

Well I knew she didn't kill this 'him', or certainly didn't kill him on purpose, because - bottom line - she's Little Sarah from the office. How do we know anything? The answer is we don't; I just knew in my heart that Little Sarah from the office was not a crazed professional killer.

Sarah then breathed in sharply which I took to mean she had made a decision of some sort. 'Come on. I'll show you,' she said. She made to walk across the street.

'Hang on Sarah!' I said. 'Hold on. I will need some trousers.'

As well as my trousers and a shirt, I needed my keys, because I didn't want to lock myself out. My keys were in my bedroom along with my trousers – and this is an important detail for later - the keys were exactly where I thought they would be; on my bedside table. I am willing to state irrefutably and categorically therefore that the only item I remember being on my bedside table in the early evening were my keys. There was nothing else on the bedside table.

Sarah's car was parked across the road from my house. Much was made of the car as the evidence was gathered for the trial, so it is worth stating as a minimum that it was a neat little red Renault Clio. There was the finest film of sand over it, as there is over almost everything you touch on the island at certain times in the summer when a southerly wind catches sand from North Africa. But other than that, nothing special: it was just a normal cheerful second-hand car that a woman might buy cheap and then not put any oil in and wonder why it seizes up. It was a celebration of summer island life and the supposed carelessness of being young. There was conjecture that Sarah must have had help with the dead body because of the nature of the car. I am not sure about that. When you are desperate, you can manage the most Herculean of tasks; you're pumped up, you're adrenalized, if that is a word.

Sarah looked up and down the street and checked sight lines as to who might be able to see what we were doing.

She took another deep breath and said, 'Here goes.'

She opened the back of her car, and in the back there was a dead man.

Printed in Great Britain
by Amazon